BROTHERS OF SHADOW & DEATH

Anywhere

BROOKLYN CROSS

I will cause three showers of fire to pour on the faces of the army of the Fomor, and I will take from them two-thirds of their bravery and their strength, and I will put sickness on their bodies, and on the bodies of their horses.

But as the men of Ireland, every breath they breathe will be an increase of strength and of bravery to them; and if they are seven years in the battle they will never be any way tired.

- Figol the Druid

ANYWHERE

BROTHERS OF SHADOW & DEATH

ELEWYEN'S AWAKENING
- BOOK ONE -

BROOKLYN CROSS

To J.R. Ward
Although you do not know me, you were instrumental in helping me find
my way through a very dark time.
Because of you my passion for reading was rekindled and I found my
courage to write.
Thank you

Trademark Acknowledgements

The author Brooklyn Cross acknowledges the trademarked status and trademark owners of familiar wordmarks, products, actors' names, television shows, books, characters, video games, and films mentioned in this fiction work.

❀ Created with Vellum

ALSO BY BROOKLYN CROSS

The Righteous Series

(Vigilante/Ex Military Romance - Dark 3-4 Spice 3-4)

Dark Side of the Cloth

Ravaged by the Dark

Sleeping with the Dark

Hiding in the Dark

Redemption in the Dark

Crucified by the Dark

Dark Reunion (Coming 2023)

The Consumed Trilogy

(Suspense/Thriller/Anti-Hero Romance - Dark 4-5 Spice 3-4)

Burn for Me

Burn with Me

Burn me Down (Coming 2023)

The Buchanan Brother's Duet

(Serial Killer/Captive Romance - Dark 4-5 Spice 3-5)

Unhinged Cain by Brooklyn

Twisted Abel by T.L Hodel

The Battered Souls World

(Standalone Books Shared World Romance/Dramatic/Women's Fiction/All

The Feels- Dark 2-3 Spice 2-3)

The Girl That Would Be Lost

The Boy That Learned To Swim (Coming Soon)

The Girl That Would Not Break (Coming Soon)

The Brothers of Shadow and Death Series

(Dystopian/Cult/Occult/Poly MMF Romance - Dark 3-4 Spice 3-4)

Anywhere Book 1 of 3

Backfire Book 1 of 3 by T.L. Hodel

Seven Sin Series

(Multi Author/PNR/Angel and Demons/Redemption - Dark 2-5 Spice 3-5)

Greed by Brooklyn Cross

Lust by Drethi Anis

Envy by Dylan Page

Gluttony by Marissa Honeycutt

Wrath by Billie Blue

Sloth by Talli Wyndham

Pride by T.L. Hodel

Warning

This book is a Fictional Paranormal Romance story and is intended for mature audiences ONLY, as defined by the country's laws in which you made your purchase.

This book may contain violence, vulgar language, various kink play, MMF scenes, tobacco and alcohol use, and addiction that some readers may find disturbing.

This book takes place in a Dystopian version of the Isle of Man and has multiple accents and written in British English.

Like most other content rating systems this is only used as a guide.

Playlist

Still Breathing - Green Day
Can't Get My Head Around You - The Offspring
Bad Moon Rising - Creedence Clearwater
Home For A Rest - Spirit of the West
Wellerman (Sea Shanty) - Nathan Evans
Intuition - Jewel
Flowers Need Rain - Preston Pablo & Banx
Enemy - Imagine Dragons
I Want You to Want Me - Cheap Trick
American Wake - Bill Whelan
What Do You Mean? - Justin Bieber
Goosebumps - Travis Scott, Kendrick Lamar
Natural - Imagine Dragons
Consequence Free - Great Big Sea
There For You - Martin Garrix & Troye Sivan
Until the Day I Die - Page Avenue
When I'm Up - Great Big Sea
Irish Heartbeat - Van Morrison
SNAP - Rosa Linn
Hold On - Chord Overstreet
Radioactive - Imagine Dragons
Gypsy - Ronan Hardiman

DEFINITIONS

'Ave - Have

'Ere - Here

Appreozo - Spell to make something invisible or visible

Ass Over Tea Kettle - To flip over backward in a somersault fashion

Aye or Ya - Yes

Basalainn - Type of Demon

Bevvy - An alcoholic drink such as beer

Bodach - Pig or pigish in nature

Buggar - Brat or ill behaving

Canne - Long wooden weapon that resembles a thick stick. Can have metal or carvings along the wood.

Cannie - Cannot

Chiseler - Young or Immature

Da - Dad or Father

Daft - To be slow to understand

Dat - That

Den - Then

Dem - Them

Dere - There

Dey - They

Din't - Don't

Dinnie - Don't or Doesn't

Dis - This

District - City within a Faction

Donkey - To act in a senseless manner

Eejit - Idiot

Faction - The divisions created across the world that are controlled by those with magic

Feck - Slang for Fuck

Fir - For

Flitter - Person without magic

Gaoth - Spell that is a hard physical shove or blow

Glas bacainn - Spell that creates a temporary invisible boundary

Gurl - Girl

Hunter - Those that are Flitters and rebel against the Factions

I'ma - I am

I'za or I'z - I am

Joshin - Teasing or making a joke

Levetatio - Spell to make someone float

Ma - Mom, Mum or Mother

Naw - No

Nicked - To steal

Pairing Ritual - Where the number one and two males in triad are chosen by the spirits of ancestors long passed.

Petrobile - Spell to freeze someone in place for a short time

Samhach - Spell to make someone mute for short time

Shouldna - Should not

Ta - The or Thee or To

Triad - Three people of magic coming together in union to create a power structure to support the needs of a Faction

Twisted - To be upset or tied up in knots over something

Windie - Window (Scottish term)

Whaddya - What do you

Whatta - What are

Wit - With

Ya - Yes or You

Ya can get tae fuck - Fuck off or Go get fucked

Yer - You are

Go dtuga na spioraid rochtain agus cosaint do magus mé ag taisteal ina réimeas - May the spirits grant access and protect me as I travel in their realm

Lig do na spioraid mé a threorú agus na cinntí a dhéanaim a chumhachtú - Let the spirits guide me and empower the decisions I make

Coinnigh mo lámh agus lig dom taisteal abhaile le scian I mo lámh agus faic I mo dhroim. Is é seo a iarraim - Hold my hand and let me travel home with a knife in my hand and nothing in my back. This is what I ask.

Demon a beheith imithe - Demon be gone

Éiríonn triúr ar cheann - Three becomes one

Family Castles

Douglas - Kelly Castle

Glentruan - McGregor Castle

Injebreck - Adair Castle

Maughold - McCabe Castle

Ravendale - McKinnon Castle

ELEWYEN

Foreward

Centuries ago, our world descended into chaos as war erupted amid the masses. Those with magical abilities fought against those without, leaving the weaker of the two desperate to remain free. In the battle, we lost many, flooding our streets and waterways with the blood of the innocent.

After decades of war across the globe, peace settled amongst the people. Most forgot the years of death and destruction, though others spoke about it as nothing more than myths to be passed on to younger generations.

Factions became the new world order, run by those with magic. They outlawed guns, closed prisons, and disbanded armies. Yet crime rates were the lowest they had ever been. These mystical groups took control of the world's leading industries, from food production to machinery and technology.

However, most of these factions wanted to remain untouched by a more modern society. They chose to bypass technological advancements, allowing only the most prestigious of families to own simple machines such as cars.

Those without magical abilities became known as Flitters. And to them, nothing had changed. But to those with powers, the world would never be the same. That was a secret they kept, day in and day out.

Like any world order, the Factions understood jealousy could still bring them down. They banded together to create stronger alliances.

The most powerful of those groups became a united front, controlling what they called Faction Three—The Brothers of Shadow and Death. The Adair, Kelly, McCabe, McGregor, and McKinnon families have grown to be an immensely powerful alliance. They now have dangerous targets on their backs, for the other envious families crave their power and prosperity.

Lurking within the shadows, there is yet another group that emerged from this war. The Hunters are a rebellious sect that comes from a long line of Flitters who remember those battle-stricken days and strive to annihilate the Factions at all costs. Their mandate is to set free the Flitters from their perceived oppression.

As each ritual moon draws near, and a new triad union is

announced, the Hunters become more active. Their goal is simple: Eliminate the triads.

Welcome to Faction Three... Where you will meet the strongest and most desirable we have to offer.

Also check out book 1 in the same world by T.L. Hodel Backfire Book 1 of 3

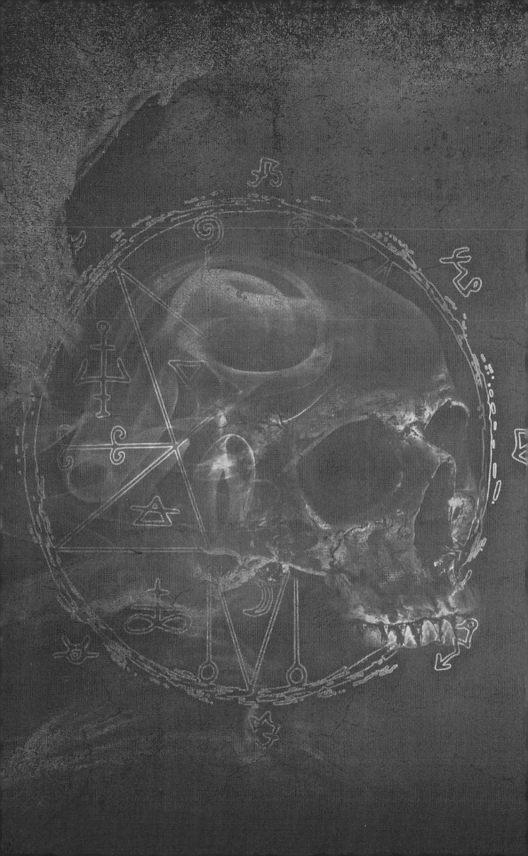

Chapter 1

Rook

"Holy fuck me," I yelled as the plane violently jerked and tossed me from my seat.

I crawled back into the large chair, pissed off that I'd been woken from my peaceful nap. The plane shuddered violently, and a high-pitched whining sound started up outside. That was never something you wanted to hear. I leaned forward to look out the small cabin window to check the plane's motor. It was trying to turn, but a mass of feathers had exploded like fucking confetti. Dark smoke streamed out in a long ribbon to join the feathers as we lost speed. The nose of the plane began to dip.

"Oh, that can't be good," I said.

A blink later, my head was slammed back into the seat. The plane tipped downward like it had reached the top of a hill on a rollercoaster and with a whine sound we streaked toward the mass of dark blue water and certain death. I could picture hitting the ocean and the plane simply disintegrating into a million little pieces, my body included.

The air mask dropped from the ceiling and smacked me in the face. I swatted the thing away, but it continued to jerk around, whacking my cheeks. I didn't want to come to this godforsaken island, and now I would die in the tin can flying me there. Flying and I had never been friends, and my inner voice screamed in my mind as my fingers dug into the padded leather armrests. I closed my eyes, trying to compose myself. No. I refused to die because of fucking birds. This was not how Rook Adair went out.

My terror calmed enough, and I managed to focus on the engine. I could picture the plane's engine mechanics and allowed my power to reach out. I was instantly able to sense the presence of multiple dead birds. The coursing adrenaline felt the same as the first time I'd stepped out onto a large stage with screaming fans. I stopped thinking about the plane crashing and pictured the crowd, and the surge of energy I got from those first notes and hearing my name screamed under those bright lights. The power tingled along my skin like little pinpricks. As a young boy, I hated the sensation of the powers that would come and go at will.

My body heated and trembled in time with the shaking plane while the *thump* of my heart slowed in my chest as my power reached out to the engine. The birds' deaths felt like smoked candy on my tongue, and I rolled the flavour around in my mouth.

A soft groan left my lips as the power wrapped around the carcasses. Although the birds were now very dead, the essence of life still clung to their bodies as if desperate to revive what would never breathe again. My power tightened its hold, the wispy tendrils

2

clenching the mangled bodies in its grip, and like a fisherman casting a net, I pulled back and drew the birds out of the engine.

I didn't need to look out the window to know that I'd see a grotesque pile of flesh, blood, and bone. Licking my lips in anticipation, I counted to three. My back arched off the seat as the power crushed the ball of flesh and turned it into nothing more than ash to blow away in the wind stream, but the essence was mine. It was tempting, oh so very tempting, to suck it up and let it course through my body like a party drug.

Instead, my mind settled, and all came to a stop. The silver chain around my neck floated in front of my eyes as the plane stopped falling, and everything hung suspended in the air like a magic trick. I guess it was, just not the fake shows of mass illusion you'd see on stage. This magic was far more powerful and far more lethal. It was also the reason I'd been sent to the island and why I was in this fucking predicament.

"Fuck," I roared as the power surged back into the engine. The tingling under my skin was almost unbearable as it raced through my body. Everything stood up, including my cock, as the magic did as I commanded. With a bang, the engine re-fired. The remaining wisps were sent to the front of the plane and slowly elevated the nose. The second engine that had stalled out re-fired, but we remained suspended in the air as the plane continued to right itself.

I would've paid money to see the reaction of anyone watching the free show. But there weren't many spectators in the middle of the ocean.

A scream ripped from my mouth as the engines roared and strained to be freed. Releasing my hold over the plane, I was snapped back and wondered if this was what it felt like to take off in a rocket ship. That was what I pictured, a small black rocket heading into space. The plane shook violently. I had to close my eyes as they began to water, and the pressure on my chest made me want to panic as it became hard to breathe.

The plane finally evened out, and we continued to sail along at cruising altitude. I gasped in short breaths as my body shook from the aftermath of the power surge. The cabin door opened, and the captain ran past me to the washroom. The door slammed into place, and I smirked at the distinct sound of his retching.

Settling back into my seat, I closed my eyes and flicked my hand, sending all the stupid masks back into their little cabinets. With another flick of my wrist, the fallen dishes and scraps of food flew to their original positions. I sighed as the weight of the power usage pressed down on me. My power was always strong, but what I'd done took way more than I could've done without the sacrifice. The only real issue was the drain when the extra boost left my system. Like taking drugs, there was a nasty side effect of using that much power all at once.

I grabbed a napkin to wipe the droplet of blood trickling from my nose. Magic always had a price to pay. I would be nauseous for at least an hour and hated feeling sick. I looked down at my cock, which was, of course, still standing at attention.

Just fucking great.

"This is a bad omen," I mumbled. "Bad, bad fucking omen."

The washroom door opened, and the captain emerged, leaning heavily against the door for a moment before he ventured into the main cabin. He paused as he reached me. His eyes were wide, and his skin was a pasty white as he dabbed at his face with a wad of toilet paper. My lip curled up with disdain.

"Did… um… did you feel anything happen?" the guy asked as he looked around the lush cabin space of the private jet. My father had designed it for these long trips. I glanced at the bed. I'd missed fixing the crystal decanter that had landed on the floor with the comforter. I pointed out the window, and the captain leaned forward to see what I was indicating.

"Something hit the wing. I think it was a bird or maybe a couple," I said as I swiped my hand at the rest of the mess. The items quickly righted themselves.

The captain turned his head. I bit the inside of my cheek to not laugh at the confusion on his face. I could almost see him asking himself if something had just moved. Being able to read his mind would be awesome right about now.

"Oh... Okay," his eyes now searching the rest of the space.

I was really regretting not bringing someone with me on the flight to fuck. Considering what my father was forcing me to do, it might have been the last time I got to fuck someone of my choice. That could've been the end of me, but at least I could've said I'd joined the Mile High Club before that happened.

I put my legs on the footrest in front of me and leaned over to pull a drink from the minibar. Even staring death in the face couldn't stop the annoyed-as-fuck feeling I had inside my chest. It felt like the annoyance would burn me up with how it raged.

Sighing, I gave the captain an irritated look. He worked for my father, so as far as I was concerned, he worked for me and should get back to work.

"Why do you look so shaken? Should I be concerned about you? Should I be calling my father? I mean, we hit some stupid bird and had a little turbulence. No big deal. What exactly do you think happened?" I asked.

I watched his face go through a range of emotions, and I could almost hear the questions inside his skull. I guess it wasn't fair to treat the man like he was an idiot. It wasn't like he could comprehend what had just happened.

"Ah… Well, I-I… we were… um…"

"Is there an actual sentence hidden in there?" I took a swig of the fizzy fruit water disguised as alcohol and gagged as I stared at the can. What the fuck had my father stocked the fridge with? The label read: *Real fruit flavour with a kick. Zero calories and zero alcohol, but all the same taste.* I had news for whoever made this undrinkable garbage. It didn't taste like an alcoholic drink at all. It tasted more like watered-down fruity piss.

"You know what? Never mind. I've been reading too many weird books lately and staying up far too late." He shuffled toward the cockpit.

"Hey, how much longer until we get there?"

He looked over his shoulder at me, and I could see the wheels turning as he tried to tell himself that what had just happened hadn't happened. I had a love-hate thing going on with those who didn't know about us, magic, or how the world worked. The Flitters—as many of the Factions called them—were all blissfully unaware that they were puppets in a much larger master's game. Many a night, I wished that I could be that oblivious. It certainly would've saved me from flying to this tiny shithole island to form one of the next power triads. Next-gen, here we come. To become part of a powerful triad was supposed to be an honour. I was told I should be excited by the opportunity, but all I saw was a lifetime of responsibility that I didn't want.

My jaw twitched at the thought. The new position in my family was bad enough, but to be forced into marriage with two people I didn't fucking know and taking over additional family responsibilities was not my idea of living. It sounded like a death sentence with two ball-and-chains. It was certainly not what I wanted, but my father didn't give a shit what I wanted. All that mattered was that I was chosen at the last union ritual to become the next head of the Adair family and join with Rhys and someone else. I had no idea why Devlin couldn't take my place. Not that he'd been any keener to take on the triad life, but being the firstborn should come with perks like passing on shit you don't want to deal with.

I waved my hand, and the captain's eyes focused on my face. "Time? How much time?"

"Sorry. We're forty minutes out from The Isle of Man," he said. "If we make it there alive, that is," he mumbled as he disappeared inside the cockpit.

Forty more minutes to comprehend the fucked-up life I was heading into and, more importantly, how I would get myself out of this mess.

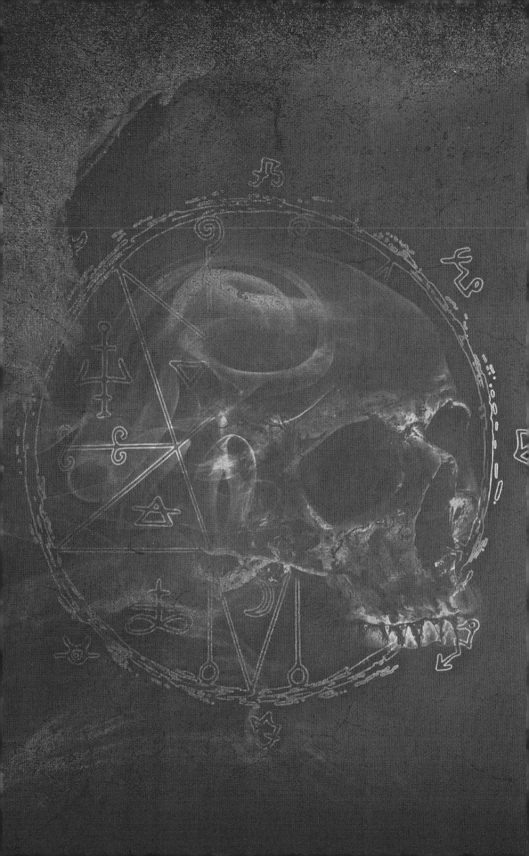

Chapter 2

Elewyen

 The trees rustled, and my hands stilled from packing my travelling pack. I shivered as a cool breeze swirled around my neck and felt like a noose trying to strangle me. There was a restless charge in the air. I didn't know what exactly it meant, but something was comin', and it was big.

 The older women in the coven were gathering and whispering in hushed tones about things like *forced mating,* and the word *enslave* had been used. There was a terrified tone in all of their voices, and they were making arrangements to improve the boundary security. I didn't know what that meant or what had set them off, and I didn't care. I'd grown up in the wild, and anything in the bush didn't scare me. I loved these women. They'd taken me in and raised me, but they were not brave of heart. Living in the wilds, you learned to swallow your fears and fight, or you were swallowed by something much larger and scarier.

If it hadn't been for them, I would never have understood the civilized world or learned to speak without growling like the wolves. For example, I learned that the massive stone homes were called castles, and those who lived in them should be avoided at all costs. They were dangerous to us. The other thing I now knew was that they had strange things that no one else seemed to have.

I'd seen them out in their small shiny boxes on black wheelbarrow wheels and asked one of the women of the coven what the shiny animals were called. They'd told me they were cars and that their ancestors told stories that, once, everyone used to have one, but now only those in the castles had them. There were so many of these differences, and I wanted to know why. Why didn't we have shiny cars to move around? And why did they have lights that didn't need fire to glow?

"Elewyen, cannie I come?" Keeva asked. I recognized the young girl's voice and turned to see her standing with her travelling cloak on and a small basket of berries. "I'z got food," she said and held up the basket for me to see.

Smiling, I sat my newly packed sack down and knelt to look the beautiful young girl in the eyes. She was the first girl I'd rescued from the villagers. It was the first time I understood what had happened to me and why I had a burning desire to help more women like me.

Reaching out, I ran my hands down the soft red locks of her hair. "Yer gettin' ta be a big lass, but dis trip I'za need ta do on me own."

Her young face fell, and her soft green eyes dropped to stare at her feet. I lifted her chin and made her look at me as I gave her a firm look. "Ya know ya wit be ma first choice in a season or two." I glanced around at the other women, like I was sharing a big secret, and got close to her ear. "Din't be tellin' the others, but I'za need ya here ta look afta dem. There be naw a one I'za trust more den da likes of ya." I gave her small cheek a kiss.

Keeva wrapped her arms around my neck and clung to me as I hugged her tight. "I'za wuv ya, Eleywen. Ya gotta come back."

Pulling back from the embrace, I kissed her forehead and then each of her cheeks. "Aye, I'za be back before Mabon. Ya best no be finkin' yer gettin' out a dancin' wit me."

Keeva smiled, but it didn't reach her eyes. "I dinnie want ya ta go. I dinnie tink I'za see ya again," she said, and a tear slid down her cheek.

Swiping the tear, I held it on the pad of my finger. Moving my other hand over the droplet, it shimmered and lifted into the air. The tear spun like a small storm, and Keeva gasped as it burst, and a small blue stone settled into the palm of her hand. Removing my knife, I made a tiny slice in my palm and gripped our hands together.

"Dion. Rabhadh. Gaol. Cleachd m' fhuil mar iobairt. Dion. Rabhadh. Gaol."

I said the spell again, and this time Keeva joined in. We closed our eyes as the heat developed between our hands. On the third round, our skin was shimmering in the sun as the spell reached its peak. When our hands began to cool, I removed my palm from hers, and two red stones now existed. I pulled a thin piece of sinew, usually used to stitch my worn clothes, from a small pouch. Then I took one of the stones from her hand and held the two pieces up. With a flick of my wrist, the sinew reformed to fit around the small stone, making a necklace. Repeating the process, I created a twin set, and Keeva smiled widely.

"Dare ya see now. If ya eva need me, ya hold dis tight and tink a me. Mines wit glow a bright red, and I'za do da same. Ya will always know if I'za need ya help," I said, tying the necklace around her neck.

She gripped the stone hard in her hand and closed her eyes. Mine immediately started to glow.

"And I tell ya another secret. Ya can think a me whenever ya want, and I'za will answer back. I luvs ya, Keeva."

"I'za luvs ya more," she said and tucked the necklace inside her tunic before giving me another hug.

"Ya mind Azula. She take good care of ya," I said.

"She smell of old cheese." Keeva made a face, and I laughed hard as I stood. "But, aye." Keeva ran her small leather-clad foot over the dirt, making a rainbow shape.

I laid my hand on her small shoulder and gave it a squeeze. Turning, I grabbed my pack and my knife, shoving the blade into the sheath on my waist. It was the only thing the coven found me with when I was not much older than Keeva. Eight, maybe. I didn't know how long I'd lived in the wild, but it was all I could remember.

Making my way to the edge of the forest and the security of the boundary, I lifted my staff in a wave goodbye to the small coven I called home. Keeva jumped on a log and waved her arms in the air like a wild little bird. Her bright red hair waved along with her arms in the wind. My heart hurt to leave her here, but this was something I had to do. Twice a year, I journeyed to find the discarded babes in the forest before some predator—animal, human, or otherwise—could hurt them.

The first village was a half a day's walk away, and as I got a little closer, I pulled my red hair back with a piece of leather and made sure it was all hidden under my cloak's hood. This was one of the better villages. They would time leaving the babes for when they knew I'd be passing through. I didn't go into the town limits but stayed near the forest, watching the villagers as they worked or played outside in the sun.

A boy kicked a brown ball in my direction. I held as still as a skittish deer, but as he picked up the ball, he noticed me standing among the shadows. Even though he couldn't see my red hair, which would tell all the villagers what I was, his eyes went wide. He ran, yelling for his friend before they both ran for the group of adults.

All heads turned in my direction. One of the men stepped forward, raised his pitchfork in the air, and shook his head no. At least he wasn't chasing me with the sharp end. I had the scar from that happening before. The women in my coven told me we were feared because we had magic, and the villagers didn't want anything to do with it. They thought we were cursed by darkness and pretended magic didn't exist or truly believed that it didn't. Anyone thought to have magic was cast out, no matter the age.

There was so much I didn't understand. Why did all those who lived in the villages hate the idea of magic? Why was a red-headed female believed to be a curse on the town? No one seemed to have answers for me. They would say it was from times of old when there was dark anger in the world and things called armies marched across the land. The number of men they talked about who lived, fought and died seemed impossible, yet their hard stares told me they were serious.

The villagers also seemed to think that we wanted to attack them. Again, this was a mystery to me. For as long as I'd been with my coven, all we wanted was to be left alone to live our lives in peace. It was the villagers who were the threat.

The shadows were getting longer, and I looked up at the thick grey clouds that seemed like an endless wave rolling across the sky. Even the spirit of wind and air was angry.

My necklace glowed and caught my eye, making me smile. Picking it up, I thought of Keeva and knew her stone would glow in return. I remembered clearly the day I found her. No older than a couple of months, she'd been left out by a tree in the middle of the woods. Keeva hadn't been left for a coven to find. No, she'd been left naked and was screaming, her little arms and legs kicking as she wailed in the early winter air. Keeva became mine, or as much mine as possible, in a coven where everyone was seen as a sister.

I had just put the necklace down when I caught a movement in the shadows from the corner of my eye. It instantly had me on high alert. Not wanting to let whatever it was know it had been discovered, I didn't stop walking.

I kept my pace even and listened for what was following me. I quickly realized that whatever it was, there were two of them, and they were not as stealthy as they thought they were. Which meant they were human and most likely thieves. Only humans were that stupid and greedy.

Glancing up, I saw a bend in the trail with a blind corner and prepared myself, knowing this would be where they would attack. As soon as my feet started around the turn, the one who was now a little ahead of me jumped out to block my path, while the second stepped out behind to block the way I'd come.

"Hey, lass, where ya be headin' all alone?" the man asked.

I didn't respond. There was no point. They were either after money or something of the female body variety, and they weren't getting any from me.

"Are ya deaf, lass? I asked ya a question."

My power prickled as the threat behind me moved closer. I squeezed the walking stick tighter, the wood firm in my hand. The guy behind me shuffled a little closer, and I waited until he was close enough that I knew he would grab me next. In a swift movement, I jabbed the end of the walking stick into his stomach. The eyes of the man in front of me went wide as I stepped forward and cracked the wood down on the hand he'd slipped inside his cloak.

With a wide, arcing sweep through the air, I brought my stick down and caught the guy behind me across the side of his face. My staff had split his face open from the top of his cheek to his chin, leaving him with a grotesque, monstrous look. He collapsed in a heap, screaming as he gripped at the open, bleeding wound.

My cloak fanned out as I spun like a dandelion seed in the breeze, but far deadlier. I dropped low and caught the man who had spoken to me in the side of the knee. He hollered in pain as he fell from the force.

"Ye fuckin' cunt," the man on his knees growled out as I jumped to my feet.

"Aye."

Like a dark spirit, I swirled and danced between the two men, landing blows in soft areas that would render them incapable of following me. No part of the body was safe, not a knee, a throat, or even the thing they had dangling between their legs.

I screamed in triumph as I brought the stick down for the final blow and knocked the man with the foul mouth out cold. He slumped forward and landed on his buddy, who was already having a forced rest. I stood up straight and searched their faces for any sign they were still awake. Failing to see any visible signs, I fixed my cloak and tucked the loose strands of my hair back, hidden from sight. Azula had taught me that we never used magic to hurt others unless it was our very last option.

Making my way around the two knocked-out men, I lined up the blunt stick with one hand at a time and brought it down hard onto the bones in the middle of their hands until the sound of snapping bones echoed. With men like that, I had to be confident that they couldn't follow me and try again when I was sleeping. I liked to ensure their hands were useless, just like their pathetic brains and little peens. I didn't think all men could be this vile, but then again, what did I know about the male species?

The fascination harboured by some of the women in the coven was baffling to me. I wasn't letting a man near me with one of those things between his legs. All they did was hurt people.

Spitting on the ground, I turned and continued on my way. Out here, you needed to be a little wild to contend with what the world decided to throw at you, and luckily, I was born a whole lot wild.

The sun was high in the sky when a roar streaked over my head. I ducked and stared up at a black bird that was so big it looked like it could swallow a village whole.

I'd never seen something so large or loud in the air before. This bird roared as it moved over the treetops. It didn't seem to take notice of me, and I couldn't stand not knowing.

"Dinnie be a donkey," I said aloud, scolding myself as I jogged after the massive bird. Even though I could no longer see it, I could hear it and followed the sound like a predator following a wounded animal. Streaking through the trees, I ran full speed to keep up with the creature. Small branches and roots hit my arms and grabbed at my feet.

Running out of the cover of the trees, I yelled as I crashed into a large fence, the likes of which I'd never seen. The metal tossed me back, and I landed on my arse while my walking stick flew from my hand and rolled under a bush.

"Serves ya right," I mumbled as I stared at the metal with holes.

Pulling myself up, my hands brushed off the dirt as I stared around the spot I didn't recognize. I'd come this way only six moons ago, and there was nothing here then. I would've known if I'd had to veer around something this large. How many times had I passed this way and never once come across this tall fence or the wide road and grey building that looked to be made out of metal as well? *How strange.*

My attention was grabbed once more when the roaring, which had faded, suddenly got louder. I stared at the creature casting a shadow on the ground as it circled, then headed for the wide road.

The women in the coven would be scolding me good for this. They were always saying I was more brazen than a polecat after their fresh fish. I couldn't help it, though. I had a burning desire to learn about everything I didn't understand. Where others would cower in fear, I would run towards what I probably shouldn't.

I was captivated as the black and silver creature roared louder, like a beast from the old tales that Azula would tell us younger girls around the fire. Its wings didn't flap like a normal bird, and its body looked like a weird fish that could fly. The sound it made was vaguely familiar. I may have heard it once or twice before, but it had seemed far off, and in the dark, I couldn't see, but this was magnificent. Just before it touched the road, I spotted the wheels like a car on the underbelly.

Man-made? Could man fly? No, don't be thick. That was impossible. Or was it? Those in the castles had cars, and they had talking boxes they would hold to the side of their head. Azula once told me that they sucked the soul out of your head if you used them too much, so they were a cursed item. When I asked why they would use them then, she couldn't answer. I didn't like answers that didn't make sense, but who else would I ask for such information?

I watched in fascination as the large, winged thing made a horrible, squealing, roaring sound as smoke rose from the large wheels. I covered my ears. As fast as it had come toward the ground, it didn't crash. Instead, it slowed down and stopped across from where I was standing. Taking a step back, I was hidden among the trees, watching as villagers ran out of the building with a tall thing with many steps. They put it up against the now quieting creature, and a gasp left my mouth as part of the beast's side opened like a great hole had been cut into its side. A moment later, a man stepped out.

My breath caught as I stared at the man. His hair was as dark as the night sky, and he had something black wrapped around his eyes, making him look dangerous. I could feel the weight of those eyes as his head turned to look around. My power tingled in my stomach, a fluttering that was as soft and fast as a tiny bird's wings. He was tall. Even when his feet touched the ground, it was easy to tell that he was tall, with wide shoulders and narrow hips. He didn't dress like anyone I'd ever met. Everything he wore was black and clung to him like the clothing was his skin. His head turned in my direction, and all the air was stolen from my lungs, leaving them frozen in place.

I had the strongest urge to touch him. I wondered what someone who looked like that would taste like as my tongue ran across my lips. I slapped a hand over my mouth for such a thought. The sudden appearance of a car interrupted my view and broke the unusual sensation. The dark-haired man didn't look happy but got in the car. It took off so fast that, within a blink, he was gone. If metal birds brought men like that, then we needed more metal birds.

Pushing away from my hiding spot, I stumbled back on shaky legs into the shadow of the trees and searched for my fallen stick. I didn't know who or what that man was, but everything in me said he was dangerous, and I needed to stay away.

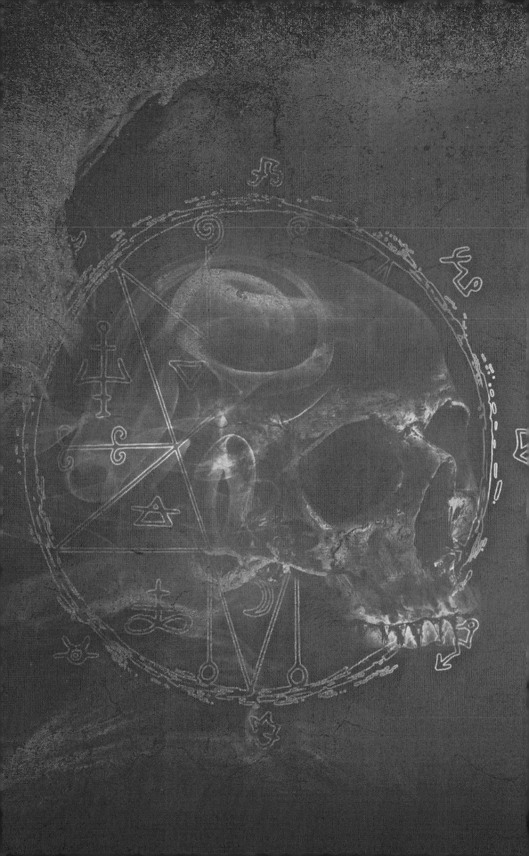

Chapter 3

Rhys

    I snarled at the staff as they walked past with more of my things. "Careful wi' dat. It be a collector's item," I said as the line of people marched on like ants.

"Rhys, are ya still twisted?" Gregory asked as he sauntered down the hall with a cup of coffee.

I hated that the man was watching this happen or that I was essentially putting him in the middle of his blood family and me. Rook was his nephew. I might have been a boy of six when I arrived here in his home, and he may be the closest thing I've had to a father since mine was stolen from me, but blood family was always going to win out in a Faction. If he was forced to choose a side, I knew where I stood, and it would be out in the bloody cold.

"How am I no' 'sposed to be twisted? I'm the older one. It be my destiny ta be da number one, and now I'm a two and forced ta leave me wing of da castle? What da fuck? Is this guy a cunt or what? I dinnie want him, and I fuckin' am no one's number two."

I snatched the guitar out of the worker's hand as he went to walk by. "No one touches me Tabitha," I said, and the servant shrank away from my glare.

"Come on now, son. Ya no how these tings work. He no more chose to be yer one than you chose to be his two." He laid his hand on my shoulder, and I shook his hand off. I was no longer a boy who needed his comfort. I especially didn't need to be comforted over this.

"No. I refuse to go through with this. I'm a McGregor, and we are never a two; but moreover, he fuckin' rejected me already. I ain't no one's sloppy seconds ta be discarded aside and picked back up whenever da fucker chooses. Fuck dis shite. I need air." I stomped away from the man who raised me and I considered family.

"Give 'im a chance, Rhys. Da spirits know what they be doin'," he called after me.

"Bah! Fuck da spirits. They can suck me meaty cock, they can," I yelled back and raised a two-finger salute to the spirits that thought they could fuck with me. There couldn't have been a McGregor spirit in on this decision. They never would've allowed it.

I'd already looked up my chosen match. His face was plastered all over the television from concerts in the Broad Faction bases over-seas. What used to be known as North America had been disbanded after the wars, now divided into twelve chunks. Each of the most powerful families of the Faction controlled a territory, even though, to the Flitters of the world, nothing had changed. It was business as usual in their pathetic little lives. Flitters didn't know that the tax money they spent came to us and that the corporations they worked for were also us. The president who smiled and waved for the people was a real person, all right, just not who they thought. He was nothing more than a talking figurehead who told them all what they wanted to hear, and it was the same all over the world.

The money was now pooled and divided equally by an accountant for each Faction. Most of the twelve stuck to their lines and didn't cause trouble, but there'd been some unrest in districts three and nine.

The Adairs, McGregors, Kellys, McCabes, and Mckinnons had come together to ensure that our power structure didn't weaken and might have stolen a few of the initial smaller lands many moons ago. But no one knew for sure, and the dead didn't willingly share their secrets.

I was supposed to be the one. I was supposed to be the power head. It was what I'd studied and trained for all my life. I would've taken our family into the next hundred years in a power position that no one would dare challenge. I always figured I would be paired and chosen, and a part of me longed to help rule. But it also meant that I had to give up the one person I'd been in love with for as long as I could remember.

My mind drifted to Mari and her smile that could light up a room. I'd buried myself in work, parties, and women to stop thinking about the one thing I could never have, and none of it worked more than a blink.

My fist hit the stone of the castle wall, and I looked at the silver rings and blood trickling down my knuckle. Bringing the fist to my mouth, I licked the blood off, moaning as the metallic taste hit the back of my throat.

"I'm gettin' fucked," I growled, then jumped into my car, putting the guitar on the passenger seat. Thinking better of it, I pulled on the seatbelt and wrapped it around my Tabitha. The small sports car revved, and the tires squealed as I peeled out of my home. Well, the only home I could remember clearly.

My hand smacked against the steering wheel, and I could feel the power rise in my chest as smoke rose around me in the car like I was hotboxing it. Taking a deep breath, I pushed down on the power that was close to raging out of control.

A McGregor as a two? I couldn't even wrap my brain around something so absurd. In all the triads that had been formed between the five families, a McGregor was always the one and the pinnacle of power. We were rarely paired with an Adair because, like the McGregors, they held the deadliest of abilities and were always number one. I think there was only one pairing in the family tree that I'd seen that was with a McGregor and an Adair, and no one knows how the union would've turned out since they killed each other before they ever reached their union night. It didn't exactly make my stomach all fluttery over the idea of being paired with an Adair, to begin with, but then to be demoted....

Not only that but this one, this Rook—what a fucking stupid name that was—looked like a knob. Stupid shaggy hair and black jeans with ripped shirts. Why would the spirits think I'd be interested in that?

I cracked my neck and wheeled the car into the Up Er Kilt Pub's gravel lot. There were already a few horses and buggies tied up outside while their owners had a bevvy. This was my spot, my safe haven from the bull crap. I sat there staring up at the sign, and for the first time, I didn't want to go back to the castle. Not tonight, not ever. I'd been in that wing since I was six. Now I was displaced and forced to start the next step of my triad with a man who had no interest in the family, the business, or, fuck, any of us. He'd made it very clear in his response to the family that he was happy to reject the union. His father had other ideas and forced him to come.

I walked into the ceremonial chamber I'd faithfully come to every three months since I turned thirteen. For me, these old stone walls were like a second home. Few felt as comfortable down here as I did. I had no blood family who wanted anything to do with me left. My only family's ashes sat in the decorative jars among the shelves and would sometimes be seen during the rituals. It gave me comfort to know that my parents were still around, even if it wasn't all the time.

"Oommmmm." Gregory started to key everyone into the chant.

My voice joined with ten others who'd come to the ritual tonight. I could clearly hear Caleb and Lincoln over the others and smirked, knowing that their competitive sides would push the other to be the loudest in the room.

The energy began to swirl. It felt different tonight, like it was super-charged. The hair on the back of my neck stood as my robes billowed around like I was caught in a windstorm. Lifting my head slightly from the cover of the oversized hood, I glanced to either side to see if everyone was being affected so strongly, but their robes stayed quiet. A stream of cool air swirled around my neck, and my snake suddenly pulled free from the confines of the tattoo on my body. It slithered down the arm of the robe, then back up, so it lay across my neck.

"Rhys McGregor, you have been chosen. Please step forward," Nigel said, but his voice was filled with a spirit from the other side.

My heart pounded hard as I took a step toward the dais. This was it! The day that I had prepared for. I'd longed for it as much as I'd secretly feared and hoped it would never happen. It didn't matter what I wanted, though. The spirits had made their decision about my fate. One nervous step at a time, I placed my foot on the top of the platform and knelt in front of the speaker.

"Rhys McGregor, you have been chosen. Do you accept this pairing?"

I swallowed hard, knowing that I had to say yes, and yet my tongue was heavy in my mouth. "Aye. I accept the pairing."

The small candles placed around the pentagram on the floor rose into tall columns of billowing fire. An invisible force that felt like hands reached out and wrapped itself around my throat. I gasped and coughed, but I knelt firm for the test and forced myself to remain calm. I was suddenly let go, and the fires returned to normal, but my snake remained dormant on my neck. I knew something was wrong before the words were spoken. Our snake was supposed to create a blood offering from the pumping blood of our heart when a pairing was accepted and sealed from both ends. My snake's dormant status screamed that I'd been rejected.

"Rhys McGregor, your pairing is Rook Adair, but he has rejected the union. This possible union will remain in effect for three ritual cycles but no more. Another pairing may or may not be made for you in the future."

Nigel fell to the floor as the spirit left his body. I remained kneeling as the shock of the words but also the pain of the rejection began to seep into my body. He rejected me?

"Ah, better luck next time, Rhys. If it's any consolation, I never thought Rook would settle down anyway," Caleb said, laying a hand on my shoulder as he left me to process.

I stood, humiliated by what had just happened and all the words of sympathy and "better luck next time." The shame that I'd just brought upon me, but also my family, was almost unbearable. To be rejected was the highest form of humiliation in a triad other than one of your union partners stepping outside of the relationship once the ceremony had taken place.

The books had said that a rejection came with pain, but I didn't understand what they meant until that night. Fiery pain woke me from an already fitful sleep. I clutched at my chest, not sure if I was having a heart attack. As the pain increased, a sweat broke out on my forehead. I tried to

26

call out for Illiam, Liam, or even Gregory, but my voice stalled in my throat, and no words would come out of my gaping mouth.

Rolling out of bed, I landed on the hard floor and tried to take a deep breath, but with every breath came a lance of pain, like someone was stabbing me with a sharp blade. I needed to get help.

Crawling for my door, I only made it about halfway when the blistering pain increased to levels that had me seeing stars and my mouth hanging open in a silent scream. I flopped onto my back and clawed at the stone floor as I fought off an attack I couldn't see and didn't understand.

"Ahhh!" A scream finally left my lips as my back arched off the ground.

The torment only got stronger and morphed, spreading all along my body. If it weren't for the fact that my eyes could still see, I would've sworn that my muscles and bones were being pulled from my body one at a time. It finally became too much, and I blacked out, only to be woken up by the same sensation all over again, but this time, I knew. I knew then that this was to do with my rejection or, more importantly, what Rook was doing now.

I'd read the books. I'd seen the words, and yet, no words in any language could describe this feeling. When a pairing was started, no matter the stage, unmeasurable pain was felt by the party that held hope for the union. If you'd agreed and the other hadn't...then you felt like you were drowning in an ocean of agony that relented briefly only to start again. I was the one Rook didn't want while he bedded another and another with no regard for the anguish he was putting me through. I hated him.

A final punishment, a kick in the teeth to show you exactly how much you were never wanted. I screamed as it felt like my heart was ripped from my chest. At some point, the spirits cared enough to let me pass out once more.

. . .

"*F*uck," I swore and yelled as I shook the steering wheel. I finally forced myself to let go before I tore it off the car. It had taken days to figure out the combination of drugs that would help numb the sensation just enough that I could function. I hated the fact that I had to take anything at all. If Rook thought that after almost a fucking month of betrayal, I would forgive him and accept him, then he had another think coming.

Leaning over, I hit the button on the small compartment and pulled out my small baggie of pills. I'd been preparing to kick the habit the moment the next ritual moon passed, and I could finally be set free of Rook. Or at least set free enough that I didn't need to take drugs to cope, but that was not fucking today.

Reaching into the baggie of colourful pills, I grabbed three. Tossing them in my mouth, I swallowed them down dry and put the rest of my stash away. Unbuckling Tabitha, I brought the guitar to my lips and gave her a kiss.

"You'll always be my leading lady," I said to the instrument and rubbed my hand down the red and white body. "Well, come on then. Let's get this show goin'."

I stepped out into the sunlight. I didn't care that it was early. I was planning on getting myself shit-faced. Then when I went home—if I went home—I was gonna tell this Rook that he could suck my cock or fucking leave, but I wanted nothing to do with him.

Reject me? No one rejected me and then put me through the wringer. I was fucking Rhys McGregor, and he was gonna learn real fast what that name meant.

The smell of stale smoke was like a breath of fresh air, and I took a deep drag of the sweet aroma. Only a few people were here at this hour, but once night fell, this place would be banging. By then, I'd be three bottles of brandy deep and singin' better than Rook on that stage.

"Well, hello, lass," I said and smacked the waitress's ass as she walked through the kitchen door. Caitlin yelped and smiled when she recognized who it was.

"Back so soon? Couldn't get enough of me cunt, could ya?" Caitlin flicked up the front of her kilt to show off the sweet little pussy I'd been buried in only a night ago. The girl never wore underwear, and I can't say that I complained much about it.

"I might be persuaded for another round. Is your friend workin' tonight?" I asked and shivered as the first round of *oh fuck yes* hit my body from the little happy pills I'd ingested. Sparkly balls danced around the room, and I watched them swirl and twist as they shifted from shades of gold to blue and then red in time to the music softly pumping through the speakers.

"Me friend? Ya mean the friend ya can't remember the name of?" She giggled, her hazel eyes filled with humour. "Aye, she be, but it ain't no night around here yet," Caitlin smiled as she walked to the bar, and I followed her like a dog scenting a female's heat. Maybe I was. My cock certainly thought we were and was making a big old tent in the front of my kilt. Laying the tray down, she turned and squealed as she bumped into me. Laying a hand on the bar, I trapped her in place.

"What would you say to an early performance?" I asked and leaned in to give her neck a soft kiss.

"Kyle, my boss, is an arse and…."

"Fuck 'im. You wanna be wit me? I'll make sure he dinnie fire ya. My money tends to speak loud." I ran my fingers down her bare shoulder and peered down the low-cut top to the treasure she was hiding beneath the thin cotton. "Especially when it's gettin' late in da month."

No one knew that the actual owner of the pub was me. It wasn't something I wanted advertised around, and the tall Scottish bloke I hired to fill the role had a nasty gambling habit. He was all too keen to work for room and board and to have his debts paid down from time to time. Too bad his debts had always belonged to me, so really, he should be happy I wasn't breaking his legs or tossing his ass in the ocean.

Caitlin bit her lip as the hand I trailed down her side slid back up her leg and under the kilt to her tight sex. Swirling my finger around, I rubbed the wetness of her arousal before bringing the finger to her lips. She opened her mouth and sucked my fingers in with a moan.

"You don't have to, lass," I said, giving her a wicked grin.

"You be an arse, McGregor, ya know dis, aye?" Caitlin didn't wait for another sarcastic reply and dragged me toward the back of the pub. My life might be crumbling down around me, but I sure as fuck wasn't letting it kick me in the teeth on the way down.

"Aye, I know."

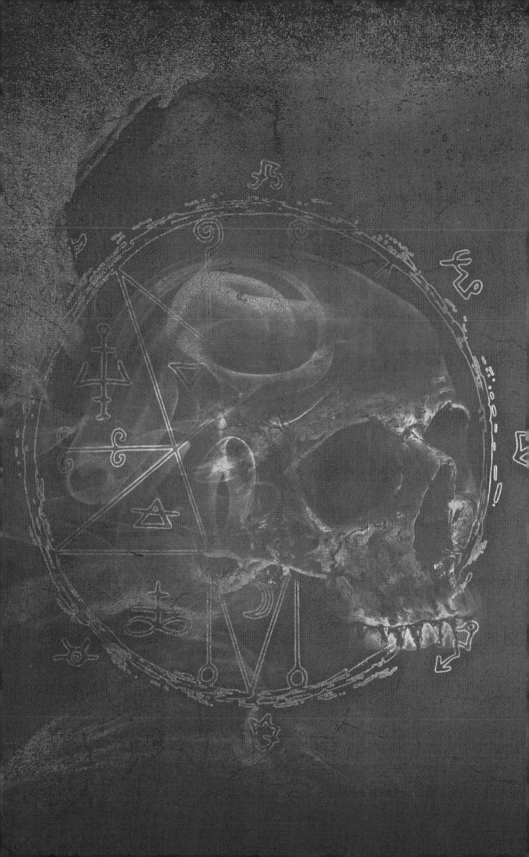

Chapter 4

Rook

You couldn't get me off this tin can fast enough. I was standing at the door, waiting for it to open before we even came to a stop. Now that I was here, the anger I'd managed to tame was brewing once more. I would find a way to pay my father and brothers back for this shit.

The engines finally began to shut down, and I could hear people yelling outside a moment before a knock came for me to open the door. The captain hadn't stepped foot into the cabin area since the near-death experience, and the fact he was still in the cockpit made me think he was saying his prayers. To a false God, mind you, but again, that was something the Flitters didn't know.

Pushing the door open, I got out of the plane and pulled off my wraparounds to look up at the dark, overcast sky. As luck would have it, a raindrop fell directly into my eye.

"Son of a bitch," I grumbled and shook my head to rid it of the water, which felt like an ice shard. I put my shades back on and stomped down the metal stairs toward the overly perky man waiting at the bottom.

"Master Adair, how good it is ta see ya. Da last time me saw ya, yer were but a wee lad," the man said.

I stared at him like he had two heads. What the hell had he just said to me? The accent was so thick that all I caught was "Master Adair" and "lad."

"Ar'ya okay, sir?"

Pinching the bridge of my nose, I sighed. "Can you repeat what you said but slower?"

"Oh, aye, certainly, sir. I. Forgotten. Ya're. No. Accustomed. Ta. Me. Accent," he said.

Giving him a weak smile, I decided to try again. "What's your name?" I asked. My eyes scanned the private airfield for any sign of the limo.

"Me name be Illiam, sir."

Waving my hand back and forth, I shook my head. "Please don't call me sir. Rook is fine."

The colour drained from his face, and he stumbled back, his hand going to his chest. His shock-white hair seemed to stand a little taller as his pale blue eyes grew wide. It was hard to tell how old Illiam was. The soft lines starting to form around his eyes said late thirties, but the way he spoke suggested that he was a fuck tonne older.

"Ave me offended ya?" Illiam asked.

I shook my head. "Um, no. Why?" I asked as the trolley of my suitcases was pushed over for me.

"Sir, it be tradition ta call ya sir or Master. Ta no do so be shameful. I'd be thrown out of da home and me wife beaten and me children sold for such a heinous crime."

"Are you serious?" I asked, lifting a brow at the man. I couldn't tell if he was serious or not. Father was hardcore on the rules we had to follow, but I couldn't picture him killing someone for not calling him sir or Master.

Illiam began to laugh, his face transforming from fear to joy in a heartbeat. "Naw, I'ma just takin' the mick outta ya." As he laughed hard, all I could think was how I might actually like the idea of him being punished after all. "Come on, den. Put yer case in da boot," he said and wandered to what I thought was the passenger side of the car until the miniature box on wheels fired up.

"What the fuck is a boot?" I yelled. "And where is my damn limo?"

Illiam stuck his head out the window and put a pair of sunglasses on. "What ya waitin' for?"

There was a click, and the trunk lifted slightly on the small car. Pulling it open, I stared at the space that would hold only one of my seven suitcases.

"Where do you expect me to fit my stuff?" I pointed to the trolley being wheeled over by one of the workers.

"Put da one in. Da rest will be brought ta da castle fir ya. Hurry on. We 'ave a schedule ta be keepin'." Illiam put his head back inside the window, and I ground my teeth together.

"I'm going to kill someone before I figure a way out of this. I can see it," I said, laying the suitcase into the thing they called a boot and then grabbed the next smallest one and my guitar. I didn't trust anyone with my baby. Stuffing the second bag in the boot, I closed the lid and had to lean on the top to get it to lock. Getting into the passenger seat, which felt completely strange on the opposite side of the car, I rested my guitar between my legs and looked over at Illiam as he stared at me.

"What?"

"Seatbelt." He pointed to the buckle, and I groaned.

"Oh, for the love…." Grabbing the strap, I buckled it and crossed my arms as I slumped down into the seat. It had no leg space for my long legs. My head slammed back against the seat as Illiam shifted the car into gear and tore out of the small airport like we'd entered a Formula One race. "Holy shit!" I grabbed for the emergency handle as the car skidded sideways out of the airport. "What the fuck? Are you trying to kill me?"

"We 'ave a schedule ta keep. Come on. I be tinkin' yer dis wild rocker dat likes livin' on da edge." Illiam removed his hands from the wheel to make air quotes with his fingers before he laughed and flicked on the radio. He pressed a button, and soon my voice was being blared into the car. "Well, come on, den, loosen up. Yer gonna get ta meet yer second. Rhys be eye candy," Illiam said and smiled. I couldn't tell if he was joking or not.

"Oh, yay for me," I mumbled under my breath.

I'd never even seen a picture of this guy, and yet we were supposed to go on some wild hunt like savages to find our woman. *Roar! Look at me. Me savage and need to drag woman back by hair to fuck and make a triad of three.* It was fucking ridiculous that this format of the triad still existed. It was beyond archaic. Why did this ritual need to continue, anyway? The world was at peace. The Flitters were blissfully kept unaware, the other Factions were happy, and we all got along. It simply made no sense.

Once we reached the main road, Illiam opened the windows and lip-synced along to the words. This was my favourite song to sing live. The crowd always got into it, and I could feel the energy flowing from the thousands singing and dancing. Never hurt that the girls in the front row would throw their underwear. I always got security to bring a few back to the room to complete my night.

Leaning my head on the door, I watched the world pass by and had to admit that the bright emerald greens of the rolling hills were stunning. The landscape opened up, and I occasionally caught sight of large castles in the distance and the water well beyond that, but for the most part, we were surrounded by vacant space. It just felt so open and empty. The roads were quiet, too quiet. Back home, the highways and freeways were always jammed, but here, it was like we were the only two people on the entire island. It gave me the creeps.

The farther we drove, the more things changed, and soon it was farmland and large clumps of forest. I never saw another living person and began looking closer at the farms we passed. There were homes, but no one outside.

"Is there a reason why no one is on the road?"

Illiam looked over at me. "Were ya expectin' ta be seein' someone?"

"What? No, I mean it's quiet," I said and gestured toward the front window to demonstrate.

Illiam smiled. "Oh! Aye, ain't it grand?" He took a deep breath. "I'ma bettin' yer no used to dis kind o' fresh air."

I blinked at the man. Forget not speaking the same damn language. We didn't belong on the same planet. I just nodded, deciding that if the man were driving me to my death, at least it would have more people.

I turned my head to stare out the window once more when we drove past a magnificent castle that even I couldn't take my eyes off. Not that I'd never admit it to my father, but I loved the look of it.

"Dat be Glentruan Castle and da home of da McGregors," Illiam said, pointing at the massive castle. Of course, it was Rhys'. I definitely wasn't saying anything about liking the look of it now. No matter how hard I tried, I couldn't peel my eyes away from the cool stone and large turrets. There was something majestic and haunting about it.

Back home, the Factions had left everything pretty much the same as it had been when the war started. The only difference was that toll booths were set up to mark borders. Those who manned them were hired by the Faction for their abilities to keep the border safe. To a Flitter, the employees simply took the money for the toll and told them to have a great day at work.

Here, though, I could feel the age on my skin. It was like the land screamed of the wars that had taken place and how they had ravaged certain strongholds more than others. My family was but one Faction in many, but we were one of the most powerful. Part of that was because, until recently, we'd always maintained powerful triads. All the main triads were broken now, with either one person or another dead.

It wasn't that I didn't understand why my father insisted I do this, but this was supposed to be my life. Turning into a miserable SOB in a suit was not how I wanted to spend my life. I had to leave everything I knew behind for this place, which was nothing more than a distant memory from when I was a small child.

"Din't be worrin'. Ya will be fallin' in love wit it 'ere," Illiam said, and I looked at the man from the corner of my eye. "Da place kinda grows on ya, if ya know what I mean. You'll see. You'll be singin' a different tune in a few days, I reckon."

I couldn't be bothered arguing with the smiling face, but I highly doubted it. The car slowed about an hour later, and we turned into a driveway with massive bushes lining either side, blocking the place from sight. We pulled up to the largest wrought-iron gates I'd ever seen, and if that wasn't enough to scream that this place stank of money and things that most didn't want to know about, then the massive guards patrolling inside certainly did. I would've thought it was impossible to look imposing while wearing a kilt, but holy fuck, was I wrong.

Each of the guards had to be well over six feet. They wore leather armour on their broad chests and thick arms and had long swords at their hips. Massive axes lined their backs. All of them had their hair in either a mohawk or braided in an array of colours, while symbols were carved into their faces. Tattoos of power were visible between the leather armour.

A cold tendril slithered up my spine as we drove through the second gate, and I knew that this one was coated in power. Taking a deep breath, I could feel the call of the surroundings, and as much as I'd never admit it, this place spoke to me in a way that no other place had. It screamed home in my head, and before we were even parked, I could feel my body recharging from the excessive power usage on the plane. I shuddered and gave a little moan as I took a deep breath. I'd never felt anything like this before.

"Ya feel it, do ya? You all do. The call here is strong on da ancestral land," Illiam said, then pushed open the door.

Stepping from the car, I had to grip the door hard as power coursed up through my feet and filled me with a sensation that caressed every part of my body. My cock was suddenly feeling very neglected.

What the hell was it with this place? I'd been near powerful objects many times, and I'd been on other cult lands and felt the pull of their power, but this was different. My body was soaking it in, like it was a strong drink and warm pussy, while I slit the throat of a sacrifice all at the same time.

No matter how this place felt, I could never see myself living in the middle of fucking nowhere. I was bright lights, booze, loud music, great shopping, and of course, I was a multiple-partner-a-night type. At twenty-four, I had no interest in settling down into a triad and helping maintain the family business. I was still young, and what about my singing career? It was just getting off the ground, and I was making it big. Other than the amazing brandy we made, I didn't even know what the fuck else we did, let alone how to maintain it. I grabbed my guitar and put the strap over my body, so it laid along my back. It was the one thing that comforted me in this strange place.

It sounded like an explosion as the trunk—or boot, or whatever it was—closed. I jolted and snapped out of the seductive sensations. Illiam was already standing by the lower stair waiting for me to catch up when the front door opened, and four people walked out. Each of them looked as if they'd travelled from a time in the past. The two women wore dresses better suited to a ball, with their hair twisted up in braids that looked like snakes coiled on their heads with the ends trailing down their backs. It took me a second to figure out they were my cousins, Belle and Mari. They barely looked like the last photo that was sent.

The two men wore similar outfits to the guards but without the armour, axes, or face paint. The family kilt of maroon and black was wrapped around their waists with eight-hole shitkickers and basic black shirts. I recognized the one as my uncle from family photos, but I didn't know the other and wondered if this was my number two. There was no pull or excitement as I stared into his pale blue eyes and hair similar to Illiam.

"Nephew, it be good ta see ya again," Gregory said.

When I held out my hand, he laughed at the gesture and pulled me into a bear hug. Stepping back, he smiled as he gripped my shoulders with his large hands. What the fuck was it with this place that it made everyone fucking massive? I mean, I was no slouch at six-three, and I was fucking cut, but my uncle looked like he crushed logs with his bare hands before his breakfast.

"Uncle," I said as he let me go.

"Naw, call me Gregory. We be family, me boy." Uncle Gregory turned to Illiam. "Illiam, did all go well and wit out incident?"

"Aye, Master. All arrangements were made, and we saw no trouble. Master Adair has been nothin' but pleasant. Da rest of da luggage be on route."

I raised an eyebrow at the slight exaggeration about my attitude and suddenly felt a little bad that I'd been such a dick.

"Excellent, cannie ya see his tings to his room while I finish introductions?"

"Aye, Master, you dinnie even 'ave ta ask," Illiam said, way too cheerily.

Illiam picked the two bags up like they weighed nothing, jogged up the stairs then disappeared through the front door of the massive castle.

"I'va never found a better servant den dat man." My uncle looked over his shoulder where Illiam had gone. "Dis is Belle and Mari, me daughters and yer cousins," he said, smiling at the two girls who had been as still as statues.

"Our pleasure ta meet ya, Rook," they said in unison, their voices tinkling on the breeze like wind chimes.

Leaning forward, I offered them my hand. Their touch was cool, soft, and as light as a feather before they pulled away.

"Liam, here, be yer personal servant picked specifically wit ya and yer needs in mind," Gregory said. "He will do as little or as much as ya require and with out question." Gregory nodded to the man that I'd thought was my second and was oddly thankful he wasn't. Not that I was picturing a life here with my chosen. I wasn't picturing a life here at all, but if I was forced to go through with this union, then I at least wanted to be attracted to the guy.

I raised my eyebrow at the wording of the sentence as my eyes roamed over the man looking at me like he was the cat and I was his fresh dish of milk. Was this to fill my time until the triad was formed? I had no idea and just gave the guy a nod.

I found it strange that my uncle was potentially offering me my own sex servant, when I was here to meet the members of my triad. I happily fucked whoever and didn't give much thought to their gender. Then again, there was a good fucking chance I was simply overthinking the entire situation.

My eyes drifted towards the open door and the lack of anyone else coming out. Why the fuck was I annoyed that Rhys hadn't come to meet me? I mean, I didn't want him, and I certainly didn't want to be here, but it still irritated the fuck out of me that he got to choose whether he wanted to see me, but I was forced to fly across the damn globe to meet him.

"If ya be lookin' for Rhys, he's no home," my uncle said, rubbing the back of his neck.

"I wasn't," I said casually, giving him a flat stare. Then what he said dawned on me. "What do you mean, home? I thought the McGregors lived at Glentruan Castle."

Gregory's face looked as confused as I felt. "Aye, they do, but no Rhys. Rhys has lived here wit me since his father—spirits rest his soul

—died. Rhys was but a wee boy of six when he and Fiona, his sister, moved in wit me. I thought Angus woulda told ya dat."

Oh, Father, sweet Father, just another thing you managed to omit to further your agenda. Now I couldn't even avoid seeing the guy while I stayed here. I managed a small fake smile, for Gregory's sake.

"Can I have a smoke and a shower before you give me that tour?"

"Whatever ya want. A grand feast has been prepared in yer honour. We be dinin' in an hour. Liam, show Rook da way ta his wing," Gregory said. "Come, girls. Let's go see yer ma before we eat."

My brow furrowed as I watched the three of them step down the stairs and head towards the massive garden area. I could've sworn my uncle was a widower, but now I wasn't so sure.

This place was already proving to be more fucked than even I could've pictured.

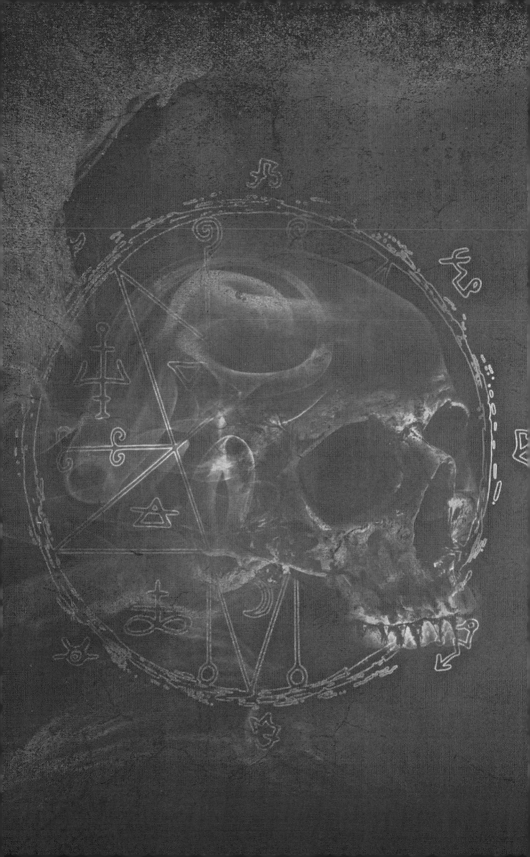

Chapter 5

Rook

Okay, the pros with the place. The food—holy fuck, did they like to feed me, and it was damn good. The service was top-notch, and my strange manservant, Liam, had my clothes put away and brought me a nightcap after he made sure the water was hot for my shower. I had a feeling he wanted me to ask him to join, but he never said a word to push me in that direction.

Had I been tempted? Yeah, the guy was good-looking, but I was bagged and just wanted to sleep.

Everything about this place was simple and relaxed but found a way to be more extravagant than even I was used to. I wasn't sure how things melded together so well, but they did. This bed was another example. I was snuggled into the comfiest and largest bed I'd ever seen, and it could easily hold six people. The bathroom was larger than the one in my father's mansion back home, and I swear the toilet tried to clean my ass for me.

Oddly, I was still having trouble sleeping.

No matter what I tried, there was an unease that was flowing through my body like hummingbird wings. My power was all over the place as well. One moment, it was quiet. The next thing I knew, my back arched off the bed as I balled the blankets in my fists and fought to keep it in check.

This place was also way too fucking quiet. I didn't like spending that much time in my head alone, and all this detached-from-the-world bullshit with no wild parties gave me way more than I'd ever been used to. Growing up, I had three brothers in the house with me full-time. It was never fucking quiet. You could be in the middle of a shit, and one of them would find a way to get in the locked door to ask a question. My gaze found the window and the dark grey clouds floating like bobbing ships outside. The quiet was also when my ability to manipulate the freshly dead spirits simmered a little brighter inside me.

All the Adair men had the ability to connect with the spirits without a ritual ceremony, but it wasn't something I practiced or welcomed. Nothing creepier than when you're banging a hot girl, and you feel your long-dead relative in the room. Fucking pervs.

I was starting to relax and doze off when a loud clatter and laughing out in the hall had me sitting up and reaching under my pillow for my knife. The large wooden door slammed open, and a man stumbled in, laughing hysterically. Four stunning women wearing what looked like schoolgirl uniforms were draped all over him. It was obvious before the scent of alcohol hit me that they were drunk, but the distinct smell of a smoky bar reaffirmed the visual.

The guy looked up, our eyes locked, and I knew this was Rhys. I could feel the tug in my gut, a stirring in my heart and my cock twitched. He didn't have to say a word for the buzz that had been a steady hum to amplify at the sight of him. I laid a hand over my stomach to try to settle the sensation. It was very difficult to runaway from yourself, but I felt like I wanted to try.

Rhys stood up straight. And despite wanting nothing to do with him, I could appreciate that he was fucking hot. Not good-looking, not even just all right. No, this man checked off all the boxes I craved in a male partner. Piercing, commanding eyes that locked me in. I forced my gaze over his body and appreciated that he wasn't wearing a shirt.

Every cut abdominal muscle, his hard pecs, and the defined arms showing had my mouth watering. Dark tattoos that stood out on his fair skin matched his black hair cut into a short mohawk. They covered the sides of his neck and travelled down the sides of his ribcage and arms. He wore leather cuffs, large silver rings, much like mine, and chains that jingled around his neck. But it was the black kilt wrapped around his waist, and the promise of what lay beneath that had my cock standing at attention once more.

Those silver eyes narrowed at me, and the room suddenly felt smaller. Rhys was a McGregor, which naturally meant he would be powerful, but what I hadn't expected was just how strong this man was. And right now, he was pissed off. And I was the target. There was no denying the waves of angry heat rolling off him, and now that the initial shock was over, my anger rose to match.

"Feck me, forgot ya nicked me feckin' room. Come on den, lassies, we best be headed ta da other side of da castle and let the pretty boy be gettin' his rest."

"Pretty boy? Fuck you," I yelled, but the door was already slamming back into place.

47

Oh, fuck no. He did not just walk out and dismiss me. Leaping from the bed, I stuffed my leg into the pair of black jeans I'd tossed on the chair. Hopping across the floor, I managed to get the second leg on and pulled them up. My bare feet smacked along on the cool stone floor as I marched for the door and threw it open. The fucker and the sexy entourage were gone, but I could hear their laughter coming from the right. This place was a damn maze, and I suddenly wished I'd taken my uncle up on a more in-depth tour rather than opting to go to my room after dinner.

I stormed around the next corner and saw them as they made a left at the end of the wide hall. "Hey, asshole!"

I jogged to the end of the corridor and turned, only to find it empty and silent. This would've been unnerving to anyone else, but being accustomed to parlour tricks, I knew Rhys was masking them.

"Appreozo," I said and waved my hand over the space.

The five of them appeared, but Rhys looked over his shoulder and smirked. "Petrobile," he said, and I was instantly frozen in place.

Son of a bitch.

By the time the immobility spell wore off, they were long gone, and he had to be masking their route because no matter what version of a locator spell I tried, it wouldn't work.

"Cock-sucking, fucking, unbelievable, arrogant…."

"Master, ya be all right?" Startled, I spun around at the sound of Liam's voice. "Me apologies, Master. I din't mean ta startle ya, but ya seem outta sorts."

"Do you know how to get to Rhys's room?"

Liam wrung his hands together and looked down at his feet. "I'ma sorry, Master, but I'ma no ta interfere wit Master Rhys or ya triad union. If Master Rhys wants ta be alone, I cannie show ya da way."

"So you can't show me the way because he doesn't want you to?"

Liam nodded. "So if I didn't want him to find me, I could ask the same thing?" Liam nodded again. "Fine, I don't want him coming to my room again."

Liam held up his finger. "Dat's no what I mean. Ya can search him out, I cannie help ya, but if he knows where ya be, I cannie stop him."

"Well, that fucking sucks since I don't know my way around this fucking place. Tomorrow, the first thing I want you to do is to take me on a really in-depth tour. And I mean, I want to see every single fucking room this place has. Do you understand?"

Liam swallowed hard but nodded his compliance. Looking around the hallway with creepy fucking armoured soldiers and weapons lining the walls, I realized I didn't know how to get back to my room. Sighing, I rubbed at my face.

"Liam, can you show me to my room?"

"Aye, Master, of course." Liam stood up straight and led the way like a prancing pony. Reaching my room, he lingered outside the door as I was closing it, his eyes once more suggesting we could be doing a lot more. Was this guy desperate, or did I look that desperate?

"Night, Liam."

"Night, Master."

Taking a moment, I stared around the room and smirked at the thought that I had taken this room from Rhys. No clue why they would make him move, and if I'd known ahead of time, I would've said I didn't care what room I was in, but now... now it was fucking satisfying.

"At least I'm annoying you as much as having to be here is annoying me," I said to the empty room.

The jeans never made it off this time as I lay back down on the bed and put my arm behind my head. Annoyingly, I couldn't stop thinking about the man who had crashed through the door. The fact that he was getting to fuck four women really burned my ass, but I ground my teeth together as I realized the women weren't the reason my dick was standing up straight. I swore a line of profanity at the ceiling, then quickly squashed the single spark of jealousy. I didn't want the triad, and I didn't want him.

I really hated this connection bullshit. The power of the chosen union was definitely coming to life, but as long as I didn't agree to the ceremony, it wouldn't happen, and we'd get back to our lives.

Waving my hand, the candles around the room snuffed out, and the room plunged into darkness.

"For the love of the dark fade, please don't let me dream of him tonight," I said, but I had a feeling the exact opposite was going to be the case.

Mari

I stared at the bonfire and watched with half-hearted interest as Crispin, Ronan, and Caleb took turns turning the fire into different animals. They were all hysterically laughing at the large fire pig running around. I took a sip of my drink, my mind wandering back to my cousin who'd just arrived... Rook.

I didn't hate my cousin—I didn't even know him—but he was here to take the one thing I loved most in this world. Even though I knew the day would come and had prepared myself, telling myself over and over to stop loving Rhys, nothing helped. You'd think that when you grew up in the same house, you'd get sick of someone or, at the very least, see them as a true brother, but nope. From the first look, with those silver eyes, I'd been lost.

"Well now, ya dinnie look too happy ta be 'ere," Riegan said as she flopped down into the chair beside me. "Lemme guess. Yer cousin Rook arrived and has finally dashed all yer hopes an dreams." She snickered.

I glared at Riegan. "Why are ya such a twat? Yer supposed ta be me friend."

Riegan snorted and shook her head. "Aye, I be yer friend. But, Mari, for fuck's sake, ya knew dis day was gonna come. Besides, I dinnie know what ya see in me cousin, anyway. Go for Ronan. Ya know he's been crushin' on ya fir years."

The wind picked up and blew the long strands of my hair around my face, making me shiver. I glanced up at Ronan, and as if his sister saying his name drew his attention, he locked eyes with me and smiled. No matter how hard I tried to envision being with Ronan, I couldn't. We were friends, but there was just no spark, no common interests, nothing that made me want to spend time with him outside of gatherings like this. All I could wonder was, why wasn't Rook paired with Ronan instead?

"You know I'm not allowed to choose my own fate, and besides, I don't have feelings for your brother," I said softly and turned my head to look at Riegan. "Besides he's cruel and who knows what he'd want to do with me," I said, keeping my voice low.

"Naw, ya prefer ta pine over my knob of a cousin." She rolled her eyes, but the anger was instant.

"Don't insult Rhys," I said. "He is a good man and will make an excellent head of the McGregor family."

"Great man, ha! What do ya gather he be doin' right now?"

The comment stung because I knew exactly what he was doing.

He was once more burying his feelings the same way I did. The only difference was that he did so by sleeping with multiple people while I was here, but at least here was not doing basalainn demon blood. My hands were trembling with the thought of a single drop on my tongue, and I quickly pulled my hands into my thick sweater and clenched them into fists.

"I know what he's doing, Riegan. You don't need to throw it in my face." I pushed myself to my feet. "Forget it. I'm going home."

Riegan snatched my arm. "Mari, dinnie go. I'm sorry. Ya know I like takin da mick out of da situation, but I dinnie mean ta hurt ya."

"You have no idea how hard it is to be born without a tattoo or red hair, Riegan. You tease, and it cuts like a knife. You have a tattoo. You'll find your match," I said.

"Yer right, I keep forgettin'."

I looked my sorta friend's face over and sat back down. "I'm not going to be good company tonight," I said.

"Aye, I know." Riegan wasn't a very warm person, but the fact that she reached out and patted my arm made me feel a little less alone.

I'd tried to move away and thought I was starting to put Rhys and what we wanted behind me. Then Ma got sick and passed to the spirit world, and Pa hadn't been himself. I moved home to be closer to him and realized I'd only been fooling myself. The distance hadn't made the feelings disappear. They simmered under the surface, waiting for the opportunity to break free. As if no time had passed, we once more became inseparable.

I jumped as Rhys's arm brushed mine, and he softly snickered. Smiling, I glanced over from the book I was supposed to be studying, then looked around the room for the teacher, Mrs. Murray. Pa had hired her to home-school us.

Rhys hid his hand but held out a small piece of paper to me, and I quickly took the offering. I loved it when he was like this. It was rare to see him not serious about learning, training, or whatever else they did to groom the guys to take over the Faction.

Mrs. Murray was in the far corner of the large library, staring up at the books. Hiding the paper under the table, I quietly unfolded and read the note. As soon as I saw the words, my mouth fell open.

"Sneak out?" I whispered, and he nodded before pointing to the door.

The large glass doors were left open to let the warm summer breeze inside. Though the curtains were drawn back, the wind still made them flutter. I looked at Mrs. Murray, who was still occupied by the books.

"I dinnie know...." I bit my lip.

Rhys held out his hand. I knew Pa would be angry, but I wanted to spend some time outside before the weather turned cold again. Smiling, I placed my hand in his, and we slowly got to our feet. We made our escape one soft step at a time but only got about halfway when Mrs. Murray spotted us.

"Where do ya tink ya be goin'?" she said.

I was going to turn around and apologize, but instead, a small scream left my mouth as Rhys began to run, pulling me along with him for a second before my feet caught on to the sudden shift in pace.

"Hey, git back 'ere!"

Laughing, we darted out the door running along the back lawn and down toward the beach. We didn't stop until we knew we were well-hidden and far enough that Mrs. Murray wouldn't be bothered coming to find us. Flopping on the grassy rise, we laughed hard until I was gasping for breath.

"We're gonna be in big trouble," I said.

"Aye, but it's worth it. Look at da clouds. They be makin' lots of shapes today." Rhys pointed to the mass of rolling white. "It be a rabbit,"

"Naw, dinnie be daft. Da is clearly a bird," I argued.

A tiny bit of sadness crept into my chest, and my smile fell. I'd had a crush on my best friend for a couple of years. Now at thirteen, I knew that *the dreams of us getting matched were just that, dreams. Standing, I walked to the edge of the water and picked up a handful of stones to skip along the top.*

"They no work when there be waves," Rhys said as I threw the first stone. He was right, of course, but I kept at it. Rhys stepped up beside me. "Is somethin' wrong, Mari?"

I couldn't bring myself to tell him what was making me sad. He was my only friend since my sister and I didn't get along. She was like oil and I the water. Gripping the stones in my hand, I stared down at my reflection in the water. "I wish I had hair like me sister. I hate me raven hair," I said, bitter, as I stared at the black colour.

"Why? It be beautiful."

Stupid tears pricked my eyes with the compliment, and I looked away from Rhys and crossed my arms. "Naw, it be a curse."

"Aye, maybe it is, but it doesn't make it or you any less beautiful."

I turned my head to look at Rhys, and his face seemed just as sad. Could it be? Could he feel the same way?

"I know we are never gonna be paired, but I wish it was you," he said.

I searched his face, and a tear trickled down my cheek. "Me too."

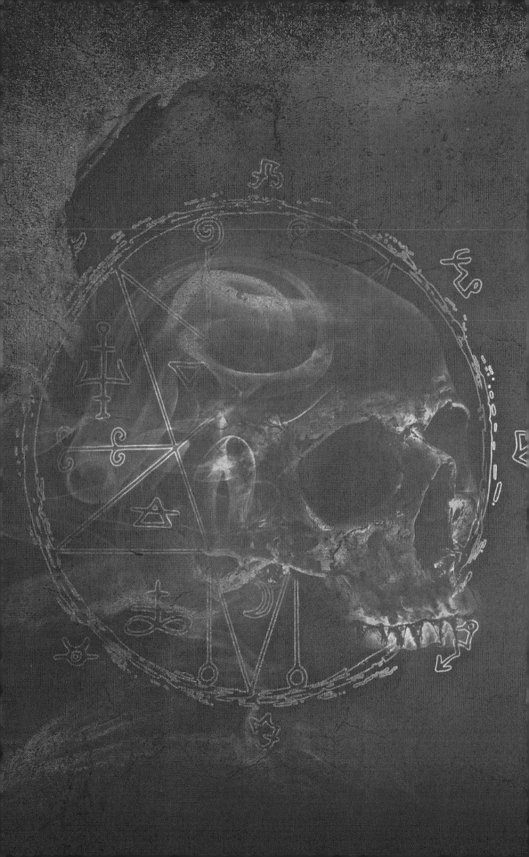

Chapter 6

Rhys

The door slammed open, and the echoing sound of the wooden door connecting with the stone was like a spike piercing through my brain. A soft murmuring of groans around me told me I wasn't alone. I peeled an eye open. That didn't help. My brain was fried from too much drink and party pills. I remembered partying way too hard and arriving back to the castle and going to my room...Rook. Shite.

The image in the doorway faded in and out as my eyes tried to focus on who was in my room. The bright blue eyes and black hair of the man standing there made me flop back down. I had no interest in dealing with this shit.

"Whateva ya be sellin', ya can get tae fuck," I mumbled and rolled over to find my face in someone's ass crack. Blinking again, I shrugged. At least it was a nice ass crack. I'd woken up to worse.

"We need to talk." Rook's voice was deeper than I'd expected, and I hated that it pulled at me.

"Naw, we dinnie 'ave ta talk," I drawled. "I be tellin' ya to fuck off. Now get out. Me head hurts."

Even with my eyes closed, I could see his arrogant face and feel him glaring at me from the door. Unfortunately, I remembered stumbling into his room—my old room—last night and the feeling of seeing him for the first time.

"Oh, for shit's sake." I groaned when Rook didn't leave. "Lassies, it be time ta go." I smacked the one closest to me on the ass, and she yelped, then giggled.

"Why he naw just join us? He's total lush," Caitlin said, her head rising from the far end of the bed. Caitlin was right. He was fucking sexy, but that was beside the point.

"Not a fuckin' chance. Go on now. Get out."

There was a collective groan as the four women—only two of whom I knew the names of—slowly got up from the bed and fumbled around to find their clothes. I swung my legs over the side of the bed and held my aching head. It felt like it would split open at any minute.

The door closed, and I stood as naked as a newborn babbie and made my way across the floor to the closet. I could feel Rook's eyes on me. It pissed me off and heated my skin all at the same time.

"What do ya want?" I growled, grabbing a black T-shirt and pulling it over my head.

I could've covered up my cock first, but I wanted him to see what he was never gonna get to touch. I was an arse like that. It brought a scrap of satisfaction for being dislodged, demoted, and rejected all in a single breath.

"It's obvious you don't want anything to do with me any more than I want to do with you," Rook said.

I turned around and leaned against the corner of the closet crossing my arms over my chest. "Is dat so?"

"Yeah, it is. Can you put some fucking clothes on?"

Instead, I wiggled my cock back and forth. It hit the sides of my thighs with a slap. "Here, an' I thought you said ya weren't interested?"

"I'm not."

"Aye," I chuckled. "News flash, mate, yer standin' in me room and starin' at me cock, which tells another story." Reaching into the closet, I pulled out a simple black kilt and wrapped it around my waist. "Just go home. I dinnie want ya here, Rook."

"I wish you'd speak normally," Rook said.

The anger that had already been simmering spiked as I fixed him with a glare. "Really now? Well, in case ya hadn't caught on, yer naw home nea more. Dis be me home and me country, and maybe I'd like fir *you* to fuckin' speak normal."

I stepped in his direction and clamped down on the instant connection beginning to form from the chosen union. I was having none of it.

"Run along home Rook. Like me said, I dinnie want ya here and me knows ya din't wanna be." I pegged him with a hard stare. "I dinnie even understand why ya be here disrutpin' me life."

"I can't. My father forced me to come," Rook grumbled. "Fucking prick."

Walking past him, I knew we were the same height without having to give him a good look. I liked that and hated that I liked it more. My hand paused on the door handle, and I shot Rook a glare over my shoulder.

"At least ya be havin' a father dat is lookin' out fir ya. One day dat won't be da case, and me hopes ya din't regret da words ya speak," I said, the anger simmering in my tone. "I could only wish me father be alive." Stepping out of the room, I wandered down the hall. The cold stone felt good on my sore feet. Way too much dancing last night.

"Where are you going? We're not done talking," Rook said and began to follow me.

I was getting the impression that people didn't say no to this guy much. The entitled and self-righteous air around him reeked worse than my last night's socks.

"Me head is needin' a coffee, and me needs a truck-load a grease ta sop up da shit me drank last night. Dis is no happenin' right now, I cannie take yer shit."

"My shit? How is this solely my problem?" Rook asked, and the frustration oozing off him made the corner of my lip curl up.

I stopped and turned to face him. His green eyes went wide as he almost bumped into me. We were, as I suspected, the same height. An electrical charge swirled around us, and it would've been easy to succumb to the seduction of the power that wanted to form and tie us together, but I just glared at him.

"Do ya think I din't know that ya rejected the union wit me long before yer were forced to come? Ya tink I be sittin' around 'ere like a sap just waitin' for yer sorry arse ta show up? Or maybe ya taut dat I be some oblivious knob dat din't know about da pairing at all." I took a step in his direction. "From da moment dat ya rejected me, I felt it. I felt every excruciating moment of it." I tapped over my heart as he licked his lips, which were too tempting, so I took a step back. "Da next ritual moon be comin'. I can only accept da rejection den, which I'ma gonna fuckin' dance doin'. So let me make dis clear fir ya since ya dinnie seem ta be catchin' on. Stay da fuck away from me. I no want anythin' ta do with ya, and in a few weeks, ya can go back ta all yer adorin' fans, and I git me room back."

Turning around I grabbed my head as it spun and marched towards the kitchen. *Shit.* I hadn't meant to let him know that his rejection affected me. I could only blame it on the fuzzy brain I was still suffering. The kitchen was quiet, but the coffee was percolating soI sat down and put my head in my hands as I waited for it to finish. When Rook stepped through the door, I could feel him, and I wished I could figure out how to cut the connection early. It was maddening and stronger than I ever thought it would be, especially with him rejecting me.

"I'm not following you. I want a coffee, and I couldn't remember how to get to the kitchen," Rook said.

He was leaning against the counter when I glanced over, and if my brain weren't screaming inside my head, I would've said fuck the coffee and left. I should leave, anyway. I could stay at one of the other castles or rent a spot for a few weeks. That sounded like a good idea. Then the temptation to touch him wouldn't be so strong. Stupid union magic was sizzling in the air and was alluring as fuck.

"I'm sorry," Rook suddenly said into the quiet room. "I don't want to be forced into a triad. It was never something I wanted with anyone, but I didn't mean to hurt your feelings. It wasn't personal or anything."

The fucker had no idea what he did to me for weeks. He was either as oblivious as a jaybird or didn't give a fuck. Either way, I didn't care. I just wanted him to keep his fucking distance and to shut the fuck up. Was that really too much to ask?

"Aye, it be what it be."

The coffee pot beeped, and I stood and grabbed two mugs, putting one on the counter for Rook. Pouring my coffee and leaving it black, I turned for the exit to the outdoor patio.

"Do you play?" Rook asked, and I turned and lifted my brow in question as I blew air on the hot liquid. He pointed to my neck, and I glanced down at the chain that held a silver pick.

"Aye, da chain was me Da's before he died, and da pick be mine. But I dinnie play dat crap ya call singin'." I smiled as his face grew dark with the insult. Turning, I marched out to the patio and sat down.

"Ah, fir fuck's sake, man, cannie ya just leave a guy alone," I said as Rook wandered out and sat down beside me.

"I just want to talk. It's not like I know anyone other than Liam and Gregory."

"Aye, but I no yer friend and no wanna talk." I took another gulp of my coffee and could almost envision the magic from the ritual seeping along the floor and wanting to wrap itself around my ankle. Nope. Not happening.

Standing, I moved across the sitting area to put more distance between us.

"Look, man, I already apologized for embarrassing you. Can't we just get over it already?"

I bit my lip to keep from divulging any more of how much he'd hurt me. I didn't want anyone except Mari to have that kind of sway over my feelings. I trusted her not to hurt me. Ignoring Rook, I closed my eyes as pieces of last night came back. Shit, I shouldn't have brought those girls here and instantly hated that I'd put Mari in the position of possibly seeing that. Fuck, I hated myself for that shit, I needed to lay off the booze and pills.

"Fine, you want to stay pissed, stay pissed. What kind of music do you play?"

What was this, fifty questions? Lifting my head from the back of the chair, I stared at the man across from me. Rook had a strong, angular jaw that was way too sexy in the soft light of the early morning. The dusting of his five o'clock shadow only added to the look. My heart thumped harder as he leaned forward, and those blue eyes locked with mine. I could openly admit that I wished this magic would go away as my skin heated and thoughts of him pushing me against the wall filtered into my brain. I needed to sit bare-arsed in the ocean, and with any luck, something would bite me cock off.

Sighing, I gave up. "I play folk, and local songs with a rock twist." I caught sight of Illiam and Liam walking by a window, talking. "Has Liam gotten in ya trousers yet? If no', he will keep at it. He be a great worker and loyal, but a bit too enthusiastic. Dere ya can keep yerself busy with him until I can except da rejection."

"My trousers? Man, you all talk so weird. No offense, but I can barely understand any of you." Rook shrugged. "Liam hinted, but nothing happened, he's not really my type. Unlike what you got up to with those four girls last night."

Usually, the jealous edge would've turned me on, and I would've poked at him until he got aggressive, which I liked from my male partners. I liked them to be in control. Doing what they wanted with my body in any depraved fashion they chose, but right now, it only infuriated me.

"Naw, ya dinnie get ta make dat kind of comment. Ya wanna whole bus of wet cunt or hard pricks? I'll 'ave 'em ordered in like a menu fir ya, but ya dinnie get to be jealous wit me."

"I'm not jealous." His tone and the look in his eyes said the complete opposite.

"Aye, ya are, and ya have no right." Rook started to argue, but I stood up and gulped down the remaining coffee in a single mouthful. It burned my throat and felt like acid in my empty stomach, but I didn't care. "I cannie be around ya, Rook. I'ma gonna ask ya one more time ta stay away from me and find someone else ta talk ta. Soon ya will be gone, and we neva 'ave ta see one another again. I cannie be yer friend. Go visit yer cousins or somethin'."

Slamming the mug down, I marched away, praying he'd fucking stay put and leave me the hell alone.

I felt like I'd been preparing for the moment I'd be chosen my whole life. I sacrificed my feelings and dreams for the greater good of the Faction because that was who I was. The person who wanted to help our people. And if that meant I had to bottle everything else important in my life and put a cork in it, then that was what I did.

Rook blatantly did the complete opposite. From the bit I'd been able to gather from the other lads in the Faction, Rook never took part in the rituals. He barely studied any of the magic or ritual books and had no interest in helping run the Faction. So, of course, the spirits would choose him and pair the fucker with me. What were they hoping? That I'd rub off on him? Well, they could all fuck off.

I loved the Faction, helping to protect those who lived here, making us stronger, but right now, I really wanted to accept the rejection and pray that I didn't get re-paired. If I made it ten more years past my thirty-fifth birthday, Mari and I could marry. I would still help run the Faction and take over as head of my family. Even if I wasn't in a triad, there were many ways I could help.

Rook needed to go home. That was all there was to it. 'Cause I was done being kicked in the teeth and expected to accept it.

Chapter 7

Rook

I had at least planned to give the guy a chance to be friends, but he'd slammed the door in my face. I wasn't the type to beg. People begged for my attention, not the other fucking way around. It was humiliating to be forced to come here in the first place, but for Rhys to act like this now… I didn't get it. I mean, sure, I rejected him, but come on… I was here, wasn't I?

I reached for my back pocket, realized I didn't have my smokes, then slumped back into the seat. As angry as I was, I couldn't take my eyes off that swaying kilt, all too aware of what he looked like underneath it.

"Don't mind Rhys. He's actually awesome."

I looked up to see Mari standing in the doorway. She looked

different without the fancy hair and ball gown. Even with the faded jeans and relaxed sweater, she had a wise aura about her.

"You don't have an accent. I didn't pick up on that yesterday," I said, relieved that there was at least one person I'd understand.

"Aye, me do, but me cast it aside when me was livin' in overseas," she said, putting the accent on thick. "I wanted to travel and go to school somewhere else, so I spent six years there before moving home again."

"So why did you come back? It's so…" I looked around at all the green and the birds singing and couldn't imagine anyone here ever having fun except for maybe having tons of sex.

The thought of sex made me think about the scene I walked in on in Rhys' bedroom. It had both enraged me and made me harder than a fucking steel pole to see him with those women. When he'd gotten up and walked towards me naked, his body on full display, I'd begun to question why I hadn't wanted the triad in the first place. There was this crazy sensation that I'd been experiencing since I laid eyes on him.

I always took the teachings about the great connection with your triad to be mystical bullshit. There was a lot of that out there. I figured the elders needed to say something to entice us to participate in the rituals. I was now discovering that it was real. My chest burned, and my stomach fluttered out of control as the power hummed with the desire to touch Rhys.

"I chose to come home last year when my ma passed away. My pa looks tough, but he took it hard. It's easy to lose yourself if you lose your triad. My pa's second had passed on before I was born, so my sister and I decided to stay close to home." Mari looked around at the gardens. "I miss her, but we go to the gardens every day to talk to her.

She wanted her ashes scattered there. It was her favourite place to sit."

"I'm sorry about your mom," I said, understanding now what happened yesterday.

"One day at a time. It's all you can do. So what about you? Do you think you'll stick around and try to make it work with Rhys?"

I shrugged, hoping it came off casual. "I doubt it. I didn't want the triad to begin with and rejected the idea, but my father forced me to come here. And as you can see, Rhys doesn't want anything to do with me."

I glanced over at Mari. Emotions flowed over her face, but I couldn't figure out what she was feeling.

"Sounds to me like you've got it bad," she said.

"No, I don't. Why would you think that?" I scowled and crossed my arms.

Mari shook her head at me. "You seem sort of oblivious to what's happening to you. To both of you. Do you even know what transpires when a union is decided at the ceremony?"

I sat straighter, annoyed that my cousin was calling me out. "If you're asking if I've ever witnessed it, then no, but I know the premise. I don't want anything to do with running the family businesses or being the next triad saviour. I just want to sing."

I rubbed at my eyes as I realized how that must sound, but wasn't life about living out your dreams? Weren't we supposed to go after what we wanted and grab it by the horns? For me, that was singing and performing. I felt alive on stage. It was all I ever wanted. Being sent here felt like a prison sentence with a cellmate who hated me for no good reason.

"Some things in life we get to choose, and some are chosen for us.

I wanted to be a ballerina, but I was born with a club foot, and it took years before I could walk without special shoes. Yet, here I am, one of the most accomplished warriors in the Adair family. Dreams shift and alter, and you have to adjust."

"I don't want to adjust. That's the thing." I pointed to the lawn and the spot where Rhys had disappeared. "I don't want any of this or him, and I shouldn't be forced to accept it."

Mari's face darkened, her eyes narrowing at me. "You have no idea how good you have it. Try being a woman in a Faction."

I opened my mouth and closed it. There was no argument. She was right. Sighing, I decided to get back to her original question. "I only know what I've been told and what I've read about the union," I said and took a sip of coffee. "I never attend the rituals."

"Okay. Then let me educate you a little. The number one is chosen first and is always the older of the pairing. Strange things happened during your pairing with Rhys. Both of you should be number ones, and yet the spirits saw fit to put you two together."

"What do you mean, we both could be number ones?" I asked and shifted around in the chair to let my leg swing over the armrest.

"Usually, the pairing is a balance. The older one is, the stronger of the union, and the younger is weaker. It doesn't have to be by great margins, but there is a distinct difference in power, ability, and personality." Mari listed off, holding up her fingers as she did. "The two of you are evenly matched in all ways, whether you want to see it or not. From what I've seen so far, you're both strong personalities with a stubborn streak. Your physical stature and power strength are very even. I can feel both of you, and it's like twin powers pressing on me."

"Okay, I get it, but I don't get why that is an issue." I took another gulp of coffee and savoured the bold flavour. It was a fucking good cup of coffee.

"It's not an issue. It's unusual and rarely to never happens. I mean, I haven't sat down and read every single pairing over the last couple hundred years, but I can't remember hearing about it. A union needs balance, and two very... um... dominant personalities don't tend to make a great union."

I laughed and smiled at my cousin, who I admit was pretty cool. She was easy to talk to and didn't talk over my head or try to make me feel like an ass for not wanting to be in a triad, yet she wasn't holding back. I liked that.

"I'm pretty sure you insulted me while giving me a compliment, but I get it."

"Oh no. I flat-out insulted you," she teased and smiled. "So, getting back to the union. The second weird thing is that even though Rhys is older, he was demoted, and you were put in his place as the number one. I'm not sure about you, but if that were me, and I'd been preparing to be a number one my whole life, I'd be pissed."

"So you're saying Rhys wanted this triad?"

Mari gave a little shrug. "Rhys has been studying the Faction rules and laws, the powers, spells, politics, etc., ever since I can remember. I'd be eating cereal, and he was studying balance sheets at eight years old. He's been ready to take the role for as long as I can remember. Then he's paired with you and...." Mari looked at me, and her face fell. She seemed sad, but I couldn't tell exactly why she was sad that Rhys had been paired with me.

"You rejected him right away. Rhys is very proud, and he was crushed. He'd never tell you that to your face, but you hurt him, and there's not much more embarrassing than being rejected in front of a bunch of council members seconds after the union is announced." Mari stood and stretched. "Not to mention the physical pain. If he'd been a weaker man, he wouldn't have survived."

"I don't know what you mean," I said, and she cocked a brow at me.

"Oh, boy...Well, I'll let Rhys explain that part. It's not for me to say. But let's just say I'm surprised he didn't run you through the moment he saw you. I mean, do you want the triad with him at all? If not, then why are you even here?"

I looked away from her inquisitive eyes. "I don't know what I want. I hadn't put much thought into it until I was forced to come here."

"Well, you'd better think on it now. 'Cause he's not going to change his mind easily. All you men think you have to watch out for a woman scorned, but you've never seen a McGregor man scorned. Good luck if you decide to stick it out," she said. "Oh, and cousin?" Mari paused, her eyes dropping to the floor. "Treat him good. If he lets you into his heart, he will be loyal and kind, and...Just don't fuck with him." She turned and walked back inside the kitchen. Everything about her was light and elegant, like a fairy. All she needed was pixie dust and wings to complete the look.

Alone again, all I could think about was what Mari had said. It left me feeling more confused than before.

How the fuck did this all get put on me in the first place? I wanted nothing to do with any of this. The potted plant sitting across the way scooted off the table and crashed to the patio floor as my power lashed out.

"Shit," I swore and rubbed my eyes.

This place was affecting me, or maybe it was the person on my mind. All I wanted was to go back home. I was supposed to be at a concert tonight for twenty thousand screaming fans. My eyes travelled over the wide-open grass with guards milling around. Instead, I was trapped here.

I never wanted this fucking responsibility.

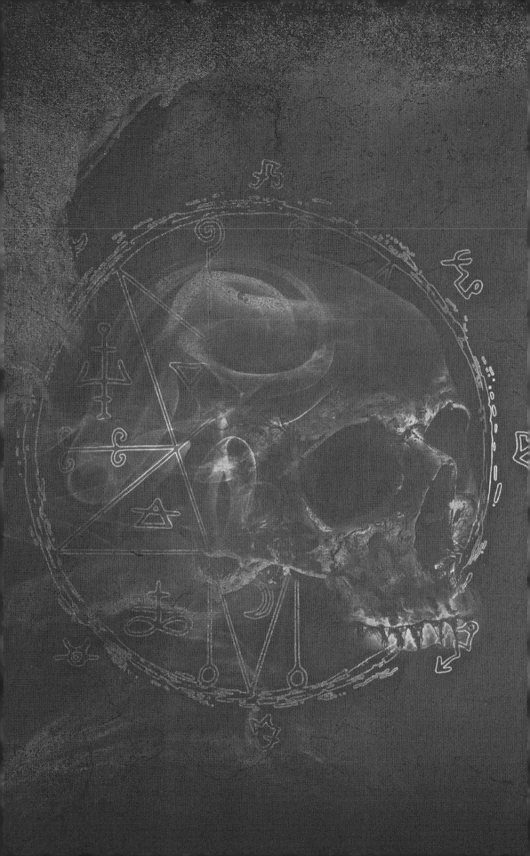

Chapter 8

Elewyen

I stretched as much as I could in the cramped tree hollow. My hand hit something soft, and a loud squeak had me jerking up, my eyes darting around to see what was sleeping with me. A bright red squirrel clung to the side of the tree trunk, chattering at me like I'd committed a sin. The little tuffs of fur on the tips of his ears were shaking comically as he turned his head one way and then the other as he told me exactly what he thought of my sleeping arrangement.

"Whad'ya want? A gurl has got ta sleep," I said, but my argument didn't seem strong enough for the furry menace. Small claws gripped a chunk of the old bark and tossed it at me. "Hey, be nice. I'za do nottin to ya," I grumbled, then slowly crawled out of my cover.

The squirrel followed and climbed the tree, its wee tail twitching as it continued to eye me with its dark eyes.

"I'za goin," I said, holding up my hands in surrender to the little beast. It scurried up into the tall branches and out of sight.

Opening my travelling pouch, I pulled out the cloth that held the food I'd made before leaving. I split a cold biscuit in two and pulled out the butter to put a small amount on one half. Wrapping it all again, I put it away, then tore off a small piece of the dried meat to have as well. Giving my shoulders a roll, I took a bite of the biscuit and was about to walk away when I looked up and sighed.

Tearing off a small piece of the buttery treat, I laid it by the entrance to the hollow tree. "Fir lettin' me sleep da night."

The villagers would've thought I was an eejit for leaving an offering to the wee animal, but I'd lived out here, and the animals had been my only companion. There were some nights that, if it weren't for a family of rabbits or a wolf, I would've frozen to death.

The sun was long past midday when I came to the next designated spot. All the locations were set outside the village limits, and this one had made a small, covered area that would protect the babes from harsh elements. I wished I could come more than twice a season, but the trip took an entire moon cycle to make it to all the spots, and only if I didn't run into trouble.

I looked around for anyone lingering in the area. Many didn't like the safe spots and would try to steal or kill the babes so that the covens couldn't take them. Red-headed women were an abomination, a curse on the couple who created the child. If they didn't get rid of the child as soon as it was born, they would be put to the stake and burned alive. When my coven, Sisters of the Oak Spirit, found me, they said that I couldn't have been left as a babe, but I can't remember anything from before they took me in.

There wasn't any movement in the small hut that I could see, but there was tension in the air like the wind was not happy. I inhaled deeply, but there were no unusual scents. I still used caution when I stepped from the woods, ready for an attack. With each footfall, the few dried leaves under my boots crunched, sending nervous energy skittering up my spine.

A large magpie took flight from a nearby tree, cawing as he flew overhead. His voice was a warning, but for what, I didn't know. I searched the surrounding forest and trail. My ears tuned into the noise of the woods.

Knife at the ready, I poked my head around the three-sided enclosure, prepared for anything. I let out a little sigh when nothing leapt at my face. There was nothing inside, but there was a mark on the ground in the grass. A cool chill flowed over my skin as I stepped inside the small space. Someone had died here, and recently. The spirits were angry, and I could feel the malice swirling inside the shelter. I knelt down and couldn't contain my gasp as I stared at the charred ground with the dark symbol. Not wanting to touch the evil thing, I felt around it and lifted my fingers to find them tainted red with blood.

My heart ached at the sight of the blood. Who could be so cruel as to hurt a defenseless child? Whoever had done this had a blackened soul. My hand gripped my knife tighter, and my thumb ran over the detailed metal of the handle. They deserved to be sent to the dark spirits and tortured for eternity.

As I stood, I caught a distinct whistling sound. I immediately dropped back to the ground. A thunk in the wooden beam behind where my head would have been made my eyes jerk up. I glanced at the arrow that could've killed me, then scurried back out of the shelter and around the other side. Why couldn't the villagers just leave us alone?

Another arrow streaked out of the shadows and hit the tree across from where I was crouched. The blood was pumping hard in my veins, but I needed to keep my wits about me. Spotting a gap in the trees, I bolted from my cover. I was about to step over the threshold into the deep undergrowth when another arrow whizzed past me. Men began yelling and calling out which way I'd gone.

My heart pounded, the thumps loud in my ears as the crashing announced that those who hunted me were far too close. I looked over my shoulder and could make out the outlines of at least six figures, maybe more. Ducking low, I ran like a deer, light on my feet as I leapt over logs and weaved around trees. The sound of a braying dog terrified me as I pushed on, desperately looking for the stream in this direction.

Bursting from the trees, I ran across an open field of tall grass and wildflowers. My feet never slowed, and in the wide-open space, the fear of being spotted amplified as I pushed myself harder. Fear snaked up my spine. They'd been lying in wait. They'd known that I or another coven member would be coming to check on the babes, and they'd waited until I was the most vulnerable before attacking. They were sick and cruel, and I could only imagine what would happen if they'd actually maimed me.

I ran up the hill and down the other side, spooking a herd of grazing deer. They were quick, but I was almost as fast and joined in the run, hoping their scent would help mask my own.

Under cover of trees again, I veered towards the stream I'd stopped at many a time to get a drink or enjoy a rest. There wouldn't be rest today. The water was cold on my feet as I splashed in and continued to bolt along with the flow of water. The slippery rocks made it dangerous, but I needed distance between myself and those hunting me down.

It was dark when I stopped running and stumbled out of the shallow water to drop to my knees and catch my breath. There was no sign that the men continued following me, but I couldn't take the chance. As soon as my heaving breaths stopped feeling like knives stabbing me in the chest, I pushed myself up and looked for a place to sleep for the night.

There was some thick undergrowth of scraggly bushes with a few large trees. I pushed my way through until I found a tree with a low enough branch I could reach. Leaping into the air, I grabbed the rough bark, and with shaking arms, I pulled myself up, sopping clothes and all. One branch at a time, I climbed up the tall tree until I was hidden among the dark canopy. I was panting hard, arms spent, as sweat trickled down my body, and yet my teeth chattered from the cool night air and the wet clothes that clung to me. Removing my pack, I sat it on the branch in front of me and almost screamed when I opened it up, and the same red squirrel poked its head out, its cheeks fat with food.

"Ya wee buggar," I said to the pesky little rodent. "What did ya get bored in ya tree all alone? Or did ya just like me cookin' that much?"

The squirrel hopped out and sat down on the branch, its stomach so full that it looked ready to have a babe. "Ya betta of left somethin' for me ta eat or we're gonna be havin' words."

Reaching into the bag, I pulled out what was left and found two biscuits and some cheese. Almost all the dried berries were gone. Swearing softly, I reorganized and picked out what I was going to eat as I tried to figure out how to ration what was left. Wrapping up what I wasn't going to eat, I closed the pouch and put it under my shirt for safe-keeping.

"Ya know, it's a good thing yer cute," I said to the squirrel that proceeded to fart, the sound like a tiny rumble against the bark. "Ya wee bodach," I mumbled.

Pulling out one of the narrow pieces of sinew, I wrapped it around my body and then the thick branch. It wasn't much, but it would help wake me if I started to fall. I quickly ate the meal, which felt like a feast to my empty stomach and laid my head back on the tree to rest. I couldn't get my hands warmed up, and the longer I sat still, the harder I shivered. The muscles in my legs were beginning to tighten, and I winced with every little movement. I opened one eye when little nails touched my hand, spotting my little stowaway finishing his climb to curl up in my lap. Once he settled, I laid a piece of the cloak over him and closed my eyes again. He was small, but I could feel the heat from his wee body soaking into me, and that gave me a small piece of comfort.

"Tanks fir keepin' me company," I said to the squirrel and gave the top of his wee head a pet with my finger. "I tink I be callin' ya Barry."

Before my eyes closed to rest, I pulled the necklace I'd made from beneath my shirt and held onto the stone. It glowed softly as Keeva answered back. Smiling, I slipped the necklace back into position and prayed that tomorrow would be better.

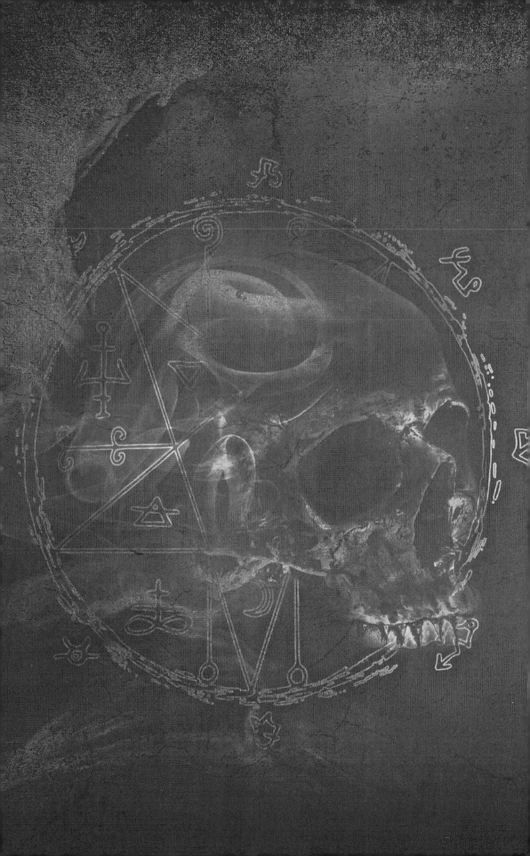

Chapter 9

Rook

  I paced the massive bedroom and felt like I was doing laps on a track. As usual, my father's secretary put me on hold. It had been a solid twenty minutes so far and counting.

  The waiting gave me time to look around the massive bedroom and appreciate the clean, crisp taste of Rhys's style. The walls were stone like the rest of the castle, but the accents were silver and black with touches of vibrant red. Everything from the frames on the wall, to the desk, to the sitting area matched. Black couch with grey and red pillows. Silver wall scones and silver framed images of modern art that I never would've pictured in a place like this. It infuriated me that I liked his taste. I didn't even know if I liked it because it was something I'd choose or if it was because he liked it. I needed to get away from this fucking magic. I would've been better off staying home and taking whatever punishment my father chose to dole out. Coming here was a mistake.

Pulling the phone away from my ear, I checked how much time had elapsed and swore. My father always did this, and I couldn't decide if it was in hopes that I would get frustrated and hang up or to prove he had all the power.

"Angus speaking," my father said like he didn't know who was on the line. I rolled my eyes.

"Dad, it's me," I drawled.

"Rook, my son, good to hear from you. I understand that you had some plane issues. The pilot quit his job after he told me what happened. Apparently, he thinks he's losing his mind, so good job," my dad said, his voice thick with sarcasm.

"Well, we were plummeting toward the ocean with an out-of-commission engine. I'm not sure what else you wanted me to do. Maybe just crash and die so your problem child would be taken care of."

"Don't be stupid. Of course not. Just something a little less dramatic would've been nice."

Bringing a fist up to my mouth, I bit it hard to stop myself from arguing with him. It was pointless. The man could argue it wasn't raining while you were being pelted in the head by raindrops until you wanted to stab yourself to end the misery.

"I want to come home. You said I had to see if I could do the triad thing. Well, I'm here, Rhys won't even speak to me, and my third is nowhere to be found. He's made it clear he doesn't want anything to do with me, and if I come home tomorrow, I'll still make my next concert."

The line was quiet, but I could still hear my father breathing on the other end. There was a tinkling of ice dropping into a glass, and I knew he was getting himself a drink of our signature brandy. I was the one that needed the drink, not him.

"Son, let me see if I can make this as clear as possible because you don't seem to be understanding what's happening here."

This seemed to be a recurring statement from everyone lately. I shook my head annoyed.

"Oh, shit," I mumbled and plunked myself down in the oversized wingback chair.

The thing was oddly comfortable, and I laid my head back and closed my eyes, waiting for my father to deliver his sermon. The word *son* at the start of the sentence was a telltale sign.

"First, the plane is already gone, and another won't land until I say so. Second, this is not a democracy, nor do you have a choice. I'm sorry if that's what you thought."

"Um... I'm pretty sure your exact words were: *go and see how it works out, and if it doesn't, you can come home,*" I said, the muscle in my jaw twitching.

"Was that what I said?"

I wanted to kill him. He'd tricked me, and now I was trapped on this large rock with no way off. I should've known better. This was exactly the kind of shit my father would pull.

"So, Rook, I know you don't like to educate yourself on the workings of... well, anything not centered around you... So I'm going to teach you a valuable lesson right now. Your third will not be drawn to you until you and your second connect. Do you understand? She is not going to waltz through the front doors and yell, 'Take me oh great Rook,'" he drawled. My nostrils flared, my fist clenching.

My father drew in a puff, I assumed, of one of his signature cigars. "Here's what's going to happen. You're going to get up off your sorry excuse for an ass. You're going to find Rhys, and you're going to do

85

whatever you need to do to convince him that you want the triad union. When you've established a semblance of a connection with him, then you can go looking for your third. Once you do, you will both need to find a way to convince her to join the union. I mean, you could force her, I guess, but we are trying to be more gentlemanly these days."

"And what if I don't or can't convince him that this is something I want? Which, let me remind you, it's not," I grumbled.

"Then you can forget about your rockstar career. In case you've forgotten, I control all the money that comes in and goes out for the family. That includes the costs associated with putting on your concerts. There are cross-border fees into the other Faction areas, and of course, I have to pay so that you're not assassinated. Yes, it also means that all the money you make comes to me first. I own you, Rook. Until you prove, you don't need daddy to hang on to the purse strings. It's time you grew up."

I wanted to reach through the phone and rip out my father's tongue or choke him with his fucking tie. I could picture his smug face as he sipped his brandy and puffed on his cigar, and my teeth ground together.

"I can sense your disdain for me through the phone, son."

"Colour me fucking shocked. You tricked me, and you fucking know it," I fumed.

"Maybe. Let me be frank and honest with you, Rook." This ought to be good. "I hoped you'd never be chosen, which is why I allowed you to gallivant all over, singing and not taking anything to do with the Faction seriously. I don't think you have what it takes to lead. I hoped the spirits would see that too. I knew Rhys would be paired. He does have what is needed to lead, and I was disappointed that

Rhys wasn't paired with Rylan instead. But I don't get a choice any more than you do. So here I am, stuck forcing you to man up."

My father's words hurt and shocked me. I always assumed he wanted me at the helm of the family, but he just openly admitted that he didn't want that at all. In fact, it sounded like he thought of me as useless and had written me off, which was why he'd been supporting my singing. Did he even think I was good at that? All this time, the one thing I thought he thought I was great at was only a way for him to keep me out of the way.

"Look, I get that you don't understand why, but here are the facts." He took another sip of his drink, and I stood to pace the room. "We're the largest Faction." He paused, and I wasn't sure if I was supposed to say something. *"Oh, Dad, what does that mean?"* my father mocked. "Well, Rook, it means that we must maintain our strength within the community by ensuring that our power source is the strongest and most secure. *But, Dad, why should we care?"* My blood was boiling as he continued to taunt me. "Son, you couldn't be bothered to pay attention to what was going on in the Factions because your head is shoved so far up your arrogant, entitled ass, and, yes, I blame myself for that, but the reality is that we have enemies. These enemies are looking for any opportunity to destroy us."

My power began to simmer and spiral like a storm in my gut as he spoke to me like I was a useless child. Just because I hadn't studied all the goings-on with the Factions didn't mean I was stupid.

"Why do you do that? Why do you treat me like I'm an imbecile?"

"I treat you the way you act." It was like he reached through the phone and smacked me. "Rook, for fuck's sake, Rhys is a top pairing. I mean, like the very top tier, grade A, can't do better, pairing. Rhys should've been the number one. I have no idea how this mess happened. When you look in the mirror, do you really see yourself with anyone better?"

My mouth fell open. "Wow, insult me and compliment him in one breath. I'm impressed. You are turning into a bigger asshole than I already thought," I growled.

"Be sarcastic all you want, but you could do worse than a man who is highly intelligent, extremely powerful, also happens to share the same passion for music, and, let's face it, he's not hard on the eyes. If I were a younger man, I would be all over him."

My nose scrunched at the image of my father ogling Rhys. It brought the same strange twinge of jealousy that I'd been suffering with since meeting the guy, and I quickly pushed it down.

"Dad, look. I know you think I will be some powerful triad that will help us save our Faction from falling into the wrong hands, but...."

"Whoa, who said I thought you're going to be a top pairing? No, I think Rhys is a top pairing. You? So far, all I have seen from you is a selfish brat acting out. If you prove me wrong, I will happily eat my words, but I doubt you will. You're too self-centred for that." My father's voice had slipped from sarcastic to annoyed with me. I was the one who had the right to be furious with him. "I still can't believe you would sit in the hall at the rituals like a spoiled child throwing a tantrum. So humiliating. You embarrass me, Rook. My first born, and you made me look a fool and shamed your mother's memory. I'm sure she's rolling in her grave watching you."

Sharp pain stabbed me in the chest, and my mouth fell open. I didn't even know how to respond. It was one of those rare moments when I didn't have a quick response. My father was straight with me for once, and in a matter of minutes, he ripped me apart and made me feel like I was an insignificant nothing.

"Real talk here, Rook. I've been in charge of the family for too long—almost fifty years too long—and I'm tired. The spirits have chosen, and it's time for you to step up. You were the one who decided to reject Rhys before the ritual was even complete. You gave it and him no thought. So am I surprised he wants nothing to do with you? No. It's your job to fix the mess you created with your hasty choice."

"Fucking great. So you're saying that the weight of the entire Faction is lying in my lap?"

"Yes, that's what I'm saying."

"And I have to get a guy who hates me to decide to spend his life with me even though I don't want a triad?" I marched across the room, my pace getting faster with the building anger.

"Yes."

"Or you're never letting me come home or sing on a stage again?"

"See, I knew you'd get it. Buck up, son. It could be worse."

"There's worse?" I asked.

"There's always worse. Remember, find a way to make him fall in love with you. Find your third, or I will have someone destroy your guitar and order all guitar makers to ignore any request from you."

My eyes went wide, and I stared at the phone. "You wouldn't dare destroy my Clarisse."

"Fail, and you'll find out, won't you? This has been a great catch-up, son, but I have to go and deal with real issues, like how to keep our borders safe."

The phone clicked in my ear, and I had to swallow down the anger before I threw the phone across the room.

Fuck me!

Chapter 10

Rhys

"What da hell is goin' on?" I asked and looked over at Gregory, who had the same troubled expression that I was sure was on my face.

"I dinnie' know," Gregory answered as he stroked his beard.

The report stated that three villages had been attacked by an unknown force. The buildings were flattened, and no one was left alive. We had no alarms go up across the island, and no one left to report anything. It was like a magical whirlwind descended on the villages, destroyed them, then took off.

"Do we know if dis be the work of da covens? Maybe dey finally had enough of livin' in da wilds."

I shook my head and stared at a map that showed the villages' locations. "I dinnie tink so. Da covens keep ta themselves and no lookin fir trouble. If anythin', dey'd hide farther from us ta keep us from takin' deir lasses. Dey not gonna make demselves a target," I said. "Naw, dis feels personal."

"Aye, like an attack," Gregory said. "But who and why now?"

I folded up the map and gripped it in my fist. "I dinnie know, but I'ma gonna find out."

"Naw, ya should'na be goin alone," Gregory said as Rook stormed into the office.

"Uncle, I need to speak with you," he said, then lifted his head.

Our eyes locked. The bloom of heat and power was instant, and I despised this connection with every fibre of my being. I wanted to be attracted to him about as much as the goats grazing outside. The next ritual moon needed to hurry up and get here so that I could go back to my life and not feel this empty damn void and the pointless spark of hope every time Rook walked into a room.

"Dinnie worry. I was jus leavin'."

I didn't even bother walking past him. It was better if I kept my distance. Walking out the terrace entrance, I could hear Gregory calling after me, but I wasn't stopping. Knowing him, he'd try to send Rook with me, and that wasn't happening. I'd rather eat roadkill than be stuck in a car with him for any length of time.

I jogged around the corner of the castle, making my way to my car, but skidded to a stop at the sight of Rook leaning against the door. Oh, you have got to be fucking kidding me!

"Standing still doesn't make me disappear," he said, looking way too smug with his lip curled up.

"Dinnie be temptin' me. Makin ya disappear is kinda what me wants. I'm just contemplatin' da how." I marched forward, and each stride brought a different image. Punching him while I bent him over my car and fucked him hard was topping the list. "Whadda want?"

"I want you to take me with you," Rook said.

I smiled, then laughed. "Aye, sure. Ya're jokin', right?"

"No, I'm serious. You can show me around, and maybe we can start over," Rook said.

My stomach did a nervous little flip. If I could, I would've growled at my own body and grounded it in a dungeon cell. The thing was acting ridiculous. He wasn't the one I wanted, yet the almighty spirits had spoken. So now here I was, pining after him like a lovesick teen. I was starting to resent them for doing this to me. Like I hadn't had enough shit happen over my life, I had to be stuck with him? They couldn't let me have the one thing I wanted. As far as I was concerned, it shouldn't matter that Mari didn't have red hair or the birthmark of the chosen.

Anger burned in my gut. "Naw, I dinnie want ya ta come, but thanks." I walked around the car to the driver's side door.

"What do you mean, naw?" Rook said as he turned to keep staring at me. "I'm offering an olive branch here. I don't know how else to apologize for what I did."

Taking a deep breath, I laid my hands on the roof of the car and stared at Rook. "Did or doin'?"

"I don't understand the question." Rook ran his hand through his hair, and of course, it only made him look sexier. He had a great jaw and the most intense blue eyes I'd ever seen. My body took the opportunity to tell me what it thought. I glanced down at the tent in my kilt. I'd never wanted to cut the fucker off until that moment.

"It be a simple enough question. Did, as in ya did it and yer sorry and wanna take it back, or doin, as in yer sorry, but ya still no wantin' dis union? Ya see, there be a difference. One leads down a road dat I'm no sure I want, but da other leads directly to me runnin' ya over with me car," I said.

Rook licked his lips but didn't say anything. His eyes screamed that he didn't want anything.

I shook my head and grabbed the door handle. I was angry at him for rejecting me and putting me through what he had. I was angry that the spirits had done this in the first place, and I was furious with myself that I couldn't get my own emotions under control. I didn't know what I wanted anymore.

"Dat be what me thought. So da answer is naw. Now git off me car."

Before I could get in and lock the doors, Rook opened the passenger side door and got in beside me.

"Whadda doin? Are ya deaf or daft?"

Rook crossed his arms over his chest and glared straight ahead, but I wasn't starting the car until he answered the question.

"I don't know," he finally said and turned his head to look at me. "I don't know what I want. I'm allowed to be confused. I didn't see myself in any kind of union for at least another four or five years. So yes, I rejected the idea, and you immediately, without even giving the idea a second thought. I'm just not sure, okay? But I might be interested," he said and nibbled his lower lip.

Fuck, he smelled good. Was the car suddenly hotter? My eyes moved from his blue ones to his lip. I suddenly wanted that lip. I wanted to grab his face and help convince him that this was exactly what he wanted, that *I* was what he wanted. Was that what I wanted? Fuck, I hated this!

We sat there for a long time. My fingers itched to touch him as the ritual connection buzzed around the small space like a charge of swarming insects.

"All right, fine. Put yer seatbelt on." The balloon of tension that had been steadily rising popped, and a subtle smile graced his lips. I had to force myself to look away, and as Rook grabbed his seatbelt, I quickly adjusted myself so that he couldn't see the annoying reaction that I had to his presence.

"Where are we going?" Rook asked as the car revved, and I put it into first gear.

I handed over the folded map and bit down hard on my cheek as our fingers touched. The spark was truly electric, and I could've sworn that everyone outside the car could see it even though there was no bright light.

Rook jerked his hand away. "What the hell was that?"

I glared at him as we pulled through the second gate. "Dat be why I din't want ya ta come wit me. Da closer we are…." I used my hand to demonstrate distance. "Da stronger da connection. I was no stayin' away simply because I want to punch ya in da face. Although, there is dat too."

"All of that from a finger touch?" Rook wiggled in his seat, letting me know he'd been just as affected as I'd been. "What the hell would happen if we…."

"Dinnie ya dare say da word. So help da spirits if ya put dat image in me head." I stomped on the gas and smoothly shifted the car through gears until we were zipping along in fifth. "Id'a be leavin ya at da side of da road, or I'd fuck ya first, den leave ya."

"Fair enough." Rook cleared his throat, then stared at the map. "What are these circled locations?"

"Villages or wadda be left a dem." I glanced over at Rook's confused face. "Someone be attakin' our island. Well, me island," I said.

Rook opened his mouth like he was going to ask a question, then looked away and stared out the window. There was no point in going into all the details with someone who had no interest in sticking around. This was my problem. These were my people to look after, and that's what I planned on doing.

Slowing, I pulled onto the road that would take me to the tiny village that sat right on the edge of the water. They had a small port and provided fish to a few of the closer villages. The road was twisty here, and I always loved how no one was on them so I could soar around the curves.

"It's beautiful here, isn't it?" Rook suddenly said.

"Aye, it is," I said, and then my heart sank as the remnants of the village slowly came into sight.

Smoke rose into the air from smoldering lumps, and I could feel death wafting off the place. Death had a different smell for us than for Flitters. It was not unpleasant, and it called to my power as I was sure it did for Rook, but human sacrifice was a sacred act and only to be performed for specific ceremonies. This was simply murder.

Parking the car, I stepped out and slowly made my way towards what was once a beautiful and prosperous village, despite its small size. This wasn't far from where Caitlin had come from, and I wondered if she had friends or family here. We'd become good friends. She was more than a fuck buddy and had a sensitive personality. This would wound her deeply. I made a mental note to see her later.

"What the hell happened here?"

"Told ya. Me island is under attack."

I walked forward, but Rook grabbed my arm. The sensation was like I'd been plugged into an electrical socket. The death called to my power, and the man beside me called to all my other desires. It was too much, even for me to handle.

"Hey, this is my family's island too," Rook said, his voice strained as he let go of my arm and stared at his hand like he couldn't understand what he was feeling.

"Aye, da Adair's do, but ya don't," I said. Rook's brow furrowed, but he didn't argue.

I looked him up and down, pushing aside the wild surge of desire coursing through my body as steady as a heartbeat. Shaking my head, I turned to walk away.

"Why do you keep doing that?" Rook asked and grabbed my arm again.

Once more, the connection erupted like a storm. I staggered with the sheer power I felt. I could feel him and his power through the connection as clearly as if I was running my hands over his skin.

I whipped around, and Rook's face said it all. His mouth hung open as he leaned forward like he might collapse from the sensation. His hand grabbed his stomach, and his eyes began to glow as bright as any moon stone. Jerking away, I stumbled back and took a shuddering breath. Every part of my body was shaking, and as wrong, as it was, all I could picture was riding Rook to the ground and fucking him as hard as I could.

"No touchin' me. What do ya no get? Da more ya touch me, da harder dis is. I only 'ave so much control." I closed my eyes. Sweat trickled down my back as I tried to suppress the power and burning desire. This was not the time or place for any of this.

"Ahh," I yelled, pushing the building magic out in a harmless, glowing ball. It sailed out over the water and dropped out of sight. Panting, I bent over and looked at Rook. He was sweating and shaking hard like he was in the midst of a seizure. His head turned slow and jerky like he was trying not to look at me, but as soon as our eyes met, it felt like I was caught in a laser beam.

I held up my hand as he licked his lips. "Don't ya dare. Rein it in, Rook," I ordered.

His eyes glowed a little brighter, and his muscles shook. A growl ripped from his mouth.

"Ah, shit," I said.

He leapt for me.

Twisting away, I turned into smoke. Rook flew through my body, grabbing at nothing. Floating the short distance to the car, I reformed. Rook's dark, hungry gaze found me, making me shiver.

"Fir fuck's sake! I no should be havin' ta do dis, ya no dat right?"

Rook ran at me like he was playing a game of rugby. I knew what would happen if he tackled me. It involved a lot of nakedness on the grass. With this much death around us, we wouldn't come up for air for days, and that couldn't happen. At least my brain was working. It was obvious Rook was lost in the sea of power and the amped-up sexual desire.

I didn't want to do this, but he left me no choice.

Lifting my hand, I said, "Petrobile!"

Rook froze in place.

"Samhach," I said, and his mouth sealed shut. "Leibheis."

Rook rose into the air like a strange balloon and hovered behind me as I walked to the edge of the cliff. Twisting my hand, he floated out over the water. Like some elaborate dunk tank, I flicked my hand, and he dropped. I lifted my hand, and he rose.

I had to admit I was having a little more fun than I should have. Seeing the shock and then fear on his face as I dropped him into the water and pulled him back up again was extremely gratifying. Even drenched like a rat, Rook still looked sexy. It was incredibly annoying, but at least the heat was gone from his eyes. In its place was fiery anger.

"Din't fuckin' look at me like dat. Ya were power drunk. Ya needed ta cool off," I said as I lifted him over land again, letting him hover a few feet away, then snapped my fingers, releasing all the spells.

Rook wrapped his arms around his body, his teeth chattering. "Y-y-y-y-ou a-a-a-ssss-h-h-h-hole. I-I-I th-think. Shit!" He shook himself off and looked down at his clothes. They clung to his body like a second skin. "I th-think something g-g-grabbed my leg in the w-water. I can't believe you fucking did that to me!"

"Be mad all ya want, but ya were about ta fuck me on da ground." I spun to walk away but stopped and turned back to face him. Waving my hand and releasing some magic, Rook's clothes shook and instantly dried. "I dinnie know about ya, but fuckin' among the smolderin' bodies of dead villagers is no' me idea of a good time."

"Agreed, but still. That's the ocean and a huge ass drop. You could've killed me," Rook growled.

Again, don't tempt me.

"Give me a wee bit more credit, aye. Me know what me doin. I've been practicing with me power since I was a wee lad, and in case ya hadn't noticed, I'ma tad powerful."

Putting space between us, I went to find clues as to who had done this. Anything would do. A power signature or maybe one of the spirits still lingered so I could ask them.

I could feel Rook moving around behind me. It drove me crazy that my body warmed, cooled, or tingled as he walked by. It felt like a grown-up version of the hot/cold game Mari, and I used to play. Except that was more innocent than the images running wild inside my skull and the incessant heat burning in my lower stomach.

"I dinnie get it. There be no soul left, no spark, just da feel of power and dis," I said, and held up a handful of ash that, at one point, had been a person. Little white bits of bone fell from my fingers, but whoever or whatever did this was able to disguise their signature.

"Why would someone do this?" Rook asked as we made our way to the car.

"Why does man do anythin? Power. They wanna war, and whoever did dis is gonna get one. I'll hunt dem down and make 'em pay."

Rook stopped walking, but luckily he kept his hands to himself this time as he spoke. "I'm here too, Rhys, and I have a right to know what's going on."

I leaned on the top of the car and stared at Rook. "Ya know ya talk a lot a shite when ya haven't spent a single day here since ya was born. Dis island is no' yours. Ya never came ta visit. Never met yer family dat lives here. Didn't come ta meet yer potential unions, and ya never cared ta know nothin' dat was goin' on until yer arse was forced ta come. Ya turned your back on us and then me. Dis island dinnie owe ya anythin', and neither do I."

The car ride back to Injebreck castle felt like it took years as we sat in silence. As soon as he got out of the car, I pulled away, then made the mistake of glancing in the rear-view mirror. Rook was staring at the back of the car, his eyes a mix of confusion and something I couldn't figure out. My hands tightened on the wheel.

"He's gettin' in ya head. Ya need ta stop thinkin' 'bout him," I grumbled to myself.

Yet the stupid connection was trying to make me feel guilty for leaving. It was trying to make me forgive him, want him, fall for him. I could feel it all like thin threads stretching from my body to his and vice versa.

"Ahh!" I smacked my hand on the steering wheel, which had been receiving a lot of abuse lately. "I dinnie fuckin' want ya! Git out of me head!"

No, I wouldn't even contemplate if we could work. The look on Rook's face when he said he wanted to try was similar to the look I made when I ate soap by accident.

The small car streaked towards the pub. I needed a break from the tension that was Rook, and more than that, I needed a release. By coming here, I could take care of my needs and see how Caitlin was doing. My fucking cock felt like it was going to explode with the power and need coursing through my veins.

A pairing was supposed to be a happy time. Instead, I was stuck with a guy who wanted nothing to do with me. I was more torn up and confused about what I wanted than ever before. The stupid connection could make me want Rook, but it didn't seem to help block my love for Mari. I thought those feelings were under control, but the triad becoming real was stirring up all I'd forced down. What a way to fuck with my head.

I parked the car, leaned over, and grabbed my stash, but I just stared at the brightly coloured pills.

"Fuck," I swore and tossed them back into the compartment. The last thing I needed tonight was anything mind-altering. I got out of my car, looking around at the modest stone homes in the distance and the horse-and-buggies in the parking area. This place may not be the fancy lifestyle Rook was used to, but this was my home, and I loved everything about it. Rook could have his screaming fans and travelling from city to city every night.

I looked down at my family ring. My father had left me this ring. It had been his father's and my grandfather's before that. I stared at the cobra head embedded in the side of the metal. My father had told me that he loved me. He'd seen me. Mari saw me. But Rook... he saw his ticket out of town when he looked at me. He hadn't said it outright, but I knew why he was here.

Caleb and Rook's brother, Devlin, talked all the time. Rook was forced to come here. He wasn't given a choice. All the guys were taking bets on how long it took before we caved or killed one another. That wasn't the life I wanted for myself. It couldn't be what my parents wanted for me. I wanted to be with someone who saw my value and respected me. I deserved that much from this life.

Rook and all his sexy temptation could go fuck himself.

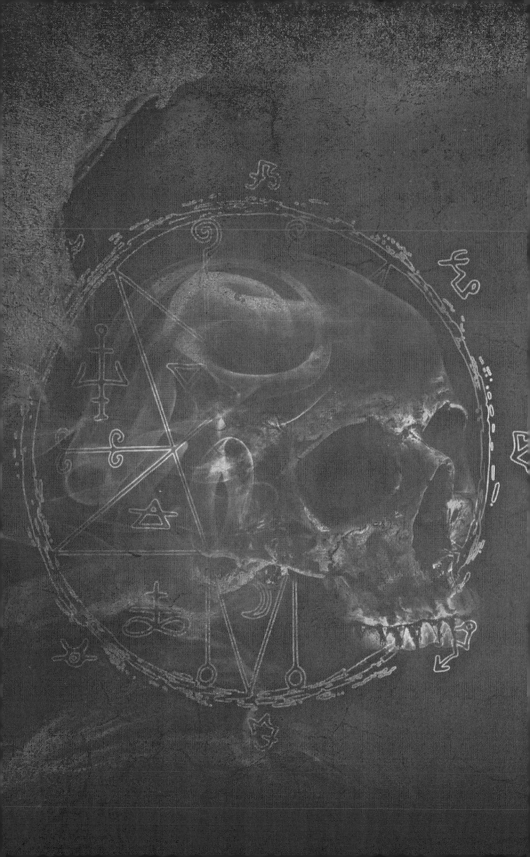

Chapter 11

Elewyen

Rage filled me as I stared at the remnants of the burnt village. The ghost-like horror and despair floated off the charred remains like a kiss of death. I stood among the thick trees on the edge of the small village and stared at the black car with the white stripes. Cars were rare. They were only driven by those who lived in the stone castles. So whoever was here was someone of importance to the island. I'd never seen one of them before. Azula had forbidden me to venture too close to the castles, and she had been in such a panic about it that I'd finally agreed.

My mind filled with images of the guy with the midnight black hair who had stepped out of the metal bird only to get into a similar car. A shiver raced up my back thinking of the man who made my

As I turned to walk away, I heard yelling and caught the hint of movement near the edge of the bluff. The ground slanted away from where I was standing, and there was no clean line of sight. Slipping into the trees, I raced across the rough terrain of rock and tree roots until I was far enough along that I could see more of what was happening.

There were two people. I couldn't see much of either of them, but they were not happy with one another. The yelling was too far away to catch, but the odd bit of a word that I heard in the breeze was full of anger.

The two figures began making their way up the slope from the cliffs, and I quickly backed deeper into the shadows of the trees. There was no way to know if these two had anything to do with the murders and the village being destroyed. It also couldn't be a coincidence that someone with a car from the castles was here before the bones of the dead had cooled.

They walked among the village and bent down. I wasn't sure what they were looking for or at from this distance, but when one of the guys stood up and turned to look in my direction, I had to grab the tree for support. It was the guy with the midnight hair from the flying metal bird. He was even more handsome than the first time I'd seen him. His eyes were so blue they reflected the colour of the sky. The second guy walked to the car, and as he did, my heart sputtered to a complete stop as his gaze scanned over the trees.

It felt like someone was sitting on my chest. I'd never felt such witchcraft before. What were these men? What power did they hold, and why did it affect me? More importantly, had they been the ones to come here to hurt these people? They disappeared into the car, and soon it was flying past where I was hidden.

For the tiniest glimmer of time, I caught sight of the two men up close. Air became solid in my lungs. My eyes trailed the car until it was out of sight, and like a rope stretching and snapping, my chest released, and air flooded my lungs.

I bit my lip and closed my eyes, trying to push down the unusual reaction to the men. The loud squeak and chattering beside my ear had my eyes snapping open and looking at Barry.

"Aye, yer no trustin' 'em eitha?" I shook my head. "Naw, I'za no trust 'em. I'za dinnie like menfolk much at all."

His little tail swished as he twisted his head to the side with my words.

"I'za no mean ya, so dinnie be givin' me dat look."

Sliding my hand in the pocket of my cloak, I pulled out a couple of berries. Barry took the offering, stuffed it in his little furry cheek, then begged for more.

"Naw, ya eat dat first, then ya cannie have more."

Popping a berry into my mouth, I made my way down the path toward the main trail, but when I got to the fork in the road, I stopped. Looking one way and then the other, I knew I should go to the left, but everything in me screamed that I needed to follow the car.

"I'za gonna regret dis. I'za see it happenin' now," I mumbled and handed Barry another piece of fruit. He poked me in the cheek with his wee nose. "Ya know, yewza pest," I grumbled. For such a small travel companion, he sure could pack the food away. "I'za startin' ta tink yer only usin' me fir da food wit da bitter winds on da way."

Of course, he didn't answer and continued to munch away on the sweet fruit. The birds were talking up a storm, and I wished I understood them better. Keeva was so good at talking to the birds, while I had better luck with woodland animals. They were speaking about unrest and a storm brewing, but I didn't think they meant the weather. A pair of bright red birds with yellow-tipped wings swirled around as they chased one another, squawking about danger and dark magic.

My hand instantly went to my necklace. I squeezed the stone and thought of Keeva. Within moments, the stone glowed in my hand, then fell silent, but my heart soared that she was all right. Not seeing her smiling face was the hardest part about coming out here for so long. Leaving her behind felt like leaving a piece of me, and I hated that I wasn't there to protect her.

The scent of smoke was still in my nose, and I rubbed at it like that would help remove the scent. Instead of growing fainter, it got stronger. The sound of a distant scream had my head snapping up. I could just make out the billow of smoke in the distance. I ran through the forest along the trail. Barry chattered in my ear, telling me how annoyed he was with having to hang on to me.

Breathing hard, I burst through the edge of the trees. My eyes grew wide at the sight of the people running and screaming, bodies glowing from intense flames. Some of them had been tied to stakes screaming as they burned. Others were already burnt beyond recognition. Those running had been doused in something, or the ropes had burnt free but not in time for them to escape their fiery end. The homes were fully ablaze, the bright orange flames dancing against the darkening night sky.

Lifting my hand, I murmured for Barry to step into my palm and carried him to the nearest tree.

"Stay here," I said to the tiny squirrel.

I took my pack off and laid it and my walking stick at the base of the tree. Not even thinking about the possible consequences, I ran toward the water well. Hand over hand, I pulled on the rope to get a bucket of water. Dashing to the closest babe that had been left in a crib left by a stake to burn with it's mother, I threw the water on the infant, even though the child had already stopped screaming.

The thick, black smoke stung my eyes, and tears instantly welled as I ran back to the well and dropped the bucket to get more water. In the back of my mind, I knew it was too late—the injuries would be so severe that they wouldn't recover—but I had to try to help the children.

The thick, grey smoke had changed directions with the wind and was blowing directly in my face, making me cough. Running headlong into it, I covered my nose and mouth and threw the water on the fire that only got bigger. It was like a monster rising from the dark fade to devour all that stood in its path.

"Please help me," a woman wailed as I ran back with my third bucket of water.

I threw it on her, but the flames only sizzled. All I could do was stand there and watch as she shrieked in pain so loudly that it hurt my ears. I slowly stepped back.

Helplessness washed over me as tears steadily trickled down my cheeks. Hearing the sound of a motor, I turned and blinked through the smoke to see the taillights of a car leaving. I couldn't make out if it was the same car, but it seemed unlikely that two cars heading in the same direction and at both fires was a coincidence.

I moved farther away from the blaze and those already lost to stare at the devastation. These same villagers would've forsaken me for simply having red hair, but it wasn't in me to turn my back on those in need. My heart hurt for those who had lived here. The ones who had done this were monsters. No…They were demons.

I hated myself even more for having any kind of pleasant reaction to the two men in the car. They were darkness conjured from the deepest depths of the fade. I needed to stop them before they killed anyone else.

Dropping the bucket to the ground, I forced myself to turn away from the last of the wailing voices as their bodies thrashed on stakes. I didn't understand why people were so cruel to one another and why they insisted on proving time and again that it was best for me and my coven to stay in hiding.

Making my way back to where I'd left my possessions, I stopped long enough to grab my stick and pack and let Barry climb onto my shoulder. He snuggled into the crook of my neck, providing a tiny spot of warmth. Silent tears fell down my cheeks to the ground below as I gently ran my finger over his small head.

He was my only comfort and the only reason I kept moving. The only reason I didn't try to run back to those poor souls. What good would it do? My powers were useless against the likes of that. Making little charms, talking to animals, and having spirits whisper messages in my ear wasn't helpful. I had no healing ability or power over the elements. I could put out a wee little wick of a flame, but what good did that do? This feeling was crushing.

I heard the dark spirits as I tried to put out the fire. Their voices were like a million small cackling demons as they took what they wanted. There was something about the sound of that fire and the screaming that shook me to my core and made me colder than death itself.

It was almost dark before I stopped or allowed my mind to play over what I'd seen. A small whimper left my mouth. Dropping to my knees at the side of a stream, I looked at my reflection in the water and didn't recognize the face staring back at me.

There were streaks of black, and my eyes were red and swollen from the smoke, making me look evil. Cupping my shaking hands, I splashed cold water onto my face and rubbed at the dark marks that ran down my neck.

Another cry left my mouth as the emotions overtook my body, and all I could do was rock and let the waves of sorrow out into the night sky. Barry kept touching my face with his little nose. I knew he was trying to understand my sadness and comfort me, but I needed to get this out. It was the only way to move on and to find and kill those who would do such a thing to defenseless children.

Once more, I could clearly visualize the handsome faces of the two men in my mind, but instead of beauty, all I saw was evil. I took a fortifying breath and began to plan how to make them pay for the way they'd hurt those babes.

Chapter 12

Rook

I paced more in the last few days than in my entire life. No one ever explained these feelings properly. The words, 'it's a connection,' didn't describe how my skin constantly crawled with this overwhelming need to touch the other person and leave me breathless. It didn't explain why my power was supercharged to the point that I felt like I could take on the world. It sure as fuck didn't hint at the reality of my mind plagued with images of Rhys's face. The fluttering in my chest whenever he was close and irrational spikes of jealousy made me want to kill anyone who'd dare to even look at him.

Why did we have this crazy connection shit anyway? Wouldn't it be easier not to feel? My soul-sucking father had tricked me into this.

He knew that my resolve would be tested, that the connection I'd scoffed at was strong enough to do his dirty work for him.

A frustrated shout ripped from my throat. The decorative items along the bookshelf took the brunt, flying off and crashing on the floor. My door banged open, and Mari stood in the doorway. Her hand was up, and her eyes glowed as she looked around the room.

"What's attackin' you?"

Running my hand through my hair, I resumed pacing. It was the only thing that helped to keep my body at bay. "No one. I'm just frustrated. Where did you come from so fast?"

She relaxed, her hands dropping. "I was on my way to the training area." She looked down at the black outfit that made her look every bit the warrior she said she was.

"This late? Is that all you ever do? Train?" I asked.

Mari's eyes hardened, and she stood a little straighter. "Are you making fun of me?"

"No, it's just...never mind. It wasn't an insult." I picked up the fallen books and began putting them back on the shelf. I really needed to get these outbursts under control. I was getting sick of cleaning.

"So you say you're frustrated. Aye, I can see that. This wouldn't have anything to do with a very sexy, black-haired, silver-eyed McGregor, would it?" she asked in a teasing lilt.

She was leaning against the door, all relaxed, but her mouth was pulled up in a smile.

"I don't get it. I don't understand this feeling. I didn't want to come here. I rejected the union, that should've severed whatever this is, but...." I froze mid-stride as my body seized with the continuously building desire that was making me crazy. Slumping, I leaned over and braced myself on my knees, my head hanging.

"Why is this happening? Why can't I get him out of my head? And for fuck's sake, why do I feel like I need to go to him? I don't want the union, Mari. You should take him. You're an Adair."

"I would take your place if I could, cousin," she said quietly. "You have no idea how much I want that," she said barely above a whisper, but I still heard it.

I looked up. Mari had her arms crossed, but she was staring down, so I couldn't see her face. When she lifted her head, her eyes didn't show any trace of what she was really feeling or thinking.

"Rook, be honest with me. Who are you trying to convince? It's obvious you're interested in Rhys. You're pacing your room like someone who is lovesick."

"Lovesick? Oh, no, no, no. I mean, it's fake. Right?" I asked, but Mari just stared at me, which was unnerving as fuck. "This emotion was only caused by the ceremony and will disappear once the ritual moon has passed and Rhys rejects the union." As I said the words, a cold panic began to claw at my throat. Sweat formed on my forehead, and I rubbed at it. What the fuck? "I don't like not being in control."

"Well, I know I'm not that old and wise yet, but I'm pretty sure no one is able to control falling in love, Rook." She took a deep breath and pinched the bridge of her nose. "Okay, this is what I do know. The unions are created, and the feelings are amplified, but they only emphasize what would have come naturally. Like a sped-up process or a homing beacon for those people to find one another."

"What the fuck? This is real? I actually like him?" I asked both horrified and excited that it wasn't all fake.

"Yes, Rook, you actually like him, but the emotion has been...."

"Supercharged," I muttered the word I'd been thinking of earlier.

"Yes, exactly. Supercharged." She shrugged. "As far as the union goes... If you think you'll go back to normal after the full moon, then you weren't paying attention to the teachings. The original union sticks with you for life. It may dull, but until a new union is chosen—if one ever is—you'll never stop thinking about who you were meant to be with." She stepped into the room as my eyes grew wide, and my breathing picked up. "Do you understand, Rook? You look freaked out." She walked the rest of the way across the room and placed her hand on my shoulder.

"I'm never going to stop wanting him?"

"Correct. Now that you've met you'll never fully stop wanting Rhys, no matter what you do." I staggered like I'd been hit with a physical blow. "Are you going to faint?" Mari grabbed my arm to steady me.

"I think I might be sick."

I sank down on the small couch as reality began seeping into my brain. My father sent me here, knowing that the connection would instantly bind us. He also knew that even if I could resist, I'd never be free of the emotions. I would forever be tortured with images of Rhys's face, forever craving his touch. He was sadistic. My father was a sadistic asshole, and I'd underestimated him.

"Rook, look at me," Mari said and knelt in front of me. "Do you really hate it here or Rhys that much that you wouldn't want to give it a shot?"

"I don't know. This place and Rhys are foreign to me. Everything is new and different, and...Why do you care so much?"

Mari's gaze dropped to the floor for a moment before she rose to her feet. There was something she wasn't telling me.

"Rook, I can never have what you have. I can never have that kind of love or connection or even the freedom to explore a relationship. Rhys is...He's special, and if there is even a small part of you that thinks you want to give this a try, then you need to go for it. Trust me. It is very lonely on the other side." She brushed away a tear, then plastered a strained smile on her face. "So, what do you say?"

"I tried earlier today. He wants nothing to do with me," I said, and once more, my heart began to beat out of control with an unexpected fear that I didn't understand.

"Boys are so fucking daft." Mari shook her head and walked across the room to my closet.

"What are you doing?"

"You want to go see Rhys, yes or no?"

"Well…"

"See what he's doing or stop him from doing it with someone else? That's what's eating at you, right? The thought of his hands on someone else's body, his lips on another while he fucks them hard."

Possessiveness gripped my chest as the image of Rhys fucking someone else rose in my mind.

"Fuck, stop that," I growled and shot to my feet as the nervous energy heaved and thrashed within me like a storm picking up steam.

"Yeah, you don't want to see him at all," she said and rolled her eyes at me. "And you aren't interested in getting under his kilt. Nope."

"Your sarcasm is noted. I just wish I knew how much of this was fake and how much of it was real," I said.

"Does it really matter?" She called out. "Most people spend their entire lives searching for a connection with another soul that is deep and passionate and all-consuming. All the things you're complaining about right now are what everyone else prays will happen to them and the majority never find."

Mari stepped out of the closet I'd spent an hour organizing just so it gave me something to do and threw a clean T-shirt at me. I caught it out of the air.

"Maybe think on this while you go shower. I'm a woman born in this family without red hair or a birthmark. I am nothing, no one. A person born without a cock, used as a weapon and tolerated by the family until I die or I'm killed off in battle. Does that sound pleasant to you? Do you think I never had dreams? That I didn't think of my union day? I didn't understand when I was little that I'd never have one. That I would die old and alone... My only hope is that someone notices me missing before my body starts to stink."

Mari marched for the door but stopped on the threshold and looked back at me. "This Faction life is a broken one, Rook. It is broken and full of broken people who are all just doing the best they can. You have the chance to have it all. You can still sing and have real love and one day be the head of your family. As Wale Ayeni said, "Be thankful for what you have. Your life is someone else's fairy tale." Now go shower. I'm going to go grab you something to wear that Rhys won't be able to resist." With that, Mari disappeared out the door.

I never thought about what it was like for the women of the family. I knew the rules, but there were no women in my immediate family back home. We were all boys, and my mother died when I was young. I suddenly felt like an asshole for not thinking about this from their side. That was one aspect the Flitters got right. They didn't have arranged connections or force unchosen women into slavery, turning them into assassins. My brothers and I nicknamed them the Butterflies. They were beautiful, and you never heard them coming.

My heart hurt for my cousin. There was agony in her voice, and if I could, I would take it away. I'd never been the warm-fuzzy type and was surprised by the emotion, which was par for the course lately.

I looked down at the T-shirt in my hands. Mari was right. This was futile. I wasn't going to be able to rest, I was too anxious to play my guitar, and the longer I thought about Rhys with someone else, the more volatile my power felt. I marched into the washroom and hopped into the shower. What I was going to do when I found him… I had no idea.

Toweling off, I stopped to stare at the tattoos of my lyrics that lined the left side of my neck. It was the first song I wrote and recorded. The first song that made me feel anything besides bitter. My father was always so quick to judge me because I didn't put more time into running the Faction, but why would I when it was the one thing I hated most?

I never saw my father unless it was at a ritual. He was always too busy to watch a little league game or help with homework. Where had he been when Devlin cried himself to sleep after our mother was killed? When Magnus graduated from school early and with top honors? When Wyatt struggled with his weight and self-image. He was nowhere. I was the one that helped my brothers grow up, so the moment they were old enough and I didn't have to focus on them, I ran and did my own thing. Everything my father did was for the Faction at the expense of our family.

Mari said I could still sing, but I found that hard to believe. My fingers trailed over the lines of script, and I couldn't help but wonder if I'd ever see a stage again. Would I ever feel like I belonged so far? This place didn't feel like home, even with the magic and the longing.

A loud knock pulled me out of the depressing thoughts.

"Are you almost done?" Mari yelled.

Wrapping a towel around my waist, I opened the door and grabbed the T-shirt.

"Well, if you walk around like that in front of Rhys, he definitely won't be able to resist you," Mari said as I pulled the T-shirt on.

"So this is what it's like when girls help a friend get ready for a date," I said, smiling. That smile quickly disappeared when Mari didn't return it, and I wanted to slap myself. "Shit, sorry…"

"Naw, it's fine. I just wouldn't know. I've never been on a date. Here, put this on, and no arguments," she said and held out her hands.

I once more found myself putting my foot in it with my cousin but wasn't sure what to say to make it better. My eyes dropped from hers to what she was holding.

"Thanks…Whoa…Nope. No, I'm not wearing a kilt," I said.

I had to admit. It was cool. All black with thick leather buckles and a large pin that was a combination of a sword with the Adair family crest. It looked kinda badass rocker. Again, something I would never admit.

"I told you, no arguing. Do you want to fit in around here and make yourself irresistible? Then put the damn kilt on, and no boxers underneath," she ordered like that was a normal request. "I'll wait out in the hall for you."

Rhys did look fucking sexy in this thing, and the thought of the quick access made my skin burn hot. I needed a fucking T-shirt that said, "Shit, I swore I'd never do but did." The material was a lot heavier than I thought it would be, but it was oddly comfortable.

"What shoes?" I called out.

"Your shit kickers," Mari answered.

I gave myself a once over in the mirror and hated to admit that I looked fucking badass. I could wear this on stage, and the fans would go crazy. Especially those in the front row as they clamoured to see if they could catch a peek underneath. That thought made my lip curl up.

"So where are we heading, anyway? You seem pretty sure you know where to find him," I asked as I stepped out into the hall.

"That's because I know where he is. *Up Er Kilt Pub* is where he always goes when he wants to unwind," she said and smiled, but it didn't quite reach her eyes.

"You really know him well." I watched her face closely.

"You could say that. I mean, he's been here since he was six, and I was five. We grew up together. His sister Fiona and my sister Belle are closer in age, so they kinda paired up, and Rhys and I paired up to hangout."

There it was. It wasn't the words Mari said. It was the look in her eyes and the slight blush across her cheeks. It screamed they were more than just friends.

We jogged down the steps to the front door and made our way outside, but I grabbed Mari's arm before we made it to the car.

"Tell me something. Are you in love with Rhys?"

Mari's smile evaporated, and she looked away but not before I caught the sheen in her eyes.

"Mari, I don't understand. If you're in love with him, then why are you helping me?"

"I guess my poker face needs work." I released her, and she leaned back against her car. "Fine, yes, you found out my not-so-secret secret. I've been in love with Rhys for as long as I can remember." She crossed her arms over her chest. "And why? Because loving him doesn't change how the Faction or the union pairing works."

"Fuck, Mari. I don't even know what to say. Do you hate me for coming here?"

She laughed, and the sound was bitter, but I didn't get the feeling she was laughing at me.

"No, I don't hate you. You didn't ask for any of this any more than the rest of us. Is this excruciatingly difficult? Fuck yes." She shook her head. "I don't know how to describe this to you. I've lived with him my whole life, and it's part of the reason I moved overseas for so long. My heart wanted something I knew I'd never have. Even though I know I need to let go and move on...I can't erase my feelings any more than the two of you can stop the connection from building."

She shook herself like a duck shaking off water and grabbed the door handle. "Like I said, I'm nothing but a girl. I wasn't the Adair chosen. Hurry up before he's fucked his way through the whole pub."

Once more, I was left speechless. Mari was in love with Rhys and clearly wanted a union with him. But, because she didn't fit the mould, the two of them never could've contemplated it. I looked into her eyes and knew I wouldn't be so stoic. In her shoes, I'd tell the world to go fuck itself. I would not drive the chosen person to be with the person I loved.

"Well, are you gettin' in, or are you going to stand out there lookin' like a wart on a frog's arse all night?"

"You know, you kind of remind me of me," I said as I slipped into the passenger side of the car.

"Are you tryin' to insult me now?" she teased and laughed.

I took a moment to stare at her profile, and it hit me that we could've been siblings instead of just cousins. Her hair and eyes were the same colour, and we even had the same shaped face, though hers was more feminine.

She cranked the radio as we pulled out of the driveway, and I smiled as one of my favourite songs began playing. We easily fell into singing together. It wasn't fair. I realized at that moment just how unfair this was, and if it ever got to the point where I could change laws, I was fucking changing the one that kept our Faction women so suppressed.

Mari tapped her fingers in time to the song on the radio, and in no time, we were pulling into a unique-looking pub that I could've sworn had once been a hobbit home. The round wooden door with the old-fashioned windows gave it a homey cottage vibe.

I opened my door and stopped. "Are you not coming in?"

Mari shook her head no. "I'm sorry, Rook, but I just can't go in there."

My face scrunched up as I took in her pain-filled eyes. "Mari..."

"No, don't. I'm making my peace with what's happening, but even I have my limits." She wiped at the tear sliding down her cheek. "Please go. I need a few minutes alone."

I stepped out of the car. But the window slid down, and she called my name. I leaned on the door, looking at her.

"I like you, cousin. I'm happy that if it was going to be anyone other than me with Rhys, that it's you who was chosen."

"I can't wrap my head around why you're helping me. I wouldn't be this generous."

"If not you, then who? It will never be me. It was never going to be me. At least with you, he has a chance to have something real, and I guess you're kinda cool, but don't let that go to your head. I will deny it if asked."

She smiled, and I realized how pretty she was. Not in a creepy I-wanted-to-fuck-my-cousin way, but I couldn't help wondering if Rhys had hoped that they could be together as well. I was torn by the mixed emotions this information brought, swirling to the surface.

"Thanks, Mari," I said and closed the door.

I stayed where I was and watched the car zip out of the parking lot. It took a moment to sink in, but only one other car in the large gravel space. I slowly turned in a circle, and there were a good dozen horse-and-buggies and another area like a large pen with more horses standing around, but not a single car other than Rhys'. Well, I no longer had a ride, didn't look like I could hitch one, and there was no way in hell I could remember how to get back to Injebreck to walk, so I'd better find a way to make this work.

I rolled my shoulders as I walked towards the front door, just as someone came out. The music was loud, and punched me in the face as the couple laughed and staggered by. They didn't pay me any attention as I stepped inside and let the door close behind me.

I didn't have to search hard for Rhys. My blood pressure shot through the roof as my eyes locked on the man on the stage. The connection I'd been trying to fight erupted in my chest, forcing me to stagger against the wall for support.

His voice was deep and rich, and the song he was singing made me want to jump up there and sing with him. The corner of my mouth curled up. Maybe the spirits did know what they were doing.

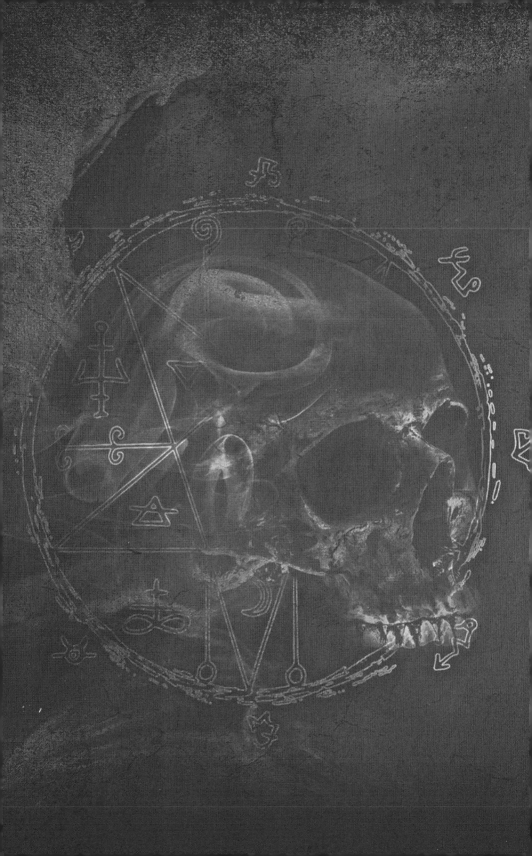

Chapter 13

Rhys

The music was pouring out of me tonight. I'd given up trying to decipher what I felt or should feel. I let myself go and didn't think about anything else. My foot tapped along with the mass of feet stomping and hands clapping in time to the upbeat song. I hit the pedal, and a filthy sound blared through the speakers as I started into the riff part of the song that always brought a cheer.

There was nothing quite like this. The world narrowed into a single moment of peace and erased the feeling of being crushed by the weight of my responsibilities. I'd always been an island floating on my own, weathering any storm, but right now, at this moment, I wanted a few minutes of calm before I needed to take the head winds on again. For me, that could only come from music. The lyrics about needing a vacation from my life were fitting and called to me in a way they never had before.

"You have to excuse me. I'm not at my best!" The whole room hollered at the same time. I closed my eyes and let my body move to the music. "Faster!" The crowd, which had stuffed the pub from one end to the other, screamed, and I stepped forward and let my fingers shred, playing solely by feel. Glancing over at Owen, he took the signal and the lead while I slid Tabitha off, gently propping her on her stand, and picked up the fiddle. The song was taking on a life of its own that only a room with this much energy could create.

Pointing to Caitlin and her friends, they pushed their way up onto the small stage and began dancing, their feet moving in perfect time to the song. The people in the first few rows hooted louder as their kilts flicked into the air as quickly as their feet, giving everyone an even bigger show than just the dance.

I spun the fiddle and tucked it under my chin as we smoothly shifted from the foot-stomping folk song to a crowd favourite. The cheers went up as a couple of the locals who had their hard taps on jumped up on the stage to join in on the fun. I couldn't keep the smile off my face as the pace picked up to the point where my muscles burned in my arm, but still, I pushed on. The burn made me feel alive and free of the binds that held me like shackles to my duties.

I had a laundry list of things that annoyed me about Rook, but what annoyed me the most was how he managed to spend his life avoiding what I was groomed to do. Even without my parents, the importance of my role was impressed upon me, and I took every second seriously. He'd shrugged off all that we were, travelled the world without a care, and got to perform like this every few days. He was living the life I could only dream of. I didn't begrudge him not wanting to give it up, but it was yet another kick in the teeth to be paired with him. Worse yet was to be rejected by him and then unable to stop the growing bond that would forever tie us together until another match was made.

The idea that I could have these feelings for the rest of my life and never be quenched was a torturous prospect that clawed at my heart. It was selfish of me to worry about something like that. I'd watched all the women in the family born without a birthmark or red hair suffer with this same plight.

My thoughts drifted to Mari and her bright blue eyes and sweet smile that could light up a room. If I'd been allowed to choose, I would've married her the moment she turned eighteen. We were best friends, and even though she didn't say it, I knew why she left for school. I couldn't blame her. I felt the same.

We were star-crossed, like Romeo and Juliet, destined never to have what we wanted. Keeping more distance had been safer. Dating and not thinking of her had been safer, but in the end, nothing changed. She was still the girl my heart longed for, and the overwhelming sadness I saw hiding under her mask of indifference did nothing to soothe my doubts.

Our eyes would lock over breakfast, and I could feel her pain. It matched my own. Between Mari and now Rook, I think it was time that I moved out for good. Permanent space was needed between me and the entire Adair family.

"Yeah," I yelled as the song ended. I held the fiddle up as the sea of people jumped around and held up mugs of beer. And that's when I saw him. *No, he couldn't be here.*

This was my safe spot, the one place I came where no one from my life at the castle bothered me. My eyes locked with the man leaning against the far wall, and my mouth ran dry as they raked over his body. The black T-shirt fit his tall, fit frame and defined shoulders, while the kilt he'd found made him look dangerous and, if possible, sexier than he already was.

All the emotions I'd been trying so hard to keep locked up and pushed down clawed their way back up from where I'd stuffed them. I stood frozen in place, trying to figure out how to escape. I couldn't be near him. Everything was still too raw from earlier. I groaned as images of pushing him up against the bar flashed through my mind.

From up here on the stage, it was easy to see the attention he was getting, and for good reason. He was the walking embodiment of a ragin' hard-on, and both women and men were already looking to make a move on the newcomer.

Jealousy stormed to the surface, and I growled under my breath as my body reacted to him. I quickly sat the fiddle down and signaled that I was getting a drink, leaving the stage in a rush. I pushed through the throngs of people feeling like a rat in a trap.

There was no exit at this end of the pub, and I desperately wanted out, or at least my mind did. My body, on the other hand, was all too keen to claim what was mine.

Leaning against the bar, I raised my hand, pointing to the tap for a pint, and smiled as familiar hands wrapped around my waist. Caitlin, my rescuer. She didn't know it, but it didn't matter. I turned in her arms and grabbed her face, crashing my lips against hers. I tried to take all of my built-up frustration out on her, but as sweet as she was, she was not who my mind conjured as our lips moved. She moaned into my mouth, and I pushed her back against the wall, not caring who was standing around to see.

I fumbled with the front of her kilt and groaned as her hand wrapped around my cock. My little victory was short-lived as a hand gripped my shoulder, almost bringing me to my knees.

My eyes snapped open, and I tried to take a deep breath as the power I'd barely managed to wrangle earlier erupted to all new levels in my system. The look on Caitlin's face told me what I'd see if I turned around. I'd seen those eyes glowing. I'd seen them as they tried to burn into my soul and capture me. I didn't dare turn around and look into them, or we would end up fucking on the bar.

"No one touches what's mine," Rook said.

Caitlin shrank away from the menacing tone in his voice.

My jaw clenched tight, my body shaking, as I tried to control the connection swirling out of control. My eyes found Caitlin's again.

"Get out. Get. Everyone. Out," I managed to force out as fog began to cloud my mind.

She was one of the few Flitters who knew what I was and what I was capable of. She swallowed hard but didn't move.

"Go. Now," I growled.

She darted away from the wall. She could've started yelling, but I had no idea what was going on behind me. The entire building could be on fire, and it wouldn't matter because Rook was touching me. I braced both hands on the cool stone wall.

"'Ave. Ya. Gone. Mad?" I said, then gasped as his body pressed up against mine.

"I'm not going to play this game with you, Rhys. I'm not a patient man," he said next to my ear.

"Fuck you, Rook. Let go of me and get out," I growled, even as another wave rocked me, making me gasp.

"You. Are. Mine," he commanded in my ear.

Shivering, the hair all over my body stood to join the aching shaft between my legs.

"No, I'm not." I tried to step to the side, but between Rook's strong hand and the power wrapping itself around me as it tried to bind us together, I only managed a few inches. "Fuck, Rook, just go.

You get to have your life back in a few weeks. Why are you torturing me like this?"

Rook pushed hard against my body, and my shaky arms gave way. We collided with the wall, and the little breath of air still in my lungs was forced out. I was trapped between the hardness of his body and the cool stone, and it felt so right. It felt dangerously perfect. My eyes closed as more of my resolve slipped, the power turning into sparks around us.

"I'm your number one," he said, his hands sliding along my arms until his fingers linked with mine.

"Stop. It. Rook," I panted out, even as everything in me screamed, begging to continue.

"Make me," he said, his lips brushing against my ear. He rubbed his body against mine, his hard cock calling to me as it rubbed against my ass.

I had to shake my head to clear some of the fog so I could think straight. With a strength that I didn't know I possessed, I pulled in the power that was building around us. The reflection on the wall told me my eyes were glowing as well, and with a roar, I pushed back with the power like it was a hand. Rook was forced away from me, and I finally drew a deep breath. I spun to face him, furious.

"How dare ya! How dare ya come into me spot and do dis!"

My hands balled into fists as I glared at my chosen. Rook was what I'd always wanted from my male partner, everything I could want. But he was only here because he was forced to be, and he didn't plan on staying.

Marching forward, I gave his chest a shove, and he staggered back from the blow. "What are you tryin' ta do? What da fuck is yer issue?"

Rook stood straight, his shoulders squaring as his jaw twitched, and it was the first time since I'd met him that I understood how domineering he was. The power coming off him was different from my own, yet we were equally matched. His eyes were fierce and more determined than I'd been expecting. He balled his hands and stood like he was ready for a fight. And fuck, it turned me on more. I stifled a groan as I pictured tackling him to the floor.

"I'm claiming what's mine."

Prying my eyes away from his, I realized that we were alone. I marched to the bar and grabbed the drink I hadn't gotten a sip of yet, chugging the fucking thing down.

"Aye, I'm sure," I said and glared his way, but the damage was done. I'd never get the feel of his body out of my mind. "I'm outta here. Stay outta me spot."

"No." His voice was as sharp as a sword's edge. He snapped his fingers as I took a step and ran into an invisible wall. "Why do you keep doing that?" he asked.

"Doin' what?" I glared at the man I wanted to strip naked and taste.

"Running. Every single time I try to have a conversation with you, you take off." Rook gestured towards the door. "I thought you said you'd been hoping for a triad and this union. Well, here I am, putting in the effort, and you're running again."

"I'm no' runnin'." I backed away from the wall of magic and turned back to face Rook. "Fine, I was runnin'."

"Did you even hear what I said to you? I'm acknowledging the pairing." He stepped forward, and his eyes instantly burned a little brighter. "I said I'm claiming what is mine."

"Aye, but what does dat mean? Are ya stickin' around? Are you goin' to make dis yer weekend home? Are ya plannin' on bein' exclusive ta da triad? How do ya see dis goin'?" I didn't back down as he came to stand toe-to-toe with me.

"I don't know. I don't have all the answers, but...." He cupped my face, and the earlier connection that I'd managed to wrangle into submission ripped free of my tight hold and slammed into my body like a boomerang on the return. I sucked in a deep breath as my back arched with the unbridled surge of power and desire flowing through my body.

"What I do know is that I want to do this," Rook said.

I knew it was coming. I could've tried to spin out of the way or punch him in the face—both options were tempting. But I didn't do either of those things as our lips met.

The world stopped. Between one breath and the next, it felt like an eternity had come to pass. It was as if the world paused to acknowledge what was happening here. The power erupted in a smoky swirl that twisted between us. At any other time, that would've fascinated me, but instead, Rook was all there was.

His eyes bore into mine, the glow in his blue depths almost blinding. My hands copied his, and I grabbed his face as the kiss became more insistent. The power whirling around us tightened its grip and pulled us closer like a rope—or maybe it was a noose. I didn't know yet, but the resistance I'd been clinging to evaporated.

"You are mine," Rook said as he broke the kiss, but our lips remained in contact. "You are mine, and that means no more fucking other people."

My back hit the wall, and I groaned as he became more demanding. Rook had taken full control, and I was eating it up. I rarely allowed myself to be pushed around, but I wanted him to dominate me. I could easily picture him tying me up, flogging me, spanking me, choking me, and cutting me. I was down for all of it and more with Rook.

His body brushed against mine, and even with the heavy material of the kilts in the way, I could feel that he was as hard as I was. Our cocks rubbed against each other, and I shuddered in his hold.

"Ta be yours means dat street runs both ways," I growled as Rook broke the kiss. "Naw more fuckin' around fir ya either."

His lips brushed my throat, and his teeth sunk into my neck. He began to suck, marking me as his. Ten minutes ago, I would've told him to fuck off, but every cell in my body screamed with pleasure.

Gripping his messy hair, I pulled him closer and groaned as his tongue swirled along my skin. There wasn't a single part of me that didn't feel that this was where I was always meant to be. Connection or not, this man was my match.

Groaning, I slid my palms down his chest and around his waist until I found his ass. I gripped it hard and pulled him into me until there was nowhere left to go. With the feel of his cock pressing against me, a shudder rippled through me as I pictured taking him down my throat.

"Oh fuck," I cursed and tilted my head, giving Rook more space as he broke the seal on my neck. His tongue traced a wet line up to my ear.

"Does it look like I want anyone else?" Rook said, sending shivers racing through my body.

"I dinnie mean now…Oh, fuck it."

I growled and pushed Rook back, then pulled him around, so he was the one with his back against the wall. Our eyes locked, and my world shifted. I sucked in a shuddering breath.

"I'm gonna fuck you so hard that ya won't be walkin' straight for a week," I said with a smirk.

"Bring it," Rook said, giving me the same look. "But whatever you do to me, I'll do to you twice as hard and twice as long."

His eyes glimmered with the challenge, and his hand wrapped around the back of my neck, holding me firm.

"Who I am might scare you." Rook gripped my lower lip between his teeth and bit down hard enough that the pain shot down my spine and made me groan.

"I crave to make you scream," he said, releasing my lip. "I want to make you bleed." He gripped my hair, his fingers digging into my scalp, and I knew what he would say before he said it. "Under all this, I'm a sadistic fuck, and no one has been able to take me yet. Will you?"

It felt like Rook was consuming me as he devoured my mouth, and I matched his intensity. We broke apart, gasping, both of us sizing up the other.

"Please tell me dat be a promise and no just ya talkin' tough," I said.

Before he could answer, I became the aggressor, attacking his mouth and exploring every inch with my tongue. I was met with the same aggression, the desire building at a rate that threatened to incinerate us. The hottest day in the desert couldn't compete with the heat burning in my body.

Rook groaned as his hands ran down my back. Sparks ignited beneath my skin, making my muscles flex everywhere he touched. It was too much, and yet, I couldn't get enough. Breaking the kiss to catch my breath, I leaned my forehead against his.

"I need to get ya back ta Injebreck. This is no' da place I wanna do this, and there be danger outside of da walls."

"Danger?" Rook asked.

And as if he'd conjured them, the door to the pub burst open with a bang. I felt them as soon as they stepped inside, and I spun and threw up a barrier to protect us. It was not a moment too soon, as arrows meant for our hearts bounced off the shields and landed on the floor.

"Who the fuck are they?" Rook asked as the room slowly filled with Hunters.

"Witch Hunters. Those dat know about da Factions and dinnie like us very much. How do ya no know about 'em?" Rook's mouth opened and closed a few times, and I shook my head. "It din't matter right now. Do ya know how ta fight?"

"With some spells and my knife."

"It'll have ta do."

I shivered as I released the concealment spell around my body. Rook whistled low as the leather armour, sword at my hip, axe on my back, and knives strapped across my chest were revealed. I never left the castle without them on me.

"I didn't think I could be any more turned on, but holy fuck. I might bust a nut just looking at you."

I glanced at Rook from the corner of my eye and found him gawking at me. I smirked. "Stay here and kill any that make it past me. Oh, and din't be lettin' dem touch ya wit their arrows or knives. They're laced with poison."

The group fanned out across the pub and slowly started to advance.

"You're going to fight them? Rhys, there are like ten of them. Why don't you just burn them up or something?"

My sword rang with a distinct trill that sent a shiver down my spine as I drew it from its sheath. This was my father's sword, and whenever I drew it from its resting place, I felt his essence inside the blade. My thumb ran over the delicate wires that formed the McGregor family crest. Pulling my phone out, I hit the unlock and pressed Mari's name before tossing the phone to Rook.

"Dat will only attract more. Do as me said and kill any dat pass me, but otherwise, dinnie get in me way. Tell Mari what be happenin'," I said and cracked my neck. "All right, ya fuckers. Ya wanna dance? Let's dance."

Stepping forward, I released the shield, unable to hold it and fight. I could only hope that Rook paid attention to some of his training. Arrows and blades sailed through the air. Holding up my free hand, I used the armour on my arm to block the ones I couldn't knock out of the air with the sword. The group pulled their dual long knives and moved as a unit as they descended on me with a unified precision that told me this group was experienced.

With a roar, I attacked the Hunter closest to my right and blocked a blow from the left with the thick armour that protected my forearm. With a twist of my sword, I sliced the first Hunter across his wrist. He jumped back with a yell. Jumping, my foot connected with the guy I'd blocked the blow from and sent him flying backwards and over a table with a crash. I ducked away from the knife coming for my face, and my blade blocked another blow.

The sound of metal on metal was loud as the ultimate dance began. Spinning, I caught a Hunter coming in behind me and dragged the sword across his stomach. With a scream, he dropped to the floor, trying to hold his insides in place. I leapt over the blade coming for my legs and caught the next attacker in the arm. A shrill scream filled the pub as both knife and hand went flying, severed by my sword. I remembered my first fight with Hunters and how scared I'd been. How if it hadn't been for Mari and a little bit of dumb luck, I wouldn't be breathing now.

I turned to block another attack and caught a fist in the face. Stumbling back, I got my sword up just in time to stop the knife from sinking into my heart. Soon, the battle of blocks and hits became a blur, one blending into another.

They were good, too good, and I was wearing down faster than I could take them out. I was going to have to resort to magic, and I hated the idea of sending up a beacon like that.

Panting, I stumbled back from the group and noticed that Rook was exchanging blows with one of the guys. Their knives were locked in a stalemate. Pulling one of the throwing knives from the sheath strapped to my chest, I threw it at the back of the man Rook was fighting. He yelled as it pierced him through the back, and I hoped that was enough to give Rook the advantage as I turned back to the seven remaining Hunters.

"Fuck," I mumbled.

I was preparing to use my magic when two of the guys in front of me began to spit blood. I smirked and stepped back as the bodies fell forward to reveal Mari. Belle was standing in the doorway, looking as fierce as her sister. The Hunters jumped away from the newcomers, and suddenly the playing field was a lot more even. On the island, it was mandatory that everyone, part of the Faction, learned to fight. The handful of unchosen were something far deadlier. Mari was one of the silent killers, but that didn't mean that Belle couldn't fight just as fearlessly.

My heart soared at the sight of her in her fighting gear, bloodied short sword in hand, and a fierceness in her eyes that could rival any man I knew. There was no one better I'd want by my side in a fight.

"I hear ya have gotten yourself in a wee bit a trouble," she teased.

"Took ya long enough ta show up. Taught ya might 'ave gotten lost on da way," I said cheekily as she drove her sword into the stomach of the Hunter charging her.

She was as fluid as water as she spun and brought the sword

around to decapitate the man before he even registered the first wound. We smoothly slipped into position to have one another's back.

Mari moved with all the grace of a ballerina, her hair in its pony-tail whipping around as her blade sank to the hilt in the next Hunter's chest.

"I was just making sure there were some left fir ya. Ya know, wearin' 'em down and such," I teased back as my sword connected with another blade.

"Aye, is that what you were doin'? Looked more like you were baffled by all the sharp pokey things coming at you."

"Oh, a cock joke? Me sees how it be," I said, laughing at her.

"Me dinnie know why me had ta come. There was only a speck to wipe away, and me was in da middle of me mani-pedi," Belle complained as she dropped the man she'd been fighting to the floor, his throat slit. His eyes were wide as his mouth gaped, trying to draw a breath, but she stepped over him like he was invisible.

"No whining at me. You know you like it," Mari said as Belle grabbed a full beer off one of the tables and chugged it down as the last remaining Hunter ran for the door.

"Oh, I dinnie tink so," I said and switched my grip on the sword.

With a yell, I threw the sword like a javelin. The sharp sword stayed true, sinking deep between his shoulder blades. The Hunter fell to his knees and coughed up blood before falling face-first on the floor, silent.

With the threat neutralized, I turned to see Rook's eyes darting around the room, taking in the carnage, then fixing on the dead man, sightlessly staring back up at him. His eyes were a little too wide, and he had a death grip on his knife.

"I think this might be his first rodeo," Mari whispered as she followed my stare.

"Aye, I tink yer right. Cheers for comin'," I said.

Her eyes were sad as she looked at Rook's hand, then up into my eyes. Those blue eyes always reminded me of a cool winter storm, but her tongue was always devious.

"You don't even have to ask. You know that I'll always come for you, no matter what," she gave me a smile before making her way to her sister.

"Yer made of pure gold," I whispered under my breath so only I heard.

"Belle and I will start clean up. You better go talk to him." Mari nodded in Rook's direction, snapping me out of my thoughts. Rook was staring at us, but his expression was hard to read.

"Dis been a weird night," I mumbled as I headed towards Rook.

"Aye, that it has," Mari answered.

"Are ya okay?" I asked Rook, then kicked the Hunter's blade away from his hand, just in case. "Was dis your first dust up?"

"Dust up? I fucking killed a guy," Rook said, looking at his blood-smattered hand. His eyes fixed on the decapitated head that had rolled not far away. "Is this a normal Saturday night for you all? You seem completely normal, killing a group of people."

"Aye, ya did. And aye, it be normal from time ta time. But if ya hadn't killed 'em, ya woulda been on da floor instead." I looked around at the blood and damage. It was going to be a few days before the pub could reopen. "Come on. Let's get ya back to Injebreck. Hunters tend to travel in large groups. Dis won't be all in da area."

Reaching out, I lifted Rook's hand and had to suck in a deep breath to battle back the instant desire. "Give me da knife."

Rook's hand slowly opened, allowing me to take the blade.

"Mari, is anyone else comin'?"

"Yeah, twenty on clean up. If you need to go, we got it covered til they arrive."

Nodding, I wrapped my arm around Rook's shoulders and guided him past the dead men sprawled on the floor. I paused long enough to pull my sword from the back of the man lying in the doorway, give it a quick wipe, and put it back in its sheath.

Rook was quiet until I got in the car beside him. Then he looked over at me, his eyes unreadable. "Is it really like this all the time?"

"Ya mean wit da Hunters and burnt villages and everythin' else?" Rook nodded. "Aye. Sometimes better, sometimes worse. Ya really had no idea?" Rook slowly shook his head no and leaned his head back on the seat. "Whateva ya father has been payin' to keep dis from ya, it was a lot. The world is no' a fun place all da time, Rook. Ya've kinda been livin' like a Flitter wit all da glitz and glamour. Ya know it all be fake, right? No' da fans, but da rest? As heads of da Faction, we are always at war, and assassins can be around da corner. Ya probably never knew it, but yer pa woulda had guards followin' ya ta keep ya alive." I turned the car on and put it in first. "It's da same all over. Welcome to da real world. Dis is what our family deals wit daily."

"And Mari and Belle?"

"What about 'em?"

"They were dressed like...."

"Warriors?" Rook shook his head no. "Oh, you be meanin' assassins. Well, Mari be one, but Belle no. She jus no how ta fight, we all learn from da time we can hold a blade."

Rook's head slowly turned toward me. "I call them the Butterflies," Rook said and looked at me. "I've never seen anyone fight like that before."

"Ya, dat is exactly wat dey be. Dey look like butterflies, but dinnie kid yerself Mari be lethal and would lay her life down fir ya. When ya bury yer head in da sand, ya put us all in danger, Rook." The car revved as I pulled onto the road and flew towards the castle. "Fightin' will be da first thing ya need ta learn if ya plan on stayin'."

I felt like I was being too harsh, but he was like a newborn babe dropped in a lion's den. He had to have a severe reality check quick, or he would get someone killed, and I refused to let that happen. Glancing at Rook's reflection in the glass, I tried to picture him no longer breathing, and my heart spasmed in my chest. No, he couldn't leave the property again until he learned more and how to fight. I wasn't going to let him die.

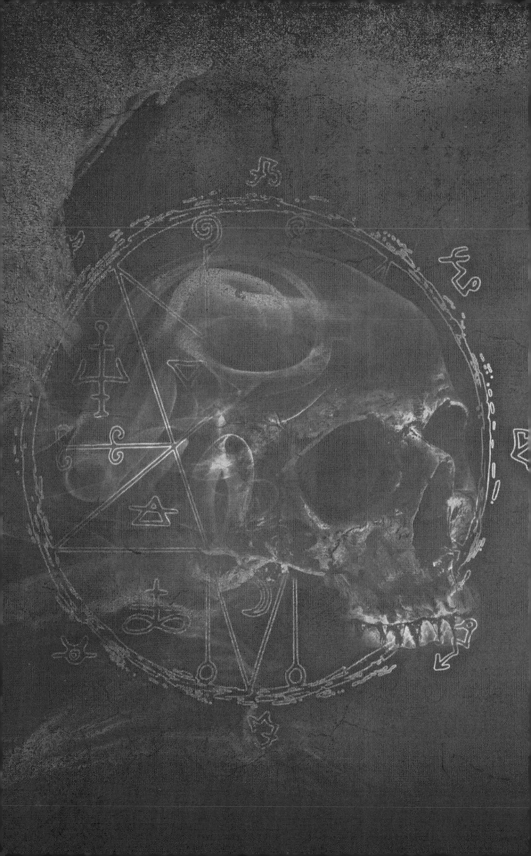

Chapter 14

Mari

It felt good to use my skills tonight. Not that it had been a big fight, and not that I wished for Hunters to attack. It simply felt good to be useful and needed. Stepping out of the shower, I wrapped a towel around my body and twirled my hair up in a second one before heading out into the bedroom.

"Sweet spirits," I yelped as Rhys looked up from where he was lying on the bed. "You better not be getting blood on my bed," I scolded, even though I knew he was in different clothes and the faint smell of his soap lingered in my room.

He looked scrumptious, laying on his back and staring up at the ceiling like he was star gazing. This felt way too natural. It was something he used to do every night before I left for school. He would get scolded and kicked out by my ma or pa. I started to wonder if he secretly liked it.

"What are you doing in here, Rhys?" I whispered like we were committing a sin.

Even though nothing had ever happened, the desire had been there for so long it felt like we were now sneaking around and doing something wrong. Maybe for me, it was. I'd dreamed of him in my bed and not just as my best friend as we hung out and talked. I was too emotionally connected to him to have him in here like this. It was far too tempting to push lines that we couldn't cross.

"Do ya remember when I used ta sneak in 'ere all da time?" he asked as I veered to the walk-in closet to find more to wear than a towel.

"Aye I do. How could I forget? Did you know my pa lectured me good more than once for finding you in here?" I said.

He chuckled. His laugh was the same warm, heart-fluttering sound. I quickly pulled on sleep pants and a warm hoodie before wandering back out to the bedroom. I stopped as soon as I left the closet and took a moment to appreciate this and pretend that things hadn't changed.

"I don't think he ever found out how you were doing it, though."

Rhys laughed hard at that. "Aye, there be too many forgotten passages. Wonder what he'd be sayin' tonight."

"Probably the same thing he always said. That it's inappropriate for you to be alone in my room late at night."

"Aye, he probably would."

Rhys still hadn't moved. I'd long ago put little glow-in-the-dark stars on my ceiling. I liked the feeling of lying outside even when I wasn't. It made me feel free of all that I was and couldn't escape. Rhys had been equally captivated by them and snuck in to stare at them.

"I would come in 'ere all da time an' stare at da stars," he said.

"I know. You were always getting me into trouble," I said, and taking a deep breath, I pushed aside all the fluttery feelings to wander toward the bed.

"Naw, I mean when ya were gone. I'd lie in 'ere every night an' stare at da stars an' wonder what ya were doin' an' if ya thought about me anymore." He slowly sat up as I sat on the other side of the bed and pulled my knees up to my chest. "Did ya?"

"Think about you?" He nodded. "Of course I did. Don't be daft." I smiled, and he smiled back.

What I didn't say was that he was all I thought about. I'd finish classes and end up sitting in my room with nothing but time. I explored when I could and shopped when I was able, but it all felt hollow. It passed the time but didn't provide any real comfort or substance to my life. It was as if I was on the outside looking in at a world I didn't belong to and yet had nowhere else to go.

The distance from Rhys had made it easier to not long for him every second, but the loneliness made him clearer than any photograph. It was a terrible thing to love someone I could never have, and in many ways, it was worse to know he felt the same.

"What are you doing in here, Rhys?"

He sighed and shook his head before standing and going to the window. "I dinnie know what I be doin'. I spent me whole life preparin' for dis moment, an' now dat it's here...I just...." He crossed his arms over his chest.

"Why are you second-guessing yourself? You're going to be a great leader." Needing to do something, I stood and wandered around the room, lighting candles. I could've easily done this with my magic, but there was something to be said for creating with your hands, even it if was just lighting a little flame.

He turned his head and looked at me as I dared to wander closer. The look said it all.

"Rhys, I cannot be part of your decision."

"Aye, I know." He shook his head and sighed.

"Okay. Then what's going on?" No candles left to light, I sat back on the bed.

He turned, so he was leaning against the stone, and it reminded me so much of when we were kids. Whenever he was feeling uncomfortable about anything, this was the pose he made, and the little crease between his eyes would always deepen. It somehow made him look sexier, and I was tempted to take a picture.

"I'ma no longer gonna be da leader we taught, Mari. I'ma second, demoted, and to a man, dat, from what I can see, is wantin' nothin' ta do wit da Faction. I dinnie know what I'ma ta do wit dat, or if I even wanna. Is he gonna reject all me ideas just like how he rejected me?"

I searched his face and was confused. Rhys had never been one to second-guess himself. If anything, he could be over-arrogant. I was suddenly worried that there was something he hadn't told me. Had Rook said or done something other than the rejection to make him doubt himself like this?

"Rhys, this is not like you," I said.

I studied every movement. I didn't want to do this. I always felt that having empathic abilities was cheating and invading someone's personal space, but this seemed like a good time to use it. I released a little of my ability, and it reached out and tasted his emotions. He was scared. But scared of what?

"Wat if I still reject 'im at da next ritual moon? What if we manage to make it until me thirty-fifth birthday so we can choose one another? Or we can jus run now…."

"Rhys."

"Naw, I'ma serious, Mari. Maybe I'ma no' cut out for any of dis. Maybe we shoulda taken off when ya offered a year ago. Shite, what have I done?" Rhys groaned.

This was my opening. I could see it in his eyes. All I had to do was say *let's run off* and he would. Whatever drove his fear, he was willing to toss away all he'd worked for his whole life.

"Rhys," I said more firmly, and his eyes shot up to mine. I stood from the bed and went to lean on the other side of the large window. "No, you were right to turn me down. It was a desperate, irresponsible, and irrational thought. You did the right thing then, and you're not going to reject Rook and your third now. Especially now that the connection has started."

"We would be considered deserters and never allowed to return to the Faction."

"Aye, I know."

"All right, and what about Rook? You know that you'd long for him for the rest of your life, and he'd long for you?"

"Aye," he said, his voice breaking as he rubbed at his face and shook his head.

"Is that really what you want to do? You never struck me as the man who would want to hurt your union. Nor are you the type to want to hurt me. You'd never be able to commit and not feel torn about all we'd left behind."

"Fuck, Mari. Naw, I dinnie wanna do dat to Rook or me third or ya." He crossed his arms over his chest like he was trying to hug himself.

I badly wanted to offer him the comfort he needed. To reach out and touch him and be folded up in his arms as he took the strength I offered, but I stayed put and kept my hands to myself. My own emotions were as volatile as his. I didn't trust what would happen.

"Can I be blunt?" I asked.

"Aye, always."

"You know how I feel, yes?"

His eyes found mine and reflected what was in my own heart. "Aye."

"Then you know that what I'm going to say right now is not easy for me, and I don't say it lightly." I licked my lips and took a deep breath. "I don't want you to run off with me. I never did. I know what I offered a year ago, but I was having a hard time at school, was sent on a few difficult missions, my ma was dying and you've always been the one who makes me feel better. I wanted to get away from it all, and it was a terrible thing for me to ask of you." Turning my head, I looked out the window to the dark water as it slowly rolled onto shore. "Not only that but—I can't believe I'm saying this—I really like Rook. He's an ignorant ass, but he has potential," I said, and we smirked. "More than that, I think the spirits got it right. You two are made for one another."

"Mari..."

I held up my hand. "No, you need to listen to me. I understand that you're unsure about what the future will hold with the new power dynamic—you've always seen your union one way—but that doesn't mean that everything you've been working for will be destroyed. Rook strikes me as smart and a good person under the jerkish exterior."

Rhys snorted, and his eyes lit up a little.

"I also know how he crushed you when he rejected you. As hard as you've tried to hide how much it hurt, I can see it in your eyes."

"Aye, ya always could see me better than anyone else."

"The pain he caused has scared you. You are scared to open up to him now, and don't even bother trying to deny it. It's also making you hesitant about all the other unknowns left to come. But none of that matters anymore, not really. He's here now. He wants to try now. Not only that, but the Faction needs you. Your family needs you. You and I both know that your uncle is not cut out to lead, and Ronan is...well, Ronan."

Rhys smirked.

"Besides, if you really do love me, for no other reason, I need you to get in as a respected council head of the Faction so that you can do what you always said you would and change the laws."

"I do want ta do dat," he said, and he looked up from the floor and straightened his spine. I could feel his resolve returning as the fear began to ebb away.

"I'm also confident the magic ties that are drawing the two of you together now will turn into the real thing. Rhys, you have the opportunity to fall in love with him if you give the two of you a chance. Trust me. He is squirming like a worm on the end of a line for you."

He moved his hand over his chest. "It be so much. I canna even explain it."

"I think the reason why the books don't explain it well is that no one can put into words or they don't want to freak out everyone with how it consumes you."

He turned so he could look me in the eyes, and it took all my strength to keep my face neutral and my eyes focused on his face. It was way too easy to tumble down the rabbit hole of fantasies otherwise.

"Da guilt is overwhelmin', Mari. I'ma feelin' like I led ya on all dis time, knowin' dat we could never be. I can feel da emotion seepin' in for Rook, and den I feel guilty dat I'm hurtin' him and da triad by lovin' you."

I bit my lip hard. That was the first time Rhys said he loved me out loud, even though we'd both felt the same way for years. I could feel my throat wanting to close up and choke me. He didn't seem to notice that he said it, and I quickly spoke before it became awkward.

"You have nothing to feel guilty about, but this can't happen anymore. You will always be my best friend, but it's not fair to anyone for you to come to my room like this. It's not fair to you, me, or your new triad. It leaves too many doors open, and I'm one you need to close."

His eyes filled with pain. "I know. I just..."

"I know," I said, cutting him off. I couldn't hear him say the words. "I love that you'd even consider running away for us to be together, but it is always the coward's way. You, Rhys McGregor, are no coward." We fell silent, and I stared out the window at the sky that, for once, wasn't overcast. "How is Rook?"

"Shook, but otherwise fine. I made sure he was asleep before I left him to go change."

A smile tugged at the corner of my mouth. That was the Rhys I knew. The man didn't even realize his own depth of caring.

"I dinnie understand why Angus has kept so much from 'im. He be as shocked as a newborn babe takin' its first breath, an' I dinnie think dat be fair ta 'im," Rhys said, his voice holding a hint of anger. He didn't recognize how much he'd already started to feel for Rook, and I wasn't going to point it out. That was something they needed to explore on their own.

"No, it's not fair. Do you want me to train him?" I offered.

"Yer sure?" Rhys asked as he pushed away from the wall and came to stand in front of me.

Was I stupid for not taking him up on the offer to run off? Maybe. Maybe I'd regret it, but it was the right thing to do.

"Yeah." I rubbed my hands up and down my arms. "I have the

feeling the two of you are going to need it. Trouble is on the horizon, Rhys. I feel it in my gut."

Everyone thought my powers were battle-oriented, but only Rhys knew I had the gift of sight. I'd seen our life together if we'd run. I'd seen the Faction we'd go to and our kids. It wasn't just a dream. It could've been my reality if we'd taken that fork in the road, but to take that road meant many others would die. I couldn't be that selfish.

Rhys would hate himself because he had no idea all I'd seen since coming home. There was very dark magic at play, and it was blocking a lot of my ability, but one thing was certain, Rhys needed to stay with Rook, and they needed to find their third as soon as possible. They were going to need one another.

"Aye, den let's git 'im up ta speed as quick as ya can. He is gonna need ta learn from da best." Rhys's intuitive eyes searched my face. "Ya getting' anytin' specific? Ya look ta be worryin'."

"No, not any more than usual. All I know for certain is that you need to take care of one another and find your third and bring her into the fold. You're all at risk, more than at any other time in history or any other triad. That much, I know for sure. If any more comes to me, you'll be the first I tell. Tomorrow morning, get him down to training, and I'll start working with him."

"I dinnie deserve ta 'ave ya in me life, Mari. Sleep sweet," he said.

"Sleep well, Rhys."

I watched him leave and waited until the door closed before I sagged against the wall, letting free the emotions I'd been holding back. Crawling onto the bed, I buried my head in the pillow and let the tears flow. I'd seen enough of the future to know that we'd just passed a significant fork in the road of my life. I knew what it meant for me and what my future held. Holding myself tightly, I took a moment to grieve all that was lost.

I was so tired. The constant bombardment of images and feelings was sometimes more than I could handle. Everyone thought my drug abuse stemmed from depression, and I let them believe it. It was easier and simpler that way. I didn't want anyone other than Rhys to know what I could do. My power was coveted, and no one should know what I saw and be able to manipulate it to their will. I was barely strong enough to do what was right all the time.

The demon blood quieted my mind and let me rest. Everyone took for granted the calm of only their voice, of not seeing the world burn or survive. I saw it all, and what I saw terrified me.

I was shaking and would cave again soon. I was too close to my breaking point. There was only so much I could take.

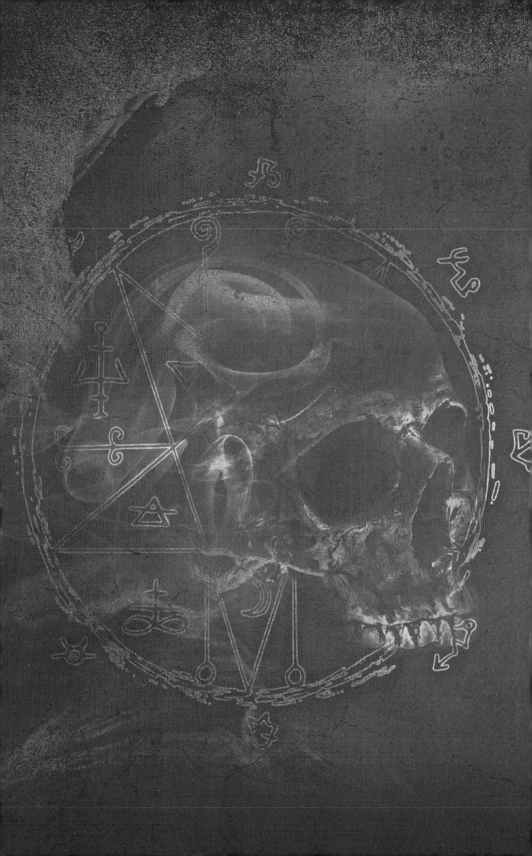

Chapter 15

Elewyen

I awoke shivering and with a squeaking in my ear. My eyes snapped open. Barry and I were curled up in the old den I found, but the rumbling in the distance told me a storm was closing in. Barry squeaked again and poked me in the cheek.

"I'za know yer hungry. I'za hungry too."

I slowly pushed myself into a sitting position and pulled the long cloak open enough to get at my travel bag. I'd taken to lying on it at night, so my little travel companion couldn't take more than his share of food. Stealing wasn't something I liked to do, but I was drawn into the last village I passed by the smell of fresh baked goods. There had been a loaf of bread cooling just inside of an open window and a jar of what ended up being raspberry jelly. I felt guilty for stealing them and disappearing into the woods like a terrible thief.

Opening the flap, I pulled off a small chunk of the bread, then used my knife to spread some of the jam on it before cleaning the blade and putting everything away. I took a bite of the bread, and if a squirrel could scowl, Barry did so now. He sat on my knee, his tail twitching as he stared at me.

"Yer pushy, Barry. Naw respectin' gurly squirrel is gonna wan' ya wit dat attitude," I said, breaking off a piece of what I was eating to give him. He snatched it from my fingers and ate it like he'd never eaten in his life. Little bits of jam were smeared all over his face, and I giggled as I watched him try to lick it off.

"At least ya be fun," I said.

Leaning against the dirt wall, I thought about last night and the strange dreams that had come to me. I was missing someone, but I didn't know who. I kept reaching for them, but I couldn't see them clearly, and they would disappear before I could touch them. I was wandering around in a fog, lost and grasping at nothing.

I'd woken up in a cold sweat more than once, and now I wondered if I was coming down with a fever. The thought became more concerning because whenever I woke, I thought I saw someone sitting in the den with me, but his face was out of focus. Was he a spirit trying to communicate with me? Or was he a figment of a fever dream? I had no idea. He kept trying to tell me something, but there was no sound, and then he'd disappear.

At one point, he was drawing in the dirt with his finger when I woke up, but he disappeared as soon as I looked at him. The only solid part of him I'd been able to see before he'd faded was his hair. It was as dark as the night sky.

I gave Barry a little more of the bread, then stuffed the rest in my mouth before he could beg any more of it away from me. I was a sucker for a cute face.

Lightning flashed outside, followed by a loud roll of thunder. I pulled up the hood on my cloak. I didn't mind harsh elements, but I'd never been a fan of storms. Something caught my eye, and when the lightning flashed again, it revealed lines carved into the dirt floor that hadn't been there before.

A shiver travelled up my spine. I stared down at the ground where I'd seen the apparition. I'd never known of a spirit that could do more than whisper words, yet there on the dirt floor were two identical letters. I wished I could read to put a name to the letters. I'd seen them in lines of words on the villagers' wooden signs sticking in the ground. Reaching out, I traced the letters with my finger and memorized the strange message.

*R*ook

The door banged open, and I sat up straight, grabbing the knife from under the pillow.

"Holy fuck, Rhys! Do you ever walk into a room peacefully?" I grumbled and flopped back down. "What time is it, anyway?"

"I like dat yer armed. There be hope for ya yet," he mocked. I was too damn tired to be bothered snipping back. "Ya know, me taught ya might be a wee bit happier ta see me, considerin' I saved your arse last night, den tucked ya in ta bed like ya were a babe," Rhys drawled.

I glared at him, but of course, that smirk and his deep voice flowed over my body and made my cock harden. It was like he had a direct line to it.

"You're never going to let that go, are you?"

"I reckon not for a while. But then, of course, there was the whole 'yer mine' speech, unless dat was just da power ridin' ya at dat moment and nothin' more."

Of course, he had to mention that. My mind instantly conjured images of how he'd felt and tasted and how I'd wanted to do a whole lot more until the night went very sideways. Grabbing the blanket, I flung it off and pointed at the raging morning wood I was sporting.

"Does this look like I want to take it back?" I pulled the blankets back into place. "I was up all night thinking about all that happened last night. I think I fell asleep like ten minutes ago."

"As fuckin' hot as dat is, and as temptin' as ya are, I'm no' gonna join ya in me bed. We 'ave work ta do. So, get up and meet me in da kitchen. I'll be nice and let ya get a cup of coffee first."

"Work?"

Rhys stopped just before he walked out the door. I really did hate that he looked so calm and cool as a damn garden vegetable while I was burning with desire from the inside out just looking at him. What the fuck was it with those black kilts that looked so damn sexy?

"Aye, and dinnie be takin' time to relieve that itch ya got. I didn't get to rub mine out, neither da ya." Rhys rubbed his chin. And even that small movement sent an electrical charge through my body. "Oh, and I'd wear somethin' comfy—trackie bottoms or somethin' of the like."

"What the fuck? How is this fair?" I asked and swung the blankets off again.

His eyes immediately flicked from mine to take in the whole package. "Dinnie worry. If I have it me way, ya'll be screamin' under me soon enough," he said stiffly, and then he was gone.

"Really? You're going to say that and leave me like this? What kind of heathen are you?"

His laugh echoed along the hallway, and I groaned as I slipped from the bed. Unbelievable. I was partnered with a sadist. Fucking wonderful.

"Comfortable, he said. Trackie bottoms?" I grumbled as I rummaged through the closet. "What the hell are they, anyway? Track pants or jogging pants, maybe?"

I pulled out a black T-shirt and a pair of black 'trackie bottoms' and wandered into the washroom to do my morning routine. I was very tempted to ignore Rhys and take a few minutes to get rid of my hard-on, but I figured he'd know somehow and torture me more. The image of him in leather armour crossed my mind, and I doubled over and grabbed the edge of the sink.

Fuck, this was torture. Anyone who said being the number one was the best had never been through this. It felt like the worst case of blue balls mixed with a healthy dose of magic keeping it that way.

"Good mornin', Master. Would ya like me ta help ya wit anythin' dis mornin'?"

I jumped at the sound of Liam's voice. "Holy fuck, Liam! Don't do that to me."

"I'm sorry, Master. I didn' mean ta startle ya," and he took a step farther into the room. His hands were neatly folded in front of him, but his eyes were trained on the tent in my pants.

"Liam?"

"Aye, Master?"

"Let me give you a rundown of what will happen if you touch me. The first thing that will happen is Rhys will find out, and I'm guessing he'll be pissed off. Now I don't know about you, but I think he's fucking scary when he's angry. Do you want him hunting you down to cut your cock off because you touched me?"

His eyes went wide. "Naw, of course, no', but ta service ya is part of me job until da triad is formed. Master Gregory said ta give ya whatever ya needed. Dis 'as been me job in da house for many years."

I cocked a brow and leaned my hip against the stone counter. It seemed odd that Gregory would encourage Liam to offer himself up to me. Did he also offer himself up to Rhys? Did that mean he accepted? The rage in my chest was alive and well with the thought of someone else touching what was now mine.

"Who exactly have you serviced, Liam?" I asked, my anger quickly escalating the longer I stared at his handsome face. I wanted to growl at the thought that Liam had taken Rhys down his throat. The possessive, crazy sensation that had started the moment I saw Rhys the first time apparently had no intention of lessening.

"Almost all da males dat pass through da house."

I pushed away from the counter, a growl leaving my throat. "Oh, really? Is Rhys one of these males?"

Liam licked his lips and stumbled backwards out the door as I continued to advance on him. There was no reason to be angry with the man, but I couldn't seem to stop the desire to rip his head from his shoulders.

He held up his hands as he dropped to his knees and continued to back up like an animal would until he hit the bed.

"Please no hurt me," he whimpered.

"Answer the fucking question, Liam. Have you serviced Rhys before?" I cracked my knuckles, not sure what I'd do if he answered yes.

"Naw, Master Adair."

My shoulders instantly relaxed, but my chest was still tight with emotion as my hands clenched and unclenched into fists.

"Are you lying to me?"

He shook his head no. "Rhys neva 'ave sex wit anyone from da house. I dinnie know he was even havin' sex at all til a month ago. He be very private." Liam lifted his eyes to mine and licked his lips. "He kinda got more... active when... um... when da chosin' ritual happened," he said, and then winced away like I might hit him.

That was interesting. I knew Rhys had been upset by the rejection, but it sounded like he'd become a lot more promiscuous. Not that I could judge. Before I arrived here, I usually had three to four people a night. This had been the longest I'd gone without fucking someone in a couple of years.

"Okay," I said and stepped back from the man who had only been trying to help me. I was going crazy. This place made me insane. The connection was like trying to hold back the wind.

Pulling on my sneakers, I made my way down to the kitchen. I could hear Rhys laughing and wandered in to see him and Mari at the table, throwing bits of food into the air and trying to catch what they threw up like they were children. Just like that, the jealousy was back.

I blinked, and a memory that was not my own flashed through my mind.

"Naw, I'ma no doin' it. It be foolish," Rhys said.

"Yer jus chicken ta lose ta a girl," Mari snarked back as she held up a blueberry.

"Am not."

"Are too." She flicked her long hair over her shoulder. "Rhys, da boy dat's scared to lose a game to a girl."

Rhys's face turned bright red. "Take dat back. It no be true."

In answer, Mari tossed the blueberry into the air and caught it, smiling. "Den play da game. First ta miss has ta do da other one's chores fir a week," she said.

"Fine, I'll play da silly game."

I staggered a step as the memory released me. I'd never had that happen before. Mari looked over from the table, and our eyes locked. The piece she'd tossed in the air hit the floor. Had she given me the memory by accident? I had no idea. Was that even possible?

Rhys tossed a piece of muffin into the air and caught it, laughing. "I win. Ya missed." Rhys looked over his shoulder to where I was standing. "Ah, yer here. Good. Took ya long enough," Rhys teased as he smiled at me.

My jaw twitched, the strange jealously overriding everything else, including his happy look.

"Liam paid me a visit," I said, not expanding on what happened or why, but it was like all the oxygen had been sucked out of the room as Rhys slowly stood from the table.

"Did he now?"

I poured myself a coffee and pretended to ignore Rhys, but I could see the glower on his face out of the corner of my eye.

"And anythin' special happen dat ya feel yer needin' ta share?"

"Nothing I want to share with you," I said and took a gulp of the coffee. Why I was getting so much enjoyment out of pissing Rhys off, I didn't know, but I was relishing the jealous look in his eyes.

"Well, I always did hear he had impeccable skill. I might be needin' ta pay 'im a visit meself," he said, and my power flashed with the threat.

My glare found Rhys. Mari sat perfectly still except for her eyes, which bounced between the two of us, a partially eaten muffin halfway to her mouth.

"He said it was his job to make sure I'm happy and comfortable with my stay."

"Ah, I see. So wat yer sayin' is your claim last night be bullshit. Good ta get da truth out there, den." Rhys looked down at Mari. "I'll leave 'im to ya." Rhys marched out the open glass doors.

"Fuck," I growled and slammed the mug down. The hot coffee went everywhere. Shaking the steaming liquid off my hand, I wandered to the door and looked out, but Rhys had disappeared. Angry and wanting to vent on someone, I turned on Mari.

"This is all your fault," I snarled.

"My fault? What exactly did I do?"

"You told me that you love him, and then you made me go to that stupid pub. Now I've got all these fucked up feelings that I can't seem to get control of. I mean, what were you doing, anyway?"

"I'm pretty sure we were eating, talking, and laughing, none of which are jealousy-worthy unless, of course, you never want him to speak to anyone ever again," she said and crossed her arms over her chest.

"Don't be ridiculous. Of course, I know he's going to talk to people. It's just...."

"Ah, it's because it's me. Right? That is what you're saying?" I ground my teeth together as she waited for a response. "Well, Rook, a couple things. First, this is my home. It has been since the day I was born. That man who just walked out the door, and I could've run off at any time, and trust me, we've been tempted." It was like she slapped me in the face. I knew how she felt, but to have confirmation that Rhys had the same feelings made my chest tight.

"Do you have something to be jealous about?" She shrugged. "Maybe. I mean, we share a bond that, as of right now, you can't match, but the keywords there are *as of right now*. Ya need to work at it with him to have an actual relationship." My eyes narrowed into a glare, but she only smiled back. "I actually like that you're this invested. It's good."

"Well, at least one of us likes it. I'm already sick of all this connection crap, and it's only been four-eight hours. My cock won't chill out, and I'm jealous about everything. And now you're telling me the two of you wanted to run off? How am I supposed to take that?"

Mari leaned back, her eyes fixed on me like she was staring through me. "I was hoping for more thankful."

"Thankful? Of what? You admitting you love what's mine and him feeling the same? Not fucking likely," I said, rinsing off my hand.

"Rook, let me bring something into focus for you. For twenty years—years, not hours—Rhys and I have been each other's person. Who do you think he cried to when you rejected him? Who do you think had to listen to him scream in pain night after night while you fucked whoever you wanted?" she said, her voice turning into a snarl.

My eyes snapped to hers. What was she talking about? What pain was she referring to? I wanted to ask but swallowed back the question as her power filled the room.

"Who do you think told him that he should give you a second chance to prove that you're worthwhile? Who will still be telling him that after this conversation?" She smacked her hand off the table, and not only did I jump, but so did all the plates and bowls.

"I-I…"

"Shut it." She slowly stood from the table, fury strong in her gaze. "I've spent most of my life pining over that man, and I will spend the time I have left breathing doing the same thing while I support your union and train you to make sure that neither of you dies. But what I don't deserve and will not accept is you walking in here acting like an asshole and accusing me of causing your jealousy issues when you haven't done shit to build or connect in your relationship other than grace us with your fucking presence."

"You know what? You're right. I never wanted to come here in the first place, and all I want is for my life to go back to the way it was. Maybe that could've happened if I hadn't listened to your stupid advice," a cookbook flew off the shelf and smacked the wall beside Mari with a bang.

Both Mari and I stared at where it lay, the pages fluttering. I hadn't meant to do that and was as shocked as she looked. Mari turned her head towards me, and the look in her eyes had me wishing I'd swallowed my last sentence. She marched forward, and willpower alone kept me from stepping back. She lifted a finger and poked me in the chest.

"Let's get something clear, Master Cousin Rook Adair," she said sarcastically. "You're actin' like you're still suckin' on yer mama's tit," she fumed, her accent coming through. "Ya better be growin' up and ya better be doin' it quick, because dat man"—Mari pointed to the open door—"is no' gonna play yer jealousy game because ya can't keep yer shit in line." She poked me again, and I took a step back as her blue eyes flared. I instantly felt how strong she really was. "If ya ever speak ta me like dat again, ya won't have to worry about consummating a union, cause ya won't 'ave a cock to consummate it with. Are we clear?"

My mouth ran dry. "Yes. Crystal." She went to walk away, and I couldn't help myself. "I saw you two," I said. Mari turned to look at me, and I licked my lips. "I saw you two as kids. You were laughing and smiling at one another, and you were talking him into playing a game of catching food you tossed in the air. That's what set me off."

She sighed. "I'm sorry. My powers are unstable at the moment. I must have given you the memory. Issues of being a telepath that's forced to push my powers down." She shook her head. "That's all it was: a memory. I'm not his future, Rook, even if we share a past. I don't know how I'd feel if roles were reversed, but what I do know is that I'd be trying to make things work with Rhys rather than lashing out at him."

I rubbed the back of my neck. "I'm sorry."

"Good, then do yourself a favour and stop blaming me for your issues and look in the mirror. The man staring back at you will have the answers. If you really want Rhys, that is. Now grab a bite and meet me outside," she said, turning and marching away.

"Do I want to know what you're planning to do to me?"

Mari looked over her shoulder and smiled, the anger completely gone. How did she do that? I'd be angry for days if one of my brothers got up in my face.

"I prefer to leave it as a surprise, but I'd suggest not pissing me off anymore, or I may decide to kill you and bury your body."

Well, that was comforting. I'd managed to piss off Rhys, and now he thought I'd fucked Liam, and then I rounded it off by antagonizing my one friend here. I also had a feeling she really would follow through on her threat.

"Good job, Rook. Give yourself a big old pat on the back," I said. "Does this ever get better?" I asked, then jumped when someone answered.

"Aye, it does," Gregory said as he walked into the kitchen. I decided that everyone needed squeaky shoes so I could hear them coming. He clamped his large hand onto my shoulder, and the corner of his mouth lifted with a ghost of a smile. "When I be first paired wit Gerrit, it was da same wit us. I was da one, and he was me two, and me emotions were all over da board. I wanted him, and then I hated 'im. I picked fights wit 'im over nothin', and den would throw him over da couch and...." He cleared his throat. "Ya git da idea. Da point is that it's normal ta feel outta sorts and dis be extra sensitive."

Walking to the open door, I leaned against the frame and ran my hands through my hair. "What do you mean by extra sensitive?"

"I'ma sorry, I overheard some of da fight ya and Mari were havin'. I'ma gonna say somethin', and it may be outta line, but I'ma gonna say it, anyway. Dinnie be tryin' ta make Rhys choose between ya and Mari. He will come around and be yers all on his own, but if ya try ta break up dat friendship, it's gonna backfire."

I hated that he was right. If someone had tried to give me an ultimatum or force me to do something, I would dig in my heels on principle. This was a little different, but I understood what he was saying. I would just end up pushing Rhys away.

"Maybe if I'd wanted all of this in the first place and had just accepted him at the ritual, all of the tension between us would've been avoided. I've never been insecure before. Is this what it's like?"

Gregory laughed, and it came out like a loud boom. "Aye, it is, and ya, yer tryin' ta fuck it all up ta push 'em away. Dinnie worry. Rhys will forgive ya."

"How can you be so sure?"

Gregory's face sobered, and he looked over at me. "Because I see da way he looks at ya. Whether he wants ta be or no, Rhys is developing feelings fir ya." Giving me a clap on the back, Gregory wandered back into the large kitchen. "But I won't be guaranteein' he won't be da one bendin' ya over as punishment for pissin' 'im off," he said and laughed again. "Who be makin' da mess on da counter," he mumbled as he wiped up the mess I'd left of my coffee.

I smiled at my uncle as he began to make himself breakfast. "Gregory, do you mind if I ask how Gerrit died? My father doesn't talk about it."

Gregory's hands never stilled as he cracked eggs into a bowl, but the earlier smile faded. "Like all da men dat 'ave died in our family," he said and looked up at me. "He was murdered."

I swallowed, trying to get rid of the sudden dryness in my throat. "He was your two, and he was murdered?"

"Aye."

"And my father's pairing with Ailill, he was my father's number two."

"Aye, I think ya might be catchin' on," he said softly.

"I was made the one… that means…." My heart suddenly fluttered with panic.

"Son, dis life dat was forged hundreds of years ago now, it's no' an easy one. I din't ask for it, and neither did yer da, but we do it to keep da family, our people, and our way of livin' safe."

Gregory leaned against the counter and looked at me. For the first time in my life, I felt the weight of this responsibility.

"Whadda think will happen if anotha Faction takes ova?"

I shrugged and felt stupid that I'd never thought about it.

"All of us will be da first to go. They will no' want any livin' blood that be a threat for a revolution to be left breathin'. Whetha ya knew it or no', ya were always part of all dis, and the threat to all in yer triad is real."

"Will someone try to go after Rhys first?"

Gregory stood straight and looked up at me. "What do ya think, son?"

I rubbed at the spot over my heart, the pain hitting with the thought of someone hurting him or worse. "Will they come before the next ritual moon?"

"Hunters and otha' Factions can decide to come any time, but aye, yer weakest until ya complete the first ritual. Ya be strongest once all tree of ya are in union."

Panic was beginning to form as I scanned the large green area, unable to see Rhys. "I should go find Rhys."

"Rhys be fine. He will be where he always goes when he wants some quiet time. Ya can find him by da water. He has a wee spot where he likes ta sit." Gregory pointed out the door toward Mari with the spatula he was now using for his scrambled eggs. "Ya betta head on out, otherwise it won't be da otha' Factions ya will need ta be scared of."

Mari was talking to one of the guards on the lawn. The fact that she was pointing like she wanted guards in other locations did nothing to settle the unease sitting on my chest.

"Thanks for the talk," I said, pushing away from the wall to make my way toward Mari. I had no idea what I was in for, but as she picked up two long sticks from the pile on the ground, I had a pretty good idea and groaned. This would not end well for me.

171

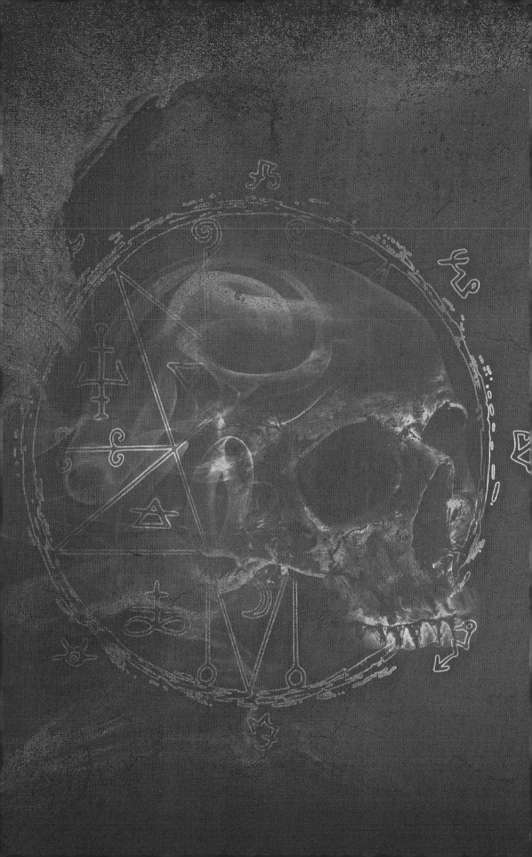

Chapter 16

Rook

"Ooof."

The air exploded from my lungs as I landed on my ass for what had to be the thousandth time. Breathing hard, I stared up at Mari. She hadn't even broken a sweat.

"Dear spirits, tell me we are done. If not, just kill me now," I moaned.

"We are done for today," she said, taking pity on me. "But you're terrible. Not even mildly good. I'm really shocked you're so bad, actually. Why your father never made you learn to fight is beyond me, but I was a better fighter by five."

I glared at her while pushing myself up, then winced as every muscle screamed. There wasn't a single part of my body not covered

"Gee, you don't say. Thanks for pointing out the obvious," I grumbled.

I didn't bother to tell her that my father had tried to make me go to class to learn, but I'd refused to do anything and had sat in the corner, not participating. In hindsight, that may not have been such a wise decision.

"Training will be every morning until you get better," she said.

"Thanks, but I'd rather take my chances than get beaten by your twig again," I said.

Mari whipped out her knife and flicked it between my legs. It sunk to its hilt in the ground.

"Oh, fuck!" My eyes went wide as I took in the hairsbreadth of space between the sharp blade and my cock, which had tried to shrivel up and hide.

I tried to shuffle away, but she was quick. The canne in her hand was suddenly pressed under my chin. I flinched.

"Consider this your last warning. You speak to me like that again, and next time, I won't miss. When it comes to training, I'm in charge, and what I say goes until I say otherwise. Tomorrow at seven, you meet me out here, or I'll come in and get you." She slipped the cane from my chin, spun it in her hands, then bent over and grabbed her blade.

Squatting, she pointed the blade at me. There was this brief—terrifying—moment when her eyes locked with mine, and I truly thought she had changed her mind and was going to cut me up, regardless.

"You have talent, but you've never bothered to learn. Not bothering to learn makes you weak. Weak in this life is not an option. You will be training with me every day for three hours until you're not a fuckin' danger to everyone around you. So get used to the welts, learn to love 'em until you can block the blows. Once you're done with me, Rhys will take over your training to teach you the sword. This is non-negotiable."

She stood in a fluid motion. "I will not allow you to put Rhys's life in danger because he will do whatever he needs to in order to protect you. As noble as that sounds, it is better if you can protect each other. Yes?"

"Yes, you're right," I said.

Mari turned and marched away.

Groaning, I pushed myself up to my feet. "Well, that was one ass-kicking. Might as well go get my second round in before the day is over," I mumbled, rolling out my shoulders.

Picking up my canne, I placed it on the rack and limped across the lawn towards where Gregory said Rhys liked to go. Cresting the small rise that led down to the water's edge, I stopped to take in the beauty. Sunsets and shimmering water had never been things I'd cared about, yet I couldn't stop staring. The magic and history of this place reached inside me and made me want to do things I'd never thought about before. Things I'd always taken for granted.

I scanned the entire area, looking for Rhys. I was just about to turn away when a glint in the sunlight caught my attention. Off to the right, so far away that I could barely make him out, I spotted Rhys on a dock. I was completely mesmerized and found myself walking toward him without giving it a second thought.

He'd taken his shirt off and worked with the sword I'd seen him use last night. He looked like he was performing a deadly dance as he moved along the wooden structure. The sharp blade arced through the air. The sun caught the metal and caused it to shimmer like a beacon. There was a sheen of sweat on his body, and his face was tight with concentration.

No matter how we had come to be, there was no denying that the old me—the one before the pairing ritual—would still be drooling for a taste. I didn't need a connection to appreciate the sight before me.

Rhy's every movement showed the sheer strength of his fit body. Muscles flexed in his forearms, in each cut line of his abdomen, and the tapered Adonis V that disappeared beneath the black kilt. The tattoos lining his sides, arms, and shoulders, the chain around his neck, and the leather cuff at his wrist, added to the look. He was dangerous. That's what my mind and power told me.

And I wanted every inch of him.

I wanted to lick the sweat from his body as I fucked him hard. I wanted to see how much he could take and when he would scream, it was too much. He would never yield. Submit yes, but yield no, and that made me shiver as the image of Rhys tied up while I pounded into him flashed before my eyes.

Heat flooded my body, and the emotions I'd been bottling reared their head again. I cleared my throat, and Rhys's eyes flicked in my direction, but he never stopped moving. I couldn't turn away, and my eyes landed on the mark I'd made on the side of his neck. The dark, purplish beacon that told everyone he was mine.

"If ya got somethin' ta say, den git on wit it," he said.

My initial reaction was to be bristly back, but I reined it in. I'd already mouthed off more than my fair share today, and it had almost cost me my dick.

"I didn't sleep with Liam, and he didn't give me a blow job or anything else," I said.

I considered it a win when Rhys stopped moving and placed the tip of the blade on the dock to lean on the handle. He was breathing heavily, his glorious chest rising and falling, and I had to force myself to keep my eyes on his face.

"Ya mind explain' what that was 'bout in that kitchen, den?"

Smart or not, I stepped onto the narrow dock and made my way towards Rhys. With every step, the connection grew until I was breathing just as heavily from the sheer willpower it took not to reach out and touch him.

"I…" I ran my hand through my hair and crossed my arms over my chest. "I was jealous," I hated that I had to admit it.

"Aye, for what?"

"Are you really going to make me say it?"

Rhys shook his head, confusion written on his face as he stood straight and lifted the sword to continue his workout.

"You and Mari, okay? There, I said it. I guessed how she felt yesterday, and she admitted it. Plus, I've seen the way you look at her. I'm not blind. I know there are feelings there."

Rhys nodded.

"Aye, dat be da truth. We spoke last night about us. Did she tell ya dat?"

My muscles flexed. "No."

"We did. I offered ta leave wit her," he said like they'd been talking about the weather and not becoming defectors.

My mouth fell open. "You what?" The jealousy was brimming, but so was something else. Anger, sure…Fear, maybe? Concern over what it would mean if he chose to do that, definitely.

"Aye. Rook, ya be thinkin' dat I was mopin' around here, waitin' for ya to waltz in and announce yer here. Now I know ya dinnie wanna come at all. Ya still woulda been travelin' da world and fuckin' whoever ya wanted if yer father hadn't forced ya ta come. Am I wrong?"

I ground my teeth together, my jaw cracking. "Yes, that's right," I finally said.

"Den what makes ya tink I didn't have me own plans dat din't include ya? We are both havin' ta give up somethin' we love to find our own ground, but Mari is not da issue. She told me no. She told me she likes ya and tinks we're good tagetha. I tink she mighta been drinkin'." Rhys smirked, and I couldn't stop myself from mirroring him.

"All right, fair. I have been pretty arrogant. I'm kind of used to people falling at my feet."

Rhys barked out a laugh. "Ya dinnie say."

I smiled. Every emotion possible soared in my body as those eyes, which felt as intimate as his touch, searched my face.

"Why are you looking at me like that?"

"Come closer. Me wants ta show ya something," he gestured for me to step up beside him.

Taking the final steps closer felt like walking across coals as the temperature continued to rise. If I didn't fuck Rhys soon, I was going to lose my mind. My heart thumped hard behind my ribs while blood soared through my veins. By some miracle, I didn't pass out.

Rhys turned to look out to the mouth of the cove, and as I turned too, our shoulders brushed. The connection licked up my body as my power began to rise like it had at the pub. I clenched my fists together. My knuckles cracked as I fought the wild urge to ride his body to the ground.

"Whadda ya see?"

Rhys pointed at the water, and my confusion helped clear some of the out-of-control desire. Leaning over, I mimicked his position and looked down at the dark water. I couldn't see anything but our reflection. Rhys turned his head and looked at me, and even through the rippling water, I could feel his stare. Every part of my body pulled tight as I beat back the need to touch him and finish what we started last night.

"I don't see anything," I answered through gritted teeth.

"Aye. See, that right there is the problem," he said. "Look again."

Once more, I stared at the water slowly lapping its way towards the dock. Once again, all I saw was us.

"You see 'im." Rhys pointed to my reflection. "Dat right there is fuckin' Rook Adair."

I looked at Rhys, and my world narrowed. Thin tendrils of smoke floated around his shifting silver eyes. It was the only thing that belied that he felt the power building between us. His features softened before he spoke again.

"Ya may 'ave met 'im. He be a go-for-what-he-wants, rockstar type." He leaned in close, and the energy coursing between us made me shudder. My cock strained behind the track pants. "If yer really wantin' dis and all it means den ya 'ave no need ta be jealous," he said, his breath hot against my ear.

"You sure about that?" I asked as I swallowed the lump in my throat.

"Aye. If yer serious about stayin' and makin' us work, den so am I. Whadda say ya wanna start over?"

"No more running?"

Rhys chuckled as he passed behind me, his shoulder brushing my back. My mouth ran dry as I watched Rhys slide his sword back into the sheath at his hip as he walked away. I wanted to say something, but logic and wit had jumped off the dock and were paddling around in the dark water looking for a life preserver.

"Na, me runnin' days are done. I'ma gonna go shower," Rhys said casually as if the electric connection between us wasn't coiling and sparking like a goddamn storm. The air was almost shimmering as it swirled in loops, trying to pull us closer.

He took a couple of strides, then looked over his shoulder at me. "In case dat wasn't clear, dat be an invitation," he said and smirked.

My long strides ate up the ground before my brain registered what he said. I felt more nervous now than at fifteen when I had sex for the first time. We didn't speak another word back to the castle. My eyes stayed firmly ahead, but his presence was all-consuming. Every one of my senses was overloaded. The scent of his skin, the sound his kilt made as he walked, and the memory of what he tasted like on my tongue.

This was a complete loss of my sanity. Something I never wanted, and yet here I was, practically dragging Rhys to his room. All I needed to do was grab his arm and run to complete the image.

Fear gripped my chest as Rhys opened the door to the castle, and we stepped inside. What if I lost myself completely to this man? What if I stopped wanting the things I dreamed about and handed myself over like a lapdog, a slave for his every whim and pleasure? There was no way for me to know what would happen once we did this. That connection had not been anything like what I was expecting, and so far, no one had been very forthcoming with answers that made sense. What would happen once the binding ritual was performed? It was obvious we couldn't trust what was in the history books.

Rhys pushed open another door, and I suddenly realized where we were. My feet froze at the threshold of the bedroom. I was a type A personality, always in control of every aspect of my life. At least, I thought I was. My gaze flicked up to Rhys, who stood holding the door and looking as confused as I felt.

"I don't think I can do this," I said and stepped back from the room, even though every molecule in my body screamed to step inside.

Rhys crossed his arms and leaned against the open door, and even though his eyes stayed calm, I could feel his energy shift to annoyed.

"What be wrong? I taught we just agreed ta try fir real, ta put da past in da past."

"I can't lose myself to you," I said. "I don't want to lose who I am to become this triad." My gut pulled painfully at the hurt look on Rhys's face.

"Aye, I see. So da dance beings again? Ya know, I dinnie think I wanna be on dis ride no more meself. At da next ritual moon, I will be acceptin' your rejection. I dinnie wanna play games." Rhys stood straight and backed away from the door, his hand ready to flick it closed in my face. "Fir da good of us both go home, Rook. It be clear yer no interested in a compromise. It cannie all be me dat is givin' somethin' up. It be obvious dat wat yer wantin' is always gonna be yer priority an fuck everyone else." He shook his head. "Dis is no' gonna work."

A new fear filled me, one that had my hand stopping the door before it could close. I should've been terrified that this meant never getting to travel and sing again. Instead, I was scared of never seeing his face again. The inner workings of my emotions were mystifying even to me. I couldn't let him close the door. It felt final like I'd lose my last chance to make this right, and I didn't know what to do.

He looked around the edge of the door. His eyebrow raised as he stared at me, standing like a statue with my arm propping the door open.

"What da feck are ya doin'?"

A growl left my chest as the inexplicable power tied to our

connection rose like a beast inside me. The door slammed open with a flick of my wrist, and I stepped over the threshold.

"You don't get to dismiss me like that. I'm your number one," I said and stepped close to Rhys.

His eyes flared, his own power coming to life. "Aye, den start actin' like it."

Whatever held me back before snapped, and just like at the pub, the only thing that mattered was having him for myself. The uncertainty and fear were wiped away with a need so strong that it burned like a fire and incinerated all other thoughts. Our lips crashed together as I grabbed his face and drove him back until he was trapped against the wall.

Rhys groaned in my mouth, and his hands gripped my ass tighter until there was no space between us. The only word to describe what I was feeling was frantic. I was frantic to taste him, not let him go, to find a way to make this work, and prove that I was the number one.

I slid a hand down his stomach and gripped his cock through the heavy kilt material.

"Ohhh, fuck," Rhys groaned.

"Fuck, I want you," I mumbled against his lips as I fumbled with the material, desperate to get access to his skin.

"Then stop talkin' 'bout it and make me yours," Rhys said, his eyes daring me to walk away.

Pushing away from the wall, I looked around, unfamiliar with his room, and spotted the washroom. I grabbed his hand and made it as far as the door when a knock sounded. I almost shouted in frustration.

"Kinda busy at da moment," Rhys called.

"Rhys, it's Mari. I need ya," Gregory said, his voice laced with panic.

Rhys pulled away and went for the door. "What's goin' on?" he asked, whipping it open.

Gregory was distraught and began talking so quickly that Rhys had to grab him and tell him to slow down so he could understand. His eyes were filled with tears as he ran his hand over his bald head.

"She's gone."

"She goes out all da time. Why are ya so worried?" Rhys asked.

Belle was suddenly at the door and pushing past her father. She shoved Rhys in the chest so hard he stumbled back. A growl ripped from my throat, and I took a threatening step toward my cousin, but the look in Rhys's eyes held me firmly in place.

"This be your fault," Belle yelled and hit Rhys again. "You shoulda moved out. Ya knew how she felt, and ya stayed. What did ya think would happen when he showed up?" Belle pointed at me. I wasn't sure what was happening, but I knew it had to be bad. I'd barely seen Belle since I arrived, and she hadn't said more than two words to me. "Ya gotta go git 'er, yer da only one dat knows where she would go."

"Ya mean she's gone ta da demons? But how? I got rid of all dem. And how do ya know fir sure?"

"She told me she was goin' ta go see Riegan. But I just talked ta Reigan, 'cause I was gonna join, and Riegan never had plans wit Mari. There be only one reason she'd lie. Dis is yer fault." Rhys grabbed Belle by the arms and held her as she fumed. "I dinnie wanna loose me sista', I'ma still dealin' wit da loss of me Ma," she said, her lip quivering.

"Aye, I'll go git her. Dinnie worry." Releasing Belle, Rhys pulled a T-shirt from a drawer and then ran around the room, strapping on an assortment of weapons.

"Can someone tell me what the hell is going on?" I blurted out.

"I'll tell ya later. I promise. I gotta go," Rhys said. He grabbed a

183

cloak draped over the back of his chair and came over to where I was standing. "I'm sorry, I gotta go."

"All right. We'll talk later."

Nodding, Rhys ran out of the room with Gregory and Belle close behind him.

Walking over to the bed, I flopped down on my back to stare at the ceiling. Maybe there was something to be said about forces trying to keep us apart. It certainly felt like something strange was going on, but then again, everything about this place felt strange from the moment I arrived.

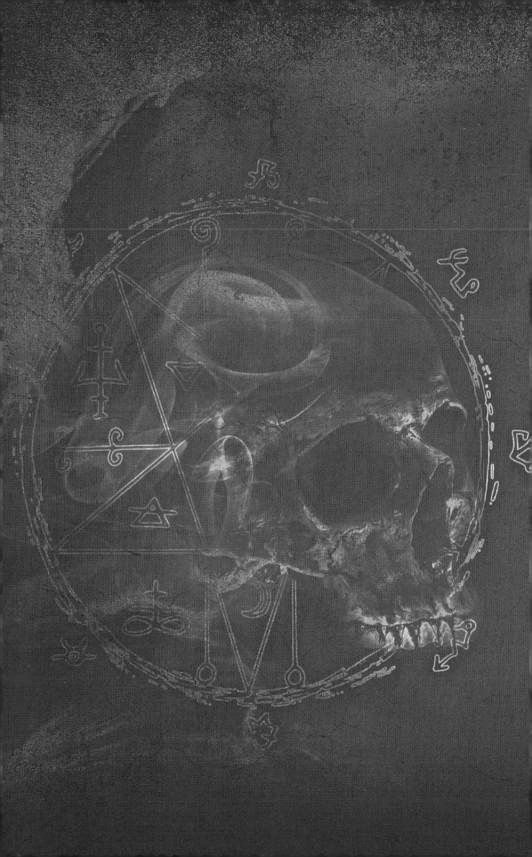

Chapter 17

Mari

My hands were sweating as the car headlights lit up the deserted road. This was the one thing I couldn't get used to here. Overseas, everything was still technology-based. Everyone had cars and trucks and cell phones. Stores were open until late or all night long, and you could get a good cup of coffee and meet up with a friend anytime.

Not that I had many—or really any—friends except for Fiona. Rhys's little sister was a ball of wild McGregor energy, but she was also just young enough that she didn't want to hang out with her older cousin all the time.

I wasn't sure why the Faction decided to keep our area here and on the mainland so primitive, but again, I was just a woman. I didn't get to ask those questions and expect a straight answer. Even my d chose to keep Belle and me in the dark about what was happening around us.

I pulled off the road at the trailhead and shut off the headlights. In the complete darkness, I took a deep, steadying breath. Rhys had done a good job closing all the portals to the dark fade. Too good of a job. It had taken forever to find an old witch with the ability to make this crack in the veil possible and a ton of money to convince her to make it happen.

"This is stupid. You should just go back home," I said, then winced as the pain erupted behind my eyes. "It will pass. It always passes." I laid my head on the steering wheel and took a couple of deep breaths as the images and emotions flashed behind my eyes.

Pain. Longing.

Love. Joy.

A woman screamed as a hand cracked her across the face.

A baby crying as it lay alone in the darkness.

A man stabbed to death for his wallet and the ten dollars he had inside.

I love you.

I hate you.

You've got the promotion.

A scream echoing as a man falls from a building to his death.

Gasping, I held my head and fought it back, but the migraine that had been coming on for weeks had me in its grip, and I couldn't focus enough to make it stop. Tears streamed down my face.

"I'm sorry," I mumbled to no one and everyone.

I fumbled for the door handle. I knew I shouldn't do this, but I had to. I couldn't take it anymore. As soon as the door was open, I pulled myself out and fell to the ground on all fours. Forcing myself to stand, I closed the door. I knew I should take my cane, but I could barely see with the pain erupting behind my eyes.

If they were going to kill me, they would kill me. I had to take my chances. Putting my hand in my pocket to make sure I had the red ruby as payment, I shuffled away from the car. It was pitch black in every direction.

"Shite," I swore and wiped my forehead with my shaking hand. I held out my palm. "Ignitious luminous." A small flaming ball appeared in my hand. It was not much bigger than a bouncy ball, but it would do. "Lead the way," I whispered. The little ball rose into the air and drifted in front of me. Hopefully, it understood what I wanted. I was too exhausted to care where it led me as it bobbed ahead and gave me something to follow.

It felt like I'd been walking forever when I heard the hissing of the demon. No matter what people said or didn't say, demons always hissed softly, and the sound made the hair stand on the back of my neck. I shouldn't be here. If my family found out, they were going to be pissed. There was a good chance Rhys would never speak to me again, but they didn't understand. No one understood what I went through and how hard it was to wake up every morning with the entire world's emotions and experiences in my chest. I had to push them down and try to forget what I saw or felt.

I'd gotten so much better at harnessing it. Three years since, I had to take anything of any kind to keep my ability under control, but I was out of the meds I found overseas. The smuggler wasn't coming to the island for at least six months, and I couldn't last that long.

The little flame rose higher into the air showing a small clearing with the mouth of a cave. I could see the dark shape of the demon waiting outside the opening. Stepping closer, I didn't look at the demon directly. They were hideous at the best of times, but the images I'd get from staring into their eyes were enough to make me want to end my life.

"Paaaasssment?"

"I have your payment," I said and pulled out the ruby.

The hissing increased as it got excited. All gems held powers that the Flitters didn't understand, but the rubies had dark properties that demons loved. They were coveted, and you could buy yourself anything from those who practiced dark magic with a ruby.

The demon turned into the cave, and I flicked my finger so the little light would follow. Walking behind the demon was slow going, and my anxiety grew the deeper we went. The tunnel opened up into a roundish room that had doors. I'd never seen a place like this. It looked like some sort of cell.

"Where is my vial?" I asked, refusing to go further.

"Stoooooorrrage, innnnn daaaaareee," the demon hissed, then pointed at a door.

"Then go get it. I'm not going in there," I said.

The words no sooner left my mouth when black hands gripped my arms on either side as another clamped over my mouth.

"Yeesssss, youuuuuu arrrrrrr."

I struggled hard in the hold of the three demons, but it was useless. They were much stronger, and my energy and power were so taxed that I could barely stand, let alone fight. The demon I'd been following opened the door it had pointed to and then reached up and pinched my little flame. I was once more plunged into darkness as the demons dragged me forward.

I screamed, the sound coming out muffled as I tried to break free. The hold I had on my ability broke free, and I screamed for another reason. All the emotions and visions of the world found me like a beacon. The agony was nothing I could've ever explained to someone. My back arched as the demons slammed me hard onto the floor. All my bones felt like they were breaking and knitting back together as the power flowed. My hands clawed at the hard dirt floor as I fought to keep the ability at bay. The threat of what the demons wanted was forgotten.

The hand covering my mouth lifted, and my screams echoed in the hollow, cavernous space. Suddenly one of the demons gripped my cheeks hard. I kept my eyes clenched tight and screamed again as the images intensified. I lurched in the demon's hold as the sensation of a car crash and the deadly impact hit me. That image was replaced with the kiss of a lover I didn't know. Then I was hit with overwhelming sadness as tears trickled down the cheeks of someone standing by a grave. Every memory and sensation that accompanied them attacked me at a blinding pace like I was their victim.

The taste of demon blood hit my tongue as what felt like a small vial was stuffed into my mouth. I should've been thrilled—this was what I'd come for—but I was horrified. The vial I wanted to purchase would've lasted me months to years with a single drop taken only when needed. Instead, the entire vial was dumped in my mouth. I tried to turn my head and spit it back out, but the grip on my face kept me from doing either, and the liquid slid down my throat.

And then they left me. The door slamming in place reverberated around me and through me.

"No," I coughed and tried to put my fingers down my throat, but it was already too late. Too much of the blood would kill me within hours.

"I'm sorry," I said again, but this time I meant it for Rhys. He was the one who helped me get clean before, and I promised him that I would only use the herbs we grew. But they stopped working long ago, and I didn't have the heart to tell him. Tears fell from my eyes as the darkness began to take over. "I'm so sorry I lied to you. I…"

My face hit the dirt, and I could feel the voices pushed back as my heart rate slowed.

Thump, thump.

Thump… thump.

Thump…

I let my eyes close and fantasized about the life I always wanted. If I was going to die, what did it matter now?

Then all went dark.

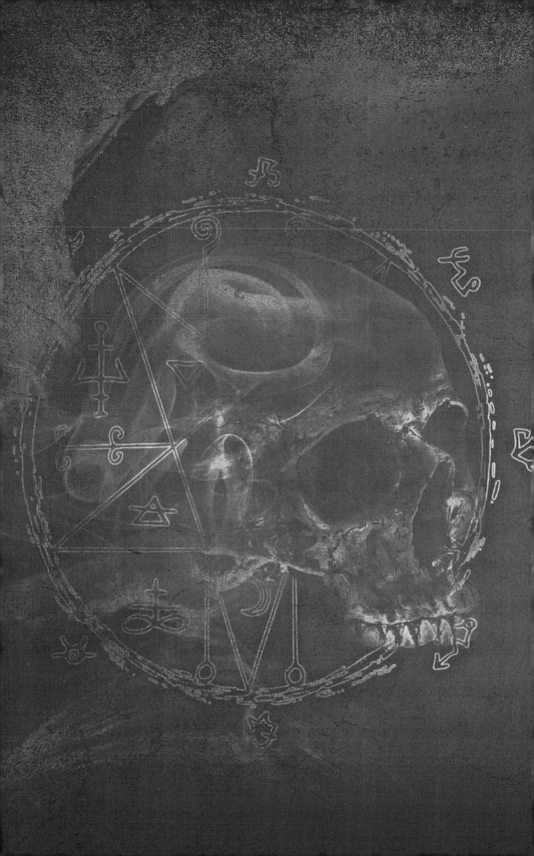

Chapter 18

R hys

With a wide sweeping arc, I brought my blade down through the last of the demons. I hated them almost as much as I hated Hunters. These demons, the Basalainn, fed off tiny pieces of human souls. One drop of their dark demon blood would transport your mind and leave you in unadulterated ecstasy. When you woke up, your body was more relaxed and rejuvenated than you could ever feel from sleep alone. It started as an innocent trade, a minute's worth of your soul in exchange for hours or days of bliss. That was until you were addicted and kept coming back far too often.

I knew why Mari took it and why she'd succumbed years ago, but I thought she had found a better way to deal than coming to these creatures that couldn't be trusted.

The wars had created the holes initially, and a wide assortment of demons had clawed their way out of the dark depths. The elders had fought most of them back to where they'd come or killed them. A few had still remained but I banned these creatures from residence here, but I hadn't been diligent enough lately.

This was part of the reason Mari left the island in the first place. It was toxic here for so many reasons. I was one of those reasons, and I held the secret to the other. Her da and Belle blamed me for her addiction, and if it kept her safe from those who would look to exploit her, then I would happily take the blame.

I knew Rook coming would be tough on her and cause more stress. I should have left right away. I didn't know if it would help, but it couldn't have hurt. After last night's conversation, I knew I loved Mari, but more than that, I didn't want her to be alone. The rules were firm. Unless a woman born into the Faction was blessed with a birthmark or she was a witch with red hair, then they were to remain unmarried and were turned into weapons. Those weapons were never allowed attachments, children, or anything else that could be used against them. Assassins for a cause. The Faction's cause.

Mari had been sent on more missions and killed more high-level targets than she would ever tell me. I always knew when she was going, though. She wore the same outfit, packed the same travel bag, and refused to speak to me for a few days afterward. It was no life for any of the unchosen, but it was especially hard on her. Her abilities made her more vulnerable than anyone realized. I didn't know how to keep her safe and still form my triad without the two colliding and destroying relationships on both sides.

It crushed me that this was her life. She deserved better. I had plans to change the rituals and free the women so they could find love. But to do that, I needed my triad, and so far, it had not gone the way I envisioned.

I knew all too well what it was like to want this kind of escape, not to feel the weight of everything crushing me, just for a little while.

Breathing hard, I ran into the dank underground tunnel. Touching the wall, I could feel old torches lining the rock, and with a thought, they all lit. There weren't that many, and the wicks were low, so they didn't cast much light, but it was enough to see where I was stepping. I'd done a quick locator spell as soon as I got into the car and didn't like where this spot was located. It was far enough away that they wouldn't be seen and yet was easily accessed with endless trails. The problem was that it was a long hike from the nearest road. It was the perfect spot for people to go and never return.

Three of the seven doors were open and empty. Reaching the fourth door, I opened it and prepared for an attack, but none came. I did the same to the fifth and the sixth, and panic set in. If Mari wasn't behind the seventh door, where was she?

My hand wrapped around the metal handle of the heavy wooden door, and saying a little prayer to the spirits, I yanked it open.

There she was, lying on the dirt floor, her eyes black as night as her head lulled from side to side, her body twitching from the effects of too much demon blood. A long dark smear stretched from the corner of her mouth down the side of her neck. I'd seen this before. Too many people died from overdoses before I killed the demons and closed all the portals—or thought I closed them all.

"Fuck, Mari. Yer no' dyin' on me."

I quickly sheathed my sword and pulled out the small pouch I grabbed before leaving. It was the only concoction I'd come up with that beat back the demon's effects and pushed the blood out of the body. Pulling the small blue bottle from the pouch, I lifted Mari so she was leaning against me. Removing the cork with my teeth, I spat it to the side, then forced her mouth open and her chin up.

"Drink it, Mari. Dinnie choke," I said as I poured the syrupy elixir into her mouth.

Her face was covered in dirt, and she had a massive bruise. I would worry about that later. I wished I had healing abilities. There were so many things I could do, but healing wounds or helping those that were ill was beyond those in our Faction. Only one Faction could heal and make potions that would fix just about anything. But they stayed to themselves and never wanted alliances with anyone.

She tried to turn her head away, but I held her jaw firm and forced her to take every last drop. When it was empty, I put the bottle away and stood to pick her up. A soft hissing sound caught my ear, and I pulled one of the long knives from my chest. The cavern was once more plunged into darkness.

They didn't know who they were dealing with, I was Rhys McGregor, and I owned the darkness. Slicing my hand with the knife, I licked the blood from my palm, and instantly, the tiny blood offering allowed me to see in the dark as if it were day.

The Basalainn was the largest I'd ever seen, but the size didn't matter. All that mattered was that it was sent back to the depths. The creatures reminded me of something shapeless and yet like tall insects at the same time. They had oddly shaped heads with rows of sharp teeth, and their long, spindly arms reminded me of an ugly octopus.

It thought it could sneak up on me, so I figured I would play along. Stumbling out into the open space of the cave, I put my arms out as if searching for the wall. The creature fell for it and lowered into a crouch to pounce.

They were surprisingly easy to kill, but only if you put a blade through their skull. Anywhere else, they could heal and regenerate. As soon as the demon leapt off the ground, I spun and grabbed it by its slender throat. Without wasting a moment, I jerked my blade into the squishy underside of its jaw. The knife sank to the hilt, and the five eyes of the demon bulged as black spittle sprayed my chest. My hand twisted back and forth, making sure to destroy the brain.

"Naw one hurts me family," I growled out.

When the demon finally stopped twitching, I tossed it to the side, where it would quickly decay and turn into dirt.

That was six demons that had slipped through a crack. Six that I hadn't gotten word about, and it bothered me that I hadn't known. I tried to keep a finger on the pulse of everything on my island. I had guards whose sole job was to bring me intel like this, and they'd been completely quiet. I was going to need to have a discussion with them.

"Luminous," I said, and the few torches that lined the halls lit once more.

Mari moaned and curled into my body when I slipped my arms under her, and my heart pounded hard. Her face was too pale, and dark circles rimmed her eyes, but the demon blood she'd taken was beginning to drip from her nose, which meant the elixir was working. I took heart in that.

"Let's git ya outta here."

I marched out of the tunnel and through the low entrance, picking up a jog. The trail was a dangerous one. Hunters loved to use these sections, but it was the most direct route back to the cars. When I was younger and looking for a fight, I came down here to see if I could run into one. A couple of years made a huge difference in perspective about what was smart or not smart. Those had certainly not been my smart years.

There was a fallen log across the trail, and with a leap, I kept running. I would have to come back later to get Mari's car. Placing Mari in the passenger seat, I buckled her seatbelt and ran to the driver's side.

It was a rough ride out to the main road, but once pointed toward home, I quickly put her into fifth. Mari had been very quiet. Other than the odd little moan, she didn't come around. I needed to get her in an ice bath as soon as possible. The demon blood hated cold. It was like it needed the heat to incubate and take what it wanted from the host. It would leave Mari's body faster if I could get her cold.

The twisty road was dark and vacant of any sign of life, not that I expected anyone from the Faction to be out this late. My eyes flicked up to the rearview mirror as three lights pulled out of an old road. This couldn't be anyone good. I stared at three motorcycles, the engines revving loudly as they gained on me. Fucking Hunters.

"Fuck," I swore and slammed my hand on the wheel. "All right, ya fucks. Ya wanna do dis again so soon, do ya?"

My small sports car looked normal enough, but it had built-in armour, an extra-large engine with boosts, and if needed, she also had a few tricks up her kilt—little modifications I'd managed to make myself after watching the old 007 movies. They may have been hundreds of years old, but I still enjoyed watching them. They were a guilty pleasure of both mine and Mari's. We'd fallen asleep on the couch multiple times to a marathon of the movies that none living would remember except those at the head of Factions. Television, movies, and most music were restricted once the Factions took control of the world. Only Factions had access to guns, and the penalty for owning one was death. Anything that might make the

Flitters question who was in power or start a revolution was wiped out or controlled.

"Come on, den. Don't be chicken," I said to the single headlight closing in on the right.

Swerving to the left, I blocked the second bike from passing. Then pulled the wheel hard to the right and slammed into the front tire of the motorcycle on that side. It flew off the road, disappearing into a farmer's field.

The thud of something hitting the back of the car made me jerk my head around. A bolt stuck through my rear window. One of them must have had a high-powered crossbow.

"Ya fuckin ruined me windie. Is dat how ya wanna play it?"

Placing my arm out to help hold Mari in place, I threw the car into neutral, then stomped on the brake. Tires squealed as the motorcycle behind me crashed into the back of the car. The driver flew over the roof and landed on the ground in front of me, rolling for several feet before coming to a crumpled stop. The other motorcycle managed to swerve and fly past.

Revving the engine, I tossed it into gear and punched the gas. The smell of burning rubber filled the car. I drove over the downed Hunter and sped after the last one standing.

"Let's see how much ya like ta be followed," I growled as we closed in on the bike.

The Hunter began weaving from one side of the road to the other, but I wasn't new to this game and smirked as I shut the lights off. He looked back over his shoulder. His eyes were wide as he stared, but unfortunately for him, he couldn't see in the dark like I did. I had just enough power riding me to see him clearly and feel his terror through the dark visor on the helmet as I revved the engine louder.

Smirking, I geared down and stopped. Waving as the idiot, still looking over his shoulder, drove right off the cliff and into the ocean below.

"Serves ya right, ya fuck."

Putting the car in first, I made a wide turn and continued home. Reaching out, I touched Mari's face. Her skin was burning up, and the twitching was getting worse.

"How much did ya take?" I asked as we pulled through the gates. All I got in response was a soft moan.

I wasn't shocked to see Gregory or Belle outside, but I was surprised to see Rook sitting on the step. As soon as the car stopped, I hopped out and ran to the passenger's side. Gregory might have been her father, but he'd never been good with the ill or injured. After his wife died, he became worse and could barely look at those who had a sniffle.

"Come on, beautiful," I said softly, unbuckling her seatbelt and lifting her into my arms.

"Oh dear spirits," Gregory said. His hand flew to his mouth, and his eyes squeezed closed. He turned away like he was going to be sick when he saw Mari's face with black blood running from her nose and smeared across her cheeks.

"She needs an ice bath," I said, jogging up the stairs.

"Rhys, where are ya goin?" Gregory asked.

"My room, it be closer to da kitchen. I need ice, as much as ya can git me," I said and twisted my way through the halls until I stood outside my door. Before I could adjust Mari, Rook opened it for me.

My eyes locked with his. "Thanks," I said.

"What can I do to help?" Rook asked.

"Plug da tub and turn on only da cold." Carrying Mari into the washroom, I shrugged off my cape.

"Okay, now what?" Rook turned to face me with concern in his eyes as he stared at Mari's body draped over my arms.

"I need ya ta hold 'er," and handed Mari off as gently as possible, then ripped off every piece of clothing other than my kilt.

"I don't understand. What are you doing?" Rook asked as I took off her boots and pants, then pulled the hoodie over her head.

"Ya see da black on er face? Dat be demon blood. I need ta git it outta her system," I said. "Stay 'ere."

I went to the closet where I had the last of my antidote stashed. Opening the box, I groaned when I saw only one bottle left. This had to work. Running back, I popped the cork and held Mari's head up to pour the second bottle down her throat. I had to shake her head and rub her throat to force her to swallow. Scooping Mari from Rook's arms, I stepped into the half-filled tub of freezing water. Luckily, I'd grown up where the water never got warm. If you wanted to swim and didn't have a heated pool, you learned to bear the cold. There was no hesitation, and I sat down and stretched out my legs in the giant tub, holding Mari with her back against my body.

"I'm not asking because I'm jealous, but why are you getting in with her? Won't that defeat the purpose of getting her cold?"

"Aye a little, but she will likely start seizing at some point. It be much harder ta keep her from slipping under da water an' swallowing it down if I don't hold her like dis."

I smoothed back her long dark hair and gave the top of her head a chaste kiss. "Come on, Mari. Dinnie let dem 'ave ya yet," I whispered in her ear.

"I'm sorry. How did she end up fighting a demon?" Rook shook his head. "None of this is making any sense. You answer a question, and all I have is more questions."

Gregory and Belle came rushing in, and Rook backed out of the way as they dumped four large buckets of ice cubes in the bath, then took off to get more. Once they were gone, I sighed and laid my head back against the wall.

"Dere be a type of demon dat likes ta frequent da islands out dis way. Dey sneak on when someone be doin' magic and wait for a wee crack ta form. Da demon's blood be a hallucinogen, but stronga. Picture da best high ya eva had and multiply it by ten, but ya get no side effects when ya wake up aside from feelin' like ya had da best sleep of yer life. There also be no of dat random seeing dead shit or tings crawlin' on ya. Yer want ta lie in a field a flowers, yer there. Ya wanna have da best sex all night wit someone, den it happens." I gave a little shrug. "It happens in yer mind, but it feels real. Ya be wakin' up wonderin' fir a moment if yer fantasy came true."

"Fuck, that sounds awesome," Rook said. The exact response that got Mari and so many into trouble in the first place. "So that is what Mari wanted to do? Get high? That doesn't sound like the Mari I've met."

I loved that he was giving her the benefit of the doubt. Not simply jumping to her wanting to take drugs or, worse, trying to end her life. I knew she was stressed, but I couldn't imagine her doing such a thing.

"Aye and no. It is also a blocker. It allows fir yer mind ta quiet down and lets ya sleep. If ya 'ave insomnia or severe panic attacks, it helps block the stimulation."

"Oh...So what is she trying to block...Oh! You mean...this is about *us*?"

"I dinnie know," I said, but I feared that, in a way, it was. Stress made her ability unstable, and the triad starting to form would certainly be more stress. "Maybe, maybe not. She has taken it before, but it be possible. Dere is one drawback, aside from havin' ta pay in rubies for it." Rook's eyes went wide. "The other and more lethal payment for this incredible blood is a trade, one drop of blood fir one minute of yer life."

Rook's face shifted from shocked to horrified as his eyes locked on Mari, then flicked back to me. "How many times can you take it?"

"Dat's da catch. No one really knows. For some it be a thousand, anotha only fifty. We dinnie know how much time we each 'ave left. Fir example, me time could be tomorrow and da blood speeds dat up ta today. Each drop is a game of chicken wit death and I can be sayin fir certain dat da reaper be starin' ova yer shoulder."

As I suspected she would, Mari twitched and then thrashed violently, her body splashing water onto the floor. I had to wrap my legs around hers and hold her arms down tight as strange noises like high-pitched screeches ripped from her mouth.

"Holy fuck, she's got black shit pouring out of her nose." Rook's eyes grew wider as he stared at her face. "How much did she take?"

"I dinnie know," I said as her body arched. It took almost all my strength to hold tight to keep her from hurting herself. More water splashed out of the tub and hit Rook in the chest as she became increasingly more volatile.

"This has to be because of me, doesn't it?" Rook stumbled back from the tub until his ass found one of the plush chairs in the washroom. "I mean, she was fine before I got here. Now she's taken this shit and may die because I came here. Because I was an asshole to her."

"We dinnie know 'er reasons, but I'd say it has more to do wit the reality of what the rest of 'er life would look like as a woman born into the brothers."

Mari's body fell slack against mine, and I took a deep breath and waited for the next round. I could only pray that she had enough fight in her to kick this before it had time to take her life.

Gregory and Belle raced in with more ice and dumped the buckets.

"How she be?" Gregory asked panting hard.

"I dinnie know yet," I said honestly. I'd never seen anyone have this much black demon blood come out of them and not be possessed.

"Belle and I will stay to help," Gregory said.

"Naw, I think it be best if I do dis meself."

Gregory looked like he was going to argue.

"Please, dis is somethin' I need ta do on me own. If her condition worsens, I'll send Rook to come git ya."

Gregory's eyes filled with tears as he continued to stand there, eyes fixed on Mari's face like he was staring at a ghost. Belle grabbed her father's hand and led him from the washroom, but she glared at me the entire time. She didn't have to say a word. If Mari died, she'd never forgive me, and I'd better watch my back because she'd be coming for me.

Once the door was closed, Rook slowly stood. "Do you want me to go too?"

I shook my head. "Naw, I'd like ya ta stay, but I need ta say somethin'," I looked away from his eyes. "Ya may no 'ave anythin' ta worry about, but I want ya ta know I get yer jealousy. I do want us ta work, but I cannie give up on Mari as part of me life unless she no wants me ta be her friend no more. If ya can't handle dat...den I dinnie know where we stand."

Rook knelt by the side of the tub and used a cloth to wipe the black mess still dripping in a steady stream from Mari's nose.

"You're really in love with her, aren't you?" he asked softly.

I swallowed the lump in my throat and prepared to say words no one had heard except her. "Aye, I am."

Rook sighed and pinched the bridge of his nose. "I wish she wasn't my cousin. It would make things so much easier."

"Aye, it would."

Mari's ragged breathing was slowly returning to normal, and I knew we weren't out of the woods, but the worry in my gut lessened slightly.

"I need to ask another question," Rook said as he moved Mari's head so he could continue to clean her face. His acting so caring towards her had my heart warming a little more for him. I nodded for him to continue. "Mari mentioned something earlier and then said I needed to ask you about it. She said that I put you through pain. What does she mean?"

Searching his face for any sign that he was lying, I didn't see any and shook my head. "I wish ya had spent even a few minutes learnin' about da union, Rook."

His hand stilled, and his eyes found mine. "Are you going to tell me, or just continue to tell me how stupid I am?" he bit out. I could see the hurt in his eyes, and there was resentment there that had nothing to do with me.

"I dinnie tink yer stupid, Rook. In fact, I tink yer very smart, but I din't get why yer so in da dark when it comes to yer Faction." I lifted a shoulder and let it drop.

Rook squeezed out the washcloth and began to wipe at Mari's ear. It was starting to bleed black as well. "I refused to study," he said quietly. "It's a long story. Let's just say daddy issues."

I cocked a brow at him, but he didn't continue. "All right. Well, ta answer yer question, when da ritual happened, and I accepted and den you rejected, no' much happened right away. There be an ache and, of course, da embarrassment, but later dat night, and den every night since, the moment yer hand touched another in a sexual manner, I felt it."

Rook stopped wiping, his eyes snapping to mine. "You what?"

"Aye, I felt it, and no' in a fun way. The pain is extreme, like me heart was bein' ripped from me chest. I had ta start takin' somethin' to dull da effect."

"Fuck, Rhys...I...I had no idea."

I laughed a little, unable to help myself. "Did ya tink I was pished wit ya simply 'cause me ego got bruised? I'ma no sensitive flower, Rook, but I see now why ya taught I was bein' dramatic."

Mari began to mumble, and once more, she was gripped by a seizure. Black blood flew from her mouth like she was possessed. A primal sound that could only be from the dark fade ripped from her throat, and it made me shiver. The icy water was making it hard to hang onto her.

"Push on 'er shoulders to help keep 'er still," I growled as I strained, and Rook jumped into action. It was incredibly hard to hold someone thrashing and not hurt them. When she finally settled again, I slumped against the large tub, breathing hard, and Rook sank to the floor.

"Why is shit so complicated all the time?"

I smirked at him. "If me had da answer ta dat, I'd 'ave da answer ta all da mysteries in life."

Chapter 19

Rhys

Once I was as certain as I could be that all the demon blood was out, I turned on the shower and washed Mari.

"Can ya hold 'er for a moment?"

Rook stood and grabbed the black housecoat hanging on the back of the door before closing the distance. He hadn't said much after our talk, and I wasn't sure what to make of the silence. I helped him get Mari's shivering body in the house coat before undoing the buckle on my kilt. It landed with a thud, soaking wet and dripping like a tap.

The warmer water felt like a million pinpricks to my chilled skin as I washed off. I grabbed a plush black towel from the rack and stepped out, wrapping the material in place. I glanced at Rook, expecting to see a heated stare, but his face was passive as he stared

"She's a good person, isn't she?" Rook suddenly asked.

"Aye, I tink she is. Let me grab a pair of bottoms and I'll take her from ya." I grabbed a pair of comfortable pants from the bedroom before returning to Rook. Our arms touched as I reached under Mari to take her from him, and we both froze as the connection was made.

His arms felt so warm against my very cold ones, and the electrical charge had me sucking in a ragged breath. I quickly took Mari, before the connection had time to flare and make us do something stupid. I was happy that Gregory and Belle had listened and decided to leave. Some things never got easier to talk about, and this entire situation was one of them, especially since they didn't understand the whole story.

"So what are you going to do now?" Rook asked.

"Da worst has passed, but now she needs ta get warm and rest," I said.

I lowered her down gently in the centre of the bed, then pulled the blankets up to cover her body. Shuffling myself around to sit beside her, with my back against the headboard, then looked over at Rook. He was staring. I didn't sense that he was angry, but I couldn't read him either. The minutes ticked on, and finally, I couldn't take the silence or the look he was giving me any longer.

"What are ya thinkin'?" I asked.

Wandering over to a chair, Rook sat down and leaned forward until his arms were on his knees and his eyes fixed on the floor. "I don't know what to think anymore. I keep running through how we got here and the whirlwind that the last couple of days has turned into, and I'm just not sure where to begin."

"Fair enough."

"I'm not a feelings kind of guy, and this connection has me all up in my feels to the point where I feel like I'm stuck in a twister."

I smirked at that. It was exactly how I felt—confused, anxious, excited, angry, and possessive, only to start all over again. "Aye, I get that. That be part of the reason I spoke ta Mari last night. Dis is new fir me too. I may have wanted to go forward wit da triad, but it dinnie mean I knew what ta expect or how I'd be feelin'."

Rook sat back and rubbed at his eyes. "Fuck. Do you think any of this is real? Mari told me it is just my normal feelings I'd have for you enhanced. Do you believe that?"

"Aye, I do. Ya woulda been my choice if I'd been given one. I'ma no gonna lie, I din't be thinkin' dat in da beginnin', and I still be strugglin' wit da demotion, but yer definitely me match." I looked down at Mari and had never been so happy to see a rosy colour returning to her face.

"I probably would've picked you too, but don't ever fucking tell my father that. Last thing I need is him telling me. I told you so," Rook grumbled, making me chuckle.

"Aye, yer secret be safe wit me."

Mari began to whimper, and her eyes fluttered open. I smiled as I stared into her pretty blue eyes.

"Hey ya, beautiful. Yer back," I said softly.

She reached for my face and laid her hand on my cheek like she was making sure I was real. Her blue eyes filled with tears.

"You weren't supposed to come get me. No one was to know," she said softly. "Oh, dear spirits, I'm so embarrassed. I…"

"Stop, we will talk about it, but no' right now. Besides, dere be no point in sayin' ta no come get ya. Ya know I'll always come fir ya. I 'ave yer back and you 'ave mine. Dat was da deal."

A tear trickled from her eye, and that single tear held more weight as it touched my arm than all the water and ice in the tub.

"I need to tell you what happened," she said, her voice rough with the pained emotion that was like another million little cuts to my heart.

"Naw, ya don't. It be me that's fecked up wi' things. I'm so sorry, Mari." I kissed her palm.

"No, Rhys. I really need to tell you. It...." She turned her head and spotted Rook sitting in the chair. Her body tensed, and all the emotion she'd just shown me pulled back as her mental dungeon doors slammed into place.

"I...ah...I shouldn't be in here. I'm sorry. I need to go," she said, fighting my hold. I let go of her, and she flipped the blanket back and jumped out of bed like I burned her.

"Mari, dinnie go til yer stronger," I said and rose from the bed, but she wouldn't look at me. She stumbled to her feet, then fell to her knees.

"No, this is wrong. I need to go. I'm sorry, both of you. I'm so sorry." She lurched forward and smacked away my hand. She only made it two steps before her legs gave out again.

"Please, Mari, let me at least help ya to yer room," I said, kneeling by her side.

"No, I'll be fine. The effect will wear off in a minute."

"Da no be da point," I argued.

Rook stood from the chair, his face unreadable. He walked toward us, and my muscles flexed. There was no way to tell if he meant to hurt Mari, so I stepped close to her, just in case.

He squatted in front of Mari, and even though she was in a weakened state, she straightened her spine and stared him in the eyes.

"Mari, I'm going to give you tonight because I like you, and you've been kind to me." The corner of his mouth lifted. It was the sexiest look I'd ever seen. "I'm also doing it because I'm not a fan of the old rules and what that means for you, but mostly I'm going to do this because before I arrived, I rejected Rhys." Rook's eyes lifted to mine, and my heart rate tripled. "I didn't understand what that meant, but you were right when you said you were here looking out for him, and I'd just arrived and was acting like you all owed me something. I'm sorry I've been a jerk and a terrible number one so far."

I nodded since Rook seemed to be talking to me as much as he was to Mari.

"Rhys and I haven't completed phase one of the ritual, so this moment is something I can do before Rhys and I officially join, which I intend to happen very soon." His eyes remained on mine as he spoke, and it was fucking hot to see him step out and own his new authority.

Rook's gaze returned to Mari. "After that... I can't, and I won't give my blessing. Aside from whoever ends up becoming our third, there is no way I would ever feel comfortable sharing Rhys with you when I cannot be involved."

"I don't know what you're trying to say," Mari said, but I understood.

My heart swelled for the first time with emotion for Rook, not driven by constant desire. I was able to see something long-term. I was able to see the man and a worthy number one. The attraction had been instant, but the hurt of the rejection hadn't begun to fade until this moment.

Whether Mari wanted this or not, the fact that Rook was willing to let the two of us have tonight while still wanting the union meant more than anything he could've said. Words were cheap, but this was an offering. He wanted to start over, and this was his olive branch. Rook wanted to give us a gift and prove his worth as a number one, especially now that he was aware. I knew firsthand this would be excruciatingly painful, and I didn't wish that pain on anyone.

"I'm saying that I'm going to leave this room, and this is your one night together with my blessing. Take it or leave it. It's your choice. I want you to understand that I've decided to stay. I've rescinded my rejection, and I'm going forward with the union. As the future number one of my triad, I'm offering you this gift. Unless, of course, Rhys has changed his mind in the last couple hours about the union?"

Rook looked up at me with the question, and I slowly shook my head back and forth.

"Aye, I'ma still wantin' da union," I said.

"I want that for both of you. This is a terribly bad idea, Rook. I get why you're doing this, but…." Mari argued, but Rook stood.

"You're right. It is a bad idea. I know the risks, but I need to show faith in Rhys and prove that I'm sorry for the pain that I've caused."

"Rook…" Mari shook her head as she pushed herself up enough to sit on the edge of the bed.

"Cousin, don't argue with me. This is the only time I can offer you this gift. It is the only real thing I can offer. Money is meaningless, and I have nothing else. Take the gift, don't take it, but I choose this," Rook said.

Rook lifted his eyes from Mari and locked them with mine. Between one breath and the next, he'd transformed. No more was he the guy conflicted and uncertain about what he wanted. The eyes that found mine made me want to be his number two without question or hesitation. As our eyes remained locked, I knew I would kill for him, die for him, and one day I would love him.

"Can I talk to you out in the hall?" Rook asked.

I rose and followed him out the door. Rook's jaw twitched, the muscles flexing in his neck as he paused at the threshold and looked back at Mari.

"I don't like the rules, and maybe one day I can help get them changed, but I don't know when that will be. So if I were you, I'd make the most of this, Mari."

"Yes," she said softly.

Nodding, he stepped out into the hall, and I closed the door behind us.

"Thank you," I said before Rook could say anything.

He ran his hand through his hair. I could tell he wasn't comfortable with this, despite all the bravado he'd just shown, but he was willing to do it anyway. "Can I ask you why the two of you never had sex before? I mean, it's clear how close you are, and you could've snuck around at anytime. I don't get it. I would've just said fuck it and done it before all the connection crap."

"Ya want da honest answer?" Rook nodded. "I have two reasons. The first is simple, I hoped when she went overseas, she'd find someone that the family would deem acceptable, and she's worth more to them as a virgin. Stupid but true." Rook shook his head. "It will be da same for us. The woman we be paired wit will be a virgin. Da blood sacrifice at the final union ritual is tradition among all da Factions, not just us. If I slept with 'er, I was wipin' away 'er last hope to find someone to spend her life wit. I'm no asshole enough ta do dat."

"Okay, and the other one?"

"Because it woulda been too dangerous. I 'ave told ya dat I love 'er, and if we'd been intimate all dis time, then ya wouldna' had time to reject me 'cause I woulda been doin' it to ya instead. Naw, scratch dat, I wouldna even been in da Faction no more."

Rook looked ready to march back into the room and call the whole idea off as his eyes darted between me and the door. "Do you think that is still a concern?"

I stepped close to Rook. Laying my hand on his shoulder, I gave it

217

a squeeze. "I be loyal, Rook. I said dat I would go forward wit dis triad. I accepted it at da ceremony, and I accepted yer decision ta stay. Ta me, dat means my decision is made, but if me heart had already been locked in dat long and dat intimate with Mari, no connection to anyone was gonna change it." Rook licked his lips and still seemed uncertain. "If we complete da first ritual, ya will see dat ya dinnie 'ave anythin' ta be worrin' about."

"When not if," he said, his eyes firm. The fact that he finally owned who we were to become was fucking hot, and it made my gut quiver and my heart pound harder.

My lips curved up as I cupped his face. The connection made our eyes close with a groan before I laid my lips against his. I instantly wanted to take things further, but I forced myself to keep the touch light.

"Thank you for doin' this. I 'ave no words ta tell ya how much it means ta me dat yer willin' ta sacrifice somethin' like dis for me," I whispered against his lips.

Gone was the light touch as my back pressed up against the wall with a thud. Rook was demanding, his tongue seeking entrance, and with a groan, I opened for him. I wasn't sure if he'd changed his mind as he pressed his body up against mine, making me pant as he stole the air from my lungs with the ferocity of his kiss.

The connection magic struck like we were hit by a car as it flared around us. I gasped, and my hold on Rook tightened.

He broke the kiss, but Rook's hand wrapped around my throat and squeezed just enough that I knew what kind of lover he would be. I was in control of all aspects of my life, but when it came to a male partner, I wanted to let go. I wanted to be used, told what to do by Rook who I had a gut feeling would know what I liked and how to push me to my sexual limits. The anger and passion burned like twin flames in his eyes and promised me pain. Pain that I craved and would only ever find with him.

"Just remember, you're my number two. Mine, and no one else's. Tonight is it. You must promise me," he snarled.

"I promise ya on me da's grave dat ya will never need ta worry."

Rook nodded and pushed away from the wall. "You better get in there and maybe put a protection spell on the room. My jealous side has a nasty streak, and I can't guarantee I won't come back here."

There was something entirely too sexy about that statement. "Ya know dis is gonna hurt like a fukin bitch, right?" I pointed to my heart.

"You went through this every night for the month before I arrived, right?"

"Aye, I did."

"Then I think I handle one night. Just put a boundary in place," he said as he marched away.

"Fuck," Rook yelled when he walked around the far corner of the hall.

As terrible of a person as it made me, I loved that he was possessive and gave me this gift without guilt. It showed me more than any pretty or sexy words ever could.

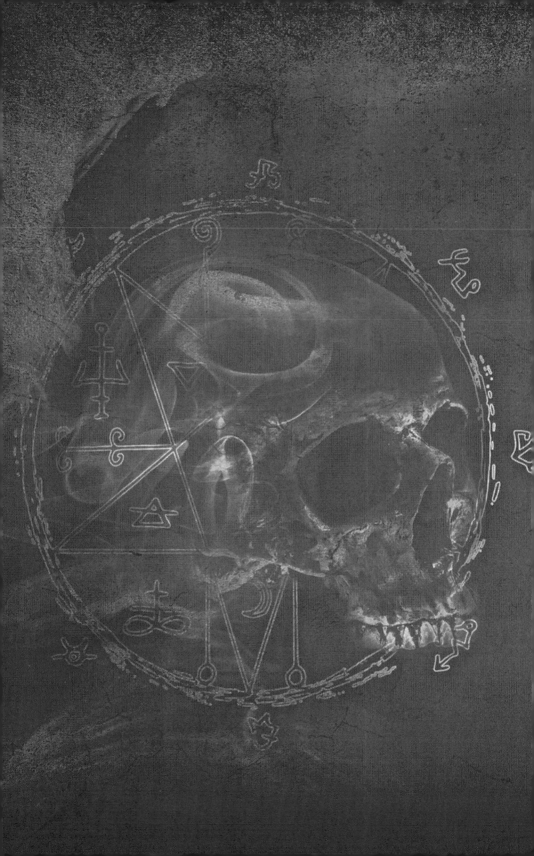

Chapter 20

Rhys

Stepping into the room, I wasn't sure what I was expecting, but Mari in one of my black T-shirts hanging on her like a dress was not it. She was bent over, going through my drawers with her adorable ass in the air. The door clicked closed, and she jumped, clutching a hoodie.

"Whadda ya doin'?" I asked.

Mari looked away and turned in a circle before she spotted the woolen socks she pulled from the drawer and left on the bed. She marched over, trying to put the hoodie on at the same time.

"I used some of your toothpaste. I hope you don't mind, but that demon taste was stuck in my mouth," she said as she pulled the hoodie down. Her face appeared lodged in the arm of the thing.

"Mari, did ya not hear Rook?"

She still didn't say anything.

"Fuck my life," she growled, trying to get the hoodie fixed.

I closed the distance and pulled on the hood to free her head. She pulled it down and into place before sitting on the edge of the bed.

Squatting in front of her, I grabbed her shaking hands as she fumbled with the thick socks.

"Ah, screw it! I don't need socks," she tried to stand, but I held her wrists firm.

"Mari, ya almost died. We need ta talk."

"Sure, but not right now." She jerked away from me and made to bolt for the door, but she wasn't getting out of at least talking.

"Glas bacainn," I said, holding my hand out to the door. It locked, and a barrier went up into place.

Mari spun around and looked at me, her eyes wide. "What did you just do?"

Before she could think about her options, I held my hand out to the washroom door. "Glas bacainn," I repeated.

The door slammed closed, and another barrier went up. The final spot was the window—not that I expected her to jump from this high up, but I wasn't giving her any opportunities to prove me wrong. Mari was strong, but she would be weak from her ordeal and I had a lot of tricks and kept them up my sleeve.

"Rhys... No! What are you doing?"

"We're needin' ta talk." Mari crossed her arms over her chest as I walked toward her. "Ya almost died on me, Mari."

"That's not what was supposed to happen!" she yelled as the tears began to stream down her cheeks. "I was attacked. They forced me to take the whole bottle. I was only going to buy a bottle and take a drop. I swear to you."

"Attacked? By whom?"

"The demons. I don't know why. They never said, but they purposely overdosed me. It's how I got this." She pointed to the bruise on her face. "I didn't try to kill myself, Rhys. I swear I didn't."

"I need ta find out who opened dat portal. Dey will 'ave da answers," I growled, anger overriding everything else as I pictured those disgusting demons hurting Mari.

"Um… I had it opened. I…" Mari held herself tighter. "I needed some of the blood and knew you wouldn't like me going to them. I shouldn't have gone behind your back. I'm sorry. I just wanted to deal with this on my own."

Marching away, I ran my hand through my hair. "Mari, ya know how dangerous dis magic be. Why?"

"Why?" She held her arms out, and I could see the anger beginning to burn in her eyes. "You can't understand what it's like to be me. I don't want to live in pain all the fucking time anymore. I'm tired of waking up and fighting my ability and this lonely existence without any reprieve. Every single day is a struggle just to breathe and not feel like I'm suffocated by the solitude, the voices, or the pain. I feel useless all the time and try so hard to be a good person, and yet, it's constant torture. So yes, I wanted a little bit of peace. Even for a few hours. To be able to take a deep breath and not feel it all pressing in on me."

Her eyes locked with mine, and the raw emotion there took my breath away.

"For just a little while, Rhys, I want not to feel your love pressing in on me and never be able to have it," she said, gasping for air.

Unable to stand it any longer, I stormed across the open floor and pulled her into a hug.

"I didn't want to die. I didn't go there to die. But when all went quiet... I wondered if it would be better if I did."

"Dinnie say dat," I said into the top of her head as I gripped her tighter. "Please, dinnie, ever say dat. I'ma gonna push hard to have the rules changed so ya can find yer happiness, Mari. Ya deserve ta find someone dat can love ya back with their whole heart. And if it makes me a selfish man, den so be it, but I cannie live with out ya in dis world."

"Rhys, you're destined for far greater things than worrying about me. You and Rook and your third are going to make your mark on this world. I cannot tell you what, but I've seen it. That needs to be protected." She pulled back and looked up at me. "That's why I don't think I can do this. I want to, but... I can't put that at risk."

"I dinnie love him—not yet. Ya cannie come between somethin' that isn't yet established."

"But you will, and if I fuck that up...." She sniffed and looked away.

"Aye, I will at some point, and naw, ya won't," I said honestly, but the words were sour on my tongue. Mari was everything I'd ever wanted, and because of who we were, we were never to be. It wasn't fair. "I told Rook dat no matter what, I would remain loyal and go forward wit da union. Ya know I be a man of me word. Wat happens dis moment will no change dat fact. If ya no want it den fine, I'ma never gonna make ya do somethin' dat yer no wantin', but dinnie make yer decision tinkin' yer gonna mess up da triad."

A small smile graced her lips. "Good, that's good."

"Do ya remember when I was tryin' ta learn how ta ride a bike for da first time?"

Mari sniffled but then giggled. "Yeah, I remember you falling on your arse over and over again."

"Aye, and what did ya say ta me when I said I wanted ta give up?" I asked and stepped back so I could see her face more clearly.

"I said that a girl wouldn't cry because we are made of stronger things. I was a little shit," she said and laughed as she wiped at her face.

"Naw, ya were right. Ya've always been made of stronger stuff, and if not fir ya, I woulda been a whiny brat." She rolled her eyes at me, and I grabbed her face and made her look me in the eyes. "Dinnie look away, Mari. I mean every word. Yer da reason I am da man I be now, and yer stronger than ya give yerself credit."

"I'm sorry. I never should have tried to go there alone, and I shouldn't have hired that witch to open the portal. All I did was create a mess for you to clean up."

"It be fine. I'm no' angry. I git it. I told ya I'd keep yer secret, and I'll take it to me grave."

She covered her mouth with her hand and closed her eyes. "I'm going to miss us so much. The thought of losing you for good hurts in every part of my body. My heart feels like it's being ripped out. I shouldn't say that. I shouldn't. But I needed to get it off my chest. You are my heart, Rhys, and I want the whole world for you, but it doesn't stop this from hurting."

I laid my lips on her forehead and breathed in her scent. "I dinnie want to make yer life harder, but I cannie deny that I wanna take wat I can fir us tonight. If ya dinnie wanna stay, den, I'll release da doors, and ya can go. Just tell me what ya want."

"I don't know if I can. I want you so bad, but all I can think is that it's only going to make it harder tomorrow to know that tonight was all there will ever be."

Sighing, I stepped back and nodded, even though I didn't want to let her go. I wouldn't force her to put herself through any more pain because of me.

"If dat's wat ya want, I understand but ask yerself dis. Ar'ya seein' da triad in shambles? Dat dis moment ruins it all?"

Mari crossed her arms and walked over to the door but stood staring at the wood. I waved my hand, releasing the barrier. Mari reached for the door handle, her body shaking. "I still see the triad," she said and slowly turned to face me. "You've always loved me and been here for me."

"Aye, I always 'ave, and dat won't be changin'. We will always be friends and allies, and ya can come ta me any time," I said. "Ya will always own a piece of me heart."

Grabbing the bottom of the hoodie, she pulled it and the T-shirt off in one go, dropping them to the floor. I took in the sight of her body, the way her dark hair tumbled over her shoulder, and stopped mid-waist. She was a warrior with strong legs and cut muscles but in a perfectly feminine way. I'd dreamt of seeing her like this and not forcing myself to look away. Her skin had always been fair, but tonight she looked like the moon had kissed her skin. I groaned as the desire hit like a punch to my gut.

"I know I'll be punished for this, but I want to know what it's like to be with a man who loves me. I'm tired of holding on to being a virgin for some mythical man. I hate the rules, and I hate what the family and the stupid triads are doing to all of us women, but I do love you, Rhys. I have since the moment we were old enough to understand the word, and if I'm going to give myself to anyone, I want it to be you."

"Yer Da would neva punish ya," I said, my voice rough.

"Maybe, maybe not, but either way, I don't care, at least not right now."

Mari moved away from the door as graceful as any dancer. Her toes were light as a feather as she stepped towards me. My mouth was dry, and I couldn't think of a single intelligent thing to say to what she'd said while staring at her.

"I love the way you look at me," she said as she stopped close enough to run her hands over my shoulders. "I've lost count how many nights I've dreamt of this, how many nights I snuck from my bed and came down to your room hoping to change your mind about preserving my innocence for someone else. Only the images of who you are to become kept me from raising my hand and knocking on your door."

I shuddered as she pressed her body against mine. Her fingers traced up my neck, soft as a breath of air. "How many nights I touched myself thinking of you."

"Dear spirits," I groaned. Gripping her ass, I pulled her into my body, and it was as if I'd stepped into a slice of paradise.

"Did you ever think about me? Did you ever pleasure yourself while dreaming about me?"

"Dinnie ask crazy questions, Mari. Of course me did. Every damn night. No matter wat mischief I got up to wit others, it was always you I wanted."

She smiled. It was the sweetest expression, and a rosy blush spread across her cheeks. We'd never even kissed. So many times, I was so close to throwing everything out the window, but we always remained firm.

"I'm gonna kiss ya, and I'm not gonna stop until day breaks tomorrow."

Not giving her time to answer, I dropped my head to hers, and that first taste of her sweet lips was something I would remember and treasure forever. Mari melted into my hold, her arms wrapped around my neck tighter as she opened her lips to let me explore. She was a cool rain in a drought. My heart had been suffering for so long that I didn't know what I was missing until this moment.

Mari moaned as our tongues gently battled. Breaking the kiss, I looked down into her eyes and pushed the long hair over her shoulders so it draped down her back and left her breasts exposed to my greedy eyes.

"Oh," she whimpered as I cupped her breasts.

"I intend on savourin' every last inch of yer body," I kept my eyes locked with hers as I lowered my mouth to the hard little nipple that was begging to be sucked.

Mari's body shuddered, and I gripped her waist to keep her steady.

"Oh, Rhys," she moaned.

Her head fell back, and her hands fisted in my hair. I loved how she responded to my touch. When I switched to the other nipple, she moaned louder, and my hands gripped her ass to keep her from falling over as her legs shook.

"I fear my nipples will crave this touch forever," she whispered.

I sucked harder, making her cry out. Lifting my head, I savoured the look on her face. Stepping back, I smirked as she whimpered like she was afraid I would stop. That wasn't happening.

Remembering Rook's warning, I recast the spell on the door before taking Mari's hand and leading her to the bed.

"Sit down," I said.

Mari perched herself on the edge of the bed. She looked exactly how my dreams had conjured her in my mind. Sweet, a little shy her first time, but eager as she craved to try everything. Her eyes were glued to the tent in my pants, and I slowly moved my hips back and forth. Her eyes followed along.

"I think I have too many layers on," I teased, and she nodded, making me smile. "Do ya wanna do it?" She looked up at me. Her brow knitted in confusion. "Take me bottoms off?"

She reached for the edge and paused, her fingers barely touching the material. Lifting her chin with my finger, I made her look at me.

"Dinnie be nervous. We've waited a long time for dis. Own dis moment with me. For tonight, da rest of da world dinnie exist."

Her stunning blue eyes shimmered with conviction as her fingers gripped the elastic waistband.

"I like your kilt better," she said, making me laugh.

"Aye, so do I." I smiled at her, then groaned as she pulled the pants down. Her hand immediately grasped my cock.

"Oh, fuck."

She didn't even hesitate and slipped the head into her mouth.

"Sweet spirits, where did ya learn ta do dat?" I asked as she swirled her tongue around and began to suck hard.

Mari moaned her answer, but I couldn't pick out a single word.

"Take more if ya can," I encouraged.

Her mouth had a touch of its own magic. After a couple of attempts, she managed to do what many wouldn't even try. She took me all the way down her throat.

"Mari, fuck, yes. How did you learn to do this?"

"Is it not right?" she asked, her hand wrapping around my cock and continuing to stroke. "The movies overseas showed that this was what you'd like."

I laughed and then smiled down at her. "Oh, I be likin it. Da movies are no' wrong."

A wicked grin lifted the corners of her mouth. "So you want me to do it again?"

"Aye, do it again. Suck me hard and take me all da way down."

Mari did exactly that, and my head fell back on a groan. Unable to help myself, my hands gripped her hair, and I began rocking my hips to her movements. I'd never felt anything so good. It was like she was ravenous. I gave her control as she picked up her pace. Shocking me further, she slipped her hand between my legs. I groaned when she found all the sensitive spots that drove me wild.

I stepped back, but Mari tried to follow me, her eyes still fixed on my cock, which was ready to explode.

"Naw, stop. Yer gonna make me come too soon. Fuck," I swore, taking a deep breath and trying to control the need that had taken over so quickly.

"Do you not want to?" she asked, her eyes worried.

Kicking off the pants, I knelt in front of her. Cupping her face, I kissed her hard. There was no holding anything back, and every ounce of everything I felt for her poured into the single act. Mari's moan turned into an adorable whimper as I nipped her bottom lip and sucked it into my mouth.

Coming up for air, we were both panting hard as I laid my forehead against hers. "I do, far too much. I just really wanna savour dis time wit ya."

Mari squealed as I grabbed her ass, pulled her to the edge of the bed, and forced her to lie back. "Dis is somethin' I'va been dreamin' 'bout for a long time."

Starting at her knee, I kissed the soft skin that felt like satin against my lips and slowly drew circles up her leg with my tongue.

"Yer so soft," I whispered as I got closer to the sweet pussy I'd wanted since we'd both been old enough to know how we felt. Mari moaned, her legs trembling as I closed my eyes and tasted her for the first time.

"Oh my... Oh dear, I never," Mari panted, making me smirk.

Running my hands up her legs, I pushed them farther apart and dove in like a starved man. I was starving, and she was my first meal in years.

"Fuck, Rhys," she squealed and wiggled against my mouth as my tongue swirled and dipped inside her.

I was determined to taste every inch of her body and pulled up on her ass to get an even deeper angle.

"Oh my. Oh, dear spirits," Mari moaned as her back arched off the bed, and her hands found my hair.

"Aye, right there. Oh, Rhys, this isn't fair. You're going to make me...." She ended the sentence with a yell as she came in my mouth. The taste of her was like honey-dipped magic on my tongue.

I clenched her ass harder, my fingers pressing into her soft skin as I devoured all she gave me. Her screams of pleasure were music to my ears, and it wasn't until the final wave of her climax subsided that I stopped and let her body relax.

Mari was panting hard, her chest rising and falling quickly, her arm lying over her eyes as she lay splayed for me. I committed every part of her body and the look on her face to memory. This was a moment I never wanted to forget. Pushing myself to my feet, I gripped my cock and stroked it slowly to the sight of her. Every part of me ached to be inside of her.

"Slide up da bed," I said.

Mari moved her arm from her face, and her eyes locked on what my hand was doing. Licking her lips, she did as I asked and pushed herself to the middle of the massive bed.

"I'll be gentle with ya."

She nodded and spread her legs for me to settle between them. I hovered over her and took a moment to appreciate the beauty of the woman who had stolen my heart years ago. It was a double-edged sword for me. I was getting what I'd always wanted and saying goodbye at the same time.

Her dark hair fanned out around her, and she bit her bottom lip—her nervous habit. Eyes the blue of the sky glinted in the candlelight of the room. I kissed her long and slow, letting her experience all that I felt for her.

Reaching between our bodies, Mari gripped my cock and made me hiss with the feel of her hand. She stroked me and then rubbed the head of my cock on her clit.

"Aye, ya like dat?"

She nodded.

"Dis is gonna hurt a little, but it'll fade," I said and wiggled my hips to apply pressure to what she was already doing.

"It will hurt more never to know the pleasures at all. Please make love to me, Rhys. I don't want to wait any longer."

"Ya may want ta grip da blanket."

Mari's eyes grew wide, but she grabbed the blanket in her fists as I lined myself up. I teased her a little and let her get used to my girth, but as soon as I felt her relax, I took her in one go and then lay still as she screamed.

"I got ya. Da worst is over," I murmured and nibbled softly at her neck as she whimpered. "Relax, Mari. Let yerself relax, and da pain will go away."

Her walls gripped me hard, begging for more, but she wasn't ready. I sucked on her neck and traced little designs along her skin with my tongue until I could suck on her sensitive earlobe. I was careful not to leave a mark.

"Oh yeah, Mari. Ya feel so good," I whispered into her ear. "Yer beautiful and so perfect." I laid a few more soft kisses over her pounding pulse as her body relaxed.

Her walls continued to clench my cock, and I had to battle back every instinct I had to pound into her and take what my body was craving. Lifting my head from her neck, I laid my lips on hers and waited for her to respond. As soon as she opened for me, I kissed her languorously. Nothing was being left unsaid between us tonight.

Mari moaned, and her arms slid around my neck as she became more insistent, yet I still didn't move. She needed to be ready because I didn't know if I had enough control to hold back.

"For da love," I growled out as Mari thrust up into me before wrapping her legs around my waist.

"Do it. Make love to me. I want this," she said, grabbing my lower lip between her teeth. The pressure of her teeth was just enough pain that my cock surged, and the last of my restraint threw itself out the window.

"I'm gonna do more than just make luv ta ya, and I want you ta bite me every time you come. Bite me hard. Dinnie worry about hurtin' me. I like da pain, and I heal quick," I said.

She gave me a sassy grin and rose enough to twirl her tongue around the chain dangling around my neck until the guitar pick was lying on her tongue. That was seriously the hottest fucking thing I'd ever seen.

Backing out of her slowly, I watched to see if there was any pain, but it had melted away. She closed her eyes and tilted her head back, her mouth hanging slightly open. She looked exactly how I'd dreamed. My heart filled with so much joy that we got this moment.

As I picked up the pace, Mari began to moan and dug her finger-nails into my shoulders. It was a shot of adrenaline straight to my cock with the bite of those nails. I loved pain during sex. Her nails dug deeper as my thrust became harder, making me groan.

"Ah, fuck, Mari. Yer so tight," I said.

I wasn't even sure she could hear me as her moaning turned into screams, her body arching off the bed. I knew she was close just as her body clamped down hard around me. She opened her eyes and lifted her head to bite my peck. The climax hit, and she screamed. I did, too, as the extra pain and pressure squeezing me pushed me over the edge of sanity.

My thrusts became frenzied as I drove her toward a second one.

"Rhys, please don't stop," she begged, and every muscle flexed with her request as I forced the climax that had been on the cusp of releasing back down.

With a quick twist and a squeal from Mari, I flipped us so she was on top.

"Ride me da way ya need, Mari. Use me." I wrapped her long dark hair around my fist and loved how she responded with a moan, her blue eyes wild with need. "Do it, beautiful. Fuck me the way ya want."

She needed no more encouragement and braced herself on my chest as she tentatively began to move.

"Can I try any position?" she asked shyly.

"Of course. Whateva ya be wantin'."

Mari shocked me when she pulled her feet up under her body and began to move on my cock in time with our breathing.

"Fuck," I yelled.

The new position forced me deeper than before. The sight of her breasts bouncing was drawing me dangerously close to the edge of release all over again.

"Fuck, Mari! I can't hold back much longer," I said through clenched teeth.

I reached between her legs to play with her clit, rubbing in little circles. She gasped and bounced faster on my aching cock. The female body was a marvel to me. I envied how they could come over and over again so close together.

"Yes, yes, yes," she called out, her body freezing in place as she came. As soon as she slumped, I rolled us over again and put her legs on my shoulders.

"Ya better hang onto me," I growled and immediately pounded into her as hard as I could. Sweat trickled down our bodies as I let myself go.

It felt like time stood still as I came.

"Mari, fuck," I groaned as I finally gave in.

With each thrust, I came again until her legs slipped off my shoulders, and I collapsed on top of her.

Silent tears streamed from her eyes as I kissed her lips softly.

"I love you so much," she mumbled against my lips. "Thank you for this. Thank you for this gift."

Even though the words were on my tongue to reply, I couldn't let myself say them anymore. Smoothing back her damp hair, I kissed the tip of her nose.

"I feel selfish takin' dis moment wit ya."

Mari lifted her hand and placed it on my cheek. "I know you do, but don't. I wanted this with you. I wanted to know and feel something real."

"Aye, I know, and I swear ta ya dat I'll get da rules changed." I kissed her tenderly and then rolled us over so I could spoon her. "Ya need ta promise me somethin', Mari."

"It's okay, I know. I'll never try something like what I did tonight again. If I need anythin' from now on, I'll let you know, and we can figure it out."

I pulled her tighter into me. "Ya better. No more slinkin' off into da dark. There be too much unrest and dark tings afoot ta be doin' dat."

"I know," she said and sighed.

"Rest up. I plan on makin' use of da time we 'ave left."

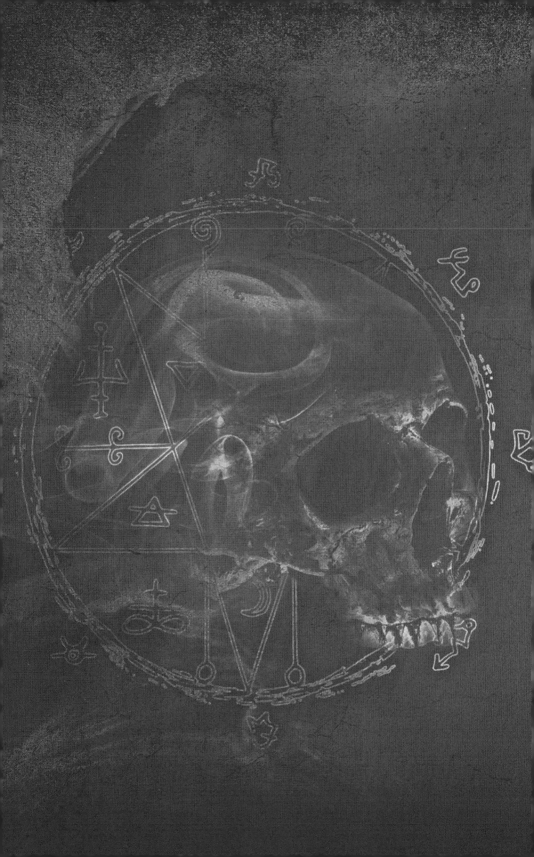

Chapter 21

Rook

I slammed my fist off the rock wall in my bedroom as the pain gripped my chest again. It had been a dull ache that I managed to push aside until now. I wondered if Rhys was as tough as he seemed while I ate dinner and washed it down with a beer. I watched the stars and enjoyed the quiet night then real agony started.

The pain hit so hard that it felt like someone had taken a sledgehammer to my chest. I almost fell off my chair. I knew that whatever was going on in that bedroom had been stepped up to the next level. My fist found the wall again as another scream ripped from my mouth. I was caught between a burn-the-world-down-around-me rage and the most excruciating pain imaginable. If I hadn't been able to see my chest, I would've sworn that my heart was being torn out.

Rhys had gone through this pain. I put him through this when I rejected the pairing and blocked the connection as soon as I felt the link. I suddenly hated myself so much for not taking the time to learn the power of the magic within the Faction and, more importantly, the repercussions of my actions. How was Rhys able to look at me, let alone forgive me? I remembered clearly. Each night was filled with two or more partners and multiple rounds, like one long party. The fact that he was still sane was astonishing.

I leaned against the wall and let my feet slide until my ass found the floor. There was so much clarity. I understood why Rhys didn't greet me when I arrived, why he was so reluctant to be in the same room as me. He looked at me like I burned him when we touched, and he asked Mari to leave with him. I saw it all like a fucking light-bulb flicked on.

"Fuck!" I yelled as it gripped me again, and I tensed against the sensation. It eased once more, and it felt like the pain was letting go of my soul. I gasped and took a deep breath. My muscles shook, and sweat trickled down my forehead into my eye. Insult to injury was what that was.

I wiped the sweat away from my eye before running my hands through my hair. I laid my head back against the cool stone and tried to prepare for the next wave that was sure to come. If roles had been reversed, I would've gutted him on sight. Embarrassing me would've been bad enough, torturing the fuck out of me...I'm coming for your head. But, then steal my room and touch my things, I would've shackled him up and made sure his end was painful. I would've found every torture device available and used it on him until he was screaming and begging me to kill him. So really, I was getting off easy.

"Ahh," the scream was pulled from me, and I collapsed to my side, holding a hand over my chest to make sure the skin wasn't really beginning to tear apart. Tears were not my thing, and I couldn't even remember the last time I cried, but they ran freely down my cheeks now.

How had all the men in the family who'd lost one of their triad survived this pain? My respect notched up slightly for my father. Whether it was by death or choice, the pain of the connection being interrupted or severed was the same. Again, these were things I knew but had never taken as more than dramatic build-up in the books I was forced to read. I snubbed my father, I snubbed the Faction, and I hurt Rhys in the process.

A knock came on my closed door.

"Go away," I yelled, then bit back another scream as the excruciating sensation throbbed brightly.

"But, Master, yer screamin'," Liam said.

"I know I am," I panted out. "Go away."

The door rattled like he was trying to get in, but the spell I'd put into place held. I knew that Liam would try to distract me if I asked. The idea had merit as the anger replaced the pain, but the guilt was sitting right there, staring at me. I did this to prove my loyalty to us going forward. It would diminish or wipe out all the goodwill this sacrifice had built if I let Liam do anything to me.

"Liam, I said go the fuck away! Please, just leave me alone!"

"But, Master, I need ta make sure yer no bein' attacked."

I sprawled out on the cold rock floor, sweat dripping from every part of my body as the next round began to build again. There was never enough time to fully relax before being hit by the invisible force that stopped my heart and made breathing impossible.

"I'm not being attacked. Now please go away. I just want to be left alone."

"As ya wish, Master," Liam said.

I slumped. Another wave hit, and this one was the worst yet. My head swam as little black dots danced in my eyes.

"I'm sorry, Rhys. I didn't know it would hurt so much," I mumbled before I passed out.

J woke up in the same position I passed out in, without knowing if it had been five minutes or five hours. The ache was still there but dull now, like a distant memory and not as sharp.

Turning my head, I looked out the window. It was not yet light out, but the sky was shifting from the dark black of night to the greys that promised sun. I pushed myself off the floor and stumbled to the bathroom, feeling like I'd been out for an all-nighter and drank way too much while being punched repeatedly in the chest. Which fucking sadist had come up with the triads? Who thought creating a bond that would torture one another was a great idea? I stood up as I considered the ramifications of being paired with the wrong person. What if a person got paired with someone who was sadistic? There were certainly enough sadists in history and our family trees. Did they set out to torture their partners?

I couldn't picture Rhys doing that to me. Regardless of last night and what I'd given my blessing for, Rhys was noble. He would never cross that line to get back at me for any reason. I'm not sure I could say the same. Rhy's cousin, Ronan, on the other hand…I'd heard the stories and the whispers of him going too far with his form of sex and how his father, Rayland, had to bury a few bodies. I had an affliction for pain. I liked to give it and hear the screams, but I wasn't quite that bad.

I shivered at the thought, suddenly so much happier that Rhys was my match.

I'd hardly scratched the surface of what we were supposed to be and the responsibility that was yet to come.

Testing the water temp, I quickly stripped and stepped into the warm spray, letting it soothe the sore muscles. Once clean, I stepped out of the shower and let myself air dry while going on the hunt for clothes.

Mari was supposed to be training me again today, but I had no idea if that would still happen after last night. I quickly pushed the image aside, knowing anger of my own making would flare if I thought about Rhys with her again. Would I be okay with her now that she'd been with Rhys? I didn't know. I wouldn't until I saw her face. The sad reality was that if she were any other girl we both wanted to fuck, I wouldn't have given a single shit. It was the part where I wasn't involved that was driving the train of anger.

Grabbing my smokes, I decided to go for a morning walk since the castle would be quiet for a while yet. The morning had brought a thick dew that glittered like a blanket of diamonds on the grass. It didn't take long to reach the far side of the inlet where I'd found Rhys working out yesterday. I turned to stare at the castle. There was something eerie about the tall structure, with strands of fog floating around as if it were from a ghostly realm. A cool breeze travelled over my body, and I suddenly wished I'd put on a hoodie for the walk.

There was a perfectly groomed walking path that I set out to follow. I assumed it circled the property all the way around. It soon became clear that the trail stretched farther than I originally thought.

Stopping I leaned against a tall tree. Pulling out my smokes, I flicked open my lighter and lit up the little stick to take my first drag in what felt like forever. Holding out the smoke, I stared at the glowing orange end. Rhys didn't seem to smoke, and the last few days had bounced from one chaotic event to the next.

I should give up this habit—one day, it would kill me—but today was not that day. The only sound in the thickly wooded area was the morning birds singing and my lighter as I flicked it open and closed and let my thumb roll over the starter, making the flame dance to life.

There was a snap of a twig a moment before a loud yell yanked me out of my calm reverie, and I turned my head just in time to see a hooded figure with a stick about to take my head off. Instinct that I didn't have a day ago had me dropping low and spinning out of the way as the stick, which looked like a rough version of the canne, hit the tree right where my head had been. Another yell and I was jumping out of the way of a strike that would've been a painful kidney blow.

"Whoa, Mari! I get it! I need to be prepared for anything," I said as I dodged another blow from the hooded figure. By the sound of the voice, it was female, and my only guess was that Mari had decided to teach me a lesson.

"You'd think you'd be a little more appreciative after what I went through so you and Rhys could have last night."

I wasn't quick enough, and the stick hit my hands, sending my favourite lighter flying and disappearing into the thick shrubs and undergrowth.

"Hey, back off!" I growled as the stick hit my arm, but I managed to block the more painful blow. "I get the point."

She twirled the stick over her head and dove low, swinging it like a helicopter blade for my ankles as she spun in a circle.

"Fuck!" I jumped over the stick, ducked the next time it came around, then jumped back in a flip that I didn't even know I could do, landing in a fighting stance. How the fuck had I just done that? There was no time to marvel over what just happened as she at me came again. I was pissed now.

She picked up the pace of the blows, but I managed to dodge or block each one and started to become the aggressor, forcing her to step back.

"Is this what you want? To see what happens when you piss me off?" I growled.

A responding growl came from inside the hood. It sent a shiver down my back. That shouldn't have been as sexy as it was. Great. Now I was into my fucking cousin after last night. Lusting after my cousin was so a no-go, I had to talk to Rhys about this.

She ran at me and took me by surprise, knocking me to the ground as her fist found my jaw. She landed a hard right hook that rattled my teeth, and my anger spiked.

"What in the actual fuck!"

"Ya dezerv ta die." She said, and I didn't recognize the voice. A strand of red hair slipped from inside the hood. Everything inside me froze for a blink as I realized this was not Mari, and whoever it was out for blood.

Her fist found my face again, and my anger went from annoyed to full-on rage. I was in survival mode now. This was no test. I growled and shoved the unknown opponent off me, sending her rolling across the dirt. She didn't stay down. She jumped up, spinning the stick in one hand. I had to admit she looked badass.

My power flared to life when she ran at me, and I waited for the right moment. As the next blow streaked for my side, I stuck out my arm and caught the fast-moving weapon in my hand. With a yell, I pushed her back until she slammed against the tree where I'd been relaxing.

Reaching out, I snatched the hood and yanked it away from her face. Green eyes, the colour of spring grass, greeted me, and I sucked in a gasping breath as we stared at one another.

"Mine," I whispered as a spark of something that hadn't been there a moment ago flared inside of me.

There was a flash and a tingling under my hand where I gripped her. Even as my mind continued to reel, my body and power recognized my third. I had a million questions about this connection, but that would have to wait until later.

She snarled at me, and I caught the flash of a blade.

"Petrobile," I said, and she froze, the blade coming for my face.

"Rhys started out hating me. Why not you too?" I grumbled as I stared at the tip of the sharp knife.

I could feel her trying to fight the spell, but I forced the decorative blade from her grasp and cut the tip of my finger before tucking the knife through the leather of my belt. Swirling my finger in the air, I drew a small ball of power to the surface, then touched her forehead and drew a bloodied symbol that enhanced my power and kept her secure.

"I'm sure this is not how you saw your morning going, but next time, mind your own damn business and let a guy have his fucking smoke," I said.

I glanced around for my lighter, but I had to concede it was lost forever. Fucking great.

Stepping back from the tree, I picked up the fallen stick. "Leib-heis," I said and smirked at the terrified look on her face. "Looks like this triad thing is going to happen." Her eyes narrowed at me. "Yeah, I get it. You're probably not interested in that." She'd dropped a small pouch, and I picked it up and looked inside to make sure there wasn't anything dangerous. I only saw some crushed berries. "Sorry about your berries," I said and dropped them into the pocket of her cloak.

Sorry about your berries? I used to have swag and game. What the fuck?

I took a moment to look my third over. She was covered in dirt and smelled like it, but she was beautiful. Even with the glare that said she wanted to cut my cock off, I couldn't deny the obvious.

"Listen, I didn't want to come here, either, and I didn't want to meet Rhys, but I did, and I'm shocked that I'm kinda happy about it. Hopefully, you'll feel the same in time. I hope."

Turning, I walked toward the castle with a floating redhead in my wake. Another thing that I thought was bullshit. My father would say that you needed to go into the forest and hunt down your third. Like, what in the actual fuck? Was it like a fox hunt? Were we supposed to travel around hunting down the right redhead? It seemed ridiculous, and I'd tuned him out.

I was going to have to crack a book one of these days. I could see it coming. Surprises were not my thing, and this place had thrown way too many my way in a short window. It was time I took this shit seriously.

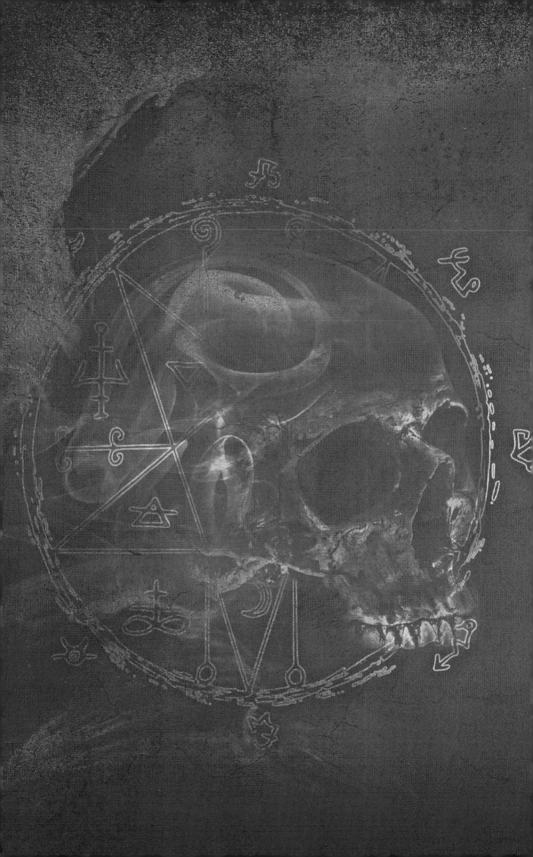

Chapter 22

Elewyen

    I'd only seen red when I saw the man who had burned down the villages with the babes still alive. He deserved to die, and I didn't give it thought when I attacked before the flame in his hand could do any more damage.

    I blame the irrational emotions on the fact that I spent most of last night in a strange bout of pain that had me doubled over. I'd never experienced anything of the sort before, and if I hadn't been so far away from my coven, I would've sought Azula out for help. One moment, I felt so sad that I burst into uncontrollable tears. The next, I was suffering from an invisible fire clutching my chest. There was a strange need with the pain like I needed to find something. It reminded me of the spirit voices that would call to me but with no words spoken. Between the bouts of pain, I made my way toward the source. There was no telling what I would find, but I needed to know. I needed to make it stop.

I hadn't been expecting to find this man or for him to be so powerful. My coven wasn't that strong. I was the strongest by far, and even I didn't compare to the power wrapped around me, squeezing like a fist. It was so strong that it was making it hard to breathe. I had no idea where he was taking me or why, but it couldn't be for anything good. Men like him didn't take you for good reasons. Men never had good intentions. It had been ingrained in me that those with decent souls were a myth. No, men took you to hurt you and to destroy everything they touched.

The path opened to reveal a wide stretch of water, edged with gardens and a small house, but it was the massive stone structure that I could only see the top portion of behind the hill that had my eyes going wide.

No, not that castle! Please, don't take me in there. I begged inside my mind since my mouth couldn't move. My mind conjured a wide assortment of tortures, from burning my body to cutting my skin off in long strips to feed the magpies. I didn't want to die, and Keeva needed me.

Azula called the men from the castles heathens of the worst kind and said that only those who wielded dark power lived inside. They sought to steal our power and fill us with their seed, so we were forced to bare them more red-headed babes. I never understood this. There were too many tossed away in the forest. Why not save them if they wanted red-headed babes? I shouldn't have been surprised that this was where we were heading, considering he landed in a metal bird and used a car to get around.

"I have to tell you this is not the way I thought we'd end up meeting," the man said and looked over his shoulder at me. He said it like we planned to meet. What plan? I did not know him. "I also thought it would be a lot more difficult to find you, but I guess this means I don't have to traipse around the island searching for you. Knowing Rhys, he would make me do something like ride a horse. I would definitely break my neck. Now that I think about it, that probably would've been his plan."

I had no idea what he was rambling on about, and I could barely understand the words he was speaking. His eyes were as blue as the water and just as deadly to drown in.

He looked back and once more referenced finding me quickly. Why was he searching for me? What did I have that he wanted? He didn't want a red-headed babe, did he? Fear gnawed at the back of my throat.

He continued talking about a triad, but his accent was just too bloody thick to understand him clearly. We rounded a bend that led toward the massive structure, and panic gripped me as surely as his power had. Large men wearing leather and a savage appearance wandered the property. They all stopped to look over as we drew closer. They wore the marks of dark magic on their skin, and their eyes glimmered with the power they held. If I could've moved, I would've shivered and run for the forest. This was not a good place.

I could feel the death that remained on everything. It blanketed the grass and trees like those who had died here still lingered.

"I'm not sure what the protocol is. So, for now, I'm going to lock you up since you don't seem thrilled about this or to see me in general. Don't need you cracking me around again with this." The man held up my weapon, and I wanted to grab it and beat him over the head with it.

"Liam," the man called out as we stepped into the castle's cool shadow and then through the biggest doors I'd ever laid my eyes on.

251

It was just as stunning on the inside and just as useless. Who needed all these things? What purpose did they serve? What was the shiny thing hanging from the sky by more shiny things? I wanted to run back to my forest and my hut with the rest of my coven.

"Liam," the man that had me yelled again, and someone came running from another room.

"Aye, Master, I be sorry for bein' slow, wha can I…Oh my. Ya found yer third," the man, who I assumed was Liam, said.

I could understand him better but didn't know what he meant by a third. The only thing I knew of that was a third were the three pillars of sacrifice, and panic lanced my heart at the thought of being sacrificed on the full moon.

"I did. Do we have a room that she can't escape from?"

Liam tapped his chin. "I tink da dungeon would be best. Magic dinnie work down there, and da cells 'ave all been recently redone. She cannie be escapin' from dare."

"Perfect, lead the way."

My heart pounded out of control, the beats loud in my ears as his boots thumped on the stone floor. We wound our way through an endless number of hallways and stairs that led farther down, away from any windows. The darker it became, the more my fear took hold of my mind.

It was like he was taking me to the Dark Fade through a portal in the floor. At the thought of never seeing Keeva again, my soul ached almost as bad as what happened to me last night. I never meant to leave her alone. What would she think when I never returned? Would she think I abandoned her? Would she try looking for me? I didn't want her to leave the safety of the coven, but I knew she would. Keeva had the tenacity of a warrior in her small body.

Liam opened a thick metal door, and the room beyond smelled

terrible. Damp mould and old piss permeated the air. But there was something else as well. Death. It smelled like rotting carcasses, like whatever went in there never came out.

"You'll be needin' ta secure her before we walk through da door. All spells will stop workin' as soon as we walk over da threshold."

The man who had the spell on me turned to look at me, and the strange swirling of butterflies took flight in my chest. "Great, round two it is."

The man, whose name I still didn't know, dropped my stick and knife onto the floor, then proceeded to put his hands inside my travelling tunic. I tried to growl at him and move, but nothing happened other than my body flushing hot as his hand roamed over my stomach, hips, and then down my legs. He found my other two knives and dropped them to join the others.

"Well, you certainly like your sharp objects, don't you?" He smiled at me like I should know what that meant.

Those captivating blue eyes had my pulse pounding. I couldn't understand the sensation and figured it was my fear. It was the only thing that made sense.

My eyes followed him as he walked behind me, and my body trembled inside the spell. Not being able to see him was worse than staring into those eyes that sucked me in. He wrapped an arm around my waist, pinning my arms down to my side. His other arm went around my neck. Then he pulled me sideways in the air like I was nothing more than a bird.

"Go get the cell ready," he said.

Liam dashed through the door and opened one of the other barred doors. "Ready."

Two steps later, the man's arms around me tightened until I couldn't move or breathe as he walked through the door. I knew the moment the spell had dissipated and tried to fight, but the position and tight grip made it impossible. He was too strong, and my throat was almost completely closed off.

"I'd save your strength. You're going to need it," he said as he walked into a small room. The temperature dropped, and I shivered like we were walking hand in hand with the dead. They were locking me up. The realization that I wouldn't be able to escape and get back to my coven or Keeva had me fighting twice as hard.

The man lifted me so my feet touched the floor, but he shoved me before I could get my balance. I flew across the space and fell onto a straw bed. He backed out of the room and closed the door. The sound echoed in my head. I was locked in. Even though it was futile, I ran at the bars, my hands reaching through to grab at him. Hurting him and making him pay before he killed me was all I could think of as I screamed like one of the phantoms that I was sure occupied the place.

He jumped back out of the way of my nails.

"I'ma gonna killz ya. Ya feckin', murdarar," I yelled, my hands wrapping around the metal bars and shaking the door.

"Well, ya certainly got a lively one," Liam said.

The man who had captured me looked at Liam with a look that I couldn't decipher before he shook his head and walked out. The little flames in the torches along the far wall flickered as the outer door closed and sealed my doom.

The room felt like it was closing in on me. I stumbled back, my ass finding the thing that was supposed to be a bed, and hot tears trickled down my cheeks. The magic in this room had stripped me of my power. I'd never felt so naked before. It was natural to reach inside myself and touch the place that held the gift. My lower lip trembled, but I refused to show more emotion than I already had. I needed to keep strong.

This was all my fault. Why hadn't I just left the man alone? I had to stick my nose into village business, and now look at me. Here I was, locked up for trying to avenge those who had lost their lives when they would never have done the same for me. How many times had I been chased with pitchforks or arrows skimmed me? How many times had I been attacked by men who thought I was an easy target? The villagers had never shown me an ounce of kindness. Not a piece of bread, a smile, or a hand to find the babes. They were as much my enemy as the man who had taken me. Yet I felt drawn to this man and angered by what I'd seen. No matter what they would've done for me, it didn't feel right to let them all die the way they had without punishment.

My small pack rustled, and Barry poked his head out.

"Ya come fir da trip, did ya? I'ma tinkin dis is one trip yer gonna wish ya had no made." Barry ran up the front of my tunic and sat on my shoulder where I could pet him. "I'ma glad ya did, though."

Pushing myself back so I could lean against the wall, I pulled my feet onto the bed and let the tears fall silently on my knees. The emotion clogged my throat. I pulled the hood up on my cloak and tried to bury myself in the material like that would somehow make the nightmare go away.

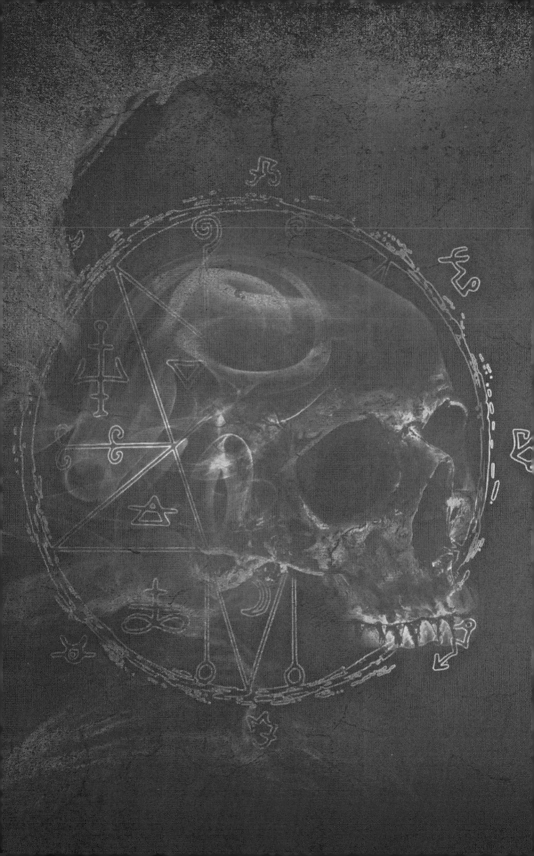

Chapter 23

Mari

If there was a better word than euphoric, I didn't know it, but that was how I felt. I was walking on a cloud, and it didn't matter right now that what happened with Rhys would never happen again. It only mattered that it had. For one night, I got to live out my fantasy and be held by the man I loved. It was the shortest fairy tale story in history and the most perfect. At least to me.

Jumping out of the shower, I looked at myself in the mirror. I looked different. More of a woman, maybe? Whatever it was, I couldn't wipe the smile off my face. Wandering out into the bedroom, I dug out my training clothes when a hard knock sounded at the door.

Turning, I stared at the wood. "Who is it?"

"Mistress, your father has sent us to get you," the guard's voice said. I recognized his deep baritone but didn't know his name. The guards all went by a letter, and I thought his was Zed.

Not sure what was wrong, I pulled on my clothes and tossed my hair in a ponytail before heading for the door. Yanking it open, I found four guards standing outside. None of their faces showed any emotion.

"What is going on?"

"I was not informed. We are just to come get you," Zed said.

Closing my door, I stepped out into the hall, and the men surrounded me as Zed led the way. The last time I'd been escorted anywhere was when I was fourteen and left the property to do some shopping on the mainland. I glanced up at the guards, but they kept their eyes straight ahead, their hands resting on the hilts of their swords.

"Has something happened? Was there an attack on the castle?" I asked.

"Not that I'm aware of, Mistress Adair."

They led me toward my father's side of the castle, but we didn't head to his chambers. We stopped outside of a door that I'd never entered. Zed knocked, his meaty fist sounding like a giant was banging on the thick wood.

"Come," my da called out from inside, and Zed opened the door for me.

As soon as we stepped through, I knew that something was off. The room was set up like his office but larger, with old leather-bound books and the ritual items I was never allowed to touch. One wall had thick metal shackles with chains, and a shiver travelled down my spine. My eyes grew wide as I stared at the strange space. What did my da need with a room like this?

He stood in the middle of the room and stared at me as the door slammed into place. I jumped and looked over my shoulder. Two of the four guards had remained inside and now guarded the door.

"Da, what's going on? Are you all right?" I asked, taking a step towards him, but he held up his hand. I stopped. His face was cold, a look he'd never directed at me before. "Am I in some kind of trouble?"

"Aye, Mari. Ya are," he said, his voice devoid of emotion.

I suddenly wished that I had a weapon. The guards at my back were making me antsy, and my da's attitude wasn't helping.

"Okay, you mind telling me why?" I asked, crossing my arms over my chest.

"What do ya think ya were doin' last night?" he asked, his eyes finding mine.

My mouth dropped open as I realized what he meant. The rules stated that if one of the unchosen created attachments or threatened a triad's pairing, they would be punished. It was an old rule that I didn't even think they followed anymore.

"What I was doin was private business," I said, my overseas accent slipping as the anger rose inside me. I wasn't interested in sharing my intimate time with Rhys with him or the guards.

"Mari, dinnie be daft. What is da eighth rule fir a woman born of Faction but who has no birthmark or red hair?"

My eyes darted around the room again as my blood pressure rose along with the blush across my cheeks. "It's no dat I dinnie know da rule."

"Then what is it?" Da persisted.

My teeth ground together. "Dat I'm ta remain pure and untouched until a suitable match can be made. I am ta remain unattached until such time the match can be made or give meself wholly to da Faction in service to da council as dey see fit. The service will include Faction business and da ending of lives da Factions deems necessary ta eliminate," I said. "But ya cannie be serious. Dat rule is archaic, Da, and I had no one who was interested, and I'ma already doin Faction work. I be holdin up me end of da deal." He stood silent, hands on his hips like a statue that sprouted from the stone. "Da fir spirits sake, ya talked ta da other Factions that be our allies, and day din't have no'one." I held my arm out towards the window. "When I was overseas, I dinnie find anyone. A match was no comin."

"Dat does no' matter," he said.

"Ya, it does. I deserve ta have a bit of a life," I said, anger notching higher.

"Naw! Ya deserve what yer given, and ya coulda ruined a triad parin'," he yelled.

I stepped back. I'd never seen Da like this. In all my twenty-four years, he'd never raised his voice at me.

"Da, what has gotten into ya? I did nothin wrong, and ya used ta want more fir me and Belle and da rest of da women in da Faction."

"Yer sister will be matched in a ritual one day," he said and walked over to the desk. "But no' you. And now ya've ruined even da small chance I had of pairin' ya up and sendin' ya off."

My eyebrows shot up. "Pairin' me up and sendin' me off? What am I, a farm animal?"

"Naw, they be worth more at dis point," it was like he'd slapped me across the face.

I stumbled back as the shock rode me. I'd been here for him since my mother died. I made sure he ate and slept. That he walked and talked to people. I read books with him. We sat and played chess and talked about everything except Faction business, but now I barely recognized the man standing in front of me.

"Ya din't mean dat," I whispered.

"Ya need ta be punished, Mari. Ya need to pay fir yer sins. Dat is da order of da Faction. It is what da rules dictate. Dinnie make dis any harder on yerself."

"Punished? Yer no seriously gonna punish me?" I took a step back, and a large hand gripped my shoulder. My adrenaline spiked as my da picked up something black from his desk. "Fir havin' sex? Da, this is crazy. Please din't do this," I begged.

"Tie her to da wall."

"Git off of me, or I will break yerr neck," I snarled at Zed.

Even weaponless, I was a threat. That was why Da had sent four guards. Zed looked uncertain but removed his hand. What I was capable of was well known amongst the guards.

"What do ya plan ta do ta me?"

The long end trailed from my da's hand, and I realized he had a whip. Was he serious? He was going to whip me.

"Ya cannie be serious?"

"Aye, Mari, I am. It be da rules. Yer ta receive twenty lashins and never ta do it again. If ya break da rule again, then it will be forty lashins and solitary confinement fir two weeks. Da punishment gets worse da more ya disobey."

"So all da Flitter women can fuck all of ya men as much as ya want, but I can't have one night fir me? I cannie have one night with someone I love and will never have again?" I screamed. I'd never felt this level of rage, and the chains rattled on the wall as my power rose and filled the room.

"Mari..."

"No! Ya din't think I've seen da parade of partners ya've had in dis house, including Illiam, since Ma died? Ya think I dinna know about da parties dat Caleb has or da circus of women that Rook, Rhys, Crispin, Ronan, Lochlan, or anyone else has slept with?"

"Dat no matter. Da rule states—"

"Fuck da rule!" I screamed, my temper flaring as the chains lifted away from the wall. It was a rare thing that I got this angry, but the fury burned bright inside me now.

My da looked at the wall and licked his lips. "Da rules are in place fir a reason, Mari. Ya must follow dem, no matter if ya like 'em or no'. Ya were born an Adair. No matter what, I luv ya as me daughter. But right now, I am no yer Da. I'm just a man dat is set to punish ya fir disobeyin' da rules dat the many generations before ya put into place," He said quieter. "Mari, ya disrespected yer cousin and his triad wit what ya did."

"Shows you how much ya know. Rook gave his blessin'." My hands clenched into fists. "Go ask him if ya din't believe me. He wanted Rhys and me ta have da time together. If he's okay wit it, why can't ya be?"

He shook his head. "Why ya gotta make dis so difficult?"

All I could see was red, and the candles around the room flared as I screamed at the top of my lungs to release the frustration. My da took a step back, and I could feel Zed and the other guard move as far away as they could get. No, I wouldn't let this get to me. They wouldn't break my spirit.

I pulled the cool shield of indifference up from inside of me and wrapped myself in it. "Oh yes, how dare I, the simple, useless, and completely worthless woman born in this house, dare to speak out about being whipped for no good or logical reason? Well, since I'm so useless, the next time you need someone's throat slit, go do it yourself," I growled. "I will do your bidding no more. You want to kill me, then kill me, but I will not be your assassin for hire at the price of my soul."

"Mari, dis be exactly why no attachments can be made, yer already emotional." I bit my lip, so I didn't leap at the man wearing the face of my father. He sounded like a typical sanctimonious windbag. "Ya need to learn yer place again. Ya have forgotten da ways dat ya were raised. Always wit da wild heart and sharp tongue. Ya need ta remember who ya be talkin' to."

"Oh, I know well who I'm talking to. The question is, do you?"

He swallowed hard, and I watched his throat move as he did. The flames dimmed to normal, and the chains clattered against the wall as my power released them. Could I kill my da? I didn't know, but I was mad enough that if I had a knife, I wouldn't trust myself.

I sucked all the anger inward and forced myself into a steely calm. "The only reason I still live under this roof is because I choose to. I want you to remember that, and now I'm no longer sure I want to. Now tell me, how did you even know?" My voice came out cool as a winter breeze.

"How dinnie matter. What does is dat ya did."

I took a step towards my father. Zed moved behind me, and he would've tried to grip my shoulder again, but my da held up his hand to warn Zed off. It was a good thing too, or I was going to break every bone in his body, starting with the wrist. Once I was directly in front of my da, he didn't look so certain of his conviction.

"I'll stand by your wall and take your lashings, but not because you told me to. I'm doing it to prove to you that I'm more than just a woman. I'm stronger than all the men in this castle combined." My da's brows arched, but he didn't argue. "I also want you to remember that each time the leather touches my skin, it only makes me stronger, and I will remember what you've done until the day I die." I gently laid my hand over my da's heart, his eyes softened, but it was too late.

"And I will *never* forgive you, not even for a moment. If Ma were alive, she'd be disgusted with the man you've become since her death. You are no pillar of honour, so don't lay your head down at night and try to tell yourself anything different. They will be lies of a snake's tongue." Whipping the shirt over my head, I dropped it at his feet. "Women will rise from the shadows you've placed us in, and when we do, I'll ride the horse that takes all the men like you to the dark fade."

I marched over to the wall, wrapped my hands in the chains, and braced for what was to come. Living this life, I was conditioned to take pain. They honed me into steel wrapped in flesh and bone.

The whistling of the whip sailing towards me cut through the air a moment before the sharp bite hit my back. I closed my eyes as the sting forced tears to my eyes. By the fifth one, I had to bite my lip hard to keep from screaming. I refused to make a sound. I would never give him or the Faction my screams.

I gave up all my hopes and dreams and became a weapon for them. Working diligently to help protect those who lived on the Island. I would never regret my time with Rhys and gladly take a thousand lashings to have that night again.

"Twenty," Da said.

Taking a deep breath, I turned and marched toward my da with my head held high. Bending over made my back scream in pain, but it only fueled my anger. I grabbed my shirt and stood to stare into my da's eyes.

"You are no longer my da. You are just another man wielding power he shouldn't have, and remember, I will never forgive you for this," I said, then turned and marched towards the door. I glared at the guards until they moved out of the way. Pulling my shirt on, I was proud of myself for not wincing.

If I wasn't already convinced that Rhys and Rook needed to be in charge, I was now. They couldn't take power soon enough.

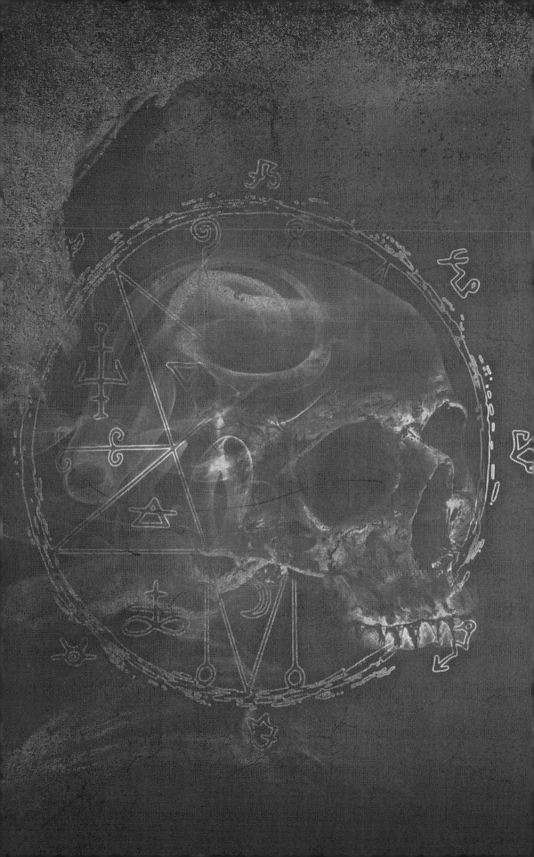

Chapter 24

Rhys

I smiled as I wandered down the hallway towards the kitchen area. I hadn't felt this alive in forever. The hardest thing I 've ever done was walk Mari to her room this morning. I kissed her until we were lightheaded, knowing it was the last time. Goodbye was bittersweet, but my heart was thankful for the time we shared.

But reality was calling, and I wanted to find Rook to thank him and make sure he was okay. I heard Rook grumbling before he rounded the top of the stairs from the large entranceway. He looked angrier than a badger poked at with a stick.

He glanced my way and swore a few times as he marched towards me. My eyes scanned over his face, and there was no hiding the bruise forming on his cheek or the fact that he was covered in dirt

He looked like he decided to roll around in the flower bed. If it weren't for the scowl on his face and the fact I hadn't felt anything, I would've sworn he'd just had a wild night of sex.

"Wha' happened?" I asked.

"I'm really starting to hate this fucking place. That's what happened," the anger palpable as he stormed past me.

Turning, I caught up to him and glared at the side of his face.

"I mean can't a guy just have a morning smoke? No wonder the guards look like a herd of giants when everyone here wants to kill you."

"Wha' da fuck do ya mean?"

"I'm pretty sure the meaning is clear. This place is fucking crazy. No, scratch that. Everyone who lives here is crazy." He looked over at me, and his eyes shimmered with power and anger.

Reaching my room—which, I guess, was his room now—he pushed open the door, and it slammed against the wall.

"It might have been a lie that I was living overseas, but I loved it. People adored me, and I got to sing every night. I had fans draped off me, ate at the best restaurants, and slept in whatever bed I wanted. Fuck, I could pick up a remote and turn on a television or blast my stereo any time of day or night." He turned in a circle, his arms out to his side. "This place is not only crazy, but it's still in the stone age. You have people wandering around in armour and weapons like we live in the Middle Ages, and people beat you with large sticks. Bring on the fucking blue pill, 'cause I wanna go back."

"So we're doin' dis again. Ya know ya change yer mind fasta than a lass changes her undies."

I smirked as he glared. It was way too much fun teasing him, but I did want to know what happened. Sighing, I closed the door as Rook continued to fume and toss clean clothes out of the closet.

"Ya look like ya decided to go a round or two wit a cat. Does dis have anythin' ta do wit last night?"

"No, it fucking doesn't." He stopped and looked over at me, his eyes softening a little. "I'm never fucking going through that again, and I'm sorry. I really had no idea what was happening to you."

"Aye, I know."

We stood quietly, staring at one another. Rook seemed to want to say something else, just like I did, but neither of us said a word.

As if the spell holding him broke, Rook stomped out of the closet and scooped up his clothes before making his way to the washroom. He didn't close the door in my face, so I took that as an invitation and followed him into the spacious room I loved. Everything was set up just how I liked it, and I never took for granted the luxurious shower and massive clawfoot tub that overlooked the back gardens. It had been a little getaway spot for me when I needed to soak and relax.

Rook stripped out of the tight black jeans and T-shirt, and my eyes went wide. Heat, as well as the hard-on, were instant as my eyes traced over the hard contours of his body. I couldn't stop staring at his ass, which looked perfect for gripping. I itched to touch every inch of his body. The binding spell instantly flared like a wick set on fire.

He turned on the water, then hopped in the shower. And dear sweet spirits, my mouth watered. It didn't matter that I had an arduous workout last night. I was up and raring to go. I'd never been so happy for the open-concept shower with no doors. The unobstructed view of his muscles, dark tattoos, and mouth-watering cock was for my eyes only.

"I be needin' ta ask... Do ya regret what ya did for Mari and me? Cause yer actin' like ya do."

Rook placed his hands on the tiled wall and sighed. "Yes. No. Shit. No, I'm not, but, fuck, I can't think about it. I can't even look at you without wanting to punch your face."

I burst out laughing and earned myself another glare. "Ya tell me about it. Weeks, Rook, fuckin' weeks. The pain nearly killed me. I had to block ya outta me mind and started markin' X's on a cally until da next ritual moon when I could be acceptin' da rejection. Every goddamn day it be da same pain ova and ova. Ya think one night be bad, try dat on fir size. Yer lucky I didn't meet ya at the air strip, stab ya with me sword and be sendin' yer body back ta yer da and trust me, it was temptin'.'"

He turned and leaned against the tile, and I couldn't keep my already travelling eyes from roaming over my chosen. No matter what we thought of the ritual or the spirits and their choices, they did know how to pair.

"If I'd known, I would've at least met you first. I'm a fucking piece of shit most of the time, but I'm not that bad." He ran his hand through his wet hair, and I desperately wanted to be those droplets of water.

"I thought I was going mad last night. Doesn't help that I'm a bit of the jealous sort, and I don't like to share what's mine unless it's by my design." He crossed his arms over his chest and looked away from my stare.

I smirked. "A bit of da jealous sort, ya say?"

"Fuck off," Rook said, but the corner of his mouth tugged up.

I pulled off my shirt and tossed it aside and those magnetic blue eyes, which looked so much like a rippling body of water, locked with my own.

"Do ya know what happened last night?" I asked, kicking off my boots.

"I'm pretty sure I can guess. I don't need you giving me a blow-by-blow about you and my cousin," Rook said, making me shake my head.

"Naw, no' about me and Mari. I mean about me and ya." My hand went to the buckle on my kilt. His eyes dropped to my hands while his tongue ran over his bottom lip. I let the kilt fall, and the relaxed muscles all flexed. It felt like the room's temperature had risen a few more degrees.

"No, I don't know," Rook said, but his voice was soft, like he hadn't committed to the words as he stared at my body. I liked that look on his face.

Stepping forward so that we were both under the spray, I stared him in the eyes. "Ya made me tink dat ya jus might be a good number one after all, dat ya be made wit honour even if ya try ta hide it."

"There is something we should talk about," Rook said, then groaned as I cupped his face. The connection power raced faster around the small room. Even the water seemed to sizzle as it came into contact with the energy.

"It be important?" I asked.

Our lips brushed, and I softly nipped at his lip. I needed us to take this step forward. The connection magic was intense, and the chemistry was off the charts. I wanted to know if I could genuinely fall in love with him. It was too much to think about, so I would start with him and then our third when we found her.

He licked his lips. "It can wait," his voice as ragged as I felt.

"Good."

Rook swallowed hard as I dropped my hands to either side of his body, and the heat seeped into my fingers. We groaned in unison as the connection healed the hurt between us. That was the beautiful and dangerous thing with a fated connection. Some people were truly sadistic and could purposely hurt their other two partners over and over, but the connection would repair the damage with close proximity time and time again.

"Ya know what else?"

"What?" Rook gripped my hips, mirroring my position, and pulled me closer.

"Ya made me think dat there be more layers ta Rook Adair den da self-centred twat who arrived," I said, making him smirk.

"Fuck, it feels so good to be near you," Rook closed his eyes. The glittering magic whipped around us faster as it twined us together. "Why didn't it hurt before I came here?" he asked.

Dropping my head, I nipped at his neck and drew lines along his skin with my tongue, making Rook groan.

"I don't get it. I don't fully understand," Rook said, then sucked in a gasp when I gripped his ass. "Explain it to me."

With a growl, he pushed me backwards slowly until my back came into contact with the cool stone of the shower wall. I gripped him tighter.

"You're so fucking distracting," Rook mumbled as he attacked the spot where he'd already left his mark. "You make it hard for me to think straight."

I smirked and closed my eyes, soaking in the bond that had been calling to me for weeks. The power that had made me feel like I was somehow drowning in the middle of a desert. There was simply no relief until now.

Lifting his head, Rook gripped my face and forced me to look at him. "Explain to me why it always hurt for you and not for me. Tell me why when I was overseas, you suffered, but the night that I arrived, you had four women, and I never felt a thing? Explain to me why suddenly, with Mari, it was like being kicked in the chest by a donkey while having my heart ripped out?"

I smirked at his visual and let out the breath I was holding. "Because, Rook, I neva rejected ya. I always held out hope dat ya'd change yer mind, but as da days turned inta weeks, I decided dat I was gonna' accept yer rejection. Of course, dat was when I got word ya were comin'. A few more weeks and ya woulda been free of me. Ya coulda gone on livin' yer life da way ya wanted."

A bit of sadness crept into my chest at the thought of never having met him. Or more accurately, that he never wanted to meet me. This entire thing was forced upon him, and I was the consolation prize.

I tried to look away, but he forced me to keep my eyes locked on his. "That's not what I want now," he said.

"Aye? And what are ya wantin', Rook?"

Lips crashed against mine, taking my breath away with the sudden attack. Rook ravaged my mouth, and I groaned as I granted him access. Taking full advantage, I ran my hands over his back, loving how his strong body flexed under my touch. Gripping his ass, I pulled him into me, so there was nowhere else to go. It felt fucking amazing to finally be pressed up against him like this, with no clothes in the way.

"Fuck, I can't get enough of you," Rook growled, breaking the kiss.

Grabbing his shoulders, I pushed him until he was the one with his back to the wall. Taking my time, I explored his hard chest and sucked on one nipple and then the other until he was squirming and panting under my touch. My tongue traced lines down his abs as I slowly sank into a squat, not going near the hard cock begging to be touched.

There was something entirely too sexy about Rook begging. I knew he wasn't the type, but I wasn't planning to play fair. I groaned loudly and ran my tongue up the inside of his thigh. He shivered under my touch, and I felt his pulse jump and his breaths quicken. I gave the sensitive areas all around his cock special attention. First, massaging them with my fingers or mouth, then soft bites. Each time, he groaned a little louder. I glanced up at the way-too-sexy man, and his blue eyes darkened with passion.

"Stop fucking teasing me," Rook growled.

"Is dat what I'm doin'?" I smirked up at him.

His eyes narrowed into slits. There he was. The man who would happily press my face into the floor and fuck me until I screamed. That look alone drove the temperature in my body so high that the room felt like a sauna and made it hard to breathe.

"You know what you're fucking doing." Rook gripped my hair and jerked my head back, forcing me to look up at him. "Suck my cock, Rhys," he growled.

A man who could give me what I needed was like getting the best dessert ever and then finding out it came with whipped cream and a fucking cherry on top.

"Whateva ya say," I wrapped my hand around the cock I was dying to get my mouth on from the first moment I laid eyes on Rook.

A shudder went through my body as my hand barely fit around him. The image of him taking me hard from behind had me groaning as my tongue swirled around the head of his cock.

The power had become insistent. The way it whipped around our bodies felt like it was fusing us together as it amped higher. I licked the length of his cock and almost fell over as the power did the same thing to me. Looking down, I stared at my cock, amazed by what had just happened.

"What is it?" Rook asked.

"I'ma gonna say the magic is encouragin' us ta continue," I said.

The moment my mouth wrapped around his head, a burst of wild desire soared through my body and straight down between my legs. I was staggered by the force that almost made me come on its own. It had me falling to my knees and ramming Rook's cock down my throat. I groaned and choked at the same time. All my senses were bombarded with wild and intense pleasure.

"Oh fuck, yes," he said, gripping my hair harder.

My nostrils flared as I tried to breathe past the cock almost too big, even for my skills. There was a momentary panic, but I forced myself to relax and swallow. As if sensing my hesitation, the warmth of the magic slipped into my mouth and down my throat. Suddenly, I had more room to breathe, and the fear disappeared. This was incredible. I couldn't even explain it, but it was as if the connection was more than simply magic. It was an essence all its own that was made specifically for us.

The muscles lining my throat gave way as they relaxed, and I drew my head back, swirling my tongue around the shaft. Even with experience and magic, this wasn't going to be easy.

With a subtle slurping sound, I let him fall from my mouth, then looked up at him. "I want ya ta fuck me mouth. Take me how ya like."

"I like it rough, real rough," he said, waiting for me to tell him no.

"Aye, but ya cannie be too rough fir me, and I've no safe word," I said, smiling at the hungry look that crossed his face.

"You sure about that? Everyone has their limits."

"Maybe, but there ain't a limit I've found yet dat I cannie take or a pain dat I dinnie like. So, aye, bring it."

Bringing him back to my mouth, I got into a comfortable position and swallowed a few times to allow that cock to slide into my throat.

It was easier this time, and I put both hands on his legs for support. Looking up at him, I pushed forward until my nose touched his stomach.

"Fuck yes," he growled, his face becoming a dark mask of need.

Rook grabbed my hair in both hands this time, just as I suspected he would. He didn't hold back as he fucked my face. There was no mercy, and it took all my focus to match his rhythm. My throat would be raw from this, no matter what, and I loved it. I wanted to be so sore I could barely speak.

Rook finally owning the number one was sexy as hell to me. He was rough, but I wanted brutal and dug my nails into his legs, making him cry out. His hands tightened painfully in my hair, and I moaned, loving the sharp bite it brought. His rhythm became fierce, making my eyes water. Shifting my hand, I cupped his balls and massaged them as he worked me over. The continuous groaning and animal-like sounds Rook made only fueled my desire until I was aching to explode.

The mimicking magic felt divine, but I needed more and slipped my hand between my legs. I grabbed hold of my throbbing shaft and stroked myself in time to Rook's pounding thrusts. Closing my eyes, I took it all in. There was something so simple and powerful about letting go and enjoying myself, letting the magic do what it intended

"Fuck, fuck, fuck, Rhys...Shit, yes! Aahhh!" he yelled and yanked my head close to his body as he came.

My nose was pressed against his stomach, and I could feel it flex as he came down my throat. The power made a miniature explosion like it was trying to combine into one. I groaned, coming hard, and had to pull away from Rook for fear of hurting him.

I flopped, and my back found the cool tile as my body convulsed uncontrollably with the pleasure pumping through my system on a loop. With each pulse that ripped through my body, I came again, and it wasn't until Rook dropped to his knees beside me that I realized he was feeling it, too. When the sudden burst of power subsided, Rook collapsed and draped his arm over my stomach.

"If dat's from a blowy, I be ready ta see what happens when I fuck ya." I rolled my head to the side to look at his amused face. "Woulda been kinda nice ta know that could happen. I almost bit down," I said, and then coughed a little from the roughness in my throat. It was glorious, and I couldn't wait to do it again.

"Yeah, that would've ruined the mood," he said, making me laugh.

My smile faded. "Do ya still wanna go? If ya really no wanna be here, I will no force ya ta stay. I be very aware dat dis was not yer first choice, but I'm no gonna be content ta be da runner-up forever."

Rook pushed himself up, so he sat with his back against the wall, and I groaned as I sat up to look at him.

He rubbed at his wet hair before laying his arms over his knees. He looked like he was posing for a sexy magazine, and it was distracting as fuck.

"You mean like how I'm the runner-up to Mari?" He cocked a sexy brow at me.

"Ya no dat be different," I said, and eyed him narrowly.

"Yeah, I know, and no, I don't want to go. I'm not going to pretend that I love everything here and that I'm not going to miss performing, but this thing, this triad...I want to do it. I want to try."

"Ya know ya can still perform, right? Who said ya had to give singin' up completely?" Reaching out, I turned down the heat a little and sighed as the spray cooled my heated skin.

"What do you mean?" he asked, looking genuinely confused.

I snickered as I pushed myself up to my feet and held out a hand to help him up.

"I dinnie know who ya been talkin' to, but just 'coz yer in a triad, din't mean ya have ta give up all of yer life from before it. I'm no' gonna force ya ta stay here all da time and 'ave dat turn into an argument between us. If ya want ta do a concert, then go, but da numba of concerts will need ta change with our new roles, and I cannie say I'ma gonna want ya gone all da time."

"You're serious?"

"Aye. We'd also need ta take even more precautions when yer on da road, or Hunters and Factions will take advantage or try ta hurt ya." I reached for the soap, but Rook wrapped his arm around my waist before I got my hand on the little bar. I looked at him. His face was as serious as I'd ever seen.

Drawing me into his body, he stood silently and stared at me. I wasn't sure what was going on in his head as his eyes roamed my face. The only sounds were our mutual breathing and the water as it continued to spray down on us like heavy rain.

Rook placed his hand over my heart, and I glanced at it, then up into his eyes again.

"I know that I don't own this yet, but I want you to know that I do want us, no matter the shit I spew when I'm angry—and be warned, I spew a lot of crap. Also, if you ever tell anyone that I can be this sweet, I'll deny it and punch you in the mouth," Rook said.

I chuckled at that.

"I'm sorry for the pain I caused you with the rejection, and I'm sorry that the person you love is someone you can never have. I can't even imagine."

I looked away from Rook's gaze as the fuzzy feelings from what we'd just done waned slightly with the thought of Mari.

"Aye, Mari and me had always known dis day would come, and I'ma no' gonna be over her in a blink. I'ma jus bein' honest. But I've always looked forward to the day of me pairing." I placed my hand over his. "We may no 'ave gotten off ta da best start, but I tink deres hope."

I leaned in and kissed the lips that were calling to me. I was tempted to see if I could get my cock to stand again, but I realized he never told me how he'd ended up all bruised and dirty. Then I remembered he needed to talk to me.

"Ya gonna tell me now how ya got dis, or what ya were wantin' ta say earlier?" I asked, touching the bruise on his jaw.

"Oh, that. Yeah, about that." He rubbed the back of his neck, and I wasn't sure I would like what he said next with the look on his face. "I found our third, and she's kind of feral. She's the one that did this to my face."

I took a step back and smiled at the joke, but the smile slowly fell as I realized he was serious.

"I'm sorry. What did ya just say?" I tried to comprehend the words he'd spoken. I had a hundred questions and didn't even know which one to ask first.

"Yeah, I'm not sure why everyone kept saying it could take weeks or months to find her because she walked right up to me. Well, that's not exactly accurate. She attacked me and tried to kill me, but the point is, she found me," Rook said as he proceeded to wash his body.

I couldn't even form a sentence. Finding a third took time. It could take weeks or months. There had even been a few cases of it taking years. It was always the same. You needed to hunt around the island, searching for the covens that were well-hidden. If you were lucky, you might be allowed to enter for a fee to find your third. If not, you had to wait and track them down with a finder spell when they were outside the protection of the coven. The third was elusive, and they were not easy to find since the connection to a third was weak at best until the first union ritual and only solidified once the triad did the final ritual.

"How'd ya know she be our third?" I asked.

"Oh, I felt it when I yanked her hood off and looked into her eyes. I thought the word *mine*. I don't know. I just knew." Rook shrugged while I was reeling.

"Okay, back it up. Im'a gonna need a little more explainin' on all dis. How, when, where, all of it," I was flabbergasted that he was so relaxed. I also wondered why I couldn't feel her.

Rook shrugged again, then rinsed his hair. He had his back arched and eyes closed as the water beat down on his body. He was the picture of calm and relaxed, while I wanted to beat the information out of him.

"I was out for an early morning walk enjoying a smoke when she attacked me with a stick like the canne Mari uses. I thought it was Mari at first with the hood up. She's wild, though. I don't know if she even speaks English. She made no sense to me at all. The only word she was screaming I could understand was 'murder' as she tried to claw my eyes out."

"I asked ya if what ya needin' ta say was important. Ya didn't tink dis was important?"

Rook rolled his eyes at me. "She tried to kill me, and we were having a moment. She isn't going anywhere. So, no."

I pressed my lips together to stop myself from saying something sarcastic. I also couldn't help finding the humour that Rook was the only male from a triad in history who had found their third because she attacked him. At the moment, I didn't blame her.

"I'm scared ta ask now, but what room is she stayin' in, and did ya get a couple guards to mind da door?"

Rook handed me the soap as he rinsed off. "No need for guards. I spelled her to stop attacking me when she went for a knife, then brought her back here and put her in one of the dungeon cells. She's secure enough there."

"Ya did what?" My mouth fell open. "Did ya lose yer damn mind out in da forest? How are we gonna get her ta tink we're no threat when ya toss her in a cell?"

That at least explained why I couldn't feel her at all.

He shrugged again. "I don't know. I don't even know why she attacked me. Could be that we just got the crazy one. Besides, I got her here, which is supposed to be the hard part." He patted me on the shoulder and stepped out of the shower. "It's your turn now."

Son of a bitch.

Chapter 25

Elewyen

I heard voices before the outer door opened. Two male voices bickered, and by the tone, they weren't happy. They were probably arguing over who would have their way with me first. If they thought I was going down without a fight, they would find out quickly that wasn't going to happen.

"Enough. You two are impossible," a woman's voice yelled as the door opened, but no one stepped inside.

"Sorry, Mari, and tanks fir comin'. I jus tink after what dis donkey did, she is no gonna trust us as easy wit'out ya."

"Who are you calling a donkey?" the man who captured me responded. I'd recognize that voice anywhere.

"What did I just say about fighting? Seriously. If you two can't keep it together, go back upstairs and sort this shit out before walking in there or all you're going to do is scare her more."

There were a few moments of complete silence, and I wished I could see what was happening.

"Good. I'm glad to see we can all play nice in the same sandbox. Shall we?" the woman said.

A stunning raven-haired woman was the first to walk in. She wore an outfit, the likes of which I'd never seen. It was as black as her hair and molded to her body like skin. Her long hair was braided and hung over her shoulder, but it was her blue eyes that had me sitting straight. There was something very calm about her but also commanding. I'd never met a woman who had that sort of presence to her.

Then my eyes found the two men, and my heart sped up. Up close, they were unbelievably handsome, and they called to my body. I drew my feet on the bed and wrapped my arms around my bent knees. The sensation was faint until they were only a short distance away. Barry tucked himself in tighter to my neck, quiet, angry chatter coming from him.

"How did a rodent get in there?" The one with the bright blue eyes asked, and I caught enough to know that he was talking about Barry. "Do you guys not kill rodents in this place?"

"Naw, cuz yer be a feckin' cunt, an' ya froze 'im," I growled as I glared at him.

The girl smiled widely and looked at the guy with the blue eyes. "Oh, I like her. She's going to keep you in line."

I wanted nothing to do with any of them. I just wanted to go home to Keeva. Earlier, I tried to contact her with my necklace and panicked when the stone wouldn't warm. That was when I realized what they meant by this area was blocked from magic. It wasn't just the spell he had me under, but everything. It also meant that Keeva couldn't reach me, and if I didn't answer, she would worry and maybe try something she shouldn't. That thought scared me more than being captured and tortured to death.

"Do ya know why ya were brought 'ere," the new guy asked, his voice softer than I expected for his size and rugged look. The dark ink on his neck and arms, and his strange hairstyle, made him look dangerous.

I looked him over and couldn't deny he was appealing. The weird sensation I felt in my gut when I first saw them at the village kept trying to kindle but would just as quickly snuff out. Settling on eyes that reminded me of storm clouds, I answered.

"Naw, I'z dinnie nowhat yer wantin'. But it cannie be anytin' ta me likin'."

Arms crossed over his chest. He gave off a calm vibe, while the other felt like a wild animal barely contained.

"We're no' gonna hurt ya," he said.

"Ya'za got a funny way o' showin' it."

"Yeah, my cousin here is not exactly the best with manners," the pretty woman said.

She stepped up to the door, and the lock clicked open. I wanted to bolt, to try to escape, but I needed to be smart. Charging them wasn't wise.

"She was hitting me with a stick and then tried to stab me in the face. I think I was justified in locking her ass up," the blue-eyed one said, and I glared at him.

He pointed at me and gestured with his hands enough that I knew what he was saying. It wasn't that he was speaking a different language. I just never heard anything like the way he spoke.

"Ya deserve it," I said and made a spitting action on the ground. "Murdarar."

"See," he said and held out his hand toward me. "She keeps saying that, and I have no idea why."

The pretty woman stepped into the small space and squatted so I wasn't staring up at her.

"Howza we start wit dis," she said, with the same accent I was used to. I sat up a little straighter. "Me name be Mari. Dat be ma family. He be Rook. And dis..." She gestured toward the quieter one with the stormy eyes. "Dat be Rhys. We are no' gonna hurt ya," she said softly.

I stared into her eyes and wanted to believe her. It couldn't be magic, but I felt like I could trust her where I couldn't trust the men.

"Wha'z yer name?" Mari asked.

I was tempted not to tell them, but what did it matter at this point? And I wondered why, if they were planning on sacrificing me, they bothered to get my name.

"Elewyen, an' dis be Barry," I answered, pointing to my companion.

"Barry. She named the rodent?" Rook said, and I wished that I had something to throw at his pretty face.

"I dinnie tink yer helpin'," Rhys said as he glared at Rook.

There was a unique tension between them that I didn't understand. The energy floating around them was bizarre and left me with a confused taste in my mouth.

Mari opened a tiny sack that I hadn't noticed, and I pushed as far away as I could. She smiled at me, and it was soft and warm.

"Me told ya, we mean ya no harm, no matta wha' ya been taught. Me likes da name Barry. It be a good name. May I?" She opened her hand and showed a handful of assorted seeds and nuts. "It no' be much. Just some leftover from a snack, but if he be hungry, he can 'ave it."

The little traitor jumped off my shoulder and scampered across the uncomfortable bed until he sat close to where Mari squatted. I watched her closely to see if she was going to try anything, but she slowly leaned over and dropped the offering in front of Barry.

"Yer a food trollop, Barry. Ya would sell yer wee soul fir a nut," I grumbled at my companion.

Rhys stepped into my small space, and it suddenly felt smaller. "I'ma sorry, Elewyen, dat dis be how we met. I'ma wantin' ta get ta know ya betta and explain tings, but I really be needin' ta know somethin'. Can ya tell me why ya tink Rook be a murderer?" Rhys asked.

Rhys nodded toward Mari, and she stood and backed out. I didn't want her to go. There was something about Rhys that made me antsy, and I couldn't sit still. He crouched and leaned against the wall.

Of all the things I thought they would do with me, sitting and talking was not one of them. He smelled fresh, like my mint herbs, and a strong manly scent, like an oak tree, was making my head swoon. Both men were unnerving to my system but in completely different ways. I would've put more space between us if I weren't already in the farthest corner.

"Dinnie be tryin' ta pretend ya din't know wha I'ma talkin' about. I saw ya," Rhys's face scrunched in what seemed genuine confusion. "Da village by da cliffs."

"Does she mean when the two of you went to check on the village?" Mari asked Rhys.

"Aye, I tink she does." Rhys turned his attention to me. "Da ya mean the village dat was all burned ta da ground, people an all?"

"Aye,"

"Naw, we no burn da village," Rhys said.

"Naw, ya lie. Me saw ya. Furder down da road, in a car jus like ya left wit. The place were ablaze, and all da people screamin'.""

Rhys's face darkened. "Anotha?" He ran his hand through his hair and stood. "Dis is no good. Why am I no hearin' about any of dis? Where be da scouts dat keep an eye on all the happenin's?"

Mari shrugged. "I dinnie know. Da has no said anythin' ta me."

"I din't tink he knows. He woulda said if he did, but dat means da scouts either be dead, or they be turn coats. Neither be a good situation," Rhys said.

I watched the two of them interact. There was something in the stares that said they fancied one another. Rook didn't seem to like it. He was casually leaning on the bars, but his gaze was fixed on the other two like one would watch a small child.

"Do ya know what direction from da first village ya travelled?" Rhys asked, his attention returning to me.

I sat a little straighter. "Me could showz ya."

Rhys smiled, and it was warm, like sitting by a crackling fire while you were wrapped up in a thick cloak.

"I'ma sorry, but ya cannie leave until ya know why Rook brought ya here, an why it is dat yer drawn ta us. Ya can try an' deny it, but ya felt something. Dat be why ya tracked us down." He motioned his hand between himself, Rook, and me. "Ya did come searchin, ya?"

I swallowed the lump in my throat. He knew more about what happened to me than I knew myself. "Aye, me was searchin' for da source of da sadness and pain." I rubbed over my heart, and Rhys's face filled with concern.

I couldn't deny it, even if I wanted to keep that information to myself. The sensation had disappeared from being in this room, but it had been pain I followed that led me straight to Rook like a beacon.

There was some sort of magic involved, and if I had any hope of getting out of this, I needed to understand.

Rhys opened the door and stepped out, locking it behind him. I had this strange urge to ask him not to leave. His presence was peaceful, while Rook tied my stomach in knots.

"Da village be to da side of da settin' sun and a half day walk from da otha village."

"Tank ya, Elewyen. Mari, will ya come wit me to see if we cannie find da village she be mentionin'?"

Mari's eyes lit up the moment he addressed her. "Of course."

I wasn't sure I liked that. There was no reason not to like it, but again, the weird aura they had was doing things to my mind.

"What am I supposed to do?" Rook asked. He looked the same kind of angry as when I attacked him. "I should be coming with you instead."

Rhys shook his head at Rook before looking at me. "Elewyen, I be sorry, but I'ma gonna go for now. I need ta find the village ya mentioned. I swear ta ya dat we didn' burn it down." He pointed at Rook with his thumb. "Neitha did he. I'ma gonna leave 'im here wit ya. I tink ya be needin' ta have a wee chat."

"What? Did you not hear me say she tried to stab me in the face with a knife?" He crossed his arms over his chest.

I only caught every third word or so that he said. His accent was thick and fast. I lived here my whole life. Were there lots more people out there? Did they all dress and talk like him? Were there more metal birds? And what else did they have that was different from here? I knew it was dangerous, but I couldn't help the little bubble of excitement at learning something new.

"Can I speak ta ya out in da hall fir a moment?" Rhys asked.

He walked out with Mari close behind. Rook muttered something under his breath before he followed them out and closed the door. I was once more alone except for Barry, who happily cleaned up the last of the nuts and seeds.

"Ya sav any fir me?" I asked.

Barry looked up at me with his big, dark eyes, and his nose twitched as he looked between the spot where the seeds had been and then back up at me.

"Dinne be given me dat look. Ya know where da nuts wen'."

Barry climbed onto my shoulder just as the door opened, and Rook came back in alone. Whatever was said calmed him some. He didn't look so angry. Gripping the bars, he stared in at me.

"Ya scared of a wee lass?" I asked, mocking him.

"Scared? Try annoyed. You didn't have a clue who I was or if I'd hurt those people, and yet, you were trying to take my life. How does that make you any better than those who killed the people in the village?"

I just blinked at him, not certain what he was saying. But enough that he was upset at me for thinking he hurt the villagers.

It hurt my pride to admit, but I didn't think it was them either now that I had met them. People who could callously burn down a whole village had to be powerful, like these two, but they also didn't care about life. I didn't get that sense from these men. Maybe my powers were depleted to useless in this room, but I didn't need them to see the hurt and anger in Rook's eyes now or the shock Rhys got when I told him that I thought it was him.

"I'ma sowwy dat me tried ta stab ya in da face," I said.

This time, Rook stared at me, his stunning blue eyes blinking. I shook my head as I realized that he understood me about as well as I understood him. Well, wasn't this fun? The two that didn't understand one another trying to communicate.

"I think you said sorry. I'm not sure," Rook said and then mumbled something I didn't understand under his breath.

"Ya be angry at dem or me?" I asked.

Rook sighed, crossing his arms over his chest, and my eyes wandered over his tall form. He made me warm in this dank room, and I suddenly felt like I was wearing too much under my cloak.

"Neither."

"Ya be actin' like ya are."

He rubbed at his eyes. "I know I am. Look, I really don't want to stand down here in this stank. If I let you out, will you behave until we get a chance to talk?"

I was pretty sure he wanted to let me out to talk, so I nodded and slowly stood from the bed. Anything that got me out of this room that felt like death and gave me my powers back was a good thing. The door made a heavy clanging noise as Rook unlocked it and pulled it open.

"Cannie 'ave me stuff?"

"By stuff, if you mean your weapons, then no. Do I look like I was born yesterday?"

"What do beenz born yezterdayz 'ave ta do wit' me stuff?"

Rook shook his head. "I have no fucking clue what you just said to me."

Sighing, I walked towards him and stared up into his eyes. "Me dinnie know what yer sayin ta me," I answered.

He smacked his hand over his face before he stepped back out of the way. "Fucking Rhys and his fucking bright ideas. Never mind. Follow me." He motioned for me to walk behind him.

Rook had shown great skill out in the forest, but if he was a warrior, he didn't show it now. If I'd meant to kill him, I could've jumped on his back and done just that. The idea crossed my mind but left just as quickly. As much as I wanted out of this place, I only hurt those who were out to hurt me or other innocent lives. My gut screamed that these two didn't hurt anyone who didn't deserve it.

He opened the thick door and stepped out into the hall. There was a buzz in the air that I could feel, and I knew this was the only opportunity there would be to escape. Picking the spell in my head, I stepped over the threshold and sucked in a deep breath as my abilities filled me. There was no feeling to describe having your powers stripped away like that, even for a short time.

Rook stepped away from the door and snapped his fingers to close it rather than turning his back to me like I'd hoped for. Forced to improvise, I threw my arms out in his direction.

"Gaoth," I yelled and hit him with the spell.

He flew back and slammed into the wall with a thud. I sucked in a sharp breath as an ache exploded in my back. Rook slid down and groaned, a small trickle of blood smeared on the rock. The pull I felt at the cliffs returned, and it staggered me. I gripped my stomach and looked down to see if I could find what was making me feel this way. The air shimmered, and my body began to shiver.

What in the manner of all spirits was this magic? And why had it attached itself to me? I needed to get away from him and this magic as fast as possible. Yet the pained look on his face as he slouched over hurt my heart. I was torn, wanting to run, but needing to stop to see if Rook was all right.

Dinnie be a donkey. Run! Run now!

Clenching my teeth, I ran up the stairs, my feet echoing in the hallway. This place was a maze, but I managed to weave my way out by paying attention to the statues and unique decorations I'd seen.

"Dammit, Elewyen." Rook's angry voice growled out of the lower hallway like a monster coming from the darkest depths.

My stomach clenched tight. That sound made me want to run to the door and run to the man. My mind was warring with the emotions bombarding me. It was fear for Keeva that won out. Picking up my tunic so I didn't trip, I ran for the final hallway and the door that led out of this place.

Rook's feet were getting louder, and a strange thrill raced down my spine at the thought of him chasing me. It was too inviting of an image. I wasn't sure what he would do once he caught me but seeing what was under that black top of his was suddenly very intriguing.

Stop it. I scolded and sprinted harder.

Looking over my shoulder, I caught sight of Rook skidding around the last turn. He was a lot faster than I'd given him credit for. My hand got within inches of grabbing the door handle when I slammed into a spell blocking the way. A shriek tore from my mouth as my body was thrown backwards and sent somersaulting, ass over tea kettle.

Lying there, face down on the cool stone, I opened my eyes to find Rook's black boots before me.

"Looks like Rhys thought you might make a break for it. Apparently, I'm the stupid and trusting one."

With a moan, I tried to push myself up, but Rook hit me with the same spell as this morning. My body froze like a piece of wood in the winter, and other than my eyelashes and lungs, I couldn't move a single body part.

"I get it. You don't want to be here. Guess what? We had that in common. I would've run for the nearest hill when I first got here. What is it with you trying to kill me?" He dabbed at the back of his head again, and his fingers came away red. If he was going to kill me, he certainly had a reason. Guilt gripped my throat so tightly that if it weren't for the spell, I would've cried out.

"Elewyen, you do realize you could've killed me? Doesn't matter. I'm letting Rhys deal with your bullshit for tonight."

He bent down and hefted me up. Then picked Barry up with two fingers.

"You really like this ugly little thing?"

"Doonnnaaa yeeeee 'uuuurrrtt 'immm," I tried to say, but Rook rolled his eyes at me.

"If I didn't understand you before, what makes you think I'd have a fucking clue what you just said to me now?" He marched back the way we came, and my heart fell thinking about spending the night in that dark and disgusting room.

When we reached the hall to go down, he continued past until he got to a set of stairs that went up instead. I was happy no one from my coven could see this. It was humiliating to be handled like a sack of food by a man, even one as sexy as him.

It felt like forever before we reached a door that led to massive sleeping quarters. My heart hammered like a woodpecker inside my chest. Is this where he would decide to take what he wanted from me?

He walked through another door, put me on my feet, and leaned me against the wall like a stiff board.

"This is my bathroom. Let's just say you need a fucking bath. So this is what I'm going to do." He pointed to the taps on the wall. "That one is hot, and that one is cold. Soap, shampoo, and conditioner. Use what you want, but you're not coming out of this room until Rhys and Mari get back."

He placed Barry on a strange table and made his way back to me. He moved some loose hair out of my eye and stared at me.

"I really hoped we would get along this time around, but it seems you want to do this the hard way." He cracked his neck and gripped my jaw as he leaned close to my face. "Don't make me become the bad guy, Elewyen. I don't want to be, but I will."

This close to my nose, I could smell him clearly. He reminded me of the forest during a heavy rain on a stormy night, making me want to inhale deeply. Even unable to fully understand what he was saying, I caught the meaning, and my body lit up as surely as if I'd burst into flames.

Stepping away from me, he released the spell a moment before he closed the door. I heard him speak a word, erecting a magical barrier from the opposite side.

Well, shite. One dank cage for a prettier smelling one.

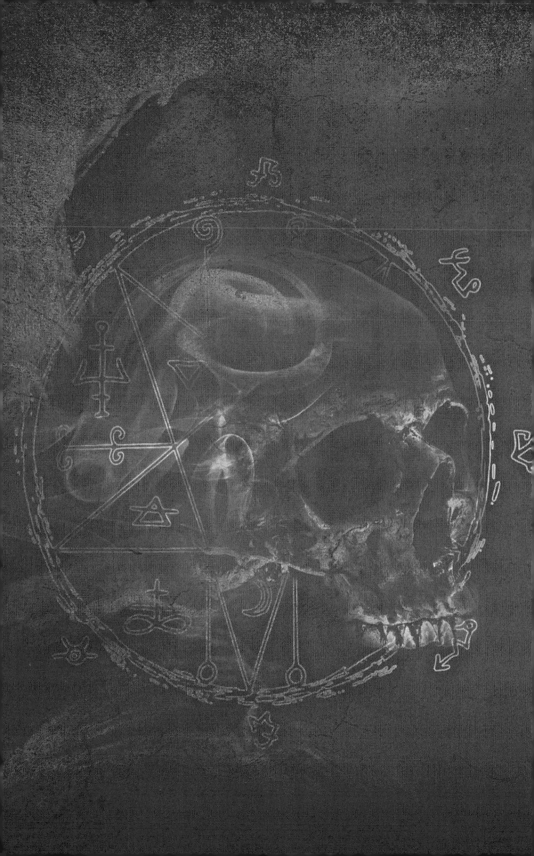

Chapter 26

Rhys

My head was swimming. Everything was happening so fast. I'm not sure what I thought would happen, but I quickly realized that Rook coming to the island less than a week ago had initiated a cascade of events. It was as if the world turned upside down and shook me until I couldn't think straight.

Rook was seeping into my pores, and a part of me loved it, but another part of me was terrified to let him in that close. Mari and I had this magical evening, and I was just coming to terms with what that meant when *wham*, now our third, had found us. That had never happened that fast before. Was the universe rushing this for some reason that I couldn't see or understand? Was it simply coincidence that had drawn Elewyen to us? She said she felt pain and sadness. Could she have felt what Mari and I did as surely as Rook? If so, I felt like an ass and hated that I'd done that to her. Rook offered himself, but Elewyen was an innocent bystander, and I put her through agony all night long.

I rubbed my eyes. I thought I was mentally and emotionally prepared for all this, but now I wasn't so sure.

Glancing over at Mari in the passenger seat, I could tell something was off. She was way too quiet and not her normal bubbly self. She sat there like the dead staring straight ahead, her face blank of all emotion. I hated that after everything we confided in each other last night, it felt like a cavernous wedge had come between us.

"I feel ya staring at me," she said and turned her head to meet my gaze.

"I be at a loss fir what ta say, but wanna say somethin'," I confessed, running my hand through my hair. The sides of my faux hawk were getting a little too long, and I needed to get them cut soon.

"Rhys, there's nothing to say. We knew all along that this was going to happen. Last night was like a gourmet meal, a once-in-a-lifetime thing. There is no looking back, no hoping that there will be a different outcome. We have to live in the moment. Your third has been chosen and is currently sitting in a cell. You don't get any more real than that."

Putting her elbow on the door frame, she leaned her head into her hand. I wanted to touch her, to comfort her, or maybe myself. It was difficult to wade through the emotions.

"Besides, we talked this all through, and we both know where we stand. I know you want to make everything all better. It is who you are to want to try, but there is no way to make this better. There is no way to incorporate me into the equation. You need to stop trying to work the problem and focus on all the other things going on.

Rook and now Elewyen are at the top of that list, then there's the island and asserting your authority as the head of the McGregor house."

Her eyes flicked to mine. "And changing these stupid laws that suppress the Faction women. It may seem unfair to put that on you, but you're one of the few who feel as strongly as the women do that it is wrong. Not just me, but dozens now and hundreds in the future are depending on your help."

"Aye, I know," I said.

We raced along the winding road, hitting puddles and spraying water from the earlier rain into the air. The sky was still a dark grey and promised more of the same blinding rain and angry thunder before the day was done.

"Do you think you can eventually love him?"

I didn't want to answer that question, but we'd always been honest with one another, and lying to her felt wrong.

"Aye, I do. Da attraction is strong, and I do like him. Over time, I know it will turn into more than simply physical pull. The pain that he created is startin' ta subside wit him here," I said, my hands tightened on the wheel. "Dat does no' mean dat my feelin's fir ya will turn ta dust."

"No. Dust is good. My hope is that you will fall madly in love with the two of them and forget about me completely."

"Is it?"

Mari looked over and shrugged. "I'm not saying this to be a martyr. I truly want it to happen. You should be happy, but I also know that with you as a head member of the council, the Faction will shift and become better. The spirits see it. That's why they paired you and Rook together. I don't know enough about Elewyen yet, but I'm sure she is perfect for you two as well."

"Where is dis comin' from, Mari? Ya've seen somethin', haven't ya?"

She looked away from my eyes, and a trickle of fear travelled down my spine.

"Tell me what ya saw."

"No. What I've seen is for my mind alone, and the rest has yet to be seen. To adjust course based on bits and pieces of a vision is dangerous. Just trust me when I tell you that you're on the right path. We are both on the path we need to be on."

"Forgive me if I continue ta worry. When ya get all cagey like dis, me mind conjures far worse tings than what's da truth."

"Okay, I will tell you this. Rook is strong, and despite his arrogant and argumentative nature, he has a good heart, but he's unguided. He's been allowed to live as a Flitter who just happens to know magic exists. That's dangerous, Rhys. It's the one thing that truly worries me about this union for you. Will he put the entire Faction at risk with his own selfishness?" She rolled her shoulder and winced. I stared at her but whatever was bothering her seemed to disappear in an instant.

"From the moment I met my cousin, I thought him an equal match in all ways, but his heart doesn't align with the Faction and those he's supposed to protect. That also means you and now Elewyen. I've seen both roads in your future, Rhys. The one where your triad is strong and the three of ya stand side by side together. I've also seen one where Rook is not around because he couldn't handle this life. Both of those versions live inside of Rook, and as the number two, it is your job to make sure he decides not to bolt."

"Yer not speakin' anythin' dat I 'ave no' already thought meself. I see both sides ta him starin' back at me from his eyes."

Mari suddenly sat straight and pointed toward a side road. "Over there. Look. There is still a thin stream of smoke behind the trees."

I steered the car on to the side road, and it didn't take long to find the next turn. We pulled up to a smoking village much like the other had been. Everything was charred and turned to ash.

"What in the spirits?" Mari said, her eyes wide as the car came to a stop. "Who would do this, and why?"

"I dinnie know." Pushing open the door, I stepped out, and Mari followed.

"You don't think this is the Hunters, do you?" Mari asked, looking around, and I knew she was assessing for any threats.

"I dinnie know. It's no' their style ta kill Flitters. They be Flitters and all for dose without magic but anythin' is possible when yer tryin' ta start a revolution. Me feelin' is that this be another Faction."

As I knelt among those who had died, it was clear that this couldn't have been the work of Hunters or even a random arsonist. The flames had burned too hot and travelled at unimaginable speeds. Magic had set this fire. There was no other way to kill this many people all in one go without them all trapped in a building or two.

Smoking posts remained where some villagers had been tied up as sacrifices. Kill the few to use the power of the sacrifice to kill the many. I hadn't seen this level of cruelty before, but I'd read about it in the books of war in the library. This had Faction One all over it. They were the Faction that controlled the elements. But why now? Why this, and why us?

"Oh shit! Rhys, look," Mari said, breaking me of my thoughts.

My eyes followed where she was pointing. As soon as I spotted the smoldering fields, my heart sank.

"We need ta go and check somethin', but I'ma prayin' dat I'm wrong."

We jogged back to the car. The worry that had begun to gnaw at my gut now sat heavy like a rock. Pulling away from the village, I whipped onto the road and flew toward the other end of the island. My eyes darting to all the driveways and roads where hunters like to hide.

"Where are we going?" Mari asked.

"Ta da grove," I said, and Mari's eyes grew wide. The colour drained from her face, and I knew she was now thinking the same thing I was.

The drive took two hours, and as soon as we got close, my fears were confirmed. Large farms had been burned to the ground until there was nothing but charred remains. All the fields that had been filled with harvest were devastated by scorched earth as far as the eye could see. Everything from wheat and corn to potatoes was laid to waste. The fires were long dead. Not even a tendril of smoke remained. It looked like a dark demon had walked upon the earth, and the earth had died in its wake.

Our Faction didn't pray to the darkness, although the few villagers who knew of our power thought so, and we never corrected them. The fact that our abilities were directly linked to death and spirits made explaining the difference near impossible. We were born of the shadow spirits and powered by the souls of our ancestors who had passed on. All the rules and pairings came from the voices on the other side. Since the Factions were born, this was how it had been.

"Oh, dear spirits," Mari whispered as we drove slowly alongside the carnage. "No wonder the hunters have been so aggressive lately. They think we did this."

"Aye, ta bad they dinnie aim their anger in da right direction. If they took a moment ta tink about it, it makes no sense for us ta burn our own people and food supply," I said.

We travelled in silence, looking and hoping that there would be at least one crop spared. There was nothing, and I was sure that if I pulled up to the villages, we would find more death. How many had already lost their lives to this greed? That was what this was, of that, I had no doubt. Someone was aimin' ta try to take over and wanted us weak and ripe for the pickin'.

Having seen enough, I did a U-turn and drove back to Injebreck.

"Shite, Mari, dis is bad."

Mari gripped my shoulder. "Don't stress. You'll get something figured out, and the Kelly's have boats. If we need to bring food from the mainland, we will."

I gave her hand a pat and was saddened and relieved when she moved it. "Aye, but what about the villagers? We can't just let the people left livin' on the island die."

"I don't have an answer for that, but you'll think of something. You always do," she said.

I'd never been more thankful for the triad and the power we were going to need for what I feared to come. I glanced over at Mari, and my heart ached in my chest. Unable to help myself, I reached out and grabbed her hand, wanting the support we always shared.

Mari pulled her hand away from my touch. "Rhys, please…." She shook her head and looked away. "We need draw new lines and boundaries. It is too dangerous and not fair to lean on one another like this."

I placed my hand on the steering wheel and squeezed hard. It was as though she was on a separate island and was slowly floating away. I desperately wanted to hang on tighter, but the door to friendship seemed to be narrowing.

"I'ma sorry, Mari. I—Holy shit!"

Four children ran out of the ditch in front of the car. Their terrified faces had my hands moving quick as they grabbed one another in a huddle. It was only by the grace of the spirits that I managed to avoid running them over and kept the car on the road. Slamming on the brakes, I looked in the rear-view mirror at the smoke-stained cheeks and torn clothes as they held one another and knew that even though I should, I couldn't leave them.

Mari and I looked at one another at the same time. We didn't have to say a word as we pushed open the car doors.

Chapter 27

Rook

My fingers lazily strummed the strings of my guitar, but even that couldn't calm the building frustration. Elewyen had finally stopped yelling at me to let her out, so that was a bonus. Did I feel a little bit bad about leaving her in the washroom? Maybe. But I wasn't letting the conniving redheaded witch out until Rhys was back.

I was starting to wonder why I decided to stay and make this work. I mean, the morning with Rhys had been incredible, mind-blowing even, but did I really think that I could change my habits enough to help run a Faction? Run the very thing I hated? Do paperwork that I hated? Sit in on political meetings and negotiations with other Factions? Maybe if Rhys took the lead, he seemed to like it. It was the number one's right to delegate, wasn't it?

More than that, I felt a brief ache in my chest, and I hadn't been able to focus on anything other than Rhys and Mari and what they were doing or discussing. Were they making plans to run off? Or maybe now that Elewyen was here, they would take the opportunity to mask their dash and were already gone. Why was I thinking like this? I wasn't an insecure person, and yet here I was, worrying.

Laying the guitar down, I picked up my cell and stared at the time. They'd been gone almost four hours. What the hell could be taking them so long?

"This is crazy," I mumbled as I stood from the bed and looked out the window that faced the front of the castle. The guards could barely be seen between the darkening sky and the line of trees that they skulked around. There was something off about the guards. I never saw them come or go into the castle. They all had a similar look and hadn't said a word to me since my arrival. They creeped me the fuck out.

I looked at the high walls and windows of the castle and wondered what it would be like to take over as the head of the family. Not that I wanted the gig. My father was welcome to it for another hundred years if he wanted it. But knowing that this place was mine, and then my kids….

"Kids? Where the fuck did that thought come from?" I grumbled.

I shook my head and turned at the sound of the door handle. I hated that I was so excited for Rhys to return. I'd never been the type who got excited to see a partner. They were supposed to be excited to see me, not the other way around.

"Naw, Mari, I have ta do it on me own," Rhys was saying as the door opened. He paused when he saw me.

There was a blast of immense pleasure and satisfaction in my chest that warmed my body all over as I stared into those silver eyes.

"Shite," Rhys swore. "I'ma dolt. I keep forgettin' this is no' me room anymore," Rhys turned to leave.

"Whoa, wait up a minute. What the hell happened out there? And you need to deal with Elewyen. I'm not going anywhere near her again until she's more...civilized, or at least stops trying to kill me," I snarled, annoyed that once again, Rhys seemed completely unaffected by me, and here I was pining over him.

"What do ya mean, she tried ta kill ya again?"

"I tried the talking thing, and she agreed she would behave if I let her out, so we didn't have to sit in the cell. Then, as soon as we walked out the door, she hit me with a spell. I have a fucking lump on the back of my head from hitting it so hard against the wall." I pointed to the ice pack I'd been using. "She's dangerous."

Rhys lifted a brow at me, and I squirmed. "I tink we all be dangerous. So what did ya do wit her?"

"She's in the bathroom, and I sealed the door," I said, pointing to the large wooden door.

Both Rhys and Mari looked in that direction.

Rhys stepped into the room. "I'ma sorry. Did ya just say ya locked her in the loo? Lockin' her up in da dungeon wasn't bad enough, ya had to lock her in da loo too?" Rhys ran his hand through his sexy faux hawk.

"What else was I supposed to do with her? I tried to be nice. What she did was a total bitch move. Then she took off for the door and left me for dead. Some number three. What is it with all of you that you hate me, anyway?" I smiled widely.

"But I loved the barrier you put in place. She landed on her ass real good when she hit that." My smile faded as Rhys continued to stare. "What? I had to do something with her."

"Did ya, by chance, offer her a meal or some clean clothes, maybe?

309

Did ya even try ta explain what be goin' on and the triad like I asked you to?"

My back bristled with annoyance. How was it that he managed to make me feel like an idiot without calling me one? I wasn't sure which was worse, my father, who outright said I was an idiot, or Rhys, who just stared at me.

"Mari, I know dis is gonna be a big ask...." Rhys started, and I felt a growl form in my throat as Mari reached out and grabbed his arm. A shot of heat shot through me, and my chest tingled.

"Yes, I can take care of her and will make sure she's still here for you to talk to when you get back, but you better get going," Mari said.

It wasn't what they said or even how they said it. It was the way Rhys immediately turned to her for help and how she readily accepted. They had this connection that allowed them to communicate without saying a word. I never wanted anything more than to have a good fuck and leave, but this triad bullshit was turning me into a raving lunatic where Rhys was concerned. Luckily, that hadn't started yet with Elewyen, but I was pretty sure that the same thing was going to happen.

"Thank ya. I owe ya one," Rhys said.

Mari went to the bathroom door, and Rhys turned to me. "If ya want ta know what is goin' on, den ya need ta follow me."

Rhys turned and disappeared out the door. Oh, hell no. I was getting some answers.

"Hey, where are you going?" I called after Rhys.

He looked over his shoulder but kept walking. It felt like the first night I was here all over again. "I need ta go pack. If ya wanna talk, then yer gonna need ta walk faster."

"Where are you going now? You haven't even told me what

happened out there," I said. My long strides ate up the ground until I was walking beside him. "Did you find the village?"

"Aye, we found it. Then we went for a drive to see if me suspicions were right, and they were. Whoever is doin' this is tryin' to starve us and kill us off or turn all the villages against us. I was wonderin' why da hunters are so aggressive lately, and I now know. Dey tink we be settin' the fires and killin' all dose people, just like Elewyen thought."

"I don't understand. How can they starve us out?" I asked as Rhys pushed open the door to his room. Conversations would be a lot easier if we just stayed in the same damn room.

"They be burnin' all da fields. All da fall harvest has been destroyed, and by burnin' the villagers, dey are turnin' our own island against us," Rhys said as he walked into the closet. I leaned against the door frame and watched him pull out a duffel bag.

"Okay, that doesn't explain where you're going?" I crossed my arms over my chest, prepared to blockade the door until I got some fucking answers.

He bent over, and my eyes couldn't help wandering. Damn, he was sexy. It was messing with my head. Rhys needed to start wearing pants. The kilt's easy access was like an all-you-can-eat buffet full of your favourite dessert.

"Earth ta Rook. Did ya hear what me said?"

My eyes found Rhys's. He had stood up, but in my mind, he was bent over and screaming my name as I pounded into him.

"Say what?"

"Were you checkin' out me arse?"

I lifted a brow and made a huffing sound, but the bulge in my jeans told a totally different story. "Just tell me what you said again."

"I'm headin' ta Maughold castle ta talk wit the McCabes and the

McKinnons. I'm sure dat your cousin Lochlan will join the meetin'. Then I be headin' to Glentruan to make preparations fir us ta go there. We will be movin' ta me home castle when I get back in a couple days."

Rhys walked towards me, but I wouldn't get out of the way. "Can you just stop moving for a moment and talk to me? I feel like I'm just an afterthought here."

"Ya mean kinda how Elewyen musta felt bein' left in a loo?"

"Okay, that may not have been my finest hour, but she was being really violent. The woman stares at me like she wants to rip my cock off. No idea how you plan on getting her to agree to be our third, and, whoa, what do you mean we're moving?"

"Aye, I'ma sure she be wantin' ta do jus that, and I be positive dat yer charmin' nature had notin' ta do wit her bein aggressive," Rhys teased, the corner of his mouth curling up.

I poked Rhys in the chest. He looked at my finger, then at me, and smirked.

"I'm getting really sick of you talking down to me."

"First, I no be talkin' down ta ya. I kinda be talkin' around ya." My brow furrowed as I glared at him. "Okie, look, Rook. I'm sayin' dis 'cause I want us ta work, I really do, and because I genuinely like ya. But if ya wanna be treated like yer sittin' at da big boy table, then ya need act like it."

My jaw clenched, and my hand balled into a fist with the insult.

"Lockin' our third in a loo while ya do whateva fir hours is no' productive nor helpful. In fact, it be da complete opposite."

"Why her?"

"Wa are ya talkin' about now?"

"Why did you take Mari and not me out there?"

Rhys sighed and shook his head. "Ya be wantin' da truth?"

312

"Yes, I think I deserve to know why you so easily shoved me to the side when we are supposed to be... whatever we're supposed to be."

"First ting, Elewyen needs ta connect, right? Dat has ta be da priority movin' forward. She no goin' ta be like us. Da third is more complicated ta bring in ta da connection. She'll feel da pull, but until she be emotionally invested, and the union ritual is complete, the connection with her will remain unstable."

"Well, yes, I get that, but...."

"But what? Yer da number one, are ya no'? Yer da one dat is supposed ta be pullin' us all togetha. Despite ya spoutin' off, sayin' yer wantin' me ta deal wit' her, it is no' me dat she needs ta feel connected to. Dat is part of da responsibility of da number one."

I rubbed the back of my neck.

"The second reason is ya still dinnie know how ta fight. Knowin' dat I may run in ta trouble, why would I be takin' ya over Mari when Mari is a trained fighter and assassin?"

He stood there staring at me, and I suddenly hated myself for not being more active in the Faction. He was right. I was useless and more concerned about him and Mari alone than I had been about my third. They were my responsibility, and Rhys was still having to act like the number one.

"Now, I 'ave tings ta do ta make sure dat our arses din't starve over da winter. So, now ya know, and ya know where I be goin'. So cannie please git out of me fuckin' way?" He went to step around me, but I stepped in his way again.

"I should be going with you. You said that I need to learn to take charge. I should be going with you and taking part if this is so important."

"Naw, I need ya ta stay here," Rhys said.

"Let me rephrase that. I am coming with you."

"Naw, ya ain't. I'ma no' takin' you," Rhys's tone had shifted, and so had the air in the closet. Anger was brewing under his calm expression. I could tell he was getting annoyed, and why that made me happy and turned on was beyond me.

"Why the fuck not? If I'm in this thing, then you need to start acting like it. We can connect with Elewyen together when we get back."

Rhys dropped his duffel and had me up against the wall, kissing me before my brain registered that he'd moved.

The sparks were instant, and the confusion swirling in my chest evaporated, only to be replaced with a hunger that only he could tame. Everything from the hair on my head to the cock between my legs stood to attention as Rhys pressed his body up against mine. I groaned and grabbed his ass, loving how the kilt balled up as I gripped him harder, and his hard muscles flexed under my touch.

Breaking the kiss, Rhys pulled back enough that he could talk, but his lips remained lightly touching mine, and he didn't pull out of my hold.

"I dinnie 'ave da time to be explainin' it all right now, but ask Mari, and she will fill ya in on what we found. I will fill ya in on everythin' else when I git back."

He nipped and sucked on my bottom lip, sending a shudder through my body. Fuck, he scrambled all the marbles in my head. Every logical thought decided to tap dance its way out the door. Rhys pressed his body closer, and I groaned. He kissed me again, and the last of the annoyance and confusion disappeared. Did he put a spell on me? Was it the connection, or was it simply that I wanted him that much?

"Fuck, I want you right now," I panted.

"I be wantin' ya, too, but what I'ma needin' from ya is fir ya ta stay here. I need ya ta try ta bond wit Elewyen and convince her dat she wants ta stay. Not locked up in a room, but as our third. There is naw point ta bringin' ya on dis trip, and I'ma only gonna be a day or two, tops. If ya wanna feel more included, go ta da library, and ask Mari what books ta read while I be gone."

Rhys moved his hips from side to side as he pressed against me, and my eyes closed as our cocks rubbed together. His lips travelled along my jaw until they reached the thumping pulse in my neck. I sucked in a ragged breath as his tongue swirled in a little circle before he sucked the sensitive spot that made me shudder all over.

"I'ma wantin' ta include ya in it all, Rook, but dis is how ya can best help us all. It be life and death important dat Elewyen decides ta stay. Be da number one. Find a way ta make her wanna be here."

His lips continued up my neck, and by the time he reached my ear, all I could picture was doing whatever he suggested as long as it ended with me dragging him to the ground.

"Rememba dat yer fuckin Rook Adair. No one can say no ta yer charm."

I knew he was placating me, but everything he said made perfect sense when he talked like this, and I nodded. Rhys groaned softly in my ear, and my breath caught in my throat as his hand gripped my hard shaft through my jeans.

"When I git back, I promise ta let ya punish me," he whispered.

The energy swirling around us rippled and pulsed. The thought of having him just like this, with his kilt on, flashed through my mind, along with tying him up and fucking him on the bed, or against the wall, or maybe bent over the couch. Fuck it. I was greedy. I wanted all the positions. I shivered with all the possibilities.

"Dear spirits, yer so fuckin' temptin', but I gotta go."

He kissed me again until my head swam, then grabbed his bag. He walked out, leaving me standing there stunned like he'd pulled off the world's greatest magic trick.

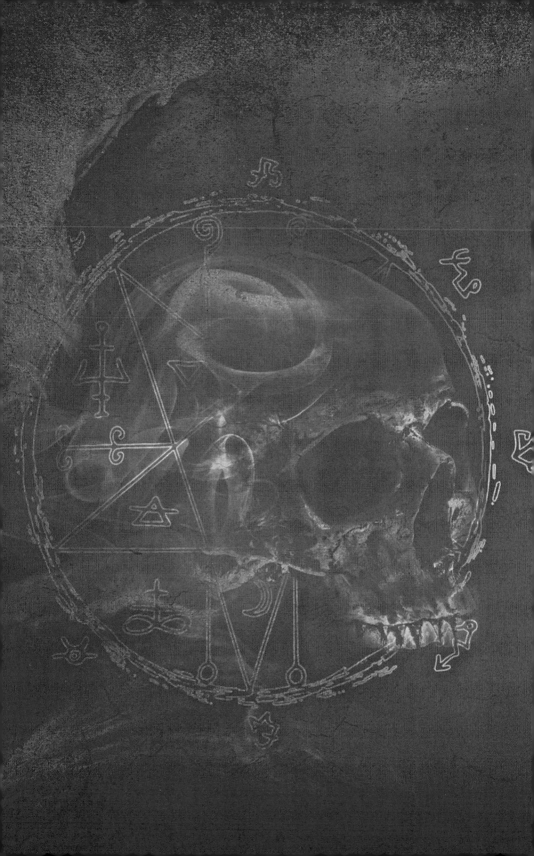

Chapter 28

Elewyen

I tried to figure a way out of this much prettier smelling dungeon, but with no success. I even tried yelling and screaming until I was short of breath, panting hard, and my throat was sore, but Rook never came back. Although, my spells worked, I had nothing that would help me get out of this room.

There was a large looking-glass over bowls that were built into a flat ledge. It was the first time I saw myself clearly in years. My face was covered in dirt, and my long hair was matted with bits of leaves and twigs from my fight with Rook. I undid the braid, running my fingers through the long strands of hair. Lifting my hand, I waved at myself while Barry was busy chattering at his own reflection like it would talk back.

"It no gonna chat back, Barry. It be only yer own self," I said.

His wee face turned up to mine, his red tail twitching from side to side before turning back to the looking glass and continuing to chat at it.

"Suit yer self." I rolled my eyes at the little squirrel.

Gripping my necklace, I thought of Keeva. My stone glowed in return, and I relaxed a little. Wandering over to the large window, I stared out at the gardens far below. It was too high to jump. I would break my legs from this height. Suddenly, I wished I could shift into one of the birds and fly away.

There was something magical about this place, and not because everything was grander than anything I'd ever seen. It was something else. The trees spoke their own language here, and the flowers had lived many generations. The large garden could've been a child's maze with so many different paths. There was a stunning woman with long red hair like mine, slowly walking around some roses. The dress she was wearing was simple and made of a pretty pale colour that reminded me of a bird's egg.

She looked towards the window, her eyes so blue that they seemed brighter than the sky itself. I shivered as she stared my way but didn't seem to see me as I raised my hand. Maybe she would help me. I got the sense that she was just as trapped as I was.

She tilted her head, and a slow smile spread across her lips as she tipped her head in a nod. Her eyes were sad like she'd just lost someone she loved, and my heart ached for her. I could feel her pain from up here. There was a tingling in my fingers, and I felt drawn to the mysterious woman.

Another girl with the same red hair and a tall man I hadn't seen on my arrival wandered toward the garden arm in arm. I didn't get the sense that they were lovers. The girl looked to be his daughter, maybe. They walked right past the woman with the dress without giving her a glance, even though she turned and looked at them. I wanted to yell, "how rude," but held my tongue as they knelt at a statue. A cool tendril gripped me as the woman approached the two kneeling figures. My mouth fell open as she stepped into the statue and disappeared.

My hand went to my mouth as I stared at the spot where the woman had vanished. I would've sworn she was a living, breathing person. I always knew that I was connected to those of the spirit world, more so than others in my coven. I heard the odd voice on the wind or whispered in my ear. Felt the cool breeze on a hot summer day across my neck, but to see someone from the other side was new, and it had happened twice in two days. Were my powers growing?

There was no way to gauge what I was feeling. Shock, confusion, and fear, it was all there, as well as excitement about the possibilities.

Stepping away from the window to give the two people privacy, I continued my exploration. Wandering to the far side, I poked at the shiny, oddly shaped objects like claws had sprouted out from the wall. They were made of metal and had spouts like a water well.

This was a strange spot indeed, and I couldn't figure out why, of all the rooms in this large castle, he had put me in this one.

I poked and touched everything. I picked up a stick with bristles like a very tiny hairbrush and rubbed the end with my finger, unclear what it would be used for. There was a bowl with colourful round balls, and I picked one up and sniffed it. It smelled like fruit, so I took a bite. The texture was all wrong, and then the sharp taste hit my tongue. Spitting, I wiped at my teeth and tongue with my finger, trying to get the taste off, but little chunks of the disgusting substance coated my mouth. There was a cup filled with what I hoped was water, and I took a swig of the substance and swished it around in my mouth before spitting it into the large bowl.

"Disgusting, blah." I shook my head and spat some more.

That was when I realized that the liquid had gone down the dark hole in the middle of the bowl.

"Wha' be dis magic?"

Stepping back, I looked at the front of the long surface and realized that the front looked like doors, but I wasn't opening them. You never knew what creatures they could be hiding inside.

Returning to my investigation, I picked up a bottle with golden liquid inside. I stared at it from every angle and gave it a little shake. Pulling up on the small silver top, I was shocked when the two sides separated.

It had a strong aroma. Placing my nose to the bottle, I gave it a sniff, then pulled my head away, shaking it with a sneeze. It smelled like...I wasn't sure what. Sort of like Rook but a lot stronger. A little bit of the liquid was dribbling out the top, and I stared at it, unable to decipher what they would use this for. Was it some magic potion? Did they drink it?

I gave the bottle a harder shake, and the top pushed in. Mist attacked me as it sprayed into the air. I started choking as droplets hit my face and stung my eyes. Tossing the bottle on the counter, I ran as far away as I could. Coughing from the intense stench trying to kill me, I banged on the rock wall and screamed for Rook to save me from the vial of poison he kept in here.

When no one came, I dove into the corner of the room and covered my face with my tunic. Barry, who'd lived through the attack as well, ran up under my tunic and began making little squirrel noises that I could only guess were sneezes. This was not a fun room, and it was filled with traps. I was terrified to touch anything else.

Wrapping my arms around my knees, with my tunic firmly in place over my nose and mouth, I waited to see if I was going to turn into a hideous creature or die in this position. I had no idea how long I sat there, but the sun had changed positions in the sky outside twice. My stomach growled, and I placed my head against the wall and closed my eyes, prepared to just go hungry, when I remembered I had half of a biscuit left. I grabbed for my bag, then swore as I remembered that Rook had taken that away, too.

"I'ma really wishin' ya shared ya nuts wit' me, Barry," I grumbled to the squirrel that was comfortably napping in my lap.

Then I heard noises in the outer room. I placed my ear against the rock wall to see if I could hear what was being said. It was too muffled, but there was more than one person talking, and my chest began to warm again. Looking down, I rubbed at the spot that was making me feel tingly. This spell needed to go away before it did something permanent to me.

When the door opened, I jumped to my feet, ready to fight whoever it was.

"Hi'za, Elewyen. Dinnie be hittin' me wit a spell or anythin'. I'ma no' here ta hurt ya," the female, Mari, from earlier said through a narrow crack in the door.

I didn't say anything, but I didn't move either, as her head poked around the corner. Her eyes were the exact same shade as the woman I'd seen in the garden. I sucked in a breath as I stared into those bright blue eyes that were intelligent and strong but warm with kindness.

"Cannie I be comin' in?" she asked slowly. I nodded.

Mari walked in, and she looked even more stunning than down in the dungeon's dim light. She wore the same black outfit that hugged her legs and black boots like what the guys wore on her feet. She looked like a warrior, with her hair pulled up high on her head and the leather straps that covered the tight shirt she was wearing.

"Would ya like me ta keep speakin' wit me accent so ya can understand me betta?"

Once more, I nodded, and she closed the door, laying her hand against the wood. I felt her power surge as a new barrier was put into place.

"Me dinnie understand what dey want wit' me. Me got nothin' ta offer, and I'ma sorry for attakin' Rook. But ya no' let me go," I said and crossed my arms over my chest.

Barry chose that moment to run down my body and across the floor toward Mari.

"Pleaz naw hurt 'im," I blurted as Barry leapt for Mari's boot.

Mari shocked me as she laughed and held her palm open. I watched in fascination as Barry ran up her body and down her arm to her open palm before sitting up and voicing his displeasure over being locked in this strange room without more food as an offering.

"Aye, I understand. Rook cannie be an arse," Mari said to Barry. "It be a good ting dat I stopped by da kitchen and reloaded me snacks."

She reached into the same black pouch as earlier and pulled out a small handful of food. Barry chatted excitedly, and Mari held her hand out towards the shelf with the stinky bottle for Barry to jump off, then placed the pile down. "It jus' be some sunflower seeds, nuts, an' dried fruits. We be callin' it a trail mix," she said, then smiled at me. "Barry be sweet."

"Aye. So ya 'ave a way wit da animals too," I said, daring to get closer to Mari.

"Aye, I do. It was me mother's gift ta me, and it has kept me from feelin' all alone many a night," Mari said and looked away from me to stare at Barry.

Even though her words were meant to be happy, her mouth made the same sad smile the woman from the garden had. Without asking, I knew that the woman was her mother.

Sometimes, I wished I knew who my mother was, but then dash the thoughts. If my parents left me in the forest to die, then they were people I never wanted to meet or call family. The one thing I knew for certain was that I raised myself with the animals until my coven took me in. My coven was my family, and those women were all my mothers and sisters. A happy warmth spread through my body at the thought of Azula and Keeva and the rest of the women.

"I know ya wanna go. I cannie see it in yer eyes dat ya wanna run for da hills and never look back, but we need ya ta stay, an' no' 'cause we plan on hurtin' ya." Mari sighed and leaned against the shelf that Barry was eating on. "'Ave ya heard of a triad?" I shook my head no. "There be too much ta be explainin', but I'ma gonna say dis. There be a lotta bad people dat are tryin' to hurt everyone dat lives on da island, as ya saw. Da ones dat burnt down da villages are attackin' many more and killin' off all da food dat was growin' in da fields. We be tryin' ta stop 'em, but ta stop 'em, we need ya ta stay."

"Wha' do me stayin' 'ave ta do wit da ones dat killed all da babes?"

Keeping a wary eye on the bottle on the counter, I took another tentative step towards Mari. I didn't feel threatened, and it was nice to speak to someone other than Barry.

"Let me ask ya dis. Do ya feel anything strange when ya see Rook and Rhys? Do ya feel a pull ta dem, like they mean somethin' to ya, but ya dinnie know why?" Mari asked.

I licked my lips. I wanted to yell yes and ask what the hell it was.

"Ya dinnie 'ave ta answer. I can see it in yer eyes dat ya know what me sayin'. Dat is the triad connection." She held up her hands and made a shape with her fingers that had three points. She turned to the shelf thing that Barry was on with a frown and pulled out another handful of seeds. Intrigued by what she was creating, I stepped close enough that I could see the shape she was making.

"Dis shape be called a triangle."

"Tree…aagale."

Mari smiled. "Tri-an-gle," she said.

I practiced it a few times until she nodded when I got it right. It felt amazing to learn something new, even if it seemed completely pointless.

"Dis seed be Rook." Mari held up a seed and placed it at the top point of the triangle. "Dis be Rhys." She repeated the process with another point. "And dis be ya, Elewyen." Mari held up the seed and placed it at the final point. "Da tree of ya together be what we call a triad of power. When yer together, yer strong." Mari closed her fist and held it up.

"But when yer apart…." She pushed all the seeds away from one another. "Yer weak. Dis power be what protects da island, and all dat live here. Dose wit power, dose without, and da animals." Mari stroked her finger along Barry's head, and he closed his eyes and rubbed against her finger. "Da ones dat are evil want ta kill all dat live here, includin' him and yer coven."

I searched her face to see if she was lying, but there was nothing about her that suggested that what she was saying was false.

"Wat ya gonna need me ta do if me stayed?" Mari blushed and looked down at her boots.

"Well, dat be da ting… Ya kinda need ta lay wit the guys," she said. "There be a ritual ta bind ya, so da power becomes one, and ya kinda need ta, you know…."

I squinted my eyes at her, not sure what me laying beside the guys, and a ritual was going to do.

Mari cleared her throat and looked me in the eye. "Ya need ta all 'ave sex, Elewyen. Da triad is formed when ya all open yerself up physically and emotionally ta become one." She held up her finger and entwined them together. "Tree becomes one power."

My mouth fell open. "Ohhh no. No, no, no. Dat no' be happenin' unless ya plan on forcin' me," I said, and my muscles tensed.

Mari shook her head no. "Aye, dey could, but Rhys and Rook no' da type. Ta make da union true and pure ya need ta consent, no' be forced. I know dis be a lot ta take in, an' dere be so much more ta explain ta ya. Can ya give us a few days? Learn all ya can, an' get ta know da guys before ya be makin' a decision?"

I chewed on my bottom lip as the idea of having sex clawed at my throat. The coven had insisted that men were not nice and that having intimate time with them would be painful because they would be cruel. That I'd become controlled by them, and from that time on, I would never be free. How could Mari, a fellow woman, ask this of me?

Mari held her open hand towards me. Barry stood up on the shelf and looked between us. I gave the wee squirrel a glance, and the fact that he trusted and liked Mari was the only reason I placed my hand in hers. Her skin was soft, and her hand warm as she gently gripped mine.

"A few days, dats all I ask before ya leave. All da lives on da island depends on it."

"Aye, I'ma stay for seven moons, but if I decide ta go…."

"Then ya can go a free woman. Dis is no' a place a torture." Mari smiled and feeling compelled to touch her. I pulled her into my embrace.

She let out a small whimper and winced in my hold. Jumping back, my hands went to my mouth.

"I no mean ta hurt ya," I said.

She shook her head and gave me a reassuring smile. "It no' be you. I hurt meself trainin', and me back is still sore. I'ma be okay. Now let's get ya cleaned up and start teachin' ya some new words," Mari said.

"Me love ta learn," I said happily, which made Mari smile, and I found myself following suit.

I had no idea what I was getting myself into or why it seemed like it was the right decision, but I would give them seven moons to convince me that this was what I wanted. In the meantime, I would map out the best way to escape if they didn't hold up their end of the bargain.

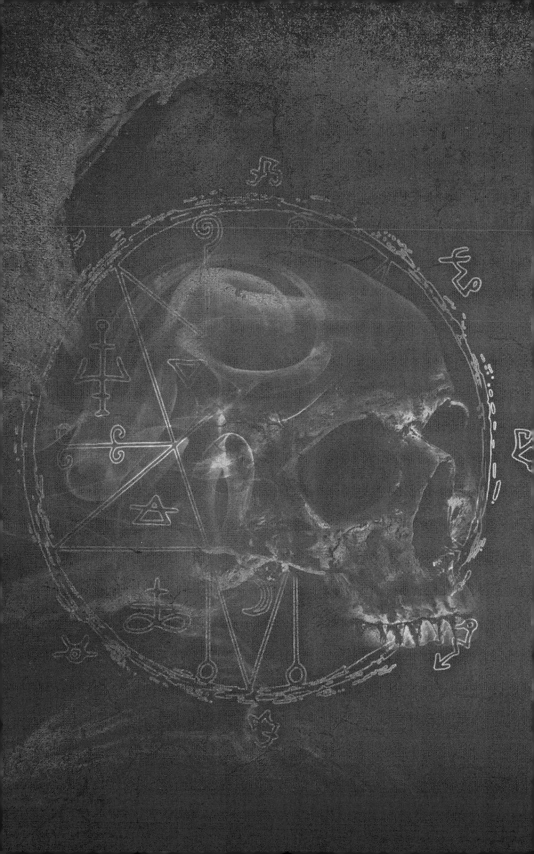

Chapter 29

Rook

Fuck Rhys. He messed with my head. I looked down at my cock, still picturing Rhys bent over in that kilt. Dammit! He made me want to do things I normally, emphatically, yelled no to. He had to have fucking magic in his touch.

My step faltered. Was he using magic on me other than the connection? I shook my head. No, that wasn't like him. In the short time we spent together, he seemed overly honest. Again, not my type, and yet here I was lusting after him like…I didn't even have words for what this felt like, but I knew Devlin, the fucker, would be laughing his ass off.

I wandered down the hall toward my bedroom and paused. A smirk pulled at the corner of my mouth. Rhys was going to find himself moved out of the other side of the castle when he got back.

"Liam," I called out tentatively. "Liam, you around?" I yelled a little louder.

It seemed bizarre to simply call out someone's name in the middle of a place like this and expect them to hear you, but there was some sort of spell. In a blink, the man was running down the hallway towards me.

Incredible. I wonder if I could put this spell on Rhys.

"Master Rook, how cannie I be of service ta ya?" Liam asked as he came to a panting stop a few feet away.

"Rhys said that we are going to be moving to Glentruan when he gets back. Where is that, and why would he want to move there?"

Liam tilted his head to the side. "Dat be Master Rhys's family castle. His uncle Rayland and cousins, Riegan and Ronan live dere. His cousin, Blaine, be overseas." Liam tapped his chin. "It not be dat far from here, an hour at most. It be right on da cliff edge, and the back of da castle looks out over da ocean." Liam shrugged. "I dinnie know why he'd wanna be movin'. He has lived here his whole life since his da died, and he no get along wit dat side of his family."

"Hmm. Start packing his room and move everything into mine. As soon as he gets back, we can move. Also, where is the library?"

Liam smiled. "Happy ta be of service. Dis way."

An hour later, I made my way towards the bedroom with a large tray of food. I had no idea who was doing the cooking in this place—it seemed to simply appear—but they were amazing. Everything from hot and cold appetizers, steak and potatoes, and even pasta was all lined up on the island for the taking. Liam said to take as much as needed.

The sound of Mari's laughter filled the hallway. Stepping into the room, I almost dropped the tray as my mouth fell to the floor. Was this even the same girl that I locked in the washroom? Elewyen's red hair fell in long waves down to her waist and glittered like rubies in the fading light. Her face was clean of dirt, and instead of looking like some mud monster, her fair skin glowed, and her smile lit up her whole face.

Mari must have given her something to wear. The short black and red kilt she wore with the bright white shirt was giving me all sorts of dirty, private school roleplay images. Her legs and feet were currently bare, and I couldn't seem to stop running my eyes up and down her body.

She was stunning. Gone was the baggy clothing that looked like pieces of potato sacks stitched together. She'd been transformed into this fucking sexy woman. For the second time, my cock was getting a workout behind my fly.

"It be no' polite ta stare," Elewyen said, fidgeting with the skirt like she was trying to pull it farther down her legs. If anything, I wanted to pull it up and sit her on the dresser.

"Wow," was all I could think to say as the shock continued to render me speechless. "You look amazing," I said.

The stirring of the connection was different with her, but I could feel it in my gut like a little ball of yarn that she was holding the other end of.

"Is the food for us?" Mari asked.

I was startled and looked over at her, having completely forgotten that she was in the room. She nodded toward the tray I managed not to drop on the floor. When I looked at her, I still saw my cousin, but oddly, I felt more comfortable than I had before. I should've felt less comfortable, considering the threat level she presented. As I looked into her eyes, I knew she wasn't. Fuck, why did everything here seem so awkward and backwards?

"Oh yeah, shit."

There was a low table near the couch and chairs that Rhys had in his room—our room now, at least until we moved. Placing the tray down on the table, I turned towards Elewyen. She tensed and took a step back. I moved slower as I stepped in close enough that I could smell the shampoo on her hair and see the pulse pounding hard on the side of her neck. Was it attraction or fear?

Lifting my hand slowly, I reached out and ran my fingers through her long hair. She swatted my hand away, and a low growl left my throat.

Mari was suddenly standing between us and gave me a look that clearly said *calm the fuck down*. Her eyes begged me to step back. I hated that, in some way, she was between me and my second and now my third. I didn't need to be governed like she was a damn chaperone.

"How about we eat, and you two can get to know one another better before you go pushing her up against a wall?"

My jaw twitched, and my hand itched to crack across Elewyen's ass, but Mari was right. I needed to keep my cool. Rhys said to convince her to stay on her own, that we couldn't force this triad together, but fuck, I wanted to lay her over my lap and pull that kilt up. Was she wearing panties?

I bit my lip to keep myself in check before nodding. I stepped back from Mari and flopped down in the large chair. Had I always been this much of a prick? My father said that I was, but I didn't believe a word that he said.

I guess it was possible. Elewyen's eyes remained locked on mine as she came over to the couch with Mari and sat down. She wasn't scared, but she was wary, and fuck, I liked that look. I was tempted to push her buttons and see how mad I could make her. There was something about the snapping green eyes that made me want to see her raging mad at me while I fucked the look right off her face.

"Elewyen has agreed to stay for seven days to see if she wants to make this work with you and Rhys," Mari said like she was our fucking negotiator.

"Is that so?" My eyes remained on Elewyen's face.

The subtle movement she made as she wiggled her ass on the couch wasn't lost on me. Good. The pull was there with her and not just me. I really needed to read up on this connection shit.

"Are you hungry," I asked and leaned forward to lift the lid off the tray that almost took up the entire table.

Movement caught my eye as something scurried across the floor. A moment later, the little red rodent that Elewyen was travelling with jumped up onto the uncovered food like it was going to dig in too.

"Oh, no, you don't," I said and snatched the small animal off the platter. "Ouch," I growled as its small claws and teeth sank into my hand.

Both girls jumped to their feet.

"Dinnie ya dare hurt 'im," Elewyen snarled like she was the animal. Her hands balled into fists as she stepped around the table.

"That thing was about to steal our food and just bit me. Who knows what diseases it has?" I said, holding the squirrel out a little tighter so it couldn't bite me again. "At the very least, it should be kicked outside."

"Ya will be givin' me Barry, or ya can be forgettin' about me stayin'," Elewyen stepped in close and glared up at me.

Fuck, what was it about everyone here being so aggressive, and why is it so damn hot?

My eyebrow cocked. "Is that so? Okay, you can have your rodent back, but only if you kiss me."

"Um…I wouldn't suggest that Rook," Mari said, but I ignored her.

If building the connection was what Rhys was after, there was no time like the present to make this happen.

"Ya wanna kiss?" Her face twisted in obvious confusion. She touched her lips, and I nodded. "Aye, for a kiss den," she said, and my mouth curled up in a smirk. "Gimmie Barry first."

I looked at the red squirrel and then back at Elewyen. "All right, deal."

Lowering my fist, I opened it for the squirrel to jump into her hand. It proceeded to make noisy squeaking sounds, its furry hand pointing at me like it was talking and telling a story before it ran up Elewyen's arm and curled up on her shoulder.

I felt a moment of guilt as I stared at the ball of fur smaller than my fist as it shook, but when Elewyen stepped in close to my body, all other thoughts were wiped away.

Cupping the side of her face, I let my thumb travel over her skin. A small current travelled where I touched and made me groan. It was different than with Rhys, softer with a slight tingle and a gentle pull in my gut, but it had the same effect on my body. I dropped my head, and my lips touched hers. There was a distinct jolt as the connection of power jumped between us. I didn't have long to relish it when a fist found my side and stole the air from my lungs.

"Oof!" Elewyen slammed both her palms into my chest. I stumbled back and crashed into my chair, gasping for breath.

"If me was ya, I wouldna start dis ting by threatenin' me companion," Elewyen said. Reaching down, she picked up two plates off the platter. "Can ya take me ta da room I'ma ta sleep? I'ma no stayin' in 'ere wit him."

Mari looked horrified, her mouth hanging open as she glared at me.

"I'ma take ya in a moment. Let me speak ta me cousin."

Elewyen stood by the door as Mari leaned over and gripped the arms of the chair as she stared me in the eyes.

"Do you not want this to work?" I opened my mouth, but Mari cut me off. "It was a rhetorical question. If you've decided that you want to go home, then go, and we will figure out how to save those on the island without you. Otherwise, don't be an arse. Try to remember that the only interaction Elewyen has had with men are those who want to either steal from her or rape her."

A growl rippled from between my lips as anger flared at the thought of someone hurting her.

"I warned you not to force a kiss from her. So next time I give you a warning, maybe try listening instead of letting your oversized ego control your actions."

Mari stood straight, and I wasn't sure what she thought as she stared at me.

"You have a lot of potential. Try not to allow your arrogance to fuck it up." She marched away to join Elewyen at the door, and just like that, I was once more alone.

In hindsight, that may not have been the best approach. I rubbed my eyes and pictured the look on Rhys's face when he found out. I never had a problem with women. They flocked to me and begged me to fuck them. Leaning forward, I grabbed one of the plates of food.

Why the hell had Rhys given me such an important task?

"Fuck. I'm not cut out for this crap."

Chapter 30

Rhys

It was late when I pulled up to the tall gates of Maughold castle. The guards made me get out to prove who I was. Seemed like a strange thing to do, considering they'd all known me for years. Getting back in the car, I waited for the heavy gates to slide out of the way.

As always, whenever I entered one of the other families' properties, a shiver went down my spine as the warning of power pressed in on me. All the properties were guarded against those that would want to hurt us, but the spells were not infallible. On more than one occasion, a Hunter had made it onto the property and killed a guard before they were discovered.

I always liked the look of this castle, lights lined the driveway. It had a garden in the middle of the roundabout with bright white flowers and a fountain that ran all year. A magic all on its own.

I pulled into one of the vacant spots and grabbed my duffel. I couldn't help wondering how things were going with Rook and Elewyen, and a bit of guilt settled in my stomach that I'd left them to figure it out while I took off. But Rook was the number one, and she was drawn to him, which meant the connection was already building between them.

I hoped that things would strengthen when we moved to Glentruan. I knew that for any real future with Rook and Elewyen, I needed to move away from Injebreck and Mari. There were too many memories tied there.

I jogged up the stairs to the metal doors, raising my hand to knock when I heard the deep thud of the massive lock clicking free. William, the servant who had worked this castle long enough to see multiple generations come and go peered around the corner. Another beauty and mystery of the castles were that they all held back time. Well, they couldn't hold back time, but it certainly travelled much slower when you remained on the property for long stays.

"Master McGregor, what a sight fir ole eyes. Come on in," William said, then pulled open the door for me to enter. "To what do we owe the pleasure?" William spent a lot of time overseas and in other Factions as he travelled the world, his accent sounded crisp and clean to my ears.

"I'ma callin' a meetin' of all dose on da council and those of da next generation. We 'ave trouble brewin', I'm afraid."

"Aye, there has been some strange things happening for sure," William said as he ran his hand through his white hair.

I used my thumb to gesture toward the door I'd just come through. "Dat be why da guards be actin' so strange?"

"Aye, we had someone sneak on the property not even a night ago and kill a guard and set fire to one of the sheds. Looks to be like they tried ta set fire to the door, but the magic that protects this castle was much stronger than they realized."

"Did ya catch 'em?"

"Sort of. Before the guards could grab him, he doused himself in petrol and lit himself on fire." William shook his head. "I have not see a person burn in years. It is not something I care to see again any time soon."

Reaching out, I placed my hand on the old servant's shoulder. "I'ma sorry ya had ta see dat." I let my hand drop as William gave me a sad smile.

"Thank you, Master McGregor."

"Where be Caleb and Lochlan and everyone else? I taught they'd all be here by now."

"Lochlan just arrived, but he be in a fine mood and has retreated to his room. He said it was for the night and that he'd be up for the meeting in the morning. He also said, and I quote, 'do not to fuckin' disturb me tonight'." William smirked.

Lochlan could be bristly at the best of times, but when he was thrown off his schedule or there was shit on the horizon, he got extra grouchy.

"As for Master Caleb, he can be found in his room with…a wee bit of a party on the go."

I rolled my eyes, knowing what that meant. Caleb loved to pretend he was in a harem, and as I made my way up the stairs, the thumping of the music was all the confirmation I needed to know what I would walk in on. Caleb also had no shame and left the door wide open for whomever happened to be wandering past to watch. He'd horrified his sister and mother enough that they never came to this end of the castle anymore.

Poking my head in the bedroom, I couldn't help but be in awe. Caleb stood in the middle of his bed with weapon straps on his body, and nothing else. His wrists were tied with black rope to a pulley system on the ceiling. There was a girl hanging onto the ropes with her legs wrapped around his head, while his face was buried in her pussy. Two more girls were enthusiastically servicing his cock. But it was the three guys behind him fucking in a train that had me shaking my head in complete wonder.

I would never say it, but the guy was a legend. Even I was envious, and I was never envious.

"Oi, asshole," I called out over the music and moaning.

Caleb lifted his head from between the girl's legs and peeked over her thigh. "Rhys, come in and join us. I gotta few ta go around."

"I'ma paired now. I cannie play with ya no more," I said dropping my duffel on my way to the bar Caleb had in his room. Pouring myself a healthy dose of scotch, I wandered over to the small couch and sat down. "I be sure ya'll find out what dat be like soon enough on one of da next ritual moons."

I visited a time or two and played with Caleb and the groups of men and women he always had at his beck and call. The castle should've been named the Palace of Lust. You could end up staying for days and crawling home with a cock that no longer worked and a head pounding like someone was inside your skull playing bagpipes and drums.

The girl on his shoulders began to scream and moaned loudly as she very dramatically came on his face. When she was finished, she flopped off his body to the side, narrowly missing the two girls kneeling at his feet.

"Gimmie a min," Caleb moaned out. "Yeah, dat be it right dere," he said.

The men behind him picked up the pace, as did the girls sucking him off. It was like a dance performed so many times that they knew exactly what was expected.

"Fuck, aye!"

I averted my gaze from the passion-filled bed before I was tempted to join in. I still had the semi-hard-on from touching Rook. It had been unbelievably difficult to leave him standing in the closet and not do more. Every touch we shared was linking us closer. I swore the reason my head hurt earlier was because of Rook hitting his head on the wall. I hadn't put it together until he explained what happened when Elewyen tried to escape.

The moaning, gasps and odd screams of pleasure continued, but my mind was elsewhere as my eyes remained unfocused on the portrait of Maughold castle on the wall. Unfortunately, the image kept wavering and all I could see was Rook's blue eyes. I had to pinch the bridge of my nose and think of all those dying to clear the images that continued to plague me.

I startled when a drop of liquid hit my hand. I looked up to see Caleb standing beside the chair, topping up my glass.

"Cheers," I said as he sat down across from me.

He poured himself a glass and put the scotch down on the table before stretching out like a cat would. The room had been cleared of people, and I was so out of it that I hadn't seen them leave.

"Are ya good? Ya don't seem yerself," Caleb said.

I stared into the swirling cup of scotch and thought about the question. "I dinnie know, Caleb. Ya know, I've been preparin' me whole life for dis moment ta help take control and be in me own triad, but now dat it's 'ere…" I shook my head. "I just dinnie know if I'ma ready for all dis responsibility. I'ma makin' decisions to save lives, but then dere be all the other stuff wit da actual triad."

Caleb snorted. "Man, ya be more ready than all da rest of us combined. Ya're who we all look up ta and want ta follow yer lead, so dinnie be tellin' me ya din't know. Of course, ya know, so what be chasin' yer tail and makin' ya feel unsure? Is it Rook? I hear he flew in ta da island. Does dat mean he wanna be part of da triad now?"

I took a sip of the scotch and let it roll around in my mouth as I savoured the bold flavours. "Aye, he says he does and be tryin'. It is intense between us."

Caleb grinned over the top of his glass. "I bet it is. Helps that he cannie be a handful. I met 'im once overseas, but he was stoned, so I dinnie tink he'd be rememberin' me. Just as well, we kinda had a bit of a wild night."

My anger flared white hot, and my eyes narrowed. Caleb immediately backed up in the seat as the air crackled around us. He held up his hand.

"Naw, I dinnie mean me and him had sex. We partied hard, is all."

I relaxed into the seat and took a steadying breath. Rook and I were not strangers to sex or multiple partners, but the idea that one of my closest friends had been with Rook, my chosen, had instantly set my blood on fire. Volatile freaking emotions were driving me crazy. I couldn't seem to keep them straight.

"Aye, he seems ta 'ave his own way for sure." I laughed, breaking the tension that had started to build. "But dat's no' the problem. Well, not entirely…I mean, I dinnie even have my triad sorted and we 'ave dis mess wit another Faction. Not ta mention Mari," I said.

Caleb was one of the few people I knew I could talk to openly about my feelings for Mari and it wouldn't leave the room.

"Aye, the stunnin' wee Adair lass ya fancy. Mari be a catch all right, but she no gonna be paired wit anyone. No' wit dat black hair and no tattoo." Caleb sipped his drink, then said the one thing I always wondered myself.

"Ya know da ting dat is confusin' about Mari? She be one of da strongest women in da family, heck she be one of da strongest of us period, and yet she no gonna be paired. It seems odd ta me dat she was no' born wit da hair or mark."

I'd had the same thought for a long time. "Aye."

I settled back into the chair and laid my head on the cushion. "Anyway, we spoke, and I spoke ta Rook about her and we came to an understandin, but I need ta be movin'. I'm finally goin' home."

"'Bout fuckin' time. Ronan is a douche and Riegan is no' much better, although they both know how ta party. Point be, ya should be at Glentruan. It be where ya've always belonged." Caleb took a sip of his drink and then stopped. "Wait, did ya say ya told Rook about Mari?" He smirked. "How did dat go?"

"Better den I taught it would. Do ya tink yer gonna be paired wit Crispin?" I asked, wanting to change the topic.

The red that spread across his cheeks told me all I needed to know about what he was hoping for. It was too bad that Crispin had never liked the idea of a triad and had never been into men. If they were paired together, there were going to be some real issues to work out.

"Ya know I've always had a ting for him, but he sees through me

345

that same way as I see out my windy." Caleb nodded his head toward the window with the glass panes open to allow in the cool night air.

"Aye, it no' gonna be easy ta convince him ta pair, but da connection in da books just no do justice ta da strength of da pull. So dat will be in yer favour."

"Aye, maybe."

We sat quietly for a long time. "If ya had ta guess, what Faction do ya tink it be that is bitin' at our heels?"

Caleb shrugged. "I dinnie know, but if me had to make a guess... I'ma gonna have to say Faction One. Da Ringolds, Quitars, and Bowen's 'ave never been our fans."

"Yeah, I be tinkin' dat, too," I said.

Faction One really hated us. Our two sides had been fighting so long now that no one knew the real reason as to why, but the animosity was as strong and pure as the scotch I was drinking. They were also close enough to launch an attack, and they had the ability of wind and rain. They were able to travel with the weather like clouds, and they were pissed that we had three areas while they only had two.

"Ya wanna sleep in here?" Caleb asked.

I laughed. "Do I wanna sleep in a bed wet from come and wild sex all night long?" Caleb smirked. "Naw, I tink I'll be takin' a room on da other side of da castle, but tanks for the offer and da drink." Downing the rest of the scotch, I stood and grabbed my duffel by the door.

"Rhys?"

"Aye," I said, looking over my shoulder at Caleb.

"Dinnie be afraid about what ya were always destined ta do. Ya'ar a natural leader, and I know dat the McCabes and da Kelly's will stand wit ya. I will stand wit ya, no matter what."

Placing my fist over my heart, I nodded to my friend and walked out the door. Tomorrow we would perform a ritual to seek the answers we needed to protect ourselves and defeat this foe, but it would be the first time that I called the meeting and the first time I would be asked to lead it. I could only pray that Caleb was right, and the rest of the families would listen to what I had to say, or there was a good chance that we would all be paying with far more than lost crops.

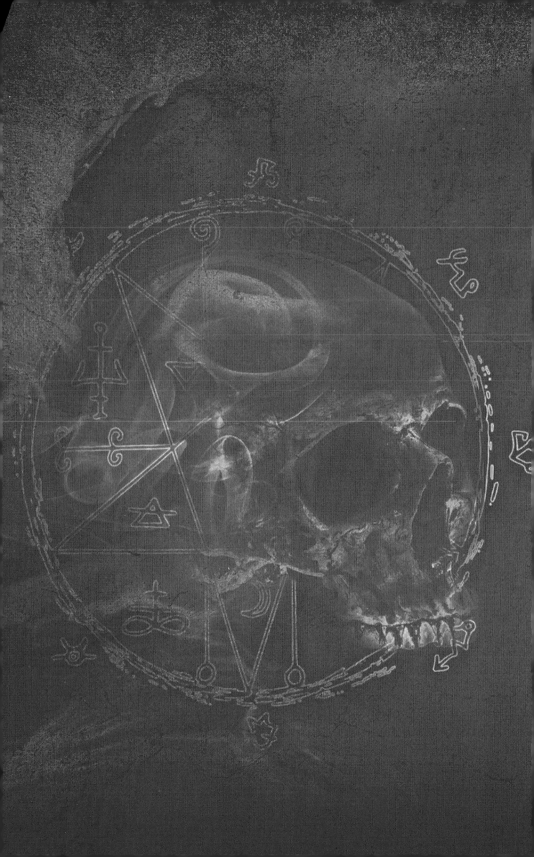

Chapter 31

Elewyen

 I layed on the massive bed staring at the ceiling while I tried to get comfortable. The thing could easily fit five or six people back home in my coven. Many a winter we all huddled inside one of the large brush huts with fur blankets and cuddled with one another to stay warm. The winters were the hardest, and we always expected for the oldest of us to perish before the snow melted.

 Turning onto my side, I looked out the window at the stars and tried to picture this place becoming my new normal if I stayed. Reaching up, I ran my fingers over the small squirrel curled up on the pillow. Barry was snoring with his nose buried under his tail. Why this wee fella decided to stick with me, I had no idea, but I was

My soul ached for things that were new, while my heart ached to go home and see Keeva. I decided that if they wanted me to consider this arrangement, she would need to come here. Maybe all the women would need to come here if they chose, but especially Keeva. She deserved a chance at a different life and not one filled with hiding in the shadows and being chased with torches and pitchforks.

That was one thing I did really like so far about this place. They didn't seem to mind my red hair. In fact, it seemed to make me special rather than a pariah. I still had to go looking for the babes left by the villagers, but maybe I wouldn't have to travel alone or on foot. Maybe the villagers could simply bring the babes here. That thought warmed my heart.

The fragrance Mari used on my hair wafted towards my nose and I couldn't stop sniffing it and feeling how soft it was. I had my first shower with water and soap, which is what I learned the round colourful balls were, and now I smelt like flowers and my skin felt different. Not that I didn't stay clean by going and bathing in the streams, but this was different.

The water was hot, and Mari rubbed my hair for me, then I sat on a soft seat while she brushed it out. Mari was so kind, and yet the entire time, I could feel her heart hurting like it was breaking. I watched her in the mirror, and although she hadn't said a word as to why, her eyes shimmered with a layer of tears.

"Ya be sad cause of yer ma," I asked in the long silence.

Her hand stilled as she showed me how to do something called shaving my legs. I never thought about taking the hair off my body, but she said that it was normal in this weird way of living. I had to admit that my skin felt as soft as a wee babe's bottom.

"Whaddya mean?"

"Yer ma be passed, ya?" I asked.

350

"Aye. How do ya know dat?" Mari asked, her eyes finding mine as she sat beside me on the comfy bench.

"She be out in da garden. I tink she be lingerin' for a reason," I explained, and Mari's eyes filled with tears. "She was admirin' da roses."

"Ya saw me ma?"

I nodded, and Mari bit her lip before wiping away tears. The corner of her mouth pulled up in a small smile. "Ya, I miss me Ma, but why ya say dat I be sad?"

Picking up her hand, I held it between my own. "I'za can feel it. Yer heart be heavy like ya suffered a loss."

Mari looked away from my eyes and cleared her throat as she pulled away to stand. "I'ma gonna git back ta yer hair. It be almost ready ta braid."

"It be Rhys, den?" I asked, not letting the topic drop.

Mari's face flushed bright pink, and she walked to the thing she called a vanity. "I tink it be best if we no talk about dat," Mari said softly.

"If ya 'ave feelin's for him, den why ya no do dis triad ting wit him?"

She held a fluffy looking piece of material to her chest, and her accent slipped back to her foreign one. "Because it doesn't work like that, Elewyen. The triad is picked by the spirits that have passed on. They choose who will be best suited together. They chose Rook, Rhys, and you. Besides, Rook is my cousin, and I'd probably kill him even if we weren't."

"Killin' him be an option?"

Mari laughed and shook her head. "Naw, it no be an option, but I'd be bloody tempted."

"Aye, I'ma tempted now," I said, making us both laugh.

Someone knocked at the door, and I sat up with a start. I waited, counting my heartbeats, when the sound of knuckles on wood came again. I looked around for a weapon and decided on a heavy-looking statue. Gripping it tight, I crept towards the door in the dark, my heart pounding harder with each step I took.

"Who be dere?" I asked, standing off to the side, ready for whoever decided to come in and try to hurt me.

"It's me. I wanted to apologize," Rook said.

My arm relaxed. I wasn't sure I wanted to see him after what had happened in his room, but I watched my hand reach for the handle as if his presence, commanded me to do so. Pulling the door open, I decided it had been a terrible idea. The dark demons had certainly known what they were doing when they created this man. My heart pounded hard as my blood heated all throughout my body in a way that I'd never experienced before the first time I laid eyes on him.

His hair was messy, and he looked like he was having as much trouble trying to sleep as I was. He had no shirt, and it was the first time that I'd seen a man's naked chest up close. I'd caught a glimpse of some men when they'd gone to the streams to bathe, but none of them had looked like this.

His shoulders were wide, and he narrowed in at the waist. The muscles on display drew my eyes along his body. He was wearing some type of black bottoms that were different from the ones he had on earlier, and his feet were bare. I found him more dangerous than when he was fully clothed. The dark tattoos of power lined his chest and shoulders before travelling down his arms.

Rook leaned against the wall, arms crossed over his chest, making them look larger. It was difficult to keep my eyes on his face.

"Hey," he said softly, and that one little word made me shiver.

Biting the inside of my cheek, I squared my shoulders. "Ya came ta say somethin'?"

Rook rubbed the back of his neck. "Can I come in?"

That was certainly not a good idea, and yet I stepped back and let him walk into the room. The large space suddenly felt too small. Like the walls had jumped inward to close me in tight with the man who wanted to devour my soul. It seemed like a wild idea and yet the fluttering in my stomach and the pounding in my chest made me want to run and hide as well as find out what else he could do. It was a conundrum.

Then I noticed the little sparkles that looked like shining dust as it swirled around our feet. I stepped away from it, but it followed.

"Wat dis be?" I asked, pointing to the swirling substance.

"It has to do with the connection between us. Old magic, stuff I don't understand."

We stared at one another, and Rook must have realized I didn't understand him.

He pointed to the floor. "Dat be magic, but it no come from me," he said and pointed at his chest as he shook his head.

I chuckled at his poor attempt at the accent, but thought it was sweet that he tried.

My eyes travelled up Rook's body. I stopped to stare at the black designs. The way they were laid out made them seem like a language made of pictures, and my fingers itched to touch him. His piercing blue eyes locked with my own. I couldn't help thinking I was in a cage with a wild animal that was scarier than any of those that wandered through the woods. Even with the door wide open, I felt trapped by his gaze.

"I wanted to say I'm sorry for threatening your squirrel," he said slowly.

"And?"

"And for trying to trick you into kissing me. I should've just kissed you instead," he said.

"Ya tink just takin' what ya want be better?" I crossed my arms over my chest.

His eyes went wide. "No, no…I didn't mean it like that…I mean, I sort of did, but in a good way, like a sexy way. I'm not doing a very good job of describing this."

I could feel his eyes searching my face, and the tingling sensation in my chest grew stronger by the second. My hand instinctively went to my chest and rubbed at the spot.

"You feel it, don't you?" he asked, his voice dropping low. He was making me warm in places I didn't understand and I wanted to rub my legs together.

Rook took a step closer, and my breathing quickened, making my head light. *Run!* My brain screamed, but my feet remained rooted to the floor as if I was nothing more than an animal in one of the villager's leg snares.

"Naw, I dinnie no what ya be talkin' about," I said stubbornly, but that seemed to be the wrong thing to say.

A smile spread across his face. It was not the sweet, kind smile that Mari gave me. No, this smile spoke of a wicked personality. Every instinct told me that Rook could bring me great pain with equal parts pleasure. An image of my nails drawing lines down his back flashed behind my eyes. I staggered back with the force of the image that didn't feel like it was my own.

"Don't lie to me, Elewyen," he said softly as he stepped in close enough that our chests were almost touching.

Heat from his skin seeped through the thin material of the sleep shirt. I was tempted to step away from the threat that he was, but my legs felt heavy, like they were made of great rocks.

"Who be sayin' dat I'ma lyin'?"

Why was I poking at him? It only seemed to make things worse, and yet I continued to do it. I craved that glint in his eyes. My tongue darted out to wet my lips, and his eyes followed the movement. I remembered all too well what it had felt like to have the soft touch of his lips against my own.

Rook leaned down, and my body tensed as his cheek brushed mine. A surge of something passed between us, and I had to lock my knees to keep them from giving out.

He made a low groaning sound as his lips stopped at my ear. "I say you're lying, because I feel the same thing right where you're rubbing. I do like this flimsy nightgown you're wearing," he said slowly. Of course now was the time I was able to pick up every word he said. Each moment he stayed this close pushed my pulse higher and made my body ache in spots it had no business aching.

"Whatta ya doin'," I asked, my voice shaking as much as the rest of my body.

My eyes closed, and I gasped when his hands gripped my waist. The heat penetrated the thin flowy material like he could burn me with his touch, and yet I shivered as if it was a brisk winter day.

Once more, my inner voice yelled that I should step away from Rook and the spell that was trying to bind me to him. I understood it now that Mari explained it, but my body wouldn't comply. In fact, it greedily wanted more. I wanted to feel his hands travelling all over my body.

Wrapping his hand in my long hair, he pulled down and I let out a yelp. It forced my head back, exposing my neck to him. I was sure he could see my heart pounding in my throat. The sound of it was all I could hear in my ears. He growled and I grabbed hold of his shoulders to keep myself from collapsing to the floor. With every sound he made my legs shook harder.

"I do really love this nightgown," he said, as he tugged on the front string that held the top half together.

355

"Pleaze," I said, not sure what I was asking for. Did I want him to stop or to continue?

The material slipped over my shoulder, and the cool air hit my breast. My body pressed into his like I was melting.

"What are you asking for, Elewyen?"

I opened my mouth to answer, but all that came out was a garbled moan as something hot and wet found my nipple. It took my brain a moment to realize that he had me in his mouth, and as he began to suck, I moaned loudly from the intense pleasure. My eyes snapped open, wanting to see what he was doing, but the angle of my head left me staring at the high ceiling.

"Mmm, you taste so good," Rook said, his voice rough. "I better stop now, or I'm going to go too far."

"Naw, dinnie stop," I said, my face and ears warmed with embarrassment.

"But I thought you weren't drawn to me?" His tongue was dancing over my nipple, and each wet swipe was like a lightning strike right down my body. "I thought you didn't want anything to do with me?"

I didn't catch all that he said, but I understood he was mocking my earlier statement. My hand raised to strike him, but he snatched my half-hearted effort out of the air and pushed. With a few staggering steps, my back was forced up against the wall. Was this what Azula meant when she said that men were mean and cruel with our bodies? If it was, then I didn't think they understood the meaning because I wanted more of this.

"Do you want me to taste you, Elewyen?"

I moaned and nodded, even though I had no idea what he meant. Rook released my hair as he stepped back from my body. Looking down, I stared at my exposed breast and felt the pulse of need aching in the tip.

"No, I don't think so. Not tonight, but make no mistake, Elewyen, you are mine, as Rhys is mine." The corner of his mouth pulled up in a devilish way, and his eyes shone in the moonlight. "Sleep well, Elewyen. Be sure to dream of me."

Rook left me standing there, confused and breathing hard, as he walked out the door and closed it behind him. What just happened? Looking up, my eyes found Barry, who was awake and twisting his head as he looked at me.

Grabbing the front of my nightgown, I pulled it closed and crossed my arms over my chest. "Din't look at me like dat. He messes wit me head," I mumbled, and looked away from Barry's judgmental gaze. At least it felt that way.

I promised seven days and thought that I would have no interest in staying, but this seemed like it might be harder than I realized. I didn't like the idea that someone was purposely hurting innocents, but there was only one innocent I was concerned about right now, and I wanted to get back to her.

I held the necklace, playing with the little stone between my fingers. I'd already made sure Keeva was okay before laying down. If I reached out again, she may think something was wrong.

Dropping the necklace, I touched my lips as I thought about what the light touch of Rook's kiss had felt like. If tonight was any indication of the influence Rook and this bond spell had over my actions, I may have signed up for more than I bargained for. Would I actually choose to stay because I wanted to?

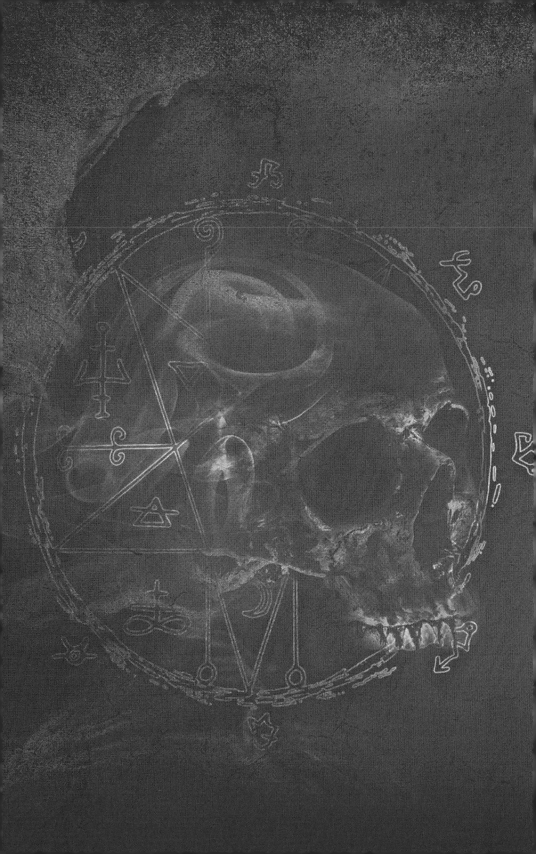

Chapter 32

Mari

I'd never locked my door in all my years living here at home, but I did so tonight. Biting down on the shirt I stuffed in my mouth, I pulled the leather top off. There was a sickening sound of dried blood pulling free from the wounds. I'd done too much, but I couldn't act any differently. I wanted no one to know about this humiliation. Tears filled my eyes in the privacy of my own washroom as the sharp pain streaked through me. It felt like my back was being burned and stabbed with every movement.

With a final tug, the leather came free, and I screamed into the shirt, the material muffling the sound. Panting hard, I stared into my eyes in the mirror. If I thought it would help, I'd kill every head of the council and let the Factions start over, but it would only throw everything into more chaos. No, killing wasn't the answer, but the anger that had brewed in my gut for years was boiling now.

Standing straight, I turned my back to the mirror and looked at the lines that crisscrossed over my skin. They were bright red and irritated, some trickled blood where the whip had broken the skin. I was most worried about infection since we didn't have much in the way of antibiotics on the island. Ma was the only one who knew how to make a potion from the red flowers and moulds in the garden. When not prepared correctly, it could kill you. The marks may fade, but what they represented would always scar my soul.

Tossing my top aside, I grabbed the container of salve off the counter. It smelled like aloe and fresh eucalyptus. This was my ma's healing recipe. She'd always been great with remedies for just about everything. I could remember her bringing one of her special broths for Belle and me when we were sick. When I hurt myself trying to keep up with Rhys in training, she used to lather the area with a thick paste and wrap it. My ma had been kind, and I'd heard her express, more than once, her fears about my future to my da when they didn't know I was listening. He always reassured her that he would never let anything bad happen to me. He lied. He became the thing he said he hated, and he became a man I no longer respected.

Taking a healthy amount of the creamy substance, I winced as I spread it on the marks I could reach. I needed help for the ones in the middle, and I slammed my hand down on the counter. No, I wasn't asking anyone for help, no one was seeing this. Out in the bedroom, I grabbed my back scratcher off the dresser. It was long and shaped like a hand. Using the rounded side, I lathered a bunch on, then smirked as it reached the spots I couldn't. See, I didn't need anyone.

I picked up the roll of gauze off the counter and started wrapping myself like I planned on trying out for a part as a mummy. With all the movement I winced and sucked in a sharp breath. One roll finished; I grabbed the second one and began the process again. I finished stripping and had just pulled on a loose tunic and warm socks when there was a knock at my door.

I stared at it like a monster was on the other side. "Mari, are ya still awake? I wanna talk to ya," my da said.

Anger flowed to the surface all over again. "I don't want to talk to you," I said, and sat down to pull on my black boots. I tied up the laces and stuffed my knives into the sheaths.

"Please, Mari, we really need ta talk about dis mornin', and..."

"There is nothing to talk about. I told you then, and I will tell you now. I will never forgive you for what you did, and you have lost the right to call me your daughter. Just go away." I grabbed the cloak off the back of my chair.

"I'ma so sorry, Mari. Please let me in," he said, and my bottom lip wavered as I stared at the wooden door. "Ya dinnie understand. I jus' want ta explain."

I grabbed my canne from where I had it stashed in the closet and stopped to lay my hand on the door. "Da, ya broke me heart dis mornin'. Ya showed me colours in ya dat I never thought I'd see. But I understand now dat those colours be yer true nature, for it is in time of our greatest tests dat our inner demons or strength be shown." I closed my eyes as the pain in my heart equaled the pain along my back.

"Ya promised to protect me, ya promised ta love me. What ya did was neither and instead ya chose ta hurt me for da only sliver of happiness I've ever taken from dis world. But, I be wantin' ya ta know, dat yer never gonna break me soul. I dinnie care about yer reasons, but I will make ya da promise dat yer neva doin' it again," I said, my accent coming through with the dark rage. "Leave me be. I din't care if I never see yer face again. Go sit wit the daughter dat is worth somethin' to ya, 'cause ya showed me yer heart fir me, and it be blacker den me hair."

I could hear him crying on the other side of the door, and all it made me want to do was punch him. How dare he cry? Before I could open the door and follow through on my violent thoughts, I went to the far side of the bedroom and grabbed the small statue that was the release switch to the hidden tunnel. It was the one Rhys had always used to sneak through to get into my room when we were kids. The tunnel hadn't been used for years, and I made a small ball of fire in my hands and tossed it in the air to light the way. Using my canne, I pulled down the thick cobwebs but stopped when they became so thick that I could barely see.

Disgusting.

Waving my hand in the air, the fireball got bigger and bigger until it touched the walls and the ceiling. Reaching back, I punched my arm forward, and the sizzling fire rolled away, consuming the webs and whatever else was lurking down here.

Reaching the end of the tunnel, I released the door, but it took several hard pushes to get it to move enough that I could squeeze out. I winced as the rock rubbed my back.

Leaping over thick roots while weaving through the trees I took off at a fast pace. Someone was blocking my sight, maybe the same person who tried to kill me. Or I think they were trying to kill me, I wasn't certain. In my demon blood-induced haze, I remembered someone coming in before Rhys found me. The voice was not one that I recognized, but he kept asking me questions, and when I hadn't answered, he yelled at the demons.

Whoever had been there wanted information from me. Even though I couldn't remember, I was determined to find out who had almost killed me. If it hadn't been for Rhys's quick thinking, I have no doubt that I would've died on that dirt floor and my body long decayed by the time anyone found me.

Reaching the caves was a long run, but I had nowhere else to be. It was times like this that I wished Belle and I were closer. A sister to lean on would've been nice, but the moment my younger sister was born with dark red hair and bright green eyes, she was treated differently. She trained with me out of boredom, but other than that, we had nothing in common. Most of the time, it felt like she would've preferred to be the only child and have all of Da's attention. I guess she was going to get her wish, because I didn't care if I never saw him again. I'd already begun to make plans to leave the castle. Where I was going, I didn't know, but I couldn't stay one minute longer than necessary.

I envied Elewyen and the covens of women who hid from the rest of the world. They lived peacefully as a unit and loved and cared for one another like people should. She was free to roam wherever and whenever she wanted and didn't have a man telling her what to do. Yes, she'd just been tied to Rook and Rhys, but Rhys wasn't the type to take up the patriarchal mantel and begin ordering her around like a servant. I highly doubted that, for all of Rook's bravado, he was like that either. Well, he might try, but Elewyen could hold her own. I smirked at the thought and what she would do to them if they even tried.

Slowing my pace as I neared the caves, I got low and snuck around the outer edge of the forest. There was no doubt in my mind that Rhys had killed all the demons, but it was the unknowns that I was more worried about. The witch I hired had been someone I used in the past for other small things and had no ties to any Faction. So how had she gotten involved?

Closing my eyes, I strained to hear inside the tunnel, but only silence greeted me. Avoiding the bright spots where the moon was shining through the tall canopy, I darted into the dark cave. I didn't have Rhys's gift for seeing in the dark as if it were daylight but being an Adair, I could see better than the average person. It took a moment, but once my eyes adjusted to the pitch-black space, I could make out the dark impressions of footprints in the dirt.

I followed the trail down to the cell I'd been kept in and knelt to stare at the mass of prints outside the door. I would've been happy to find anything that helped point me in the direction of this mystery man.

There was definitely more than just Rhys's shitkickers. His large boot with the unique tread was easy to pick out amongst the other impressions. There was a demon, a woman's boot, and another man's imprint. Pulling out my phone, I quickly took a picture of the footprints and the inside of the cell.

A glint caught my eye, something stuck in the sand just inside the cell. Using my finger, I gave it a dust off and pulled out a man's ring. It was a skull with small black gems for eyes and the letter R on the side. Holding it up, I stared at the piece that looked like one of the rings Rook would wear. It couldn't be his...could it? No, he had no reason to lure me out here. He wouldn't know the way even if he wanted to.

The sound of a man's voice echoed down the long tunnel, and I shot to my feet. Stuffing the ring in my pocket, I darted out of the cell and listened to the voice that bounced around the cavernous space. Daring to get closer, I turned and tiptoed back the way I'd come.

"Why ya callin' me? We agreed no communication." The man's voice had a deep, thick accent that was very guttural. I didn't recognize who it was.

I needed to get closer. One silent footfall at a time, I inched my way back up the long tunnel.

"Naw, me never agreed ta dat. I'z said no one would get hurt if he fell in line. Dat hasn't happened, has it?"

The voice was suddenly very loud, and a there was a flash of blue light from the tunnel opening as a small blue ball of fire was created.

Shite

Turning, I ran back the way I came. I looked at all the cells and finally darted into the one across from where I'd been held, slipping through the narrowly open door. Spinning, I stood behind the door and away from the small window opening.

"Shut da feck up! I'z be sick of yer bullshite. If tings dinnie start turnin' in me favor, ya can firget me playin' nice. Me next move will be ta kill one of dem." I shuddered with the threat. Who was he talking about? "Dat be a mistake, da demons be daft."

He was talking about me, I knew it. Who the hell was this man? My heart was hammering hard as I bent and silently slipped one of the blades from my boot. The bright blue ball filled the outer chamber with its eerie light. Taking a deep breath, I focused on calming my mind as I prepared to attack if it came to that.

"We be runnin' outta time. Ya know dat." The cell door across the way banged, and unable to help myself, I peeked through the narrow crack where the hinges met the wall. He was dressed in all black, with a quiver of arrows on his back and a sword at his hip. I knew right away by the way he walked this man was a trained warrior. I watched as he knelt and dug round in the dirt as he continued to speak to whoever was on the other end of the line.

"Ya fecked up. It be dat simple. Ya said it would work, but I 'ave yet ta see him run off inta da sunset." He stood, and before he could turn around, I moved away from the crack. "Naw, I din't want ta hear

365

yer shite excuses. Feck, feck, feck!" he screamed, and dread coiled its way around my body. "Naw, I'z no talkin' ta ya. I cannie find somethin'."

The ring in my pocket suddenly felt very heavy, knowing this must be what he was after. The sound of his boots seemed loud as he stomped out into the open space outside the cell. His shadow was cast on the wall of the cell I was standing in, and I held my breath to see if he was going to search the rest of the cells.

I could just make out the sound of the person on the other end of the phone line as they yelled back at the mystery man. It sounded like a small chipmunk, making it impossible to understand a single word.

"Fine, Iz will do it yer way, but not fir much longer."

The blue light got brighter, and I pressed myself against the rock, making myself as flat as possible. Luckily, the light began to fade as the sound of his boots travelled away from the cells. I let out the breath I'd been holding. Putting my hand in my pocket, I pulled out the ring and stared at it. Whoever this belonged to, he wanted it back, and it was definitely the person who had taken me. It made me want to know the answers this ring held that much more.

Peeking around the edge of the door, I didn't see or hear the man, but there was a strange energy left in the air from his presence. I didn't like it, and I didn't trust it. Holding out my arm, the hair stood as the electricity ran over my skin. It felt like some sort of alarm system.

Shite, shite, shite.

Slipping back inside the cell, I eased myself to the ground and tensed as my back screamed. Clenching my jaw, I leaned against the cool stone. If I was going to attempt to make it through whatever the fuck that was, I was going to need a cloaking spell. I wished I had

Rhys's ability to blend with the shadows. That was another McGregor trait, but I did have other tricks up my sleeve.

I should've just attacked him, but then I wouldn't know who he was working with or what they have planned. And if I didn't win, then I was once more a liability. Whoever he was working with didn't sound happy, and I would bet my ass that they were talking about Rook and Rhys. What the hell did he mean by *no one would get hurt if he fell in line?* Who was supposed to fall in line?

Staring at the door, I decided on the spell to use, but remained still. The man needed to be as far away as possible. He would only have put the spell if he thought someone was down here and was waiting outside to attack or because he wanted to be alerted if anyone entered the cave.

Laying my head against the stone, I stared at the damp wall across the way and the marks that had been etched into it over time. Time… that was a funny word. Sometimes it felt like we had too much and other times not enough.

My life had always felt like I was running but held in stasis. Now it seemed as though my feet had finally touched the floor, but I had nowhere to run to other than a bleak emptiness.

My eyes travelled to the four corners of the old cell that had been used back when the war raged between the Flitters and the Factions. The Flitters had it better than they realized, and I understood Rook's desire to run away from all of this. If I'd been given the choice…

I shook my head to rid it of the thoughts that would never come to be. This was my life. I'd chosen to help the Faction while I found ways to protect the women they tried to suppress. I wouldn't take that back, no matter the cost.

Laying my head on my knees, I focused on who the mysterious man could've been talking to and began making a list in my head.

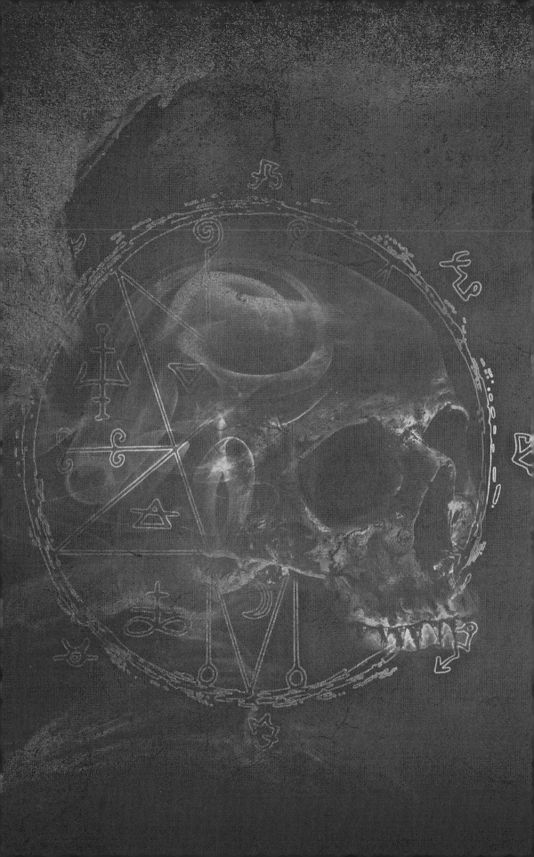

Chapter 33

Rhys

For a whole extra day, I sat around and made phone calls and negotiated assistance from our allies. Lochlan was a good help, and Caleb, when he could focus long enough, was an amazing talker. That guy could sell ice in the middle of a snowstorm.

Nigel Kelly, the head of the Kelly house had held up the meeting saying he was running late, then cancelled coming altogether. I knew the man didn't like me and would prefer any other McGregor as the head of the family. At one time, that would've bothered me but not anymore. The man could go fuck himself.

Slipping my arms into the black and burgundy cloak, I pulled the hood up over my head. Just the act of putting the ceremonial piece on seemed to bring me closer to the spirit world. I could already hear the soft chanting of those who had arrived before me echoing along the stone hallway. The sound of the multiple voices was both haunting and thrilling.

The old catacombs held a power that not even I understood. Picking up my candle and knife, I made my way toward the protective barrier that was the seal to keep both the living out and the spirits of the dead inside.

I could feel the invisible barrier and stopped to bow my head. "Go dtuga na spioraid rochtain agus cosaint do magus mé ag taisteal ina réimeas."

The air shimmered as I asked for the blessing to pass beyond the realm of the living without issue and to travel back again. Slowly kneeling, my voice dropped, and I hummed along with those on the other side of the barrier before continuing my blessing. "Lig do na spioraid mé a threorú agus na cinntí a dhéanaim a chumhachtú."

Placing my hand over the wick of the candle, it roared to life, the flame piercing my hand. I sucked in a sharp breath with the sharp pain as the flame tested my power. The skin separated and showed me the bones within my hand and the muscles that wrapped around them. It lasted but a moment before the flame died down and became small once more. I stared at my hand with fascination, as I always did, at how not a mark was ever left behind. Rising to my feet, I closed my eyes and held my hands out to my side.

"Coinnigh mo lámh agus lig dom taisteal abhaile le scian I mo lámh agus faic I mo dhroim. Is é seo a iarraim."

The long blessing had taken forever to get right when I was young. So many times, I'd forgotten a word and the barrier wouldn't let me pass. My father had made me practice the words from the moment I could speak, and now the old language spilled off my tongue with grace that filled me with pride.

The flame extinguished as I stepped through the barrier and then flared to life once more. Cold blanketed me and grew stronger with each step. As I always did, I paused beside the two memorials in honour of my parents and took a moment to lay my hand on the stones that represented my ma, my da, and of course, Robin, my father's second. Their bones lay in the catacomb under Glentruan, but each castle had a memorial for all those from our Faction who had passed on.

"I wish you rest and love in the afterlife. May your souls always be at peace." Removing my hand, I stayed a moment more to stare at the three stones.

I'd never met my parents' third. He was murdered before I was even conceived. It was inevitable that this was how I was going to end up one day. Reduced to nothing more than a stone and my spirit haunting the catacombs under Glentruan. If history had anything to say about it, then what time I had left was slim. The second was always the target, and it felt like the sands of time were already dripping faster.

Pushing the thought aside, I continued to the ritual area and glanced around the room, noticing that there were a few more missing spots. A couple I expected, like Angus Adair, Rook's father who lived overseas, but it was awkwardly noticeable that Kingsley McKinnon was not present. He was the last remaining McKinnon elder. That was a snub to my authority as the head McGregor, and my teeth ground together. It was bad enough that Nigel had decided not to show, but now Kingsley.

Shaking it off, I stepped into the middle of the pentagram and up to the stone dais and the marble sacrificial table. For this ritual, there wasn't a need for a human sacrifice, but there had been times when it was necessary. It never sat well with me that we needed to take a life

371

to save others, but if the spirits demanded it to save the masses, it was what needed to be done.

I sat the candle off to the side, and the chanting around me grew louder. The words repeated over and over with more vigour than before. The walls shook, and dust sprinkled down on the pristine marble as the power began to rise. Spinning the knife around in my hand, I closed my eyes and allowed my voice to join with the chorus. Rocking softly, my mind and body began to drift into the spirit world, and the images of those transparent wisps slowly took shape in my mind.

Laying my left palm on the marble, I stabbed through the centre of my hand until the metal tip hit the marble. The pain radiated up my arm, but I held still and allowed my mind to overpower the physical sensation.

Blood flowed freely from the wound, and the shallow lines on the table filled with the red liquid. It spread out until the entire pentagram that was in the same position as the one on the floor was filled. Lifting my hand, I held it over the flame of the nearest candle, and much like the one in the outer chamber, the flame roared through the middle of my palm. The colour shifted from a golden hue to a bright green. When it subsided, my skin was once more unmarred.

Those who were gathered chanted and swayed slightly as their hands opened a gap at the top of their cloaks, showing off their family's tattooed crest over their right pectoral muscle. The individual snakes that had been waiting patiently near the walls slithered forward and slipped into the large circular groove of the pentagram carved into the stone floor. They moved into position until they touched nose to tail.

The power ignited.

The circle began to shimmer and glow softly, which added to the hypotonic feel that washed over the room. I could feel the magic building in my chest like a chorus of a choir coming to their crescendo. The snakes took their cue in the chanting to break away from the circle and wrap themselves around the legs of their chosen. They moved in unison, spiralling their way up until they draped their long bodies upon their masters' shoulders, and the sound of their hisses became one with the men.

Holding out my arm, my snake, which had not been with the others, peeled itself out of the tattoo on my arm. The wide king cobra head flaring out as it made its way up my arm to sit on my shoulders. The weight pressed down on my neck. With its massive girth, it was the king of the bunch. The large snakes hissed, the sound drowning out our chanting. My snake moved until it looked me in the eyes, its silver depths the same colour as my own. Its mouth dropped open to show off the fangs that were as long as my finger.

"Yes, the time be now," I said.

With quick accuracy, all the snakes struck and sank their fangs into the symbol on our chests. I sucked in a sharp breath as the sharp fangs disappeared into my skin and sank deep into my body to pierce my heart. We were immune to the poison of our own snake, but they were deadly to anyone else.

"May our voices be heard," I yelled, as I picked up the candle and touched the flame to the centre of the blood on the slab and watched it ignite as surely as if it were dry kindling. "May our voices summon ya," I said. "May yer wisdom guide us, and may we find da answers we seek."

The flame swirled in a circle as it moved around the marble pentagram. The candles on the floor streamed upward until the bright orange turned white and blue with the extreme heat and touched the stone ceiling. Shadows danced along the walls, and as they did, so did our ancestors. I could see the wisps turning into bodies and faces that I recognized and others that I did not.

"Who wishes ta speak this night?" I asked, and it was Gregory who stepped forward. He lifted his head from the bowed position, and his blue eyes glowed an unearthly shade as the spirit inhabited his body.

"I do," his voice was coarse and didn't sound like Gregory, but I didn't know who we were speaking to yet.

"Aye, an' who are you?" I asked.

This had never been something we'd done in the past, but the odd, pesky spirit from another realm would sometimes end up in our call.

"Norris Kelly," came the reply.

Bowing my head, I picked up the silver chalice with liquid ayahuasca potion and added a splash of red wine to hand over.

"Thank you fir answerin' my summon, ancestor Norris Kelly," I said.

Gregory's hand reached for the chalice. He used a knife to pierce the tip of his finger, allowing a droplet to fall in before drinking a sip and passing it back. I took the chalice to the next in line, and one person at a time, they each took a sip and passed it on until the chalice made its way back to me. I was the last to take a sip, and then I returned it to the dais.

Those standing around the circle resumed their chant, but it came out as a hushed whisper as Gregory's eyes glowed even brighter until they were impossible to stare at.

"Do you know why we 'ave come and why we seek yer guidance?" I asked.

"I do."

"Please, ancestor Norris Kelly, tell us who it be that attacks da Faction?"

"Dey be hidden from our sight," the spirit replied. His answer confused me. Who could hide themselves from the spirits?

"What do ya suggest we do?"

"Protect da water. Da veins are da source of all power. Sacrifice dose dat no stand wit ya, and their blood will aid in yer enemy's demise. Collect dose wit power like rare gems. Beware of the snake that looks like the others, but its skin be a different shade. By da time da air turns from ice ta fresh wit flowers, another will join us."

My skin prickled. Were they talking about me? Was that all I had left? A few months at most? Or were they talking about Rook or Elewyen? Shite, were they even talking about us, or someone else entirely. I hated cryptic messages.

"Is da Faction in immediate danger?"

"Aye, da future of da Faction lays heavy."

"Am I in danger?"

"Yer life always be in da balance. Just some days, ya step on the rope with fire underneath, and other times on stone where the blood of others lies."

Okay, I really hated the mysteriousness with which they always gave their answers. That was the one thing that was terrible about asking the spirits for guidance. Their messages were always accurate if you could figure them out. It was like trying to decipher a complex puzzle that was always missing the final piece.

Before I could ask another question, the flames died down and the one atop the stone table extinguished. Gregory stumbled forward, but as experienced as he was to being chosen, he caught himself before falling over. Making my way around to him, I helped him to stand and looked around the circle to the faces staring back at me.

Unlatching itself from my chest, my king cobra hissed at all those in the room before slithering back down my body to once more become the large tattoo that took up my whole forearm.

In a single file line, we left the catacomb. Just before I crossed the invisible barrier, a hand gripped my shoulder. I turned to see bones. I stumbled back in shock, then looked down when I realized that something sharp was sticking out of my chest. A dark stain was forming on the robe as I stared at the spot where something had stabbed me. My eyes darted back up, but the skeleton was gone. I collapsed to the ground, unable to breathe.

"Rhys, Rhys, come on man."

I blinked, and my head hurt with the glare of lights that seemed too bright. Remembering what happened, my hand flew to my chest, but I didn't feel any wetness. I tried to sit up and sharp pain exploded behind my eyes.

"Take it easy. Ya gave us quite da scare," Caleb said.

I licked my lips. "Where did da skeleton go?"

"We dinnie know what yer talkin' bout," Caleb said.

I managed to peel open an eye long enough to see him looking around at everyone who was staring down at me.

"What happened?"

"Din't 'ave a clue. One min, yer fine, and da next, ya were on da floor and shakin'. We got ya out of da ritual area as fast as we could, an da seizure stopped."

Seizure?

"Did da ritual happen?"

"Aye, but nothin' was said. Da spirits refused ta speak and den ya collapsed," Caleb said.

Sitting up slowly, I looked around at all the worried expressions. I couldn't say for certain why the spirits didn't want everyone to hear what they said, but it could only mean one thing. There was someone in the family who was not to be trusted.

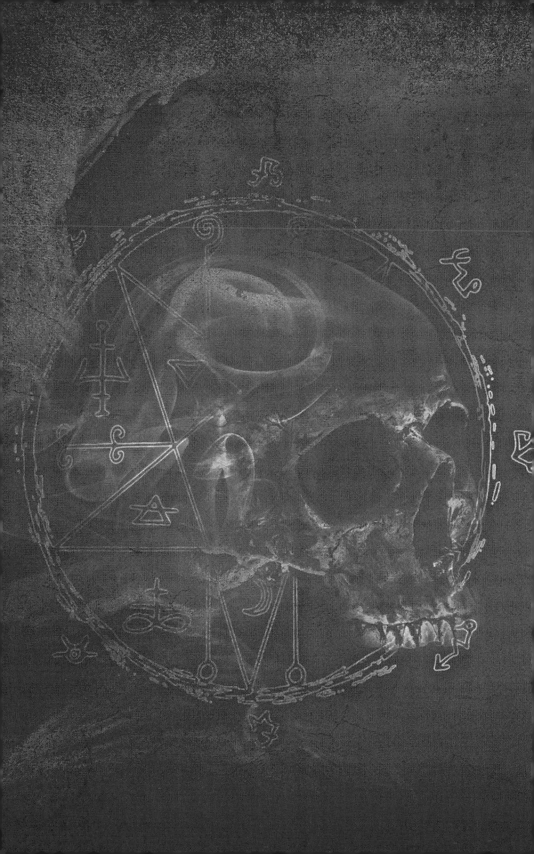

Chapter 34

Rook

Fucking hell, I had the worst case of blue balls, which only added to my royally annoyed mood. I stubbornly chose not to relieve myself of the issue in the shower, but if it didn't chill out soon, I was going to need to do something.

All fucking night, I tossed and turned with erotic dreams of Rhys and then Elewyen and then the two of them together. And finally, all of us fucking in this bed. I sat up in a cold sweat at one point, convinced that Rhys was in bed with me, his hand wrapped around my cock. I tossed the blankets off to find myself completely alone, and yet the feeling of his touch lingered like a memory.

This fucking triad was messing with every single one of my brain cells. I was a strong advocate for sex in general, but even I was starting to feel like it was all I thought about. That said a whole fucking lot.

Wandering down the stairs in my workout clothes, I followed the scent of coffee and was happy to see the full pot. It called to me like a glowing beacon of hope. Would anyone mind if I just put a straw in the fucking lid?

Finding the largest cup they had in the cupboard, I poured myself a cup and doctored it before moving to the table. A basket sat in the centre. Inside I found fresh bread, buns that were still warm, and whipped butter. Okay, my morning was looking up. I still hadn't seen a single person cooking or cleaning and yet everything was spotless, and the most amazing food was always made. I was tempted to go on the hunt just to see if I could find these mysterious workers.

Grabbing a warm bun, I spread the butter on it and was about to sit down when I heard laughter. I looked out the glass doors to see Mari, Belle, and Elewyen in the backyard. All of them were holding a canne and were breathing hard as they leaned on the weapons.

I hadn't seen Mari or Elewyen yesterday. Mari didn't seem to be in the castle at all, good luck ever finding Belle, Gregory was at the ritual with Rhys, and Elewyen refused to leave her room. That left me in a massive castle with no one to talk to. Aces all around. I managed to get a lot of reading in, and the more I learned, the more conflicted I became. We were a powerful but ruthless bunch. There were things we'd done as a Faction that were brutal and I wasn't sure I was down for. I had my kinks and pleasures but the stuff that I read was beyond sadistic.

Taking a bite of the bun, I leaned against the open doorframe, and my eyes lingered on Elewyen and her elegant features. Her thick hair had been pulled up into a ponytail on top of her head, and she was wearing knee-high leather boots that laced up the front. Looking at them was encouraging my hard-on. Add in the short kilt, tight T-shirt, and leather protectors around her wrists like the other two women, and I was full-on panting. The red and black colours suited her. It was like a complete transformation from when she'd attacked me in the woods.

It felt like a lifetime had passed since that moment. I shook my head in wonder and continued to watch as they began another round of mock battle as I ate my breakfast. Mari was in the middle and the other two women were trying to get a hit in, but she was incredibly fast. There was no move she made that was wasted and the look in her eye was as hard as steel. The smack of wood on wood was loud in the otherwise quiet morning.

If I hadn't been watching Mari so closely, I would've missed the subtle wince she made that slowed her down just enough that Elewyen landed a hard crack across her back. Mari cried out and went down to one knee. Elewyen dropped to her knees beside her as her hands covered her mouth.

"I'ma so sorry. Me never meant ta hit ya dat hard."

I'd seen her take harder hits than that and not bat an eyelash. Now my mind was whirring as I wondered where she'd been yesterday and what she'd done to hurt herself.

"I be fine. Jus' hit a bruise me already had," Mari said as she stared at Elewyen and then up at her sister.

Mari allowed Elewyen to help her stand, and she gave them a smile, but I could see the pain in her eyes from here. I filed the information away. It wasn't that I didn't trust my cousin, but there were things she was hiding. There were things she and Rhys were hiding. I felt it in the way they looked at one another. It was more than longing. It was understanding. At first, I thought it had to do with them being in love, but that didn't feel like the whole truth to me.

I stuffed the last of the bun in my mouth and watched as the women went right back to smiling and laughing with one another.

Elewyen spotted me first, and as her green eyes found mine, a blush spread across her cheeks. I tipped my head in her direction, and she returned the gesture. She was fucking adorable. I heard loud chattering before spotting the little red squirrel sitting on a branch by the small outdoor sitting area. I let out a yelp as a nut hit me on the cheek. I glared at the little menace.

"I said I was sorry, man. Knock it off," I said, as his small paws tossed another nut in my direction. This one bounced off my shoulder, but I swore and moved away from my relaxing spot. I turned and pointed at the squirrel. "Come down here and do that you demon rodent," I growled softly at the squirrel that was still giving me an ear full. "Yeah, you heard me, that's what you are," I whispered to the furry beast before turning to go out and talk to the girls. Why I had the biggest urge to turn and make a face at the small beast was beyond me, but he irritated me as much as one of my brothers.

"Mornin'," Belle said as we passed one another.

"Did I interrupt?" I asked Mari but kept my eyes on Elewyen's face.

She stared me in the eyes, even though I could tell she was still nervous. My power seemed to be hyperaware of the energy she was putting off. Most of it was nervousness, but under that, I could taste curiosity and arousal. I shuddered.

"No, your timing is perfect. You think you can take us both on?" Mari asked.

I laughed and looked at her like she'd lost her mind. "Not likely," I said honestly, and the girls smiled and then laughed.

"Okay, that may be a bit ambitious. How about one at a time, three-minute duels with two minutes' rest in between?" Mari offered instead.

"Sounds like I'm about to get my ass kicked but let's do it." I chugged back the last of the coffee. "Oh, Mari, when we're done, will you meet me in the library? Rhys said you would know what books I should brush up on."

"Sure. I need to pick out a book for Elewyen to work on. She said that she'd like to learn how to read."

I looked over at Elewyen, and she immediately cast her eyes down to the ground. "You don't know how to read?"

"Naw. I dinnie know how ta read or write," she said, and her eyes found mine, but they held emotion that I couldn't decipher.

"Not even a single word?" She shook her head no. "How is that possible?"

She lifted her shoulders and let them drop. "Me lived in da forest until da coven took me in. Dere no be any teachin' in da coven like dat. Me learned ta talk from dem, but none of dem know how ta read."

I looked over at Mari in shock. "Why is it that the covens live in hiding from us?"

"Try asking the older men in the family." She crossed her arms, but when I continued to stare, she sighed like she was letting something go. "The villagers are true Flitters and are terrified of magic. Rightly so, we made sure of that, but that means they are highly superstitious. To them, all women born with red hair are genetically disposed to be able to do magic. It's not the case, but that doesn't matter. The fear that they could perform magic is enough for the infants to be cast out, and if they live, they live. If not, then oh well."

My mouth fell open.

"I don't understand. Why do you say rightly so? We don't plan on hurting them. Do we?"

"No, but those that are living now are descendants from the time of war. All their stories and books tell them to fear the magic, fear the people from the castles, fear the technology. They banned anything like that from the villages and cast anyone out they feel may be a threat." She pointed to Elewyen. "Like those with red hair."

"Okay, I get that, but why don't the covens come to us then? Why do they hide? We don't plan on hurting them. If anything, we could help them," I said.

I could feel Elewyen's eyes on me as if she was studying me as much as I was learning about her world.

Mari laughed, but I didn't understand the humour in what I'd asked.

"Rook, you have a lot of history to catch up on. It was not so long ago that we were not very nice to the third in a triad. Like all things in these godforsaken families, the men rule, and the women are nothing more than something to be used and tossed away."

My brow furrowed at her bitter tone.

"I see the skepticism on your face, but it's all true. The men, at one time, would capture the women and bind them with magic, only to drag them behind a horse to the castle, where they were forced to live in terrible conditions. The cattle were treated better. Once the choosing rituals happened and they found their third in the bunch, they would force the woman to partake in the union ritual. There was no asking. The two men took turns raping her until she bore them a son or two. If they had a girl, it would start all over again. The entire time, the women were locked away in rooms. All alone with only a servant to prepare food, baths, or them for more sex, they couldn't say no to."

Mari made a dramatic motion with her arms as if she was trying to show off the entire castle. "All of this Rook is built on the backs of women who were forced to breed for more men and suppress more women. They cooked, they cleaned, they did the gardening, and even built the stone walls all while they slept in the barns, were fed very little, and given to the guards to fuck daily."

I took a step back from Mari. There was no way my father would have done this to my mother...Had he?

"They essentially became nothing but glorified breeders for the Faction with no lives outside of the slavery they were forced into. It was around our great-grandfather's era that there was a subtle shift. Some of the men couldn't stomach raping their third all the time, and the law was created that the woman chosen could only be brought into the triad of her own free will. The connection power also changed and once the union is complete, to hurt your third is to beat yourself. This, too, was to help protect the third from the brutal ways. The women who had been enslaved were set free, but they immediately hid from the rest of society. Also, you should know that the vote to end this way of life wasn't unanimous, and those voices are still in council to this day."

"What the fuck?" My mind was blown. I didn't pay attention to much, but I would remember learning about this. "So what you're saying is some would still do this if they thought they wouldn't get caught? Like, would my father have done this to my mother?" I asked, nervous about the answer.

I was truly horrified by the thought. I may not have known my mother well because she was murdered when I was so young, but I couldn't imagine my father treating her like that. The man was a colossal dick, but an abuser was not something I would ever put on his resume.

"I don't think so. I mean, I don't really know. It's not like I know Angus well, but I never heard any whisperings." Mari shrugged. "This all took place right after the war when the Factions were created. Like so many things after the war, things changed for the worse. It was like all the advancement that had been made by civilization was destroyed. There were only a few who dared write about what it was really like before the world fell."

Mari ran her hand down her long braid. "I'll show you those books as well. We are one of the few Factions that keep them on hand and allow the next generation to read them. With each new generation, the rules and thoughts continue to evolve, and that is the only thing that gives me hope that one day cursed women like me will get to be paired or at least be allowed to have a life."

"Mari, you're not cursed. I...."

"Rook, I mean no disrespect, but don't be trying to tell me what I am when you have not spent a single day as me. You have no idea what I've lived through or what the Faction has made me do in their name. You may see me as your cousin, as family, and as an equal, but you and Rhys and a handful of others are the exceptions, not the rule. Even my own father sees me as a commodity to be sold and has told me such to my face. When a deal couldn't be made to sell me off, I was pushed to the side and became nothing more than his sword for hire. I cannot live or breathe or sleep without permission, and I'm certainly not allowed to love or speak out of turn. Speaking to you like this right now could get me whipped, and yet I do because I'm tired of it. You and Rhys and Elewyen here are a beacon of hope for me and many others."

"Are you serious? You could be punished for telling me the truth?"

"I could be punished for looking you in the eyes the wrong way. If you chose to punish me yourself, you could do so openly here in this training area, and if I wanted to live, then I must submit." She lifted her shoulders in a small shrug. "Just because most of the rules are no longer followed, doesn't mean they don't exist and are still used when the council wants something."

My mind reeling, I turned to look at Elewyen and didn't know what to say about any of this. How was I supposed to convince her to stay here after learning all of this? If I was her, I wouldn't want to stay. This explained so much about why she attacked me the way she had. Not only did she think Rhys and I had killed a bunch of innocent people, but she'd been taught that we planned to violate her. I liked my sex rough, but I wasn't about to take it without consent. That was a line I wouldn't even cross, Devlin, on the other hand... Fuck, I could see my brother being into this shit. That worried me.

"I don't know what to say to any of this other than I'm sorry for what my ancestors have done," I said to both women.

This was what Rhys meant when he said I'd been living with my head in the clouds. I had lived a life that was a modern fabrication to placate the Flitters who lived in those areas. But under the bright lights and cheering fans was an ugliness. Had my father really been trying to shield me from all of this, or did he not think I could handle it? That was a question for our next call.

Elewyen lifted a shoulder. "Me tink we done enough talkin." She gave me a smile. "Let's fight," she said.

I caught the canne Mari tossed my way out of the air and smiled back. "All right, let's do this."

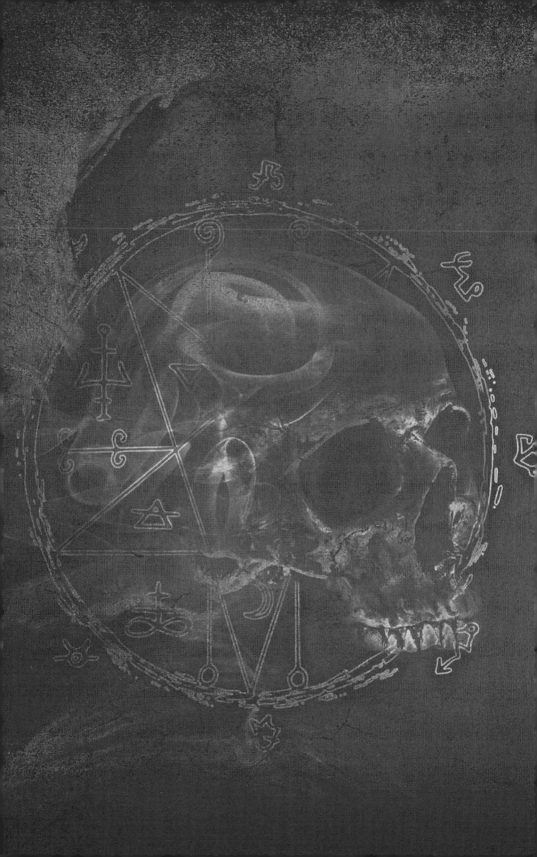

Chapter 35

Rook

Okay, I thought I was fucking tough, but going multiple rounds with Elewyen and Mari was a whole new level of pain. Not that I was going to let anyone know that. I walked away from the fight with my head held high and at least twenty new bruises to add to the others.

Washed and changed, I went down to the library and found Mari staring at the shelves with a stack of books in her arms. I closed the door quietly, but she still jumped like I slammed it in place. Her eyes searched my face as if I was planning on attacking her.

"We need to talk, and I thought that it would be best if no one else could hear the conversation," I said and waved my hand over the door to create a barrier from prying ears. One thing I'd learned in my short time here was that, for as big as this place was, everyone knew everything going on.

"Okay," she said, then walked over to the nearest table and sat the books down. "If this is about Rhys and me, you don't have to worry, but thanks again for…Well, for what you offered.".

"That's not what I wanted to talk to you about," I said.

Her eyes lifted to find mine again. "Oh, okay. What did you want to talk about?"

"What are you hiding from me? More specifically, what are you and Rhys hiding from me? I don't like secrets, and I really fucking hate being left in the dark." I leaned my hip against the table and watched as Mari's face transformed from open and friendly to a stone-cold mask.

"We're hiding nothing," she said.

Taking a deep breath, I slowly moved around the table, and as I did, her back straightened. "I'm not going to fight you, Mari," I said as I came to a stop in front of her. "But you owe me. I gave you your night with Rhys completely guilt-free, and this is what I want in return. I deserve to know the truth of what is really between you two because there is more than longing and desire. The way Rhys looks to protect you and worries about you is beyond that." I leaned down closer to her ear. "What are you hiding, cousin? What don't you want the world to know? Don't make me ask Rhys and put him in the middle again."

"You're an asshole, Rook. You know that, right?" Mari said, and it made me smirk.

"I've been told that once or twice." Pulling out a chair, I sat down and waited for her to follow suit. She shook her head as she sat beside me and clasped her hands on the table.

"If I tell you this, you can never repeat it. I mean it, Rook. Don't toss it out as a joke, and don't try to use it against me or to pry information from me because I cannot say. It is of the utmost importance that no one ever knows. Rhys is the only one who knows the truth, and it puts him at risk just for knowing. You need to promise me right now on your own life that you will never breath a word of this again." Her eyes bore holes into me, and I could feel the weight of her words.

I licked my lips. "Okay, I promise."

"No, not good enough. You need to say *I promise on my own life that I will never discuss this again with anyone, not even Rhys.* This will become something that neither of you can talk about. Words can travel even when we don't mean them to." Wasn't that the truth?

"So you're asking me to keep this secret from him, too?"

"From the moment I tell you this, you need to forget it again. Pretend you never heard it and move on. You're the one forcing me to say this, so if you want to know, these are the conditions."

Leaning back in the comfortable chair, I crossed my arms over my chest. "Fine, I swear to you on my life that I won't say a word."

Mari rubbed her eyes. "Tell me this first. Are you falling for him? Are you falling in love with Rhys?"

I narrowed my eyes at her. "What does that have to do with anything?"

"Just answer the question, please." Mari mirrored my position, and once again, I saw a lot of myself in my cousin.

"I don't do feelings."

She stared at me. I stared back.

Her right eyebrow rose.

"Yes, I am. Fine. There, I said it. Happy now?"

The corner of her mouth curled up. Leaning forward, she held out her hand. I stared at it.

"Take it. You said you wanted to know, so take my hand."

Reaching out, I tentatively laid my hand in hers.

"You ready?"

"I guess...Oh, fuck!" I swore as my mind was pulled into a whirl-wind. I had to grab the table to steady myself from falling off the chair. When the swirling colour stopped, I was standing in a room with Rhys and Elewyen. I picked up a baby wrapped in a blanket knitted with my family colours from a bassinet. Warmth radiated from me as I smiled at Elewyen and Rhys. I could feel the love in my chest, and it made my heart hammer hard.

I gasped as I was suddenly back in the library. Tears streamed down my face. Glancing up, I met my cousin's eyes. "You...you...."

"Yes, I *see*." She stood from the table, and I couldn't take my eyes off her. Rare didn't begin to describe her ability. "I knew you'd come. I didn't know about the gift you'd give me, but since you have, I've seen a lot more." She pulled a book from the pile and held it to her chest. "Love him, Rook, and never look back. Hold on to both of them tightly and protect them with all you have. There is darkness coming. Darkness I cannot speak of and most I do not yet know, but I feel it to the marrow of my bones." She pointed at the stack of books. "Read these, and if you're wise, you should brush up on all the spells you can. Take my word for it. You're going to need them."

Mari walked towards the door, and I released the spell just before she reached for the handle. A moment later, I sat alone in shock, my mind still reeling from what I saw. That could be my life? Could I really feel like that? Was that my son? No wonder Rhys protected Mari so fiercely. If anyone ever found out...I shuddered at the thought. She would never be safe.

Grabbing the pile of books, I stood and left the library. I went up to my room, my mind still trying to compute what I learned. Flopping on my bed, I draped my arm over my eyes, planning to nap away the aches and the spinning in my mind.

A knock sounded at the door.

"Come in," I called out, expecting it to be Liam.

"Ya 'ave a bit a time?" came Elewyen's voice.

Elewyen was standing in the doorway with a large book in her hands. She'd changed again into something else of Mari's. She wore a long creamy sweater that fell off one shoulder and a black kilt. I found it sexy as hell.

"For you? Sure. What's going on?"

I was shocked to see her. She blushed many times earlier, but seemed uninterested in anything else. I spent my shower picturing her in that short red skirt that kept distracting me before she would land a blow to my arm or leg. Now here she was, looking just as scrumptious as she stood in the middle of my room.

Elewyen walked towards the bed and held out the book for me to see. "Would ya teach me? Mari was gonna, but she needed ta head out. I'z wanna learn."

My heart warmed that she came to me, and I sat all the way up and patted the bed. "Of course. I'm not sure I'm the best for you to learn from, but I'm happy to try."

Elewyen got up on the bed and crossed her legs as she sat across from me. "You need to come here so we can both see the book." I touched the spot beside me.

There was uncertainty in her eyes, but she shuffled around and sat close to my side.

Taking the book from her, I looked at the cover, *The War of Twin Flames*. As good as any place to start. Pointing at the first word, I looked at Elewyen.

"The. War. Of. Twin. Flames," I said slowly, pointing at each word.

"Dee waarr a twin flames."

"The," I said, enunciating the "th" sound. "Or, as Rhys would say, da," I offered, figuring that may be easier.

When she said it again, she said it with my accent, which made me smile. I watched in fascination as she concentrated on the word I was pointing at and then proceeded to slowly copy it down on the pad she was carrying. She kept re-writing it and saying "the" over and over again. A few minutes passed before she held it up to me. "Cannie ya write how da word is ta sound, so me dinnie firget?"

"Sure or yes, which would be aye for you," I said and smiled.

She smiled and looked away from my eyes, but I'd seen a glimmer of real emotion before she turned her head.

"Wat it mean, *the?*"

"Oh…um…" I tried to think about how Rhys would use it in a sentence. "Da dog ran out in da rain." She tilted her head and looked at me. "I would say, 'the dog ran out into the rain.'"

She nibbled on her bottom lip, and I couldn't stop staring and wanting to taste her mouth. The little connection current felt delicate, like this moment between us, but it was there every time she moved. It travelled up my knee from where her leg softly brushed against me, slowly diving me crazy.

We were at it for hours, and normally, something this mundane would've made me go insane and lose interest long ago. There was something about showing Elewyen something new that intrigued me. The excitement in her eyes with each new victorious word made me never want to stop. If she wanted to sit here forever, I would.

It was well past dinnertime when we both began to yawn. "Do you want to go grab something to eat? There is always a ton of food in this place," I asked.

"Aye, I be starvin'."

"You're understanding me a lot easier," I said.

She blushed again, the red flaming her cheeks and making her look sexy and fucking cute as sin all at the same time. "Aye, I'ma... I'm a quick learner."

My brow cocked upward. "That you are."

The necklace around her neck began to glow and then stopped. She quickly grabbed the stone and stared at me like I would try to take it away.

"Why did it glow?" I asked. "I'm not going to take it. I'm just curious."

She nibbled on her bottom lip and closed her eyes. A soft glow emanated from the stone, shining through the narrow gaps between her fingers. "I dinnie know if I should say."

Placing my finger under her chin, I forced her to look at me. "I know you don't know if you can trust me, and I don't blame you, but neither Rhys nor I would do what Mari was talking about. Do we like sex rough? Sure, but...I'm talking too fast again, aren't I?"

Elewyen nodded. Sighing, I tried again. "We will not hurt you and will not take your necklace. What does it do?"

She released the little gem, and it once more lay dormant against her skin. "I'z 'ave someone back home dat I care about," she said, and I had to stop myself from growling at the thought of another man in her life.

"I thought your coven was all women?" I asked, barely managing to keep my voice calm.

Elewyen scrunched up her nose and furrowed her brow. "Aye. Da someone is a wee lass. Keeva be like me sista. Dis lets me know she be safe when I'ma travellin' in search of da babes."

It was my turn to look at her like she'd lost her mind. "You do what?"

Elewyen hopped off the bed and began walking around my large room with her hand over her eyes. "I look for da babes...that get left in...the woods," She said slowly and making sure to pronounce each word carefully.

She peered over the couch and looked around, then continued to walk as she demonstrated out what she was talking about. "I protect dem from dose dat wanna kill 'em or eat 'em."

My mouth fell open. "You mean when Mari said that the villagers cast out the babies, she literally meant small infants are just left in the forest?"

"Aye, what ya tink she meant?"

I didn't know. I thought it had been a figure of speech. "You know, I think I've had enough learning for one day. Let's go get that food," I said.

Elewyen placed her hands on her hips. "Aye, ya really are no from around 'ere, are ya?"

I shook my head. "Overseas is very different. We have lots of modern technology and television shows, and I sing music on large stages for thousands of people," I said and slid off the bed to join her.

"What is tech-nooo-loo-gy?"

I knew on this side of the world the Factions like to keep everything as anti-modern as possible, at least from those who were not part of the Faction, but I hadn't realized until now just how much had been kept from the people who lived here until my talk with Mari. How did they explain what a car was, or if they saw a plane or cellphones to each new generation? Did they just never see them, or was it something that they saw, but never had so didn't care? And how the heck did I explain this to Elewyen? My appreciation for my tutor just went up.

"I think I know how to explain technology to you," I said. "I'm going to show you."

When we got to the kitchen I pointed to the microwave and pushed the button on the bottom to open the door. The light turned on, and Elewyen took a step forward and looked inside.

"This is called a microwave. It warms up cold food."

She stared at me with wide eyes as I put a plate in, entered the time I wanted, then pressed start. The plate inside spun around, and she took a step back like it was going to jump off the counter and attack her.

"Trust me, it's safe. It won't hurt you," I said, giving her a reassuring smile.

Once it beeped, I pulled out the plate and sat the steaming food onto the counter. Elewyen walked over, then poked at the food. She yelped and put her finger in her mouth, which, of course, derailed my brain as I watched her suck it clean.

I had to clear my throat before I could speak again. "See? Now the food is hot." I made my way over to the fridge and opened it, pulling out a jug of water and sat it down on the counter. "Touch that."

She looked at me and tentatively poked at the glass. "It be cold."

"Yes, that is called a fridge. It helps food from rotting by keeping it cold."

I'd never seen someone's eyes light up so much over the prospect of a refrigerator.

"Ya mus' show me more." She gripped my arm with excitement. A blush stole over her cheeks, and she pulled her hands away as the little current that had been constant since she entered my room rippled and made us gasp.

"I like it when you touch me," I said, but stepped away and decided to keep her enthusiasm up by going to the next item in the kitchen... the stove.

Dinner had never taken so long to get eaten, and I'd never had so much fun eating. Watching Elewyen's excitement over each new discovery was priceless. I couldn't keep my eyes off her as she leaned against the counter and finished eating some berries and cream for dessert. I managed to keep my distance, but the little droplet of cream at the corner of her mouth summoned me. Elewyen stilled as I stepped in close to her and placed a hand on either side of her on the counter. Her eyes darted from side to side like she was looking for an escape.

"I promised you that we are not going to hurt you or kill you. Do you not believe me?" I asked.

She swallowed audibly.

Taking my chance, I leaned in and placed my lips over the cream. The air immediately changed with the contact and made me groan as it caressed my body. The droplet was sweet on my tongue, but the light contact made me want a whole lot more. I wanted to pull up the black skirt and sit her on the counter to devour what she could offer me instead.

"I dinnie know what ta believe anymore," she whispered.

I knew how that felt. It was only days ago that I had the same feeling when I arrived and met Rhys. I was so adamant that I wasn't going to have anything to do with him or a triad. Elewyen's hands went to my waist, and I thought she was going to push me away, but she just left them there.

"You can touch me," I whispered, staring into her spring-green depths.

When she just stared at me with those wide, unsure eyes of hers, I leaned back, gripped my T-shirt, and pulled it off over my head. Dropping it to the floor, I watched her expression carefully and wasn't disappointed as the energy around her changed. Desire burned in not only her eyes but the flush of her cheeks. As light as a feather, I trailed my fingers down her arms until I reached her hands and picked them up to place on my chest.

"I want you to touch me."

She shivered as her fingers splayed over my pecs. "I dinnie know what ta do," she said quietly.

I cupped her face, and she flicked her gaze up to mine. "I'm going to kiss you for real now. Touch me wherever you want. My body is yours."

I waited to see if she was going to stop me. Unable to hold myself back any longer, I licked across her lips, tasting the remnants of the strawberries as I asked for access. It took a minute, but she slowly opened her mouth. I groaned and held her tighter as I tasted her mouth for the first time.

She was tentative, but the power that had been so restrained began to swirl faster, like it had with Rhys. From one breath to the next, it began pulling us tighter together. Elewyen moaned into my mouth, and her hands began to move on my chest, then around to my back. It was as if she was igniting a fire everywhere her fingers trailed.

"Aw, come on. Ya got rooms, go ta one. I dinnie need ta see dis in me kitchen," Belle said, her voice grating.

I wanted to turn around and throw something at her as Elewyen jumped like she'd just been electrocuted and tried to pull away. I kept her firmly trapped against the counter, not wanting this moment to end.

I glared over my shoulder at my annoying cousin that I barely saw, but she picks now to show up. Fucking ironic.

Belle glared back at me and pointed to the large amounts of food still on the table. "I'ma wantin' me supper."

"Fine," I said.

I bent to grab my shirt, then took Elewyen's hand. She tried to tug it away, but I wasn't letting her return to the timid shell she'd been a moment before the kiss.

"I be sowry," Elewyen said, as I marched us past my cousin, irritated by the inopportune timing.

I was getting somewhere, and it all burst like a balloon. Maybe it was Elewyen's tentativeness, or maybe it was the fact we were both a little unsure about one another. The wild, desperate need that I had with Rhys had been instant. It seemed to need coaxing with Elewyen. It was still there, but just responded differently.

"Where ya takin' me?" she asked, pulling back on her hand again.

"To my room," I said.

She stopped walking, jerking me to a halt.

"I… I dinnie tink I'z ready for what ya want," she said.

Turning around, I looked into her eyes and smiled. "Just lie with me. Like sleep, not anything more, just sleep in the same bed?"

"Oh…I…" Her cheeks were bright red, and she looked over her shoulder where her bedroom was.

Stepping in quickly, I cupped her face, desperate to hang onto what we started. "You promised seven days to see if you want to stay, to see if you want to join in the union with me and Rhys. Two have already passed. If you were serious, then this is the next step. Did you mean what you said?"

"Aye..." she said, her voice wavering over the single word.

"Then let's do this. We won't do anything intimate if you don't want to, but just stay in the room with me."

"Why?"

"To see if you like it, like me, like the idea of what it would mean to be with me and Rhys for real. If you don't like me and choose to go, then at least you'll know for sure without any doubt about how you feel."

Elewyen was quiet a long time, but I wasn't giving in or letting her go until she agreed. I couldn't explain why I was nervous for her answer, but I was.

She slowly nodded. "All right, but I'z need ta get Barry. I dinnie wanna leave him locked in me room alone."

I nodded as we veered toward her room, but all I could think about was that the rodent was probably going to try to chew my cock off in the night. That was not what I had in mind, but if it was the only way to get her to agree, then I would take it and call it a win.

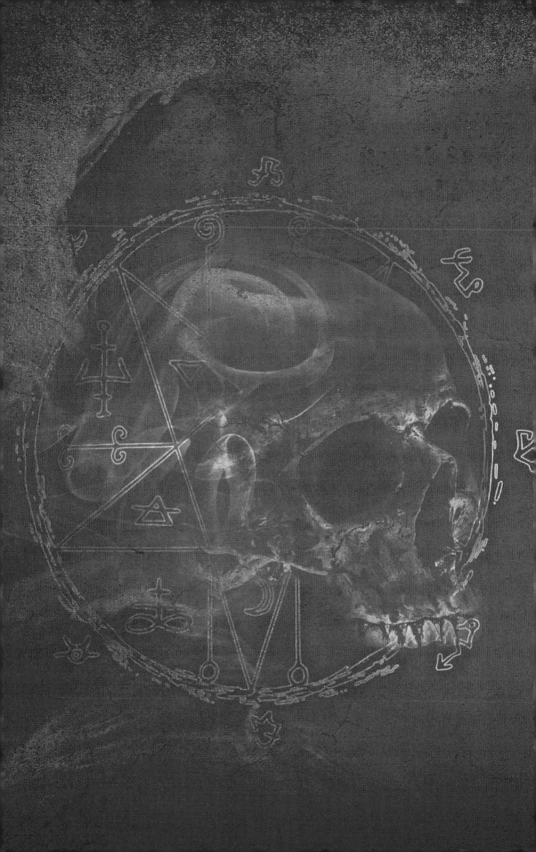

Chapter 36

Elewyen

This was a terrible idea. When he asked me to sleep in here with him, the logical part of my brain said that this was not a good idea and wanted me to say no, but the steady yearning in my heart and the heat between my thighs had ended up winning the argument. The way he looked at me seemed to confirm everything I was taught and destroy it at the same time. The look in his eyes was dangerous, and when we reached his room, and he kissed me again, the world seemed to stand still.

The strange animal growl that came from his mouth as he pushed me up against the wall made my blood run cold and boiled me from the inside at the same time. How was that possible?

"Fuck, you're beautiful," Rook said, breaking the kiss that left my head light. I barely remembered him pulling me across the room, giving me one of his tops to wear and ordering me to get changed.

The bigger confusion was why I did what he told me to. Barry was annoyed and had told me off all the way back to Rook's room. I wouldn't be surprised to find that the little bugger had chewed holes in all Rook's pants or something by morning.

My mind and my body wouldn't settle, and it only got worse when Rook dimmed the light and rolled over so that he could wrap his arm around my waist. I bit my lip as he pulled me tight into his body. The initial nervousness quickly turned into something else.

I'd never been in the same bed as a man for any reason, and I had to admit that, at least with Rook, there was something comforting about the feel of his hard muscled body holding mine. The hard pounding of my heart in my chest on the other hand was making me anxious and my body hypersensitive.

When he exhaled heavily, I shivered as my hair moved with the breath. When his finger flexed ever so slightly, it was like he hit me with some form of lightning. I was silently panting for something and had no idea what I wanted from him.

Rook lay perfectly still, his breathing even for such a long time that I thought he was asleep until he spoke.

"Why are you still so nervous?" he asked quietly.

His breath brushed against my ear. The heat in my body tripled, along with the tendrils of power that I couldn't see but could feel as they wrapped around our bodies.

"Answer me, Elewyen. Why are you nervous?"

"Ya make me nervous," I said. "Me heart dinnie wanna stop runnin'."

"Let me help you relax," he said, his lips touched my neck.

I was shocked that I hadn't passed out as my heart raced faster until it was all I could hear.

Thump, thump, thump.

"I dinnie tink yer helpin'," I said, tempted to leap from the bed even as my body begged for more. "All da women in me coven 'ave warned me of a man's touch. Day would say dat it cannie be poison to da soul. I'z was told ya be a path of notin' but anguish."

He made a soft rumbling sound against my neck that had my body pressing back into his, which only increased the sound he made.

"Is that what you believe? Do you think I'm nothing but a road of anguish and pain?"

I felt like a dog panting after a long run. "Ya be messin' wit me head and me body. Dat much me knows fir sure."

He chuckled, and as the sound vibrated down my spine, I couldn't stop the moan from escaping my mouth.

"Yer no helpin' ta calm me."

I felt him smile into the side of my neck. "Oh, but I can."

The arm he had wrapped around my waist travelled down my leg, and I had to bite my lip to hold back another moan. His hand slowly lifted the large T-shirt I was wearing pulling the material all the way up from where it had been at my knees.

My body began to shake as the nervousness worsened.

"Shhh, Elewyen, I promise this won't hurt," he said, and then ran the soft lobe of my ear through his teeth.

"It feels like ya could consume me body," I said, my voice wavering.

Rook was a mystery. I would swear he could take what he wanted when he wanted, then in the next breath, he was calm and understanding. I couldn't make up my mind which of the two was the real Rook.

I sucked in a gasp and pushed back hard into his body as his hand slid around my hip to the lower part of my stomach. He groaned into my ear as he held me tighter, and the vibration travelled all the way down my spine.

"Do you even understand how beautiful you are?" he whispered.

Other than Keeva, no one had ever said I was beautiful. Rook had said it to me twice tonight, but I didn't know what you had to look like to be considered beautiful. I thought Mari was beautiful and her sister Belle was equally so. Did he compare me to them? Was I my own kind of beautiful?

"Stop thinking so much, and just relax."

Rook's hand left my bare stomach, and I felt empty from his lack of touch until he reached around and cupped my chin, forcing me to look up at him. The moon's rays were bright tonight, and they made his eyes look even more stunning than normal as the moonlight emphasized the deep blue. The shadows that lined his face made him look like a dream and a demon at the same time. Not an ugly demon, but one that would happily lead you to sin, and you would smile and go right along with him.

He stared at me for what felt like a lifetime, and with each moment that passed, I wanted him to kiss me. The feel of his lips on mine and the emotions that his kiss brought to life in me were firmly planted in the front of my mind.

As if reading my thoughts, he dropped his head. The kiss didn't start out tentative like it had before. It was hot and deep, and his tongue demanded entrance to my mouth, I gave in wanting more.

If this was what a kiss felt like, then I couldn't help wondering how laying with him would feel. I was so engrossed in the kiss that I didn't notice when his hand left my face, but I noticed when it pressed into my stomach once more. I didn't jump as much this time, but I couldn't seem to stop pushing back into his hips.

Each time I moved, he groaned a little louder and his kiss became a little more aggressive, as if my body's action increased the desire in him. He was wearing soft bottoms, but I could distinctly feel something hard pressing into my back and knew what it was. I'd been taught by the women of the coven the parts of a man and how they worked. When I travelled, I sometimes came across men bathing naked in the stream. I hid among the bushes and secretly watched them. It was wrong, and yet I couldn't help staring at the part of them that hung between their legs. I didn't remember it looking as big as what this felt like, though.

Rook's hand grew bolder and slid down my body until it rested on the top of my womanhood. Even as anxious as I was, I wanted to know what it would feel like if he touched me there. When his hand skimmed farther down my leg, I was disappointed until he pulled up on my leg and draped it over his own.

The position opened my legs up, and every part of my body trembled. He was lighting fires under my skin, and the sensation burned in my gut. The strange tingling magic I felt when I looked at him erupted as it broke free from deep in my chest. Breaking the kiss, I arched off the bed as his hand returned to the top of my womanhood. It was too much.

"Just relax, I feel it too, but try to remain calm," Rook said as I gulped for air. He brought his face close to mine. "Look into my eyes. Good, that's it. Don't fight it. Ride the feeling. Let me help you. Hang onto me."

I moaned into his mouth as he kissed me again, and I wrapped my arm around his neck. I did feel more stable the moment I hung onto him, and it suddenly felt like he'd never be close enough.

Rook broke the kiss, and I sucked in a deep breath as his fingers found another sensitive spot that, with the lightest of touches, ignited intense pleasure. I jerked as he pressed on the area and rubbed in a circle.

"Oh…sweet…spirits," I stuttered.

His fingers dipped lower and glided through the wetness that had been steadily building between my legs.

"Rook," I whispered.

He swirled his fingertips around, and my body tensed all over, but not in a bad way. Drawing his fingers up once more to the sensitive area he first found, I couldn't seem to stop myself from pushing harder into his hand. Each little swirl of his finger loosened the grip I had on my own senses and the power that was steadily building. To lose control of either was dangerous, but to lose control of both was deadly. I should tell him to stop.

I opened my mouth to say the words, but nothing came out.

"Do you like that?" he asked, before his lips found my neck and his teeth grazed the skin.

"Aye," I said, then whimpered as his finger slipped a little bit into my body. "Oh…aye."

"That's it, Elewyen. Let yourself go," Rook said.

I didn't know what that meant, but I found myself moving my hips around and trying to get to some destination that my body was leading me to.

"Fuck, yes. You're so fucking sexy when you whimper like that. Do it again for me. Whimper for me," he said, and right away, a whimper that ended in a moan left my mouth. "Yeah, I like that. I like hearing you cry out."

His fingers were getting bolder, and soon it felt like his entire finger was sliding into my body.

"Say, fuck yes, for me," Rook whispered in my ear.

I would say whatever he wanted so long as he didn't stop.

"Feck yes," I cried out as he continued to massage the little spot that made me want to jump out of my skin. My fists clenched as I panted harder.

"You're so sexy, and I'm so fucking hard," he said, and his finger pressed harder into my body, making me cry out. "Yes, that's it," Rook growled against the pounding pulse in my neck.

I didn't know what he meant by hard, but there was no time to ask or care.

I bucked up hard with my ass as the pressure became so intense that I could no longer hold still. The magic that had been whipping around the room and warming my skin as it licked past tightened like a rope around my body. A part of my brain screamed that this should be scary, but the rest of me wasn't listening.

Rook growled in my ear as what felt like multiple fingers were now working their way in and out of me in time to my own movements.

"Come for me, Elewyen. Let your body go and come for me," Rook commanded, his voice deep and rough.

My movements became more erratic as my body raced toward something that I was desperately after. My power pushed out of the cage I kept it tightly locked in, and the room filled with a soft green light, but I had no control to pull it back. Instead, my back arched off the bed, and Rook covered my mouth with his in a kiss that swallowed my scream. I'd never felt anything so powerful. Pleasure ripped through my body in waves as strong as the ocean's tide.

With every movement his fingers made, the pleasure continued on. The power I'd been so worried about escaping swirled and entwined with either his power or the spell that was the connection. Soft green and cool white whipped around the room until they were moving so quickly that it was like the two had become one. Rook growled loudly into my mouth as the power wrapped tightly around our bodies and then pressed inward like it was physically trying to join us together.

Not so very long ago I would've fought it or tried to slow it down at the very least, but nothing was stopping this. I screamed again as an even larger crippling storm of pleasure pushed me over a steep cliff that instinctively I knew there was no coming back from.

"Oh yes, that's it. Fuck me, Elewyen, I want you so bad," Rook growled out, but I was too lost in my own floating bliss to understand why he was yelling.

My body slumped down onto the bed. I felt Rook roll onto his back. Then the blankets disappeared.

"Look what you do to me," he said.

My head felt heavy as it lulled to the side, but my eyes went wide as I stared at his hand.

"I want to fuck you so bad." Rook's eyes found mine, and there was a hungry desperation in them. "I have to do this or I'm going to do something I shouldn't. My control is hanging by a thread."

I pushed myself up to get a better look at what he was doing, and if it weren't for the floating cloud that I was riding on, I would've jumped from the bed. Instead, the explosive pleasure he'd just given me seemed to be encouraging me to continue to watch. Rook's pants were pulled down, and for the first time up close, I saw what a man's peen looked like.

It was like a giant snake attached to his body. I couldn't look away as his hand stroked the length of the shaft at a fast pace. Arms weak, I managed to push myself closer and stared in wonder at Rook. Every muscle in his body was flexed and on display. His face looked like he was angry or in pain, but I knew it was pleasure that had his jaw clenching tight as he tipped his head back and closed his eyes.

There was something entirely too mesmerizing about watching him stroke himself. To see him give himself pleasure made me lick my lips. I wanted to know what it was like to give him that look.

Not even sure where the courage came from, I reached for his body. Rook groaned and his eyes opened as my hand touched the hard muscles of his stomach, which looked and felt like hard ridges under his skin. He was strong but seeing him like this made him feel like a massive predator, but one that I wanted to catch me.

"Do you want to touch it?" Rook asked through clenched teeth.

I licked my lips, my gaze going from his eyes to his hand and back again. My hesitation seemed to be the only answer he needed as he let go and grabbed my hand off his abs. Pulling me closer to his body, Rook didn't hesitate to use his hand to wrap my own around his hard peen.

I sucked in a shuddering breath at the feel of it under my hand. His head flopped onto the pillow, and he let out a groan that made me feel powerful in a way that I'd never felt before. It was like my body was awakening to an entire side of myself that I may not have known existed, but that I wanted to explore.

His hand remained on mine and applied more pressure before he forced my hand to move along the hard length that seemed to jump under my touch.

"Yes, Elewyen, like that," he said, his voice encouraging.

Rook removed his hand, and I suddenly wasn't so sure. He turned his head and looked at me, his eyes pleading. Even though he didn't say anything, I knew what he was asking for. Getting up on my knees, I gripped him with both hands and began moving them the way he just showed me.

The top of his peen was all shiny and reminded me of how between my legs had gotten wet for him. Sliding my fingers over the wet that I assumed was his excitement, I instinctively pulled it down along his length so my hands would glide easier.

Rook's eyes fluttered closed again, and it was his hands gripping the sheets this time. "Yes…Oh fuck, I'm so close. Don't stop. Fuck, don't stop," it came out like an order to keep going.

Surprisingly, I liked his tone, and it had my legs rubbing together and my womanhood clenching for more.

As he got closer to the same ledge that I'd been standing on, the powerful magic returned. I watched as it dipped under our bodies and disappeared into the bed, only to rise on the other side, and like a needle and thread, wrapped us up together.

"Faster," Rook growled.

I did as he asked. His body arched off the bed. The muscles I was admiring somehow looked even larger as he yelled my name. I was shocked when the stream of liquid left his body and almost stopped what I was doing, but his groan let me know that this was what he was after. I continued to slide my hands along the hard length until his body went limp on the bed.

This was what the men wanted from us? This was not how it had been explained to me. The only word I could use to describe what I felt was happy. And I wanted more. I wanted to see him do that again, and I wanted to feel his hands on my body again.

Rook lifted his head and looked at me, and his lips tugged up in a smile. "Fuck, that felt amazing," he said.

A flicker of pride danced in my system. I made him feel like that. I brought that smile to his face, and I liked it. I really liked it.

"Um…Dat what ya call comin'?" I asked, and he chuckled and looked down at his chest, which had a fair bit of liquid on it.

"Yeah," he said.

"I'z dat what ya did ta me?"

"Yeah, it is."

Heat radiated from my body as I sucked in my bottom lip and looked him over. "Cannie we do it again?" I asked, my body wanted another round of that intense release.

Rook reached up and gripped me behind the neck as he sat up enough to kiss me.

"Fuck yeah, we can. There are so many things I want to do with you, but first I need to get cleaned off. So why don't I make you come in the shower?" he asked.

I had no idea what that entailed, but I trusted him so far, and I was excited to see what he had in store as he slipped from the bed and took my hand. I had a million questions about what it would mean if I decided to stay, including what would be expected of me, but they were all questions that I pushed to the back of my mind for now.

Right now, I wanted to let go, and for whatever time we had tonight, I wanted to let someone else take control of my body. I craved for him to show me what he meant by *so many things he wanted to do with me*. Was it wrong that I wanted to understand myself better, and that he seemed to have the answers? That I was putting my trust into the hands that I'd been warned to never go near? I may have been actin' a donkey, but I had a feeling the women in the coven had never met a man like Rook.

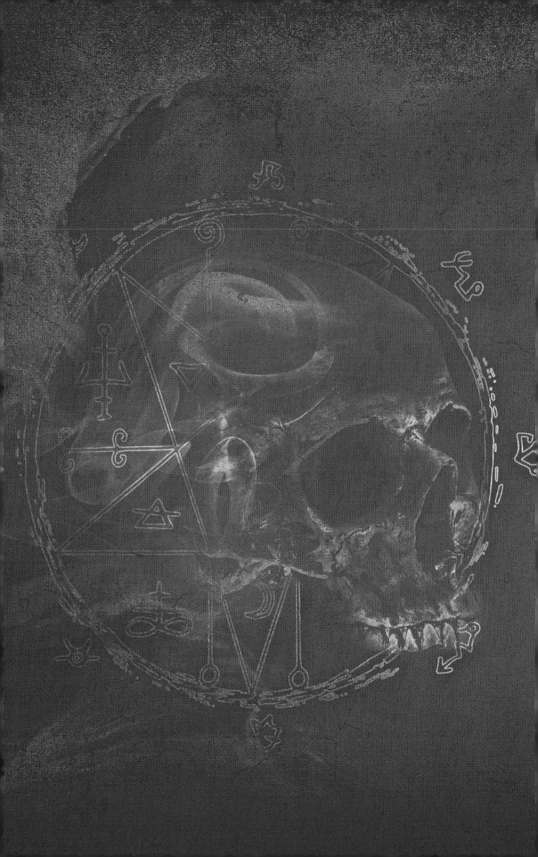

Chapter 37

Rhys

    I sat up, panting as heat began to rise in my body to an excessive level. Sweat dripped down my face, and I jumped from the bed, unsure of what was going on. My hand went to my chest, and I could feel my heart pounding like a wild animal. Was this a lingering effect of the ritual? Did I have a night terror? I don't remember. I stared at the damp area of the sheet, the confusion only getting worse with each passing second. It was like when Rook had been sleeping with people overseas, but there was no sharp pain.

    Grabbing the windows, I yanked them open to let in the cold night air and stood there breathing deeply, trying to cool my over-heated skin. The reprieve was momentary as the cool breeze seemed to enrage whatever was going on.

    "Is dis da demon fade comin' for me?" I groaned out and closed my eyes as I gripped the ledge of the window for support. I began going through everything that had happened since the ritual. Was the meal I ate poisoned? My eyes darted around the room for someone in here casting a spell, but I was alone.

"Ah," I yelled, as my power came from nowhere and ripped out of my chest to swirl around the room as my cock went from dormant to standing at full mast.

It was then that I knew that something was happening with the connection between Rook, Elewyen, and myself. It was the only logical explanation unless there was an invisible spirit in here, sucking my cock. I quickly shut that terrifying thought down. Rook was doing something with her, and I was being dragged along for the ride.

The spiritual bond and power binding us was getting stronger. I dropped to my knees, unable to hold myself up. I could just feel her on the other side of the connection with Rook, and when he groaned, the delicious sound echoed in my head. In all my reading, nothing had prepared me for this, and maybe it was because Rook and I hadn't completed our own binding first. Whatever it was, it had me falling over as the power wrapped itself around me like a cocoon and began to squeeze until it made it difficult to breathe.

Fuck, what were they doing? He better not be having sex with her. She needed to remain a virgin for the ceremony to be its strongest. Pulling myself across the floor, I reached up onto the nightstand and fumbled with my phone trying to get a grip on it.

"Fuck!" I yelled, as the phone fell off and hit me in the face before sliding under the tall bed. I felt around for it, but the power suddenly pushed its way back into my body with immense force, and my hand went to my bottoms instead.

"Holy, fuck me," I said through gritted teeth, and wasn't sure if it was me or him saying the words as I felt his cock in my hand and heard his voice in my head.

My hand wrapped around my own my cock, which felt like it might explode if I didn't touch it. The pleasure building was like nothing I'd ever experienced before, and I shuddered with the firm grip. Unable to hold off any longer, my hand worked furiously on my cock. Each stroke was an equal amount of pain and pleasure that drove me higher. Normally, I'd be all about this incredible new experience, but in the back of my mind, I couldn't help but worry about what was going on.

The connection between the two of us was undeniably getting stronger. I could almost feel his skin on mine, his hand touching me as I touched him.

All rational thought was thrown out my open window as the next wave gripped me, and my back was forced off the floor. I couldn't tell whose pleasure I was feeling. I yelled and could hear Rook's voice in my head as he screamed in the same mix of pleasure and pain.

"Rook," I yelled his name, but he didn't hear me.

There was no time to contemplate if this was normal as my ass flexed with the first round of release that flew from my cock. It seemed like an endless supply and still my hand didn't stop until the last drop had left my body.

My chest rose and fell with gasping breaths, and my heart pounded like a galloping horse. The power that had been shimmering in the air drifted down to the ground and towards me like late fall leaves before disappearing. Lying there in the darkness on the floor, a lone tear trickled from my eye.

I'd been foolish to think that I could be intimate with Mari without it affecting me. A small well of panic began to form as I realized that this was truly it. The door was being slammed shut on my

417

past, while a new door had just been flung open in my future. Visually, it was like I had been standing in the doorway and was terrified to let go of the frame. Rook and Elewyen were kicking me through whether I was ready to jump or not.

Another scream ripped from my throat as I came again when I hadn't even touched myself. I stared down at my cock and could feel a mouth that I couldn't see. My body bucked under the sensations that were mine and yet not. Was this normal? I hadn't read it in the books under the connection, and it hadn't been a question that ever came up with Gregory.

I slowly sat up and stared at the door to the shower. It seemed so far away, and I was tempted to simply flop down on the ground and stay there. But I forced myself to my feet and stumbled towards the door. My legs had never been this shaky.

Flicking on the hot water, I stepped under the spray and was just starting to feel a semblance of normal when it started all over again.

"Oh shite," I mumbled as my body broke out in the same sweat.

There was no option to go back now. Rook and I couldn't simply change our minds. We couldn't decide that this was not for us. Elewyen's presence was binding us as the three points of our triad began to merge magically. I needed to accept that and get home, move out, and complete the ritual, so I didn't end up crumpling to my knees every time they were intimate without me. At least I hoped it would stop. As powerful and amazing as this felt, it would be pretty fucking awkward in many situations.

"Fuck," I yelled as I crumbled to my side and let the water pound down on me as my hand once more stroked my hardening cock. "Rook, yer an animal," I growled.

I had a feeling this was going to be a very long night.

J was going to kill Rook. I asked him to convince Elewyen to stay. I didn't think they would be hopping into a bed together. The ritual was clear, if we wanted the triad to be at its strongest, Elewyen needed to remain a virgin. It was ridiculous, really, considering Rook and I had been whores, but I didn't make the crazy rules. I simply tried to follow them as best as I could. According to the books, the triad would still form if she wasn't a virgin, which had happened in the past, but the power dynamic was never as strong.

I winced as I reached the kitchen, and my cock brushed against my kilt. No, killing him was too easy. I was gonna cut off his cock. I lost count of the number of times the attacks hit during the night. Not only had he potentially screwed up making our triad the strongest it could be, but now every muscle in my body was sore and filled with lactic acid. My cock was raw from my own fucking hand, and I hadn't slept more than an hour, putting me in a rare mood.

"Hey, man, yer lookin' a bit stiff. Was da bed no' comfortable enough?" Caleb asked, as I hobbled my way around the kitchen like I just spent ten days on a horse.

"I'ma gonna guess dat if I'd slept in it, then it woulda been just fine," I said, and Caleb's eyebrow cocked at me.

"Do I wanna know what ya mean by dat?"

"Naw, ya dinnie wanna know. Trust me," I sucked in a sharp breath as I gingerly sat down at the table. No, cutting off his cock was too nice. I was going to impale him with something sharp and stick pins in his cock and then make it hard while the fuck was tied up. Yes, that seemed much more fitting.

"Caleb, I'ma gonna ask ya somethin', and I need ya ta be honest wit me," I said, as he sat down across from me.

"Aye, always."

"Have ya heard of anyone dat no' be happy wit me? Like someone dat would like ta see me fail, or worse?" I took a sip of the rich dark coffee and almost sighed. It tasted so good.

"Off the top of me head, no." Caleb rubbed the back of his neck and looked around the massive kitchen that could easily hold three of the kitchens back at Injebreck castle. "Well, dat's not a hundred percent true, me guess. Nigel has made it known dat he dinnie tink yer worthy to run da McGregor home, but ta wanna eliminate ya… Naw, I dinnie see it."

I didn't either. Nigel had been the most vocal about how he thought that my uncle Rayland should be taking over, but my uncle had no interest. My father had been the head of the family, which made me the next in line. My father's other brother, Riddick, had been cast out of the family long ago when he chose to marry outside of the Faction before I was born. I didn't even know what the man looked like other than for a few paintings on the walls of the castle.

"Aye, I agree wit ya, bu' somethin' seems off," I said, as Lochlan walked into the kitchen.

"Fuck, I hate politics," Lochlan grumbled as he wandered over to the pot of coffee. He'd chosen to spend a great deal of time overseas, and his accent sounded like Rook's. "I just got off the phone with Faction Four. They are refusing to let us bring any supplies through their area, because they don't want to look like they're playing favourites. So that means we'll have to deal with Faction Eleven to get food, or it will be rotten by the time it gets here. I double-checked with Falcon, who is on the mainland, and he says that the crops were poor this year. He can send some, but it won't be enough for the whole island all winter."

He grabbed a pastry off the counter and stuffed half of it in his mouth before continuing to talk. "We could fly the shit in, but that's going to get costly to support the whole island, and we can only bring in small planes or the private jets."

"Do I wanna know what Eleven is lookin' for in return?" I asked.

"Ha! They want to fuck us up the arsehole, is what they want. Not only do they want a shit ton of money for their supplies, but they're straight up dicks and demanding part of our area Twelve land."

"Could da attacks be dem? They have a ton ta gain if we need ta use 'em."

Lochlan shrugged as Caleb watched the debate. "No fucking clue, but first order of business is finding these pieces of shit if they haven't already left the island and fucking make an example of them. We need to show force. Cutting their heads off and shipping them back to their Faction would send a strong one."

I blinked as I stared at him. "Yer not serious, are ya?"

"Of course, I'm serious. They need to die and painfully. No one takes from us without paying the ultimate price." Lochlan stuffed the rest of the pastry in his mouth.

"What you're suggestin' could start a full-on war. Ya know dat, right? I'm all for punishment, and if we need ta execute dem, fine. But we need ta figure out if they be workin' for da Faction or on dere own mission. We go jumpin' da gun and sendin' heads ta Faction council members, we be doin' nothin' but paintin' a giant target on our backs."

Caleb leaned back and draped his arm over the chair. "I'ma gonna 'ave ta agree wit Rhys on dis. We no be needin' to draw any more heat den necessary."

Lochlan scoffed and picked up another pastry. "Of course, you'd side with him."

Pain forgotten, I rose from the table and laid my hands on the thick wood. "What da fuck is dat supposed ta mean?" I asked, my own anger spiking.

"Come off it. We both know Caleb would suck your cock if you asked. In fact, I'm sure he's dreamed of it a time or two. Of course, he's gonna side with you. He always does. I wouldn't have been surprised if, had he been given an R name, the two of you would've been paired."

"Sure, keep talkin' bout me like I'm no' in da room. I be fine wit it," Caleb mumbled, but I ignored him.

"Ya, it be called friendship and loyalty. Somethin' ya family might need a lesson in learnin'," I growled back, my power tingling in my fingertips with the heated emotion.

"Excuse me?" Lochlan said and glared. He pushed himself away from the counter to face me.

"Ya fuckin' heard me. Dinnie tink I din't notice dat Nigel be missin' from da ritual or dat he has made it perfectly clear dat he no tink I'm capable ta run da McGregor family. Maybe yer startin' ta tink da same way," I said.

Lochlan took a step back, his face shocked. "You really think I'd fucking turn against you? I mean, we may not always agree, but the whole family turning on our alliance and the Faction? Are you crazy?" Lochlan pointed at me. "Besides that's bull, I can't believe you'd paint me with the same brush as my Uncle just because we share the same last name. Would you want your name associated with the shit Ronan does?"

"I dinnie hear ya sayin' no, or dat you support me as head of da McGregor family," I said.

The ritual and the words of the ancestors, spoken only to me, were fresh in my mind. Someone in the room was not a friend. Someone was the enemy, and I needed to figure out who that was. I needed to know who was trying to cut my legs out from under me—out from under the Faction as a whole.

Lochlan marched towards the table, and I prepared myself to fight.

"Whoa! Naw, guys, let's no be fightin' in me kitchen. We all be friends in 'ere, and I just redecorated," Caleb said and stood to put himself between us.

"Are you calling me a traitor?" Lochlan's eyes were as angry as I'd ever seen them, which was the only thing that gave me pause. He and his family might have been the obvious choice, but the emotion in his eyes was real.

I lifted my shoulder and let it drop. "Naw, not now, but I was needin' ta know fir sure," I said and slowly sat back down, and once more cursed Rook as my cock rubbed the inside of my leg.

"You're a prick," Lochlan grumbled and crossed his arms over his chest.

"Aye, and I be takin' bets dat yer goin' ta be paired wit Leo. Yer temperaments are well suited. What are dey callin' dat now? An enemies ta lovers romance," I said, and his face went a violent shade of red.

Lochlan lowered his voice, his eyes snapping with anger. "Don't you fucking dare jinx me. I hate that asswipe. I'd rather pluck out my eyes and cut off my cock before I shove it up his ass."

I spit out the coffee I was swallowing back into the cup and laughed hard as Leo walked through the door.

"Dinnie worry. I din't plan on puttin' me cock anywhere near your tightly puckered arse either. I wouldn' wanna catch da I'ma-fuckin-arsehole disease ya seem ta spread."

Lochlan rolled his eyes before turning around to face his childhood nemesis. For as long as I could remember, they'd been at one another's throat. It would be nothing for them to throw down in the middle of the schoolyard, pull a practical joke, or even bully one another. What I saw, and what they didn't seem to see, was that there were sparks of attraction beneath it all.

"As much as I'ma always one ta enjoy listenin' ta ya argue like a good old married couple, I need ta be gettin' back to Injerbreck. I'ma gonna be movin' home and takin' da head seat at da McGregor table. It be about time," I said.

"Dat be excitin', but dinnie be callin' on me ta move yer shit. Me back be bad," Caleb teased and pressed a hand against his lower back that had abso-fucking-lutely nothing wrong with it.

"Aye, aye, yer a poor old man now at da ripe old age of twenty-four. Would ya like me ta get ya a cane ta go wit the three cocks ya had fuckin ya last night?" I teased, and all the guys chuckled. It had been a while since we were all together like this, and I wished it was for a better reason than to fend off an attack.

"Ha, ha, ha. Yer a good one, Rhys. Dinnie be such a stranger," Caleb said, pulling me into a brief hug as I rounded the table.

Making my way to Lochlan, I stopped and put my hand on his shoulder. "Yer family has control of da ports. I feel it would be wise ta shore 'em up. I tink they be targeted next, and we are gonna need 'em ta survive."

"Where are you planning on bringing food in from?"

"I 'ave a couple ideas dat I be tinkin' about. I'll let ya know if any of 'em pan out." Lochlan nodded.

"In da shadows we shall seek," I said.

"But in da darkness, we shall find," the three guys answered in stereo.

It was time to move home and make some plans to save the island and all those living on it, then kill Rook. Whichever came first. It felt strange to be excited to see Rook and Elewyen, and it saddened me that one passionate night of connecting could push so much of what I'd been feeling behind me. Guilt gnawed at my stomach that I was running off into the sunset with my new triad when I knew that it meant leaving Mari completely alone, with no one to watch her back.

Fuck, why couldn't life just be easy?

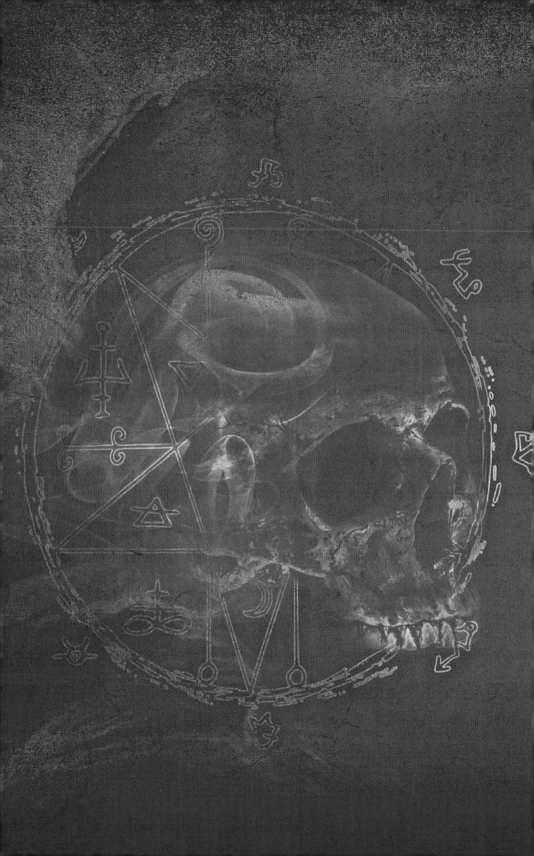

Chapter 38

Rook

There was a very good chance that I had just met my match. I mean, we were matched, but I meant in the insatiable department. It was like I flicked on a switch in Elewyen. She had been completely ravenous for the rest of the night, and we hadn't even fucked. Which was a brand-new experience for me. Either my skills were top-notch or terrible. I was going to go with the first. She just couldn't get enough.

Something hit my head, and I didn't have to look to know that it was Barry tossing something else at me. He hadn't been too impressed with the sexual escapades, and whenever we had taken a break, the furry terror had found something to toss at me. He was pretty innovative for a rodent, but so far, he hadn't chewed any

"Ya awake?" Elewyen asked, her head on my chest with her body pressed firmly against mine.

"Yeah, I haven't been able to sleep. Some sexy woman keeps waking me up," I said, and glanced down at her. Her face turned up to mine, and she smiled.

"I'z no sure what ya've done ta me," she said, and shifted her leg over mine. "Ya be thinkin' that it was like dis for all the women taken from da covens?"

I rubbed my eyes. "No, not from what Mari said. The men were not nice to the women in the past." I rubbed circles on her back. "You thinking that you might like to stay?"

I could feel her sigh. "I'z dinnie know. I cannie say dat dis is a bad way ta live, and I 'ave developed...somethin'...where ya are concerned. But ta stay? Naw if Keeva cannie come. She is a must."

"I don't see why that would be an issue, and I know that you're going to like Rhys. He is the nicer of the two of us. I just happen to be on my best behaviour," I gave her side a squeeze where I discovered she was ticklish. She squirmed against me.

The door slammed open, and we both jumped as Rhys stomped in.

"What in da ever lovin' fuck did ya do with me stuff? Ya fuckin' prick! If it wasn' good enough dat ya take me room, now ya move me shit out of da other room and hide it? Dere betta no be a single scratch on my Tabitha." The shock of his sudden appearance was replaced with anger as he once more snipped at me. "Well, ain't dis fuckin cozy," Rhys said, not letting me answer the first rant. "Def explains da shit dat kept me awake all night," he growled.

He was on a real roll today. I hadn't seen him for three nights, and this was how he came home? Oh, hell no. Rhys marched across the room to the boxes that Liam had piled in here to be moved to the

McGregor castle, but at the moment, I didn't feel like moving anywhere with him.

"Dis be all me stuff. Where be me guitar?" He looked around and before I could mention in was in the closet in a case next to mine, he began grumbling about something else and ripping open the neatly labelled boxes.

Elewyen remained very quiet as she watched him, but she didn't seem nervous about Rhys's angry outburst. She didn't draw attention to herself either as he ripped open the top of the first box and, not seeing whatever it was he was after, tossed it aside and went for the next box.

"Elewyen, I need to speak privately to Rhys. Can you give us the room?" I asked her quietly. I tucked a strand of her lovely red hair behind her ear. "This may get ugly. You don't need to see that."

She nodded and hopped up. We were trying to convince the woman to stay. The last thing she needed to see was Rhys and me throwing down, but we needed to do something, because I was the one who was supposed to have the bristly attitude, not him.

She pulled on the black T-shirt I gave her to wear, and damn, I loved how it almost came to her knees. It looked amazing on her, and I decided then and there that if she wasn't naked, this was how I wanted her to dress for bed from now on.

I swung my legs over the edge of the bed as Rhys continued to grumble and toss boxes around. Not bothering to get dressed myself, I stood and was shocked to see Elewyen approaching Rhys. Her bare feet padded softly on the stone floor as she tentatively went to him. As he reached for another box, her hand landed on his bicep, and he stopped mid-motion.

Rhys looked over his shoulder at her. His face looked pained for reasons I couldn't understand as he turned to face her. His eyes switched from white hot anger to calm in a blink.

"I'ma sowry fir whateva it be dat is makin' yer heart ache," she said, and I thought Rhys was going to cry when he broke eye contact and looked at the floor.

"Din't be sowry. Me mood is no' yer fault."

She was like a wary deer as she stepped in close to his body and wrapped her arms around his neck for a hug. They hadn't spoken at all except for down in the dungeon, and considering her original fear of men, I was confused by her sudden acceptance of Rhys. Was it because we'd grown closer?

Rhys wrapped his arms around her waist and dropped his head to her shoulder. A small inkling of jealousy bloomed. Not because Rhys was touching Elewyen, but because she seemed to be able to do what I couldn't, connect properly with him. He closed his eyes for a moment and hugged her back. It lasted no longer than a few seconds, but the moment between them seemed important, so I didn't interrupt.

A dull ache bloomed in my chest right where my heart was, and I knew that something was bothering him, but I didn't think it had anything to do with the meeting he'd gone to.

Elewyen released Rhys and left the room, closing the door behind her with Barry hot on her heels.

We were quiet until Rhys began his search all over again.

"You want to tell me what the fuck is going on with you?" I asked.

Walking to the end of the bed, I leaned against the large wooden post that held the privacy sheers. Rhys didn't say anything and instead continued to dig in the boxes and make a huge mess of the neatly folded items. I was done with this attitude and took a step in his direction.

"Hurt me," he blurted, and I froze.

"What?"

Rhys turned to look at me, and I searched his face, unable to figure out what was going on with him.

"I'ma sayin' ta hurt me."

"Man, what the fuck is wrong with you?"

Rhys' hands clenched into fists. "Ya din't understand what demons dance in me head. Da guilt dat is clawing at me soul."

"Okay, look, I have no idea what's going on. You asked me to convince Elewyen to stay, and I somehow managed to get her to almost say yes and have this incredible night." I held my hands out towards the bed. "I figured you'd come back relieved that I managed to do something you asked of me, but instead you're pissed off and now you want me to...what? Beat you or some shit?"

"I dinnie care what ya do. Beat me, fuck me, burn me, cut me, choke me, I honestly din't give a fuck what ya decide to do, just do it. I'm asking ya to do it. I *need* ya to do it."

His eyes were filled with so many conflicting emotions. The confusion in my chest was no better. I cupped his face. I never in a million years thought that I'd be the level-headed one between us in any scenario, but here we were.

"I need you to tell me what's going on," I said, and tried to ignore the surge of pleasure that coursed through my body. He made my blood sing at a higher octave with the slightest touch.

Rhys looked away and looked back, then opened his mouth, but nothing came out. He closed his eyes and shook his head. "I just dinnie know."

"Don't know what?" I asked, terrified about the answer.

"All of it," he said, and my hands dropped from his face.

"Are you kidding me right now? You're the one who has been

training and studying for this and was pissed with me when I didn't accept. Then I come here, and you tell me off and have somehow not only convinced me to stay but to actually look forward to this, and then you turn around and say you don't know? Am I living in the fucking twilight zone here? What kind of game are you playing, and why do you keep changing your mind?"

"I'm no playin' a game, Rook. Studyin' ta be somethin' and then it becomin' reality are very different." Rhys walked away and leaned against the large chair. "I genuinely want us, and more so wit each passin' day. I still wanna have da triad, but I'm a fuckin mess. On da drive back here, it all hit me. Da responsibility, da lives dat are at stake, how da tree of us bein' tagetha makes us a target, and how I may no' live very long. Den you add in da guilt me heart holds, and I be all over da place. I'ma feelin' like da world be tryin' ta eat me."

"Guilt? You mean about sleeping with Mari or having to leave her behind?"

"Both maybe I...I dinnie know," he said.

This I did believe if what I was feeling was any indication. "Unbelievable. I fucking knew it was a bad idea to let you two have the night together. I could feel it in my bones, but no... I wanted you to have your moment with her. I wanted to be the good guy, and look where that has fucking gotten us? You told me you spoke to her and that you two sorted all this shit out."

"Aye, da night together didn' help, but da feelin's were dere long before dat. Da ting is, it's no' jus her. It's everythin'. I feel like somethin' be sittin' on me chest. A panic dat I no understand."

I looked over at Rhys. He still looked like the arrogant ass, but I could feel his confusion now, and I didn't like it. I didn't want my own fucking feelings, let alone his.

"Rook, ya were wantin' fir me ta be honest wit what's going on.

I'ma no' gonna lie." He put his hands on his hips, and I knew that even though I couldn't see them, he had an endless number of weapons strapped to his body. I fucking loved it. The possessive asshole in me was going to make him understand who exactly he belonged to now.

"Last night, when ya and Elewyen were fuckin'—which may have just screwed up our triad, by da way, since she was supposed ta remain a virgin until ceremony for da full power ta take effect." Rhys rubbed his face. "Shite, what if da spirits force us ta choose anotha? Just anotha issue."

"Relax. We didn't have sex," I said, interrupting him before he could get spinning his tires.

"What?"

"You heard me. We didn't have sex. We did a lot of other stuff, but no sex. Even if I was stupid enough to do that, Elewyen wasn't ready for that step. I was fucking tempted to just take it, trust me. Point is, she is still a pure virgin." I cracked my neck. "By the way, I don't like me as the nice guy, Rhys, and I'm really fucking sick of you making me be this better person. Being the fucking number one sucks and I really hate that you're acting like I normally would. I'm the one that is all over the place and can't make a decision and I miss it." I looked over at the confusion on his face. "I know that sounded stupid."

I let out a yell of frustration.

"Point is I'm not the better person. Do you understand that? I'm the asshole. I've always been the asshole, and I take what I want, do what I want, change my mind a million times, but I do what the fuck I want. And I don't normally compromise over shit. And that now includes you. Think of that what you will, but I've allowed you to be wishy-washy since I claimed you as mine, 'cause I felt I owed you that for all the crap I did before coming here, but I'm not sharing any part of you with anyone but our third. Not your mind, your heart, or even your conflicted soul." I stood up straight and rolled my shoulders. "Call me greedy, but I want it all."

"Aye, I know," he said and rolled out his shoulders.

I ground my teeth together as other ideas began to claw their way to the front of my mind.

"But do you really?"

"Look, da point was dat, regardless of if ya had sex or no, when ya were doin' whatever, I could feel ya like ya were part of me. I ended up passin' out on da bathroom floor, and the entire time that I was enjoyin' myself wit more pleasure than I've ever had in me life, all I could tink was dat I'ma fuckin' prick for not bein' able to close da door fully on my past. I worry constantly about dose I'ma gonna leave behind." He rubbed his face. "Mari, I mean Mari, dare be no point in me pretended it be a bunch of people."

"So, what are you saying? Do you want to find a way to stop the building connection and go back to craving one another like wild animals for the rest of our lives? Because I felt you too," I said and remembered distinctly what it was like when the link happened and how I could still feel him now. "I could feel your skin on mine, the smell of your soap in my nose, your hands on my body, your hard cock in my hand."

I marched towards him, and he straightened his spine. His glare matched as my own. We stood with our chests almost touching. Our bodies were equal in size, and it didn't matter if I'd orgasmed a thousand times last night, I wanted him now. I wanted him in any position I could get him in and command him to hand himself fully over to me.

Thoughts I never thought I'd ever have. I never wanted the stupid triad or the responsibility that went along with it, but the second I met Rhys, the shift in my chest happened, and I would be fucking damned if he was getting away easily now.

"Naw, I'ma no sayin' I want dis to end. I'm sayin', I need ya ta hurt me. I need ya ta take control, and I need ta taste ya for real. I crave da pain, Rook. I need it as I need ya, and I know ya can give it ta me." His eyes ventured down between our bodies to where I was hard, and he licked his lips. "I'ma sayin' dat I need us to complete da first ritual ceremony, I need ya ta be da number one who will make me follow ya ta da ends of da earth and back again. I need ta feel dat dis is where I'm meant ta be."

I wrapped my hands around his neck and linked my fingers together, pulling Rhys until our noses touched.

"Do you know what you're really asking of me? Because I like to give a lot of pain. I like to hear someone scream, knowing it's my hand that's causing it," I growled out.

The darker part of me was peeking out, taking control. It was the part of myself that I could never wholly embrace with anyone, for fear of scaring them or hurting them too much. But I craved it. I craved it like I would crave water in a desert or air to breathe.

"Aye, I know what I be askin' of ya. I know dat ya like it, and I fuckin' love it."

I shuddered.

"Maybe we be findin' out why we were paired," Rhys said.

I couldn't agree more with that statement. No one had been able to take my brand of sex, and I always had to hold part of myself back. The binding spell flared between us and I couldn't help wondering if he might be the one who could finally take all of me.

"Do you consent to no consent? Do you consent to no safe words and no limits? You will become my toy in the bedroom to use as I want. I need you to be clear. Is that what you're saying?"

"Me only limits are no permanent maimin' me or killin' me," Rhys said.

His hand found my waist, and the connection went crazy between us. Just like last night, I was able to feel his body as part of my own. The pleasure was doubled, and the intensity ramped up to a whole new level with him in the room.

"Very well then. You're mine. I don't give a fuck what confusion or uncertainty you have left."

He made to look away, and I gripped his chin hard in my hand, my finger pressing into his skin until he looked me in the eye again.

"Understand this, Rhys. You were always mine. We just didn't know it until the ritual. Now that we do, I'm not letting you go. Not now, not ever. I don't even give a fuck if that's what you decide you want. You will have to kill me to be free."

I wrapped my hand around his throat, and he sucked in a gasp that ended with a moan as I squeezed.

The sexual energy that was swirling around the room could've choked someone as surely as my hand.

"I'm going to bend you over the couch, and I'm going to complete the first phase of the ritual by fucking you so hard that you scream my name and my name alone. You're a motherfucking McGregor and the head of your house. For the first time since I arrived, you're acting like a cunt instead, so I'm going to treat you like one and use your ass like one."

His nostrils flared as the muscle in his jaw twitched, but it was the heated look that told me there was zero fear.

"Aye. You're da number one, and I be yours," he said.

I could taste the truth of what he said in my mouth and feel the honesty in my chest.

Our lips crashed together, and like every other time we kissed, it was so charged that I wanted to devour him like my favourite dessert. Rhys's hands reached around my body and grabbed my bare ass, and I wanted more. I was going to be selfish with him from now on. He wanted me to be the number one and show him who was in control? He was about to find out.

Breaking the kiss, I fisted his hair and pulled his head back, making him bend away from me.

"Do you know what it means to be the number two?" I growled out.

"It means dat you're da final say in all Faction decisions," Rhys said, and I shook my head.

"I don't give a fuck about the Faction day-to-day shit. I don't care about the political meetings unless you want me to partake. I'm talking about with us. From now on, I control your body, mind, and heart. They are all mine. I can feel you, as you can feel me, and even your lingering love for Mari is now mine. I'm not going to walk around bearing any part of your past, and you will not bear any part of mine."

"Mari is no mistake," Rhys said.

When he tried to pull his head away from my hand, I realized he'd taken it the wrong way. Gripping him harder and wrapping my other arm around his waist to hold him firm, I forced Rhys to stare me in the eyes.

"Yes, she is. Not her as a person, but what you two did to contribute to this confusion. You need to let the fuck go, and I'm going to work all of it out of your system. I'm not sharing any part of you. You're mine, Rhys. You wanted me to be the number one and act like it? You want me to do what I want? So be it."

Not able to take it anymore, I attacked his lips and pushed him back until he was bent at an odd angle over the arm of the couch.

White hot power rose between us and shimmered off the walls even though it was daylight outside. Rhys groaned in my mouth as I dominated his body. Pulling him up straight, I went to turn him around to make good on my promise when my phone rang. I looked over at the nightstand and scowled. The annoying thing had the worst possible timing.

"Are you fucking kidding me? No one calls me."

Ignoring it, I kissed Rhys again and began balling up the heavy kilt in my hands when the phone stopped ringing, then immediately started up again. I growled as the two of us stood there with our foreheads pressed together. Once again, as soon as it stopped, it started all over again.

"Ya better git dat. Could be important." Nothing felt as important as this right now, but I also couldn't stand listening to the thing ring.

"Son of a fucking bitch. If this is nothing, I'm going to kill whoever is on the other line." Marching away from Rhys, I saw my brother Devlin's name on the display. "This better be fucking good," I said and turned around to look at Rhys.

The door was open, and like a magician, he'd disappeared. Irritation filled my chest.

"You're going to want to sit down for this," Devlin said.

Sitting was the last thing I wanted. I looked down at my cock and mentally screamed every foul word I could think of. Rhys was mistaken if he thought he could hold me off. I was going to make him mine today. The two of us were completing phase one if I had to tie him up to do it. I had visions of him running for the hills and the image Mari had shown me going up in smoke. No way in the dark fade was I letting that happen. Nothing else seemed as important as making the three of us come together.

438

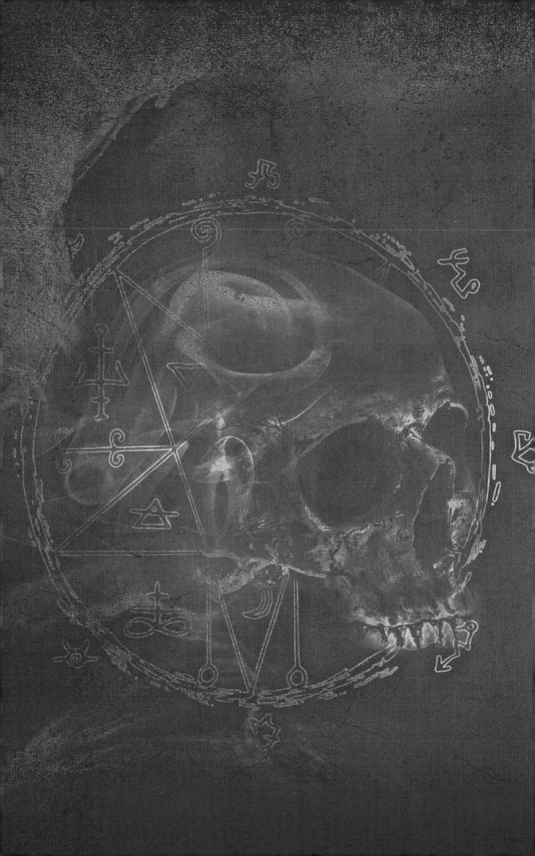

Chapter 39

Rook

"What the hell do you want? I was right in the middle of something really fucking important," I said and sat on the edge of the bed.

"Still a ray of sunshine, I see. Do you think no one else has problems in their life?"

Shaking my head, I leaned forward, so my arms were on my knees.

"It's already been a day. What's going on?"

"Are you sitting down?"

"Yes, I'm fucking sitting down. Just get on with it," I said, trying my best to keep my voice calm and even. It wasn't Devlin's fault that Rhys and I had decided to play the game of role reversal. How did I end up being the one who wanted the triad, anyway?

"You know that girl I planned on killing?" Devlin asked, and I shook my head.

"Dude, you're going to need to give me a bit more information. You asking that is like me asking if you know the girl I wanted to fuck? There is such a long list. How the hell am I supposed to guess?"

"Such a comedian, the one called Sydney," Devlin snarked back. "The point is, I know you don't want your triad, and I really don't fucking want mine, so how do you plan on getting out of yours? Can we just kill them?"

I smacked myself in the face. "Yeah, about that."

"No, bro, I'm fucking serious, and I'm sorry I was all up in your grill and making fun of you when Dad shipped your ass to that shitty little island. I was an asshole to go to the airport with the banner and bottle of Champagne, and I'm just sorry. So now, what's the plan?"

I remembered him clearly yelling congratulations when I walked through the small private airport door. He'd been holding a banner that said *Just married, now tied down forever*. There was a part of me right now that wanted to go back to that version of myself, but just the thought of leaving filled me with so much pain it almost brought me to my knees.

"Okay, first of all, why are you talking about you being in a triad? You haven't even had a ceremony where your name was mentioned," I asked, confused. Reaching down to the floor, I grabbed my discarded T-shirt and pulled it on before going in search of a pair of jeans.

"Oh, let me start over. So the night you were selected, so was I. I'm paired with Reese. Shit, you might have known if you decided to actually show up to the ritual."

"What the fuck?" I yelled into the phone as I leapt to my feet. "You were named too, and no one told me? You son of a bitch, and you have the nerve to say I keep shit from you?"

"Yeah, well, it was entertaining to watch you squirm, and I was happy to be paired with Reese. We have our own thing going. But back to the girl I want to kill. She is the sacrifice."

"The one named Sydney?"

"Yeah guy, keep up. She's the one whose father killed Mom. Then Dad went nuts trying to find? That other woman took off with her and hid from Dad for years. Remember?" Devlin said.

I knew what he was talking about, but like everything else in my life, I'd managed to keep that hurtful tidbit pushed as far away from my day-to-day thought process as much as possible. We were just kids when Mom had been murdered, and Dad had gone all crazy. I hadn't really understood his anger as a child, but the thought of someone killing Rhys or Elewyen brought an instant murderous rage into my chest. So much so that I needed to take a deep breath to calm myself down as the air around me began to crackle.

"Yeah, I know who you're talking about. What about her?" I asked, pinching the phone between my ear and my shoulder and hopping on one foot to get the other one inside my jeans.

"We found her, and the fucking little cunt is my chosen. I found the birthmark and instantly felt the connection, man. That is a no fucking way." I heard him hit something on the other end of the line, then heard a crash. "I'm not uniting with the daughter of the man who killed our mom," Devlin growled into the phone while I stood up straight and zipped up my jeans.

"I'm sorry. What did you just say?"

"Seriously, I swear you don't listen to a word I say." I pulled the phone away from my ear and looked at it as I contemplated tossing it out the window. "The fucking little cunt is my third. So how do we go about getting out of this? I was just going to choke her while I fucked her to death. A total win, win, but now I'm afraid to put my cock inside of her. She may keep me, you know, suck my soul out through the end or some shit. Besides, you know Dad. He's all like, but she's your chosen, and it doesn't matter who her father was, only that the match has been made. Blah, blah, blah. I'm not doing it. I'm not marrying that little bitch."

I quickly pulled on my socks and shitkickers while Devlin continued to rant about the girl and called her every colourful name in the book and even ones I'd never heard before.

"Okay, okay, okay... enough already. You and your rants, fuck me," I grumbled and slipped out into the hall. I was still very much on my own mission, and mine was to put my fucking triad together.

"Wait, you said her name is Sydney?"

"Oh my god, are you really going to make me repeat this again?" Devlin grumbled.

"No I'm just thinking that it's fucking ironic," I said and laughed hard.

"What? What's wrong with her name? Not that I care, it will just add one more thing that I hate about her to the long list."

I poked my head in every single room I passed, not taking any chances that Rhys was hanging out in one. "Devlin, did you not learn anything in Faction lessons? I mean, I thought I didn't pay attention. Sydney is the name of a city in the country of Australia, which is now part of Faction One. They hate us, like full-on hate us, from what I remember. Just ironic."

"No, no, it's not ironic. It's because she's..."

"All right," I barked out. "Enough with the name calling. Look, here's the thing. The girl's father is the asshole who killed mom. This

444

Sydney wasn't even born. That's like someone blaming you for something Dad did before you were even born."

"I don't think I like where you're going with this," Devlin said.

"Probably not. All I'm saying is, give her a chance. She may be annoying now, but she may also end up being a great third," I said and walked through the massive dining hall that was so large my footfalls echoed.

The tall walls held elegant portraits of family members. I had no clue who they were, but each one was framed in ornate gold frames. The table had to be custom and, with a quick count, held sixty people with elbow room and still space to run a marathon along the outer edge.

"What the fuck? I thought, of everyone, you'd be the one person that I could turn to and count on to have my back. I mean, you don't want your triad, so what the hell?" Devlin asked as he sighed dramatically into the phone.

I was passing by the library when I spotted Rhys sitting at one of the tables with a couple books laid out. They were so thick that they could've been used as weapons. I closed the door behind me and locked it in place before putting my hand over the lock and spelling the fucker closed.

Rhys looked up from what he was reading, and our eyes locked.

"So here's the thing, Devlin. I've changed my mind about my triad." I took a step farther into the room, and the air between us sizzled. "In fact, I'm looking forward to it."

"What the fuck did they feed you? Are you drunk? Did they poison you? Have you been spelled? Shit, do I need to send someone to help you? Like, are you trying to send me a cryptic message? Say yes, and I'll send help right now."

"No," I said, and yanked my T-shirt off with one hand, tossing it aside. Rhys's eyes flared as I continued to stalk towards him. "I'm actually about to fuck my second in the library so hard that he's not going to be able to sit down for a week. So if you'll excuse me, brother, I need to go."

"What the—"

I hit end on the call before turning it off and tossing it aside.

"We were in the middle of something, and you took off. I'm tired of you disappearing, Rhys. Like really fucking tired of it." Putting my hands on the table, I leaned towards him. "So now I'm going to have to make sure you know what happens when you run. You need to be punished. I'm going to shove my fucking cock so far down your throat, you're going to choke on it while I come."

Rhys wiggled in his seat. "I'ma actually really wantin' dat punishment, but I didn' run. When we were talkin', there be somethin' ya said twigged in me mind, and I needed ta find dis before I forgot. Ya are kinda distractin'," Rhys said and smiled as he turned the massive book in my direction to read. "Besides, figured ya'd need a few minutes with yer brother. I already heard about his rantin' about his triad from Caleb and just how fecked off Devlin is with who his third is. Naw offence, but yer brotha can be a cunt, so he kinda deserves it," Rhys smirked, and it made me laugh.

"What am I looking at?"

Rhys stood and came around the table, and as he did, the charge between us grew. "Fuck, ya smell good," Rhys said, and leaned in towards me, his chest brushing against my arm.

"If you want me to read this before I take you on this table, you'd better point it out now. My control is quickly slipping," I said, and didn't dare look at him as the heat rising from his skin caressed my cheek.

"Dis." Rhys tapped the page where a paragraph started and then took a step away.

"A power merge? What the heck is that?" I mumbled and kept reading. My eyes skimmed over the lines and then I went back to the top and started all over again. "What the—Is this for real?"

"Aye, it is." I watched Rhys pace around, his brow furrowed as he thought. "When ya said ya could feel me, I knew I'd heard dat before. Then when you mentioned that you were the one that couldn't make a decision it clicked and I had to come check. It was so rare and so unusual it stuck wit me from dat lesson."

"I don't get it. Why us?"

Rhys shrugged. "Fucked if I know. Nothin' about our union has made sense." He held up a finger. "I was supposed ta be da number one —all McGregors are—but naw, I'm now a two." He held up a second finger. "We be equal in almost all tings. Different powers, sure, but physical strength, power, dominance...On paper we dinnie make a good match. And now da power is becomin' one. We are becomin' one."

"Does this mean we will actually inhabit one body?" I asked, a little horrified, but it made Rhys laugh.

"Naw, not in physical body, but in all da otha ways, yes." Rhys shook his head and held his arms out to the side. "Da problem now is are ya still willin' ta be in a triad wit me," Rhys asked.

I stood straight and ran my thumb over my bottom lip.

"Tell me, Rhys, how do you feel?" I asked, as the words on the page and the long-term implications danced through my mind.

Rhys resumed his pacing in the tight spaces of the library, like a large predatory animal looking for an escape.

"Rook, I told ya before dat I want ta make da union work. Da ting is, I'ma no stupid. I'm da number two, dat means dat I 'ave a target on me back. It could be a week, a month, or even a year, but dey are comin' fir me. Dey always come fir da two first."

"Agreed. The track record is not very good for the number two, but we're going to be smarter than our ancestors were and make sure that you're better protected," I said and meant it.

I didn't want either Rhys or Elewyen to be hunted or killed, but the possibility was very real. My hand went to my chest at the same time that Rhys's did.

"It has already begun, Rook. If we complete da triad, if we choose ta do the final ceremony, den we are forever bound. Ya will feel me as I feel you, forever, in all tings. Every emotion, every touch, everythin', and if one of us dies…"

"We both do," I finished.

Rhys nodded. "It be very rare to have such a strong connection dat a merge would form. We'd be more powerful den all the couples combined, but we will be at a real risk. Dere will be very few we can trust, and even dose we tink we can, we can't…"

Rhys crossed his arms over his chest. "It means dat we cannie just leave da house ta go ta town alone. We cannie fly overseas ta visit friends or family. You cannie just go sing without months of plannin'. It means yer goin ta be more tied ta me den ya ever thought. Firget a triad connection, dis is… I 'ave no words, and no one alive has experienced it. We din't even know what da consequences be. Last night, ya said, 'oh yes, fuck me' wit Elewyen, and I fuckin said it wit ya like it be my words."

He pointed to me, and I could feel the urge to point at him. It was creepy, and yet… I wasn't scared like I should've been. Was that because he wasn't scared? Fuck, this was confusing.

"What do you suggest as an alternative?" I asked.

Rhys shrugged. "There no be an alternative other than I move out, and at da next ritual moon, I will reject da union. Den Elewyen and ya stay together and hopefully be paired again wit Ryland, but I will remain apart from both of ya. Until another second is announced, I will remain celibate. I dinnie wanna hurt either of ya."

My arms dropped to my side. "You'd do that? You'd sacrifice your own happiness and any kind of normal life or affection for an untold amount of time?"

"Aye, I would. Me life is no' worth us both dyin'," Rhys said.

I stomped across the library so fast that Rhys stumbled back, but I grabbed him by the hoodie he was wearing, and with a potent combination of fear and anger riding me, I pushed him up against the bookshelf.

"Don't you ever fucking say that again. It's not true, and I won't hear that bullshit come out of your mouth. Whether I started off wanting to do this is irrelevant. If the spirits put us together, then they knew that this merge thing could happen. So be it. If you died..." I stopped and looked away from his eyes. I couldn't believe that my emotions had grown so strong that I almost said I loved him. "Just, no. I said I'm in. You said you're mine."

In an unusual way this was exactly what I wanted. My possessive nature needed to control and know everything at all times. What better way then to feel it all as if it were my own.

"Aye, and me meant it," Rhys said.

"Then we're doing it. There are a million worse things in this world I can think of than my power and the sensations of my body being tied to yours forever."

Rhys lifted a fist and laid it over his heart. "Ya really have become da number one, Rook. Ya 'ave me respect, and I promise ta live me life protectin' ya and Elewyen, if she chooses ta stay. Dis I swear as yer number two."

The emotion in my chest was clogging my throat, and I hated shit like that. "I'm still punishing you and fucking you in this library, just because I want to. It will be the most excitement it's seen in years."

"Wouldn' expect anythin' less."

My heart hammered in my chest. My mouth desperate to taste him. Our lips met with such ferocity and emotion that it should've terrified me, but there was no longer any fear about what was to come between us. Breaking the kiss, I pushed away from Rhys, and went to the centre of the room, dragging the heavy desks out of the way.

"Wat ya doin'?"

"We're completing the first ritual right now," I growled, as I pulled the last of the desks out of my way. "No more waiting, no random emergencies, no dank, dark catacomb, no robes or anything else."

Desperation filled me, a carnal need to make this happen while we could. I jogged across the room to the massive chalk boards and gripped the thick white chalk in my hand.

"Ya were serious 'bout dat? But what about waitin' 'til da full moon?" Rhys asked.

"We don't need the full moon for phase one. We only need the ritual moon for the final union." Bending over, I began drawing the pentagram on the floor. "I don't want to wait another second to make this happen."

"But, Rook, ya just learned about the merge. If we do dis, there is no goin' back. Ya can't change yer mind tomorrow. Ya should at least sleep on it."

It was a valid point, but the thought of putting it off only added to the anxiousness in my chest. Finishing the final touches of the pentagram, I tossed the chalk to the side before fixing my stare on my second. I took a moment to appreciate him. He stood with his hands on his hips like a warrior, ready to defend me from the books if they decided to attack. His chest looked extra wide with the thick tartan he had wrapped over one shoulder and pinned with the massive brooch of a sword. The black kilt stopped at his knees and yet somehow managed to still show off the strong legs and narrow waist that I knew was solid muscle.

"Show me your weapons," I ordered.

His eyes went wide, but he didn't hesitate to drop the cloaking spell. I was already hard and dying for a taste, but the sight of him with all the battle leather and weapons strapped to every inch of his body just did something for me that I couldn't put into words.

Sorry, Devlin, you're on your own. I want what's mine.

"Take them off." My eyes feasted on my number two. I made my way around the pentagram I'd drawn to the man who was unstrapping the sword at his waist. With each step, the air crackled until it felt as if lightning had invaded the library. Rhys removed one piece of weaponry at a time, dropping them to the floor, but kept his eyes trained on me. The air felt heavy and I could feel it pressing on my chest.

Raising my hands in the air, all the candles around the room, lit or unlit, flew forward and hovered in the air. With a snap of my fingers, the wicks roared to life, then the candles dropped to the ground, evenly spaced around the outer ring of the pentagram. Fog seeped under the door from outside as I continued to call upon my power for this moment, while the shadows along the wall moved like they were alive and inched closer to the show.

Rhys straightened from taking the last of his clothing off, and other than the large knife in his hand, he was completely naked. My mouth ran dry at the sight of my second. That may have been what the spirits had designated him as, but I realized that he was truly another number one, and that was why we made sense. All the reasons that we shouldn't work were the exact reasons why we did.

I would never have respected a male I could push around. If I pushed Rhys, it was because he let me, not because he couldn't put me flat on my back. I had a vicious streak that wanted to hurt the man I was with sexually and craved the screams of pain as I pushed the limits of what he could take. No one I'd met could handle all that I wanted to give, and yet, I didn't have a doubt that Rhys would take it and beg for more.

I staggered forward as the desire spiked so high between us that I was almost brought to my knees.

Rhys spun the sharp blade in his hand, then put it between his teeth as he stalked towards me. I stood still as he reached out and unbuttoned the jeans I was wearing, then knelt to undo the boots so I could kick them off.

He rose from his knees before me, and I sucked in a shuddering breath. I'd never seen a more fierce or sexy sight. Taking the knife from Rhys mouth, our eyes locked from inches away.

"Ya sure dis is what ya want? Dis be yer last chance ta go back overseas and be done wit me and all dat is da Faction?"

"I've never been more sure of anything in my life," I answered.

The corner of Rhys's lip tugged up as he stepped over the flames of the candle boundary into the pentagram. Following suit, I stepped over the line and felt the power increase inside our protected space. I met him in the middle and held out my hands for Rhys to cut.

"Tonight, we accept da choice dat has been made by da spirits," Rhys said, as he ran the blade over my left palm. "As da second, I accept my one, and I chose to call Rook Adair mine and my number one." He dragged the blade over my second palm and then held out the knife for me.

The flames grew brighter as they waved back and forth to music only they could hear, while the fog inched past the candles to wrap around our ankles.

"Tonight, we accept the choice that has been made by the spirts," I said and pulled the tip of the blade across Rhys's left palm. "As the number one, I accept my second, and I chose to call Rhys McGregor mine and my number two." As I drew the line across his right palm, the candles turned black, and the flames that rose into the air glowed an eerie red.

Lifting the blade between us, we mirrored one another's actions as we moved in and pressed our tongues to the flat edge of the blade. I could feel Rhys's tongue as we licked the blood off from the base to the tip. The taste was divine on my tongue, and the connection roared like it was a living beast as it swirled around the room. Droplets of blood fell to the floor, sizzling before turning to smoke.

With a flick of my wrist the knife sailed through the air, the sharp tip digging into the wooden bookcase. Holding out my hands we linked our fingers together. The moment our bloodied palms met, we sucked in a sharp breath. The power that had been pulling us together from the moment we laid eyes on one another now pierced our hearts as it travelled through our bodies.

"We are the chosen, and tonight, two become one," we said in unison over and over as we knelt in the middle of the pentagram. The power was so thick that it made it hard to see the books across the room ripple like a wave.

No commands needed to be given. Rhys lay down on his back, and I followed to rest between his open thighs. We never released our grip on each other's hands. I squeezed harder, and the mingling blood seeped out the sides of our clenched palms. Rhys's eyes never left mine as I lined myself up to take what I'd been craving. Our chanting stopped, and it was as though even the power held its breath to witness what was about to happen. Only one thin tendril of golden power remained inside the circle. It felt like a delicate caress, encouraging us to continue as it licked all over our naked bodies.

"I am the shadow, born from the blood of the brothers of shadow and death," Rhys said.

"I am the death, born from the power of the brothers of shadow and death," I said.

"We are the chosen, and tonight, two become one," we said together.

I groaned as I pressed into Rhys in one hard stroke that had him arching off the ground in a silent scream.

"We are one," I growled.

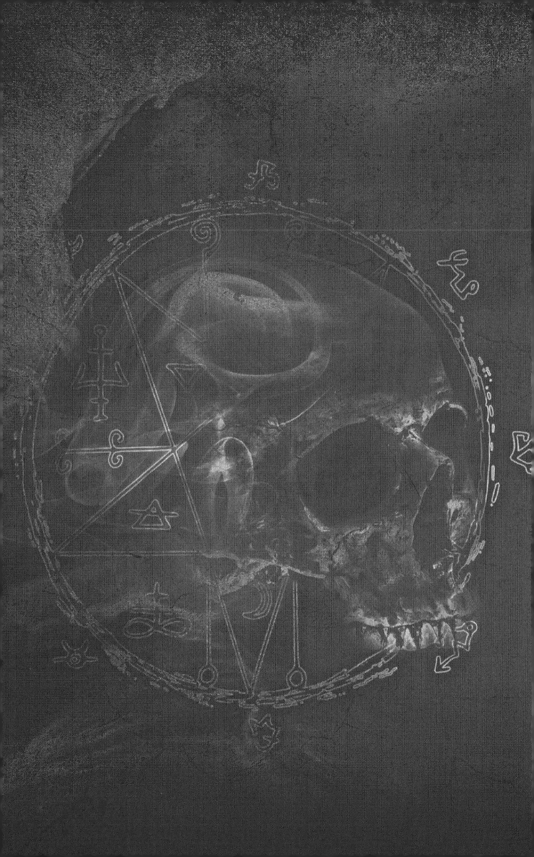

Chapter 40

Elewyen

　I wandered my bedchamber and looked at everything there was to look at so many times that I could've closed my eyes and found my way around. I was curious about the argument with Rook and Rhys, but I wanted to give them their space. I hadn't even made a firm decision to stay, let alone engage in their quarrel.

　Barry jumped around on the ledge as he looked outside. Smiling, I walked over, unlatched the large window, and pushed it open. He didn't waste a moment before jumping out and running along the vines of the climbing flowers until he reached the tree. I could hear him chattering up a storm but could no longer see him through the mass of leaves that were starting to change colour. Soon, they would be as vibrant as blood and as bright as the sun before they fluttered to the ground.

I may not want to go speak to Rook and Rhys yet, but I really wanted to do something. I had the itch to explore.

"I'ma needin' ta get out of dis room," I mumbled.

As I wandered the halls of the large castle, my mind began to wander. Last night had been mind blowing, and I figured that was only the beginning of what they could show me, but the amazing physical attraction didn't change the fact that this place didn't feel like home. What Azula told me may have been inaccurate, but my family was out there. I didn't know if this place and those who lived here would eventually feel like family.

Strolling down a random hall, I checked out each room with an open door. Most were bedrooms, but a couple of smaller rooms held unique pieces. It was like they put all the extra stuff in the smaller rooms to display pieces they had no room for on the main floors.

Continuing on, I looked into another room and was about to walk on when my brain registered what I was staring at. "What da?"

The soft lanterns on the walls were burning low and casting long shadows on things I didn't understand. It looked like the dungeon room I was in downstairs, but darker and not dirty. Chains hung from the walls and ceiling with leather cuffs on the end. There was an entire wall with what looked like weapons made from black leather and wood. I poked at the shiny silver objects that seemed to be oversized teardrops in all different sizes and then stared at the shelf that held multiple peens, like Rook's.

Had they cut them off of people and put them on display? What kind of sick place was this?

I looked around and listened for anyone coming before nervously reaching out to the shelf to poke one of the larger peens. It had a very large head with a strange curve to the thick shaft. It looked like a monster and didn't feel like Rook's flesh.

"Demon Fade magic," I mumbled as I gripped the next one in my hand to take a closer look. I was surprised by the weight of it and how it moved like it was made of something firm and yet not.

"Why is da ting blue? Did dey freeze it and den turn it into dis weird display piece?" Horrified, I put the blue peen-lookalike back on the shelf and continued on around the room.

There was a strange-looking chair that had one of those overly large peens poking up from the seat. I got down on the floor to look under the chair, but there was no person. Once more, I poked at the strange creation. This one was smooth and shiny like a polished rock. The chair had places to lock your wrists and ankles in place, and I swallowed hard at the thought of that creation stuck inside of me while I was trapped to the seat.

"Dis must be man tortures. Naw female in dere right mind would be comin' up wit a device like dat. It would destroy yer womanhood."

Even the bed looked like some sort of torture device. Leather straps and chains hung from a metal thing above, and the sheets were a deeper shade of red than my hair and shiny. There was a large cage in the corner where I suspected they put the prisoner before they decided to torture them with the weird items around the room.

Marching for the door, I spotted a flat wooden stick like the kids would play with to hit rocks. I pulled it off the rack and discovered a comfortable leather strap that went around my hand. I decided that I was taking this one as a weapon. No one was going to torture me in that room.

When I reached the end of the hallway, I was unsure which way to turn when humming reached my ears, so I followed the delicate sound. The pretty voice that could've been made by a rare songbird led me to a room with the door half open. Poking my head inside, I spotted Mari standing in the middle of the room, holding a pretty blue dress up to herself as she stared into a looking glass. Mari twirled in a circle like she was dancing when her eyes spotted me, and she stopped.

"Oh, hi." She blushed and immediately walked towards the room that I learned was a closet and held clothes. So many new words to learn.

"Sowry, I'za just bein' silly. Sometimes it be nice to pretend dat I'm still a girl without any worries."

"I'za dinnie know wat dat be like.. Whatza like ta no' 'ave any worries?" I asked, genuinely curious.

I remembered digging in the dirt for bugs and picking berries. Stealing pieces of meat left over from an animal kill so I could chew on the bone for something with more to it than the leaves and nuts. You had to get to it fresh, though. Once the little white bugs started crawling on it, my stomach would roll. I remembered standing in the cold water and learning to be quick as snake to strike and catch a fish.

I never danced until I'd been with the coven for a few years, but that was different. We all stood around an open fire and sang to the spirits for a good harvest of fruits and vegetables. Sometimes we would pray to the different spirits about the weather or give thanks for what we had, but to dance just simply dance…This was new to me. No worries was new. Not having to think about how to divide up one chunk of bread for three days was new.

Mari walked out of the closet and leaned against the door to look at me. "What da ya mean, ya dinnie know what it be like?"

"Ya dinnie need to speak wit da accent if ya no wanna. Hangin' around Rook so much, I'za startin' to pick it up, and me like da challenge. It be helpin' me ta learn fasta.'"

Mari smiled. "Okay, then. Tell me what you mean by, you don't know what it's like to be a carefree kid."

Stepping into her room, I glanced around at the pretty way she'd decorated. Everything was a soft shade of blue or grey, it reminded me of stormy skies, but it wasn't depressing. It felt like the ocean, and the clouds were meeting in the middle of her room. There were little splashes of colour, and an image of Mari with her mother hung over the bed.

"I dinnie know what ta say. Da coven took me when I'za bout eight. Before dat, I dinnie remember much otha den scroungin' fir food like a littlin' animal."

Mari pushed away from the closet and came to stand in front of me. She gave me a smile, then her eyes flicked down to my weapon. Reaching out, her finger gently travelled down my hand to the wooden piece I was carrying.

"Why are you walking around with this?"

"Ta protect meself. It be me weapon." I pointed out the door. "Dere be a whole room dedicated ta torture down da hall," I said.

Mari smiled wider and then began to laugh. She laughed so hard that tears rolled down her cheeks, and she had to stumble away and lean against the wall.

"Me dinnie understand. Dis be serious business. How cannie ya stand ta live 'ere knowin' what dey do ta prisoners?"

Mari laughed even harder and sank to the ground, holding her stomach. "Oh, dear spirits."

"Mari, dis be serious. I'ma no gonna let dem chain me up in dere an' beat me wit da strange cut-off peens. I cannie even imagine been strapped ta dat tall X or forced ta sit on dat peen in dat chair. Such horrors. Why would dey even create such wickedness?"

"Stop! Just stop talking." Mari tried to stop laughing and then burst out in laughter again. It was contagious. I covered my mouth but it did no good and soon, we were both laughing hard, yet I had no idea why. It felt good to laugh and smile just to do so. Keeva and I would make up games and laugh or when I tickled her she would laugh, but the moments were rare with so many other things that needed to be done before the sun set.

"Okay, okay, I'm good," she said and then snorted and covered her mouth as she composed herself. "It's not a torture room, it's a sex dungeon. It's where people will go for pleasure and sometimes some pain, but mostly pleasure."

"I dinnie understand," I said. "How cannie dungeon be pleasurable?"

Mari pushed herself to her feet and walked over, holding out her hand. "I'll show you, but I need that," she said, pointing at my weapon, and I bit my lip.

Mari didn't act like someone I should be afraid of and had given me a weapon outside, yet I still felt nervous giving her my only weapon. Sliding the leather off my hand, I handed it over, and she held it out to show me.

"This is called a paddle. The person using it holds it like this." She demonstrated by putting her hand through the leather and holding it like I had. "The person on the other end would get spanked, but only to the level they are comfortable with."

"Sp...aaaan...ked. Me no' know wha' dis word mean."

"Well, you can be spanked because you were naughty or because you were a very good girl. Depending on which you were, will dictate how hard you're hit."

I took a small step back. "So ya do hit people wit it?"

"Yes, but not for the reason you're thinking." Mari was quiet for a minute as she tapped her bottom lip. "Okay, look. Do you trust me enough to demonstrate on you?"

"Demonstrate?"

"Yeah, it means to use this on you, so you know how it works. I won't hurt you."

"Aye, you can show me," I said, but kept an eye on Mari as she walked around behind me.

"I'm going to smack this softly on your bottom. If it's too much, tell me," Mari said.

The thing connected with my arse, and I jumped forward. I looked back at Mari but realized it hadn't hurt. At least, not in the way I was thinking.

"Can ya do it again?" I asked.

Mari nodded. This time I watched as she pulled her hand back slightly, and the flat wooden piece made contact. The shock of it hitting sent a tingling sensation to my bottom but also to my womanhood—or, as Rook called it last night, my pussy. I still didn't understand the reason for calling it a cat. Did my womanhood purr?

"Dat be very interestin'," I said, and Mari giggled.

"That it is. I'm pretty sure that both Rhys and Rook know how to use all the toys in that room. If you want to learn, all you need to do is ask them. Trust me, I'm sure they'd be more than happy to give you the tour," Mari said, like it was a joke, but her eyes were downcast.

She pulled the paddle off.

"Cannie ya show me?" I asked, and Mari laughed again.

"It's not like the stuff in the kitchen. I can't just point it out and show you. You will want to do this with Rook and Rhys. They are your partners. Does that make sense?"

I shrugged as she handed me the wooden paddle. She walked away, and even though she didn't say anything, I got the feeling she held a lot of weight on her shoulders.

"Aye," I said.

She leaned against her bed and waved a hand at me while she smiled. "No, I'm fine. Hey, I have a great idea. Have you ever been dressed up? I mean, in a fancy dress like what I had out? That's a silly question, you probably have never seen a dress like that before," Mari said.

I shook my head, and she smiled widely, her eyes lighting up.

"Well then, I know exactly what we are going to get up to. You deserve to have a day of nothing but fun and pampering. Then we'll go for a walk through the gardens and pretend we are queens," she said, her voice shifting higher as she said it dramatically.

Mari dashed across the room and grabbed my hand before tugging me towards the closet. "I know the perfect dress for you, and it will go perfectly with your green eyes. After we will get Liam to do our nails, he is amazing at it."

The closet was almost bigger than the hut all of us women from the coven stayed in all winter. I pulled on her hand, so she was forced to stop walking.

Mari's eyes were concerned as she looked at me. "Is something wrong?"

"Naw, I'ma just wanna tell ya dat I be thankful fir ya bein' nice ta me. I know dat havin' me 'ere is no' easy, but ya 'ave been so kind. Tank ya. I'za never had a girl me age ta talk to or sit wit or anythin'." I looked down at the ground. "I like dis time wit ya."

Mari closed the distance and wrapped me up in a hug. I held her tightly and wished that I could help ease the anguish that I felt inside of her. "Yer a beautiful soul, Mari, and I'za happy ta 'ave met ya."

"I'm thankful to have met you too, Elewyen. I'm genuinely happy that you were the one chosen, and I hope that you decide to stay," she pulled back with a smile on her face. "All right, let's get you into that dress, shall we? Oh, and I know exactly what I want to do with your hair."

I wanted to give something back to her since she'd been so kind to me, and as I watched her pull out one dress after the other as she talked, I knew what I could do.

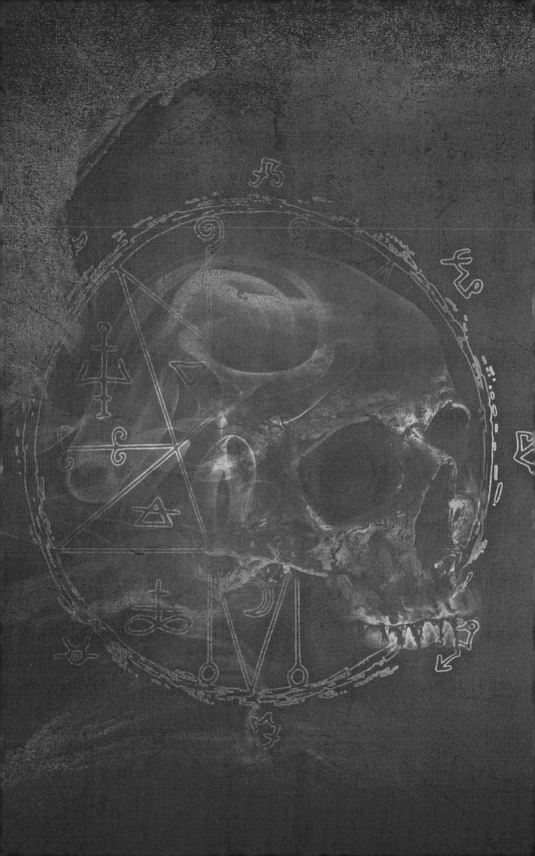

Chapter 41

Rhys

Rook flopped over, and we both rolled onto our backs to stare at the ceiling as we panted hard. I never thought sex could be life-changing, but what we'd done shifted my world. Magical connection or not, we were made for one another, and now everything was enhanced. The walls seemed brighter and more in focus. My hearing had increased to the point where I could hear Rook's heartbeat in his chest, and I felt it pounding along with mine through the connection.

My arm was draped over my eyes, and I wasn't sure I could even get it to move. A few breaths later, I shakily pushed myself up to stare at the carnage we'd created in the library.

The candles were all over the place. Luckily, their wicks had snuffed out. I wasn't sure we would've noticed if the place had caught on fire. All but one desk was overturned or on its side, and not a single book was left on the shelves. I vaguely remembered them flying around the room but hadn't paid much attention at the time. My head lulled to the right, and a soft chuckle left my mouth as I stared at the book entitled *Family Ancestors and Their Stories*. Bet they just got a heck of a show.

"What's so funny?" Rook asked.

My feelings for Rook were at the top of the list of things amplified. I went from *yes, I can picture a future with this man in my triad*, to *I can't live without him* in a blink. It was a little unnerving that I could feel how Rook felt about me. If I could feel him, then he could feel how much he and this moment meant to me. The magic that had been penetrating our bodies seemed to fuse us together in this emotional bond. I couldn't even imagine this being stronger after the final ritual with Elewyen.

Our eyes locked, and a smile spread across my face. "Apparently da ancestors be watchin'. Makin' me kinda wonder if what we did will be put in a book?"

"What?"

Laughing, I reached out and grabbed the book to show him the cover. Rook chuckled as I tossed it aside to join the other books scattered around. It looked like a miniature storm had suddenly erupted in the room, then left again just as quickly.

Staring at Rook's handsome face, I couldn't get over how lucky I was to be paired with him. We'd never met before he was forced to come here, and now it was as if we'd known one another forever. At least, that was the feeling I was getting, and it became way too confusing to analyze it too closely.

"I know what you're thinking," Rook said as he placed his arms behind his head.

"Did da connection grant ya mind readin' now?" My greedy gaze tracked lines up and down his body. I didn't think there was a sexier sight than his hard muscles on display and his still very hard cock laying against his stomach.

"No, but the look in your eyes tells me all I need to know," Rook said, his voice gravelly as he slowly pushed himself up onto his elbows. The movement made his shoulders and abs flex deliciously. He was like a three-course meal. We'd just finished round one, but I was ready for the main course.

"Aye, what does me look tell ya?" I asked, tracing the tips of my fingers along his arm and the snake tattoo.

"Come here and I'll show you," Rook said, his blue eyes heated.

The aching muscles and tiredness disappeared as I cupped his face and kissed his lips softly. Rook tried to deepen the kiss, but I moved out of the way, keeping the contact light as I teased him. When I nipped his lower lip, he cocked his brow at me. Deepening the kiss for only a moment, Rook attempted to take control, but I backed away again, and he ended up licking his own lips.

"Oh, really? You wanna play games?"

Smiling, I sucked his lower lip into my mouth, loving the flare of desire in his eyes as he groaned. My tongue traced a line along his lush bottom lip before I finally allowed the kiss to deepen. Our tongues battled for dominance. I liked pushing Rook's buttons, seeing just how far I could go before he yanked the control away.

I pushed him down to the ground and ravished his mouth. His hand found my ass and squeezed it as he pulled me harder against his body. Fuck, there wasn't a single part of Rook that didn't do it for me. Everything about him fit me and was what I needed. It was as if he'd truly been cut from the same cloth and made to be my mirror image. Breaking the kiss, I pushed his head to the side so I could even things up and give him a hickey to match the one he'd spent a great deal of time giving me.

"Fuck, yeah. Mark me, show everyone I'm yours," he gasped as I bit down softly on the sensitive skin.

His hands roamed over my back and ass. Each touch sent another charge into the air around us as it raged through my body. Releasing his neck, I moved down his chest. My tongue traced lines along his skin until I could get to his nipple and sucked it into my mouth. I decided to make him squirm under my touch. My tongue lashed at the sensitive nipple as my teeth gently rolled it.

"Shit, Rhys." Rook groaned and grabbed my hair as he pulled my head harder into his chest, forcing my teeth harder into his skin. I was definitely going to leave indents, and the idea of marking him with my teeth on such a sensitive area was as much of a turn-on as the act itself.

Making Rook swear and scream my name was becoming a new addiction. He pulled my hair hard, forcing me to look at him. It was the perfect amount of pain as he twisted his fist slightly and forced my head to tilt with the movement.

"Stop fucking teasing me," he ordered.

My lip curled up in a knowing smirk. Licking a line from his chest to his lips, I looked into Rook's hungry stare and loved that he broke the contest and attacked my mouth first.

Rook rolled me off his body with his hand still wrapped in my short hair until I was pinned on the ground under him. His body blanketed mine. The warmth that had been building erupted and turned the blood pumping through my veins into an inferno.

"Fuck me. You drive me crazy," he said in between the kisses that steadily got rougher.

I gasped as Rook yanked my head to the side. "Look at that mark," he growled possessively. My pulse jumped wildly under my skin. "I should've fucking done this before you went to the meeting, so everyone there would know who you belong to." I shivered as he drew a line up the side of my neck with his tongue. "Maybe I'll get a collar made for you."

"I'ma no wearin' a fuckin' collar. Ya wanna pet, git a dog," I challenged, and a smile broke out across his face before he laughed.

"Tell me. Did any of those fuckers at the meeting think they could have you?" Rook's breath was hot as his mouth hovered over my ear.

I could barely focus on the question with the sound of my heart hammering in my head and the feel of his cock slowly rubbing back and forth across my stomach.

"Answer the question, Rhys. Did any of those fuckers think you were still fair game?" he growled.

Licking my lips, I tried to form a sentence that would make sense. "Caleb...He...Fuck!" I swore as Rook bit down hard on my shoulder at the mention of Caleb's name. His sharp incisors clamped almost hard enough to break the skin, and my cock jumped between my legs.

"Yes, bite me. Fuck, dat feels good."

"Finish the sentence. Caleb did what exactly?" Rook growled in my ear.

He was holding himself back from stomping out of the castle and finding Caleb to beat the shit out of him. At least that was how it felt in my chest. I could feel the jealousy burning inside of him, and I couldn't help but groan. I wanted all of his jealousy. To anyone else, Rook was a fucking dick, but to me, he was a shot of whiskey with a beer chaser. The possessiveness that churned inside of him made my skin so hot that I was melting.

"He..." I panted. "He wanted me to join him in an orgy part—"

Rook bit harder into the meat of my shoulder.

"Fuck, yes!" I yelled.

The pain was an aphrodisiac to my system and more potent than any sex alone could give me. I thought for a long time that something was wrong with me for wanting this during sex, but I learned to embrace it and embrace myself. And now…Now, Rook liked to give exactly what I loved to take. My body ached in places it hadn't from our first round, and I could already feel bruises forming. I was never looking at a book the same way again.

"Do you know what I would do to any of them if they touched you?" his blue eyes darkened. The air crackled like an electrical storm was all around us and bouncing off the walls. It made the hair on my body stand.

"Naw, but no one be dat stupid," I said as he slid down my body. He reached my nipple, and I couldn't help wiggling with the anticipation.

"They better not be, or I'll kill them. Family or ally, I don't care. If they even look at you in a way I don't like, I'll rip their fucking balls off. If anyone other than me or Elewyen touches you ever again, I will kill them," Rook's voice rumbled against my chest a moment before he bit down on my nipple.

I yelled and almost came from the intense pleasure that shot straight to my cock. My body bucked up as Rook applied enough pressure that I knew there would be marks when he was done.

"Fuck, Rook," I groaned and slid my hands into his dark hair.

He kept me dancing along the cusp of pleasure and pain as his tongue swirled over the tip my sensitive nipple and made me gasp.

"Are you okay with me killing our allies, friends, and family?"

"Naw," I managed to get out through clenched teeth as Rook

moved over to my other nipple. I braced myself for what I knew was about to come.

"Then you'd better make it really fucking clear to everyone that you're off the market. Do you understand?"

He bit down, and I couldn't keep my hands to myself any longer. I needed to feel more of him. Running my fingers over his back and wide shoulders, I memorized all the dips and lines. The emptiness without him inside of me was an ache all on its own, and I pulled him as close as I could get him.

"Aye, I understand. They will all know."

He lifted his head and stared at me, his eyes narrowed in a dark glare. "Were you tempted to join?"

I licked my lips, and the pause in my answer notched up Rook's aggression. I could feel it bubbling under the surface of his skin.

"Aye, but only a moment 'cause of bein' worked up from leavin' ya in da closet."

"What would you do if I was tempted by someone outside of you and Elewyen?"

His voice was so lethal that I shivered.

"They would'na be breathin' by mornin'," I said and gripped his ass hard, loving that it flexed as he rubbed his cock along my abs.

A smirk lifted the corner of his mouth, and I couldn't take waiting anymore.

"Please fuck me. Fuck me hard," I begged.

Rook dropped his head to my chest, his tongue driving me wild. "Fuck Rook," I groaned. I felt him smile wider against my skin.

"Beg again. I like hearing you beg for me."

I licked my lips as we stared into each other's eyes.

"Besides, you came home and were an asshole earlier. If you want my cock again, then beg for it."

"Yer really gonna make me beg?"

Rook lifted himself higher, and some lingering fog drifted over my skin, leaving a cool trail, making me shiver.

"Yes, I really am."

Begging was new for me. Most of the things that had happened since Rook arrived were completely new and had kept me off kilter. I briefly wondered what his response would be if I flipped him on his back and took what I wanted. Maybe I would try that another time. Right now, I could admit that I wanted this.

"I feel you thinking it over," Rook said.

I suddenly hated that he could peel back my emotions so easily.

"Fine, I'll beg, but only cause I wanna. Fuck me, Rook. I'm beggin' ya. I be needin yer cock in me," I moved my hips back and forth under his body, trying to get more friction.

The deep chuckle that came from him vibrated along my body and out to the tips of my fingers and toes.

"You're a tough one, Rhys. You don't give in easily."

Rook braced himself on his arms, and I was captivated by the sight of him. He was a work of art. It was as if one of the statues of Adonis in the main hall had come alive just to seduce me.

"I be sorry about earlier. It's been a few very confusin' days, and da stress and connection have been swirlin' in me chest. I shouldna took it out on ya and Elewyen, though. Dat wasn't right."

"Yeah, but I can be a prick too. So I'm pretty sure that's not going to be our only fight. If they all end up with you on your back like this, I don't really care."

I laughed hard, then sucked in a deep breath as Rook's hands began to explore.

"I do like when you look at me like that, though," he said as he pushed himself to his knees.

"Yer incredible, Rook, and no' jus' ta look at."

To most, it would sound like a pickup line, but I genuinely meant it. I wasn't even sure how I'd gotten so lucky to have him as my partner. Any reservations still hovering between us were left in the hall when Rook locked the door. Then he doubled down when he said he wanted to merge our powers into one and initiated the first ritual. It was a huge risk, one that could either be a large success or cost us both our lives. The fact that he thought I was worth the risk meant everything.

Rook grabbed my knees and pushed them up. "Keep them like that," he ordered.

My chest rose and fell in time to his hand, which jerked up and down his hard cock. The sight of him stroking himself was a tease all on its own, making me grab my own hard-on. His gaze flicked down to watch my hand work. His eyes following my stroking hand was like another hand rubbing me all over.

"Do you feel how much I want this? How much I want you?" Rook asked, his gaze returning to my face.

"Aye. Do ya feel me?" I asked, and he nodded.

"It's amazing. I didn't think I'd ever want to be bonded to someone like this, but this is incredible," Rook said as he rubbed his cock along my ass to the base of my cock and back again.

"Aye, it is, and yer teasin' is drivin' me mad."

A cheeky smile curled the corner of his mouth up. "All right."

He slowly pushed his thick cock inside me. My mouth hung open with the intense fiery pain of him stretching me out again. He wasn't the type you could easily get used to, and he hadn't been joking when he'd said he liked to fuck hard. I was already sensitive from the earlier round of hard pounding, but I didn't care. A harsh throbbing spread out from where he was still pushing into my body. I groaned and closed my eyes.

"Shit, you're still so fucking tight," Rook said, as my muscles contracted and gripped him harder. "So fucking good," he said, and I felt the strain in his body as he tried to hold off from slamming into me.

With a grunt, Rook finally made the final inch, fully buried inside me. With Rook, it was the first time I could ever say I felt full. That beast of a cock flexed, and I groaned loudly, wanting him to move.

"Stroke yourself. I want to feel it," he closed his eyes as I began servicing my cock. Rook groaned with every stroke. "Fuck. That... there are no words," he groaned. "I can feel you stroking your cock when I'm moving, and it feels like you're taking me from behind at the same time. Whoever came up with this merger thing was a fucking genius. Oh fuck me," Rook growled out.

"I'm tinkin dat they no be thinkin' about dere cocks at da time," I said through clenched teeth.

I could feel exactly what Rook felt. The way his cock pressed deep inside of me and rubbed against the spot that felt so fucking good. The sensation was then topped with my hand on my own cock. It was all-consuming...He was all-consuming at this moment.

"Mmm, so fucking good," he said.

His eyes closed as he pulled back, then pushed his way inside me again. He pushed my knees out farther until my hips screamed that they couldn't go any wider, then he pushed another inch. I groaned.

"That's a sight," he said, eyes locked where we were joined, where his cock slipped in and out of me at an ever-increasing pace.

"Stop resisting and keep your fucking knees out there," he ordered, and I tried to relax my muscles enough to do as he said.

Rook leaned forward and pressed his hands into the floor by my head as he stared into my eyes. It was almost too much for my cock to feel the pleasure from both perspectives.

"Don't you dare stop stroking that cock," he growled. "You're not allowed to come until I say and not a second sooner," he demanded. "I get to choose how and where you come as your punishment."

"Me takin' yer cock once already ain't enough?" I asked teasingly. He could punish me all fucking day and night, and I would take it gladly.

"No, it wasn't punishment enough. Now don't come, do you understand?"

That was going to be tough, especially when he began pounding into me hard.

"Aye, Rook. Jus' din't stop."

The sound of skin slapping together was loud as he drove me backward on the floor with each powerful thrust. Reaching out, I grabbed the edge of one of the bookcase shelves with both hands to keep myself from shifting further.

Growling, Rook stopped fucking me. I wanted to yell for him never to stop.

"Don't fucking move again," Rook said.

I wanted to feel his ass so badly. I wanted to feel all his muscles flex as he resumed, but now my hands were as good as tied over my head.

"Did I say you could stop jerking off?" Rook growled.

"Naw, but I'ma needin' ta hold meself," I said.

His hand darted out and wrapped around my throat in a blink.

"Ah fuck," I mumbled through my constricting windpipe.

To feel the kiss of death coming and then be jerked away was a high I would never get sick of, and it had another level and meaning in our Faction. We were the brothers of shadow and death, and standing at the precipice of death made my power glimmer brighter as my desire pushed higher. The sensations coursing through my body rendered me speechless at Rook's unrelenting aggression.

"I don't fucking care. Figure it out," he ordered, his blue eyes burning bright.

I'd never seen something as sexy as that look on his face. No one had ever had what it took to make me submit as much as I craved. The only thing better would be me tied up and blindfolded as Rook brought me to that sweet edge over and over again.

One hand braced behind my head kept the brute force of Rook's thrusts at bay. My other hand gripped my shaft and matched the rhythm of his body. I loved that I could feel his hard abs rubbing against the back of my knuckles with every stroke.

"Fuck. Yer gonna make me come," I whispered through my partially closed airway.

I closed my eyes and tried to hold back the building orgasm barreling towards me.

"I said not until I say you can. I'm going to finally taste you, so you better hold it back," Rook said, his voice strained.

I squeezed my cock harder and applied enough uncomfortable pressure to ease the climax down a notch. Pain only made me want to come more, not less, so I had to hold the awkward position. My cock began to throb, making my head light with the euphoric sensations. A deep groan rumbled up from my chest as the ache increased.

A spell suddenly burst from the floor like a cascading wall of silver. It had been gold earlier, but there was no time to contemplate the reasons for the colour change as pieces of it broke away and weaved between our bodies.

"Ahh," Rook yelled as the silver power ripped through his chest.

His eyes were like liquid silver running through dark blue waters. He looked at me, and I froze.

"Oh fuck," I mumbled as Rook growled, a sound that was so feral it sent a cold shiver racing down my spine. "Rook?"

With strength that took me by surprise, Rook gripped me beneath my shoulders and stood in one fluid motion before slamming my back against the bookcase. I worried about what was happening, but that same silvery power came through the bookcase and pushed through my body. I was held in its grip, my back arching, unable to breathe.

The power pulsated between us, and I could feel my abilities increasing, along with a primal need that took control of my actions. No logical thought was left as I pushed Rook away and leapt on him. We crashed to the floor and sent books scattering as we rolled around, fighting for dominance.

I ended up on my stomach with Rook pinning my arms above my head. With a roar, I rolled us over until his arms were pinned above his head. I almost got my cock in him when he pushed up with his hips and dislodged me. Rook grabbed me by the wrist and yanked hard. I flew across the room, landing in the middle of the pentagram. The impact was hard and scattered books in every direction. I rolled over onto my back trying to catch my breath.

Before I could get to my feet or say a word, Rook clapped his hands together. My arms and legs were pulled in opposite directions until I lay before him, spread eagle. His eyes never left mine as we silently challenged one another. I opened my mouth, and he held a finger over his lips.

"Shh."

My mouth snapped shut with the power of the spell and my heart pounded hard as Rook stalked me around the circle. I could feel the power in him as it forced my power to move in sync with his. I closed my eyes and braced against the foreign sensation that left me feeling helpless.

"You. Are. Mine." Rook's breath brushed my cheek, and my eyes snapped open to find him inches away from me. The initial fear was ebbing away, leaving me with raw desire.

I nodded, still unable to speak.

Rook stood and stared down at me.

"Levetatio."

My body rose off the ground. I watched Rook as he walked around until he stood between my outstretched legs.

"You. Are. Mine," he said again, and the spell on my mouth released.

He was shifting the power structure just enough to truly be the One. Everything in me wanted to fight it, yet it felt right to let him take the lead.

"Aye. You. Be. Da. One," I replied, then screamed Rook's name as he slammed home inside me again.

I couldn't respond. Words were gone, my mind blank as his thrusts increased, and the power pushed us towards an explosive finish. I could feel the building orgasm in his body, and I utilized every ounce of control I learned over the years to hold off until he came.

"Oh, fuck! Here I come," Rook yelled, sounding like himself again.

I groaned. My back was arching and straining against the spell that had me suspended off the ground. My cock surged and tried to come with Rook as he thrust hard into me and froze in place as his release gripped him. I felt every stream expel from his body like it was my own and yelled, my body shaking as I held off the orgasm raging and demanding to be set free.

"Fuck!" It was the only coherent word from my mouth as my body trembled with the effort.

I barely registered Rook moving until he leaned forward and took me into his hot mouth. I wanted to grip his hair and force my cock down his throat, but the spell held firm.

He lifted his head to say, "You can come now."

Blood rushed painfully to my cock head when he resealed his lips around me. There had never been a sweeter sensation to experience. Now that I'd been given permission, my control dissolved as Rook bobbed up and down.

"Aye, right dere."

I tensed and tried to thrash as the sweet, bliss closed in. The subtle gagging noises and loud slurping were music to my ears as Rook kept up his fast pace.

An explosion of power rippled out of my body and created an aftershock that shook all the bookshelves and rattled the tables as I finally came. Rook took everything I gave him and continued to suck hard, drawing out the pleasure until there was nothing left to give.

Rook lifted his head from my well-spent cock and wiped his mouth with the back of his hand. All I could think was that he looked like the sexiest and most dangerous predator I'd ever seen. He snapped his fingers, and the spell sat me down in the middle of the pentagram. I gasped, trying to catch my breath. He sat down with me. I grabbed his face and kissed him hard, loving the taste of myself on his lips.

Breaking the kiss, I leaned my forehead against his. "Do ya feel dat?" I asked, picking up his hand and placing it over my heart.

"Yeah, I do. Do you feel this?" he asked and did the same with my hand.

"Aye, I do." Our hearts beat in perfect time with one another. "Da first ceremony is complete," I said and kissed his lips softly.

Rook gripped my face and pushed me to the ground like I'd done to him earlier.

"It is, and I fucking hate that I owe my father an apology," he said and then kissed me hard until we were once more breathless and gasping for air.

"Dere be a shower here in da library. I'ma thinkin' we go make good use of it, 'cause it's no' gonna be long 'til I wanna taste of yer sexy arse. Me cock is already tinglin' wit da thought."

"Is that so?"

"Aye."

Rook pushed himself up to his feet, and I took a moment to admire the man who had just gripped my heart in his fist. Rook reached out with his hand, and as I slipped mine in his, I felt like something was finally going right.

"Then let's go find that shower."

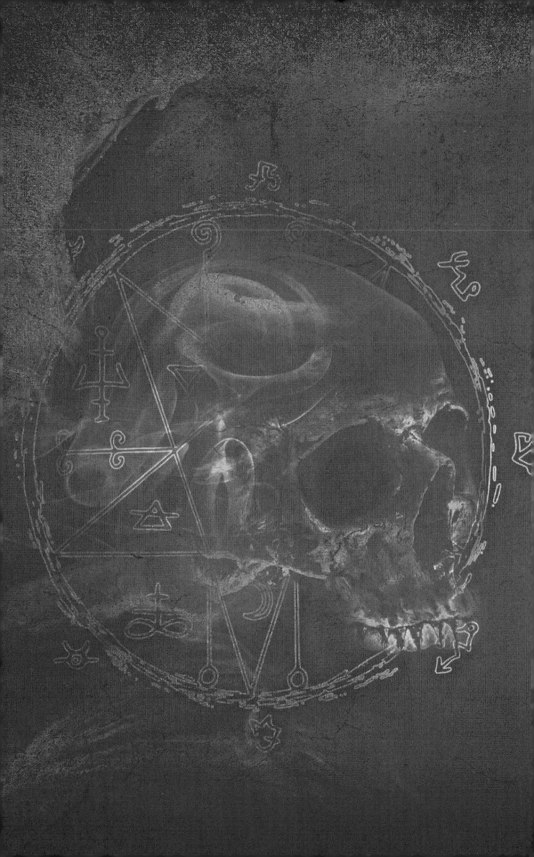

Chapter 42

Elewyen

Mari laughed as we spun in circles. The large dresses flared out in a colourful display. I gripped the wall, panting hard, feeling sick to my stomach. I fanned myself as the heat in my body increased again. It was a strange sensation. I figured I'd just been doing too much as I wiped the back of my forehead with my hand.

"Whaddya do in dis room?" I asked.

The massive room had tall windows that stretched from floor to ceiling. It was clear of furniture other than a pair of fancy chairs and a few benches. Family crests and faded banners hung on the walls and from the ceiling. A second story on one side looked down at the floor below. Glittering gold edged everything.

"This was used for balls," Mari said as she stopped spinning.

Mari looked so pretty as the sun poured through one of the large windows and bathed her in its light. She wore a dark blue dress that matched her eyes and made her dark hair flowing down her back, stand out. She looked like one of the paintings on the walls.

"I'za dinnie understand. A ball be a childs toy," I said and smoothed down the front of the rich green dress.

It glittered like a precious stone and was such a pretty colour. I wanted to keep touching the soft, rich material and loved all the golden thread that created intricate designs along my stomach and chest.

"No, not a ball like the toy. A ball was like a really large gathering of people from all over. They would come and dance and sing, and there was a huge feast you could stop and eat from all night long. That's why this is called a ballroom." Mari turned and looked off to one side, her smile slipping a little. "The last time that there was a ball here, I was only twelve, and I danced with Rhys all night long." She looked down at her feet. "I'm sorry, I shouldn't have said that."

"Naw, dinnie be sorry." I reached out and took her hand. "I'z barely know 'im. A few moments of chat while me sat in a dungeon and den a blink earlier when he return from da trip he be on." I touched my chest. "I be kinda feelz somethin, but it no be a lifetime o' memories that ya share. I'za so sorry dat dis be happenin'. Ar'ya wantin' me ta go? I no sure if me want ta stay, den da two of ya can be togetha." I shook my head. "Me know ya cannie do da triad, but da two of ya could still union."

Mari glanced at me, her blue eyes worn down and tired. I spied the bruise on her face and the pink marks on her back as she was getting changed. But she refused to say where she'd gotten them and changed the topic. I didn't know her well enough to press on something she didn't want to talk about, but I was worried for her. She was hiding far too many secrets. Secrets that weighed on her and peeked through her eyes.

"No." She reached out and pulled me into a hug. "No matter what I feel for him, we were never meant to be. Sometimes the heart just wants things it cannot have. He was that for me, but he was made for you." Pulling back, she placed both her hands on my shoulders. "Please stay. I promised I wouldn't put any pressure on you, but you're amazing, and I couldn't have asked for a better woman in all our lives." Mari ran the long braid she'd put in my hair through her fingers. "Rhys needs someone like you looking out for him. Someone who will understand that his emotions can be like a wild storm and may need taming with a gentler touch, not just with a strong fist. You are like warm, sweetened tea on a sunny day, and he needs that."

"Rook be da fist, I be da tea?"

Mari smiled and then laughed. "Yes, exactly. They are perfect together, but you will be too. You just have a different way about you, and I think he's going to need your strength, but kind heart."

"Ye be talkin like ya know."

Mari's cheeks flushed pink. "I just know him, and Rook is not all that he needs in his life. In fact, I worry that the two of them could grow toxic if not for the touch of reason. You are logical and you say exactly what you think and feel without judgement. You also have a depth of wisdom and kindness that is so important." My brows lifted, and I nibbled on my lower lip. "I know you're unsure about that, but those two will dote on you and you will have the power to make them…." Mari moved her hand in a circle over her chest. "Settle. Like ships caught in a storm, you're the anchor to keep them from drifting too far."

"Wat be an anchor?" I asked and Mari laughed, her smile lighting up her whole face.

"I guess that metaphor fell flat. Don't worry about it, just know you hold them together like a rope."

"Ah." I nodded. "Can ya tell me a bit more about Rhys? Only if ya can. I no mean ta make dis hard," I worried that I was asking too much when she'd already been so kind.

Linking our fingers, she pulled me over to a long, soft bench and sat down.

"Sure, I can do that. Rhys is a kind soul, and he works too much. He will also blame himself for everything that goes wrong and will try to punish himself when he can't fix the world. He secretly loves the bagpipes and can play them well. He can dance really well, although he pretends he can't. He likes all animals but connects with horses best, and his favourite colour is green, just like your eyes." I flushed and looked away from Mari's eyes. "I...um..." Mari cleared her throat. "I feel like I need to tell you that I spent the night with Rhys before you arrived. It may not matter to you, but I want to be honest, so you don't feel like I've kept something from you."

"Do you mean you laid with him?" The idea didn't anger me, but it pulled at my chest in a weird way.

"Yes. I'm sorry. I caved to a desire I'd had for so long in a weak moment." She looked like she was going to cry, and I gripped her hand tighter.

"I no be mad. I tell ya dat I would go fir ya." Even as I said the words, I realized I wasn't sure I wanted to leave, but I would stand by my offer if she took it. She looked so defeated. A tear dripped from her eye and I wrapped my arms around her and kissed her cheek. Unable to help myself I drew in a deep breath and let her sweet scent of berries fill me.

I pulled back and her eyes found mine again. "No, please stay. Whatever you need to make this work and make this home, I will personally see to it that it happens. Every person on this island needs you, but especially Rhys."

"Yer heart is made of pure tings, Mari. I cannie say dat me would be so kind if da woman dat be takin someone me loves from me were sittin' by me side. I'za hate dat dis be hurtin' ya."

Mari wiped away another tear that was slipping down her cheek.

"I will not lie to you, Elewyen. Each day for me is a struggle, but it's not all because of Rhys. I try with every breath to come to terms with the life I live and be the better person. Does that mean I'm perfect? No. I have had thoughts of running off with him and fantasies that I knew would never come to pass, but please know that you, Elewyen, are not hurting me by staying. You are helping me." She picked up my hand in both of hers. "I'm begging you. Please look after him. I need to step away from him, and that means that I can't be consumed with worry anymore."

I looked away from her eyes and stared out the tall windows at the water I'd seen when Rook first brought me here. The sun danced along the dark water as the waves moved slowly towards the shore.

"I'z still be getting da feelin' yer keepin' somethin'," I said, and she licked her lips.

"It's not something I can share, but I can promise you that you'll never have to worry about him not being good to you. He's a good man, a kind one, and he will fall in love with you. When that happens, he would stop an army to protect you and all you care about."

"Dis be wha' ya really want?" I asked.

"Yes, it is." Mari squeezed my hand tighter, desperation in her eyes.

"Aye, I'll stay, den, but I need ta bring me sister 'ere, an' any of da others in me coven if dey choose ta come," I said.

I'd been leaning toward staying as my decision. The longer I thought about it, the more I saw the benefit for me and the coven women. There was a lot of good that could come from the power and protection that Rook and Rhys could offer. Keeva and the other women could learn to read. And we could learn to work with this world rather than hide from it. We could explore our power, and those who wanted to find a male partner could do so without fear or judgement.

But the final push I didn't know I needed was the pleading look in Mari's eyes. I didn't want her to suffer. She was a kind soul who was fracturing inside. If this would give her some peace, then I'd do it. Letting myself trust the men was tough, but they hadn't given me a reason to mistrust what they said. I also couldn't deny that I wanted to keep Mari in my life and leaving meant that I'd lose her as well.

"Done. Whoever you're wanting to come here can."

"Rhys gonna be okay wit dem all goin' ta where we are headin'?"

Mari tilted her head slightly as she stared at me with obvious confusion. "What do you mean?"

"Rook said dat we be movin' ta a different castle. A Glen somethin'."

Mari sighed, and the corner of her mouth curled up. "Rhys is moving you all to Glentruan. That explains why all the servants were moving boxes around. This is a good thing. It means he's decided to take over as head of the McGregor family. He is becoming who he always should've been." She stood from the bench, and I rose with her. "Yes, Rhys would be fine with them going to Glentruan. It's a bigger castle and has a lot more room for your coven if they choose to come."

"I'za love dat, but does dat mean I'ma no gonna see ya anymore?" I asked, but Mari smiled.

"No, you will still see me, just not daily." Mari stared around the ballroom like she was watching ghosts that only she could see. "Did you want to see something else here at the castle?"

"Aye, cannie we go out ta da gardens?" I asked.

"Yes, it's a beautiful day for a walk outside. I go at some point every day anyway to visit with my ma. I wish she'd show herself to me like she did to you," Mari said as she hooked my arm in hers.

We didn't go back the way we'd come and instead walked out another set of large glass doors that led to the gardens around back.

"I dinnie know how ya keep straight where all da rooms and doors be," I commented as we stepped outside into the fresh air.

"Honestly, I still can't remember what half the rooms are for," she whispered, and I laughed.

We strolled along the path, and I took a moment to appreciate the different colours that kept the garden in perfect balance. Even though it was late in the season, the flowers all looked like they'd just begun to bloom. A loud chatter caught my attention, and I looked up to see Barry telling off a larger grey squirrel.

"Be nice, Barry. Dis was dere home 'fore we arrived," I called out.

Both squirrels looked at me, then scampered off, which made me laugh. It was cute to see him socializing with more than just me.

I loved having him, but it had to be lonely. I got the feeling he didn't have anyone, which was why he stowed away with me.

"Da gardens be spelled?" I asked as we walked by a tree producing buds and small flowers that would normally have happened months ago.

"Yes, my ma spelled the gardens long ago. She hated that they all died off over winter, and she didn't have a spot to walk. So this entire area remains like it is spring all year. Snow won't gather on the ground, and when the flowers reach the end of their cycle, they start all over again."

"Dat be a pretty incredible spell. Yer ma musta been powerful."

"She was. I loved her a lot. Her death was sudden illness and tragic, and I didn't know if any of us were going to get over it."

We stepped into the open area with the pink and yellow rose bushes and the walkway that led to the statue of Mari's ma.

"Mari, I'za wanna give ya a gift."

"A gift? Why?"

"Because ya've been really nice ta me, and yer da first girl other than me sister that I would call friend," I pulled her over to the statue. "I'za 'ave a power dat has been wit me as long as me can remember. Spirits would whispa in me ears, but since comin' here, dat has gotten…more." I lifted my arms and squeezed me arm muscles, making Mari smile.

"Stronger," she said for me.

"Aye, da power be growin' in a way dat I feel in me chest."

"Okay, are you scared? Because I can find someone for you to talk to." Her face pulled into a worried frown.

"Naw, da spirits dinne scare me. I wanna know if ya wanna speak ta ya ma again?" I asked.

I'd never tried to awaken and summon a spirit to the surface, but I wanted to do this for Mari.

"You can do that? You can let me speak to her?" She asked her eyes shining with excitement.

"Aye, I tink I can for a short time." I laid my hand on the statue, feeling the presence of the spirit that lingered. I waited for Mari to say if this was what she wanted.

"Then yes, please. Whatever you can give me, I will happily take."

"Da only ting is I dinnie want a bunch a people knowin' dis be sometin' I'z able ta do. Do ya understand?" I felt a little guilty leaving out her sister and da, but it wasn't something I was comfortable with them knowing yet.

"Yes, I understand a little something about secrets," she said and winked. "Yours is safe with me." She clasped her hands and smiled.

Turning to the statue, I called the power but thought about the spirit and asked her to come forward from her slumber. The power tingled in my fingertips before it sank into the shiny white stone. People thought the dead didn't need sleep, but that wasn't true. They just didn't rest like the living did. At least, that is what some of them had whispered in my ear.

Wisps of smoke began to rise from the grass around the statue. She could've been anywhere, but it felt like she was rising toward me from beneath the statue. It took time to make the image of Mari's ma clear in my mind. As she took shape behind my eyes, she slowly formed in front of me. The air around me shimmered as the woman in the white dress appeared, her face confused as to why she'd suddenly been summoned.

Mari gasped, and her wide-eyed expression told me she saw her ma. Her eyes filled with tears as her ma looked at her.

"Mari? Can ya see me?" her ma asked, the voice as light and airy as the spirit herself.

"Dear spirits, it really is you?" Mari said, tears streaming from her eyes. They reached out, but their hands slipped through each other.

"I'za sorry, I cannie make ya be able ta touch her. Dat is beyond me ability. Maybe as I git stronger, but dis took a lot ta do," I said, and both women looked at me.

"You've done more than I ever could've imagined. Thank you," Mari said, her eyes finding her ma again. To give the two women some privacy, I moved to the little bench not far away. If I moved too far away, the connection would be lost, and the image of Mari's ma would fade.

My body suddenly began to warm again. More intense this time, like a fire had been lit in the pit of my stomach. Wiping my forehead with the back of my hand, I looked at the dampness and wondered why I was getting so hot when it was so cool out. My heart felt like a small rabbit racing around inside my chest. Fanning myself still wasn't enough. I pulled on the front of the dress to relieve the heat coming from within.

I worried that I was coming down with an illness when I felt the inside of my thighs become very wet. It wasn't that time in the moon cycle. So it couldn't be that. As the wetness persisted, so did the rising temperature in my body. Then the throbbing in my womanhood started, and all I could think about was Rook and his magical fingers and tongue. Then I wondered if Rhys would be just as talented.

I sat up straighter and looked back at the castle. It was them. Whatever they were doing was causing this reaction in me. I was sure of it. It was very tempting to find them as if whatever they were doing was calling to me. But as Mari laughed with her ma, I knew I couldn't leave now and forced myself to sit still as the torturous aching increased between my legs.

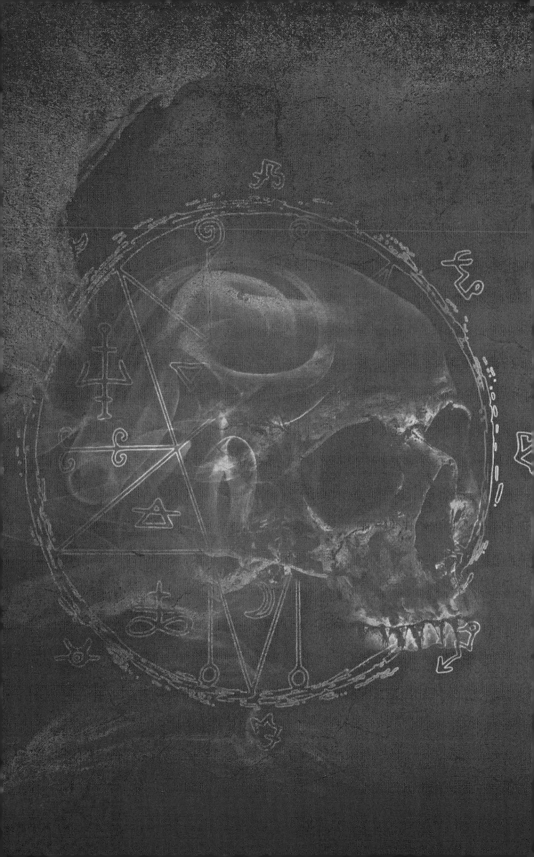

Chapter 43

R^{hys}

I didn't think this would be so hard. Watching the boxes leave in a single file, pushed into large vans, like the workers were a procession of ants, made me feel sick. Panic began to build in my chest at the thought of leaving the home I'd known since I was six. It was stupid. My castle was only an hour away, but it didn't feel like home, and the people who lived there didn't like me any more than I liked them. They weren't my family, even though we shared the same name. Any place that only reminded you of death and pain was hard to think of as home.

Mari was a lesson in love, and all those dreams secretly held in my heart had steadily crumbled down around me. There was nothing I could do to stop it. My eyes found Rook. He looked my way, and I knew where my future lay and what I wanted. I knew we would build our own castle of hopes and dreams, but it still hurt to leave.

He smiled, and I knew that no matter how much I tried to keep the pang of sadness from being seen, he could feel what was within me. It bothered me that he could feel my fears. I always battled any that cropped up alone. I was happy that people thought I was fearless. When really, I held fear for everyone and everything in my heart. Now Rook would help carry that burden. I didn't want to put that on him, yet now I had no choice.

"So dis is it, son. Ya'va come full circle," Gregory said as he walked up behind me and squeezed my shoulder.

"Aye, it would seem that way," I said.

"Ya dinnie 'ave ta go. Dis as much yer home as it be anyone else's. Besides, ya know we all love havin' ya here," he said.

I took a deep breath, fixed my gaze on the front garden, and shook my head no.

"'Tis time. Ya know it, and dis be for da better."

I never spoke of my feelings for Mari to Gregory, though I was sure he knew my heart. Everyone around us seemed to know what we both desired and tried to hide. We hadn't done a very good job.

"Aye." Gregory sighed. "I 'ave secretly and selfishly hoped dat ya woulda never be paired and ya could've been wed ta Mari. Eight more years and ya woulda been over da natural pairin' age," he said softly.

I looked at Gregory. His eyes were sad as he watched a van move out of the way for another to take its place. "I had no clue," I murmured.

"Aye. Well, no point in makin' me feelin's known when it be unlikely." He gripped my shoulder. "'Tis a shame, tho, when ya already took her worth from her," he said, his voice dropping low enough that no one else would hear. "I do hope dat dis move doesn't 'ave anythin' ta do with da punishment?"

I swallowed hard as I stared into his stern expression. "Dere be a lot more worth than their first time to any woman, Gregory. Mari's worth be more than da value da Faction puts on her," I said, conviction giving weight to my words.

How he found out about my night with Mari was anyone's guess. The walls in these old castles had ears, and news travelled faster than water. My gaze flicked to Mari, standing as far away as she could from Belle and her da. I wondered if she knew that Gregory knew when a thought began to form in my mind.

"Aye, maybe dere is," Gregory said.

I narrowed my eyes at him. "What punishment do you speak of?" My mind was reeling, and I wondered what threat those words held. Was it something he planned to do?

"It be none of yer concern now I guess. Well, I hope ya 'ave a safe move. I 'ave tings dat need tendin'."

With that, he walked away. It was the strangest conversation we ever shared and the coldest he ever treated me.

Clamping down on the worry and ache in my chest, I watched Elewyen and Mari hug like childhood friends. There was comfort in knowing that Mari accepted Elewyen. It may not have mattered if she didn't, but it made me feel better that she did. It was a purely selfish reason. As soon as Elewyen went to stand with Rook by the car, I walked over to Mari. It felt awkward and not at all like before.

"So this is it," Mari said, her face passive even though her eyes held the same emotion I held in my chest.

"Aye, it looks dat way." My eyes searched her face, and I knew that no matter how many days or years we were apart, I would remember every detail and be able to paint her from memory. "I'ma feelin' strange leavin'. It feels like I'ma runnin' off and leavin' ya alone here."

"Are you saying that I cannot function without you?" She smirked, and I knew she was teasing.

"Wha'? Naw, of course no'. I..." I sighed. "Mari, did yer Da say or do somethin' to ya fir what we did?"

Mari's eyes gave nothing away as I searched them.

"Rhys, I'm no longer your responsibility. I never was, and you need to stop worrying about me because I need to stop worrying about you. The time has officially come."

"I dinnie know if I'ma gonna be able ta do dat in da way ya be meanin'. Yer always gonna be me friend. Dat comes wit worry," I said honestly. How did you just throw away years of connection with someone?

Mari squared her shoulders, her chin rising, and her long dark hair fanned out around her as she gave me a hard stare. "I was born a woman, but no less a warrior. The moment we had when Rook first came to town was just that, a moment. We let ourselves get caught up in something that never should've happened."

"Ya sayin' ya regret what we did?"

She shook her head no. "I could never regret anything with you, but that doesn't make it any less wrong. I'm no longer the girl with pigtails with bullies and who thought monsters were under my bed, Rhys. I no longer need you to worry about me. I'm a woman who has endured the harsh reality of this world we live in, but I'll not be drowned by it. My path is my own to shape, and it is a path I need to take without you glancing over your shoulder at me."

I smiled widely, my heart full of pride. "Aye, ya've always been a warrior, but ya deserve ta be a queen. So, dis be goodbye then?"

She looked down at her feet, and I was tempted to wrap her up in a hug. It was something we would've done as friends. One night of wild passion seemed to have ruined our beautiful friendship, and I had no idea how to get it back.

"Tis far from a goodbye. Dis island be too small fir dat. It means dat we can no longer use one anotha as a crutch when we tink da monsters are too big. Yer journey be a new adventure, and I know dat yer gonna make da McGregor family great again." It made me smile to hear the sweet poetic accent I knew her to have when we were children.

"Aye, and what be yer next adventure?"

Mari looked around and then shrugged. "It be what it will be, but it will be wholly mine fir da fist time."

"Ya've always been so much stronger than I 'ave, Mari. Thank ya fir always bein' me rock and rose petals when I was needin' it most."

There was nothing left to say. I jogged down the stairs to the car, and Rook captured my stare. He seemed as torn as I felt, and once more, I wasn't sure being so tightly tied was a good thing. There were many moments I loved the idea of this joined connection, but he would feel everything I did, from the cut on my finger to the bruise I endured in training or the sadness of losing my best friend.

Looking over my shoulder, only Mari remained outside, standing still as a statue. She gave me a slight nod and then turned and walked inside the castle.

The solid wood door closing behind her felt like an end to a childhood home and the wishful hopes of a boy and a girl. For the past twenty years, I called this place home and those in it family. I couldn't explain why, but it felt like I'd just lost both.

"I'za neva been in a car ting. They be safe?" Elewyen asked as I got behind the wheel.

I gave her a reassuring smile over my shoulder and watched as Barry tucked himself into the crook of her neck.

"Aye, no need ta be worrin'. I 'ave been terrorizin' da roads here since I be thirteen."

The guards had gathered in a long line and nodded as we left the property. This was the most you ever get out of them, and I returned the gesture. We pulled onto the road towards Glentruan, and Rook reached out and gripped my shoulder.

"I be all right," I said and looked over at Rook.

"I know," he said just as my phone rang.

Caitlin's number came up on the screen, and I hit ignore. This was the longest I'd ever stayed away from my pub, and the car with Rook and Elewyen wasn't the place to have the *I cannot fuck you anymore* conversation.

The phone rang again, and Rook looked at me, brows raised. I hit the end button again.

"Who is that?"

I groaned, not wanting to say. "Ya know da girl from me pub? Ya saw her when ya first arrived. I'ma kinda needin' ta tell 'er I be off da market. I haven't been ta da pub since dat night."

The phone rang a third time, and Rook hit talk on the dash before I could get to it. Shite.

I glared at Rook. "Aye? What be goin' on, Caitlin? I'm kinda—"

"Rhys, it be da pub! It be in flames!" she yelled into the phone frantically, and my heart leapt into my throat.

"Whaddya mean?" I stupidly asked because I couldn't believe my ears.

She was crying hysterically, making it hard to understand her. "Da whole ting it be up in flames, Rhys. I dinnie know what da do," she said.

The tires squealed as I shifted the car into neutral, and cranked the wheel as I slammed on the gas. We whipped around to head back the way we just came. Rook grabbed something to hang on to, and Elewyen yelped as she slid across the bench seat. Smoke from the tires rose into the air.

"What the fuck?" Rook cursed as his shoulder slammed into mine and then into his door. I glanced back at Elewyen and then at Rook.

"Help her git her seatbelt on," I said, annoyed that I forgot to check before leaving the castle.

"Oh, I'za tink I'ma gonna be sick," Elewyen said as the car flew along the twisty road toward my hidden gem.

I glanced in the rearview mirror at her face. It was definitely green. "I'ma sorry, Elewyen. I din't want dis ta be yer first experience, but I cannie stop," I said.

Fear shimmered in her eyes, and I felt bad.

"Are you trying to kill us?" Rook asked as we raced around a hairpin turn.

"Aye, dat be me hidden agenda," I quipped back. "Caitlin, ya still be dere?"

She sniffled into the phone. "Aye, I'ma so sorry, Rhys. Dere be not enough water ta stop dis. I been runnin' a bucket from da pond, but it be no use." The line was quiet for a moment, then she shrieked. "Oh, shite! Ya scared me. Whadda doin' ere?" she asked.

"Caitlin? Who ya talkin' to?"

There was rustling and muffled arguing like she put the phone in her pocket.

"Caitlin? What be goin' on?"

I pushed the car over hills and around turns while keeping an eye out for smoke that would announce my pub's demise. A billowing black cloud rose into the air, and my heart sank. There was still the sound of two people arguing, but I couldn't make out what they were saying.

A sharp scream pierced the car, and fear stabbed through my gut. It wasn't the kind of scream that said pain. It was a scream that spoke of death. It was the kind of scream that called to my power. My magic tingled under my skin like it was being summoned.

"Caitlin," I yelled and gripped the steering wheel harder. We were already travelling dangerously fast. I couldn't push the car any faster. "Caitlin? Answer me," I yelled.

She screamed again, and the phone went dead.

My eyes flicked over to Rook. "Did ya feel dat?"

"The power call? Yeah, I felt it," he said, his eyes fixed on the road and his face as concerned as my own.

"Da sound be da call o' death," Elewyen said from the back seat.

"Aye," I said.

Every second felt like an hour until we flew around the final bend in the road. I saw no one around, which was strange. Not a single neighbour or passerby was in the large gravel lot. The car squealed to a stop. I barely got the brake locked into place before jumping from the car.

"Caitlin? Where ya be, lass? Caitlin, call out fir help," I yelled as I ran to the side of the pub, but there was no sign of her. I was forced to step back as the flames roared higher and the heat pressed into me.

"Rhys, over here," Rook called.

I ran back to the car, but Rook wasn't staring at the pub. He was looking up at the old oak tree in the middle of the gravel lot. I didn't want to look up. I knew what I was going to find. Following his gaze, rage filled me at the sight of Caitlin's body.

She was hung by a rope around her neck. The sword through her stomach and knives sticking out of her mouth and eyes told me she died painfully. This was a message to me. Whoever attacked the Faction was still on the island, and they just delivered a personal blow.

I looked back at the pub that only a handful knew about, or at least I thought so and ran through the possibilities. None of them seemed to fit. Lochlan, Caleb, Mari and Belle. None of them had anything to gain by doing this, and it wasn't in their character. It didn't make sense unless I was being followed.

Slowly turning in a circle, I let my power reach out as far as possible to see if I sensed anyone with magic skulking in the shadows, but I didn't feel anyone.

Looking back at Caitlin, my heart ached that she was caught in the middle of a personal vendetta.

"Oh, Caitlin, I'ma sorry," I whispered.

A puddle of her blood was already at the bottom of the tree, an envelope pinned to the front of her skirt.

"Who would do something like this?" Rook asked.

Elewyen stepped close to my side and slipped her hand into mine. Her eyes were kind like she knew what I was feeling and needing. The little squirrel, Barry, sat on her shoulder and gave me the same compassionate expression, and it seemed so right to see him sitting there like a little guardian angel.

"Her spirit was used fir somethin' evil. No' a bit of her lingers," Elewyen said, what I also felt.

"Aye. I'ma gonna cut her down."

Stepping away, I jumped for the lowest branch and pulled myself up. Whoever did this had help or was extremely strong. Neither option was comforting, considering the malevolence behind the act.

There were no more than five minutes from when Caitlin screamed to our arrival.

Hopping from branch to branch, I looked directly into Caitlin's face. Guilt ravaged my gut. This was on me. She would never have been in the crossfire of a Faction war if I'd never introduced her to my world. This was why we didn't bring Flitters into our lives. There was only one way they ended up.

Untying the rope, I lowered her body to Rook, who laid her out on the small patch of grass. He removed the envelope and opened it as I jumped from the branch.

"Do me wanna know what it says?"

"Let this be a warning. Finish the triad, and more of those you love will die." Rook looked up from the paper and handed it over. "Someone really doesn't like us together."

Elewyen shivered, and Rook wrapped his arm around her shoulders. Rook may have thought that he wouldn't make a good one—even I had doubted it—but he was proving with each passing day just how wrong everyone was to doubt him.

Laying my hand over the envelope, I felt for a spell or anything else to reveal who this fucker was, but nothing lingered. Whoever this was, they were extremely good at staying hidden. Walking toward the pub that had been nestled on this hill for many generations, I crumpled up the letter. No one threatened me. If they hurt anyone else I cared about, they would see just how dark I could become.

"Dis is what me tinks of yer threat," I growled and tossed the ball into the bright flames. The paper crackled and blackened immediately before turning to ash. "Do either of ya wanna get out before dis gets worse?" I turned to face Rook and Elewyen. "'Cause dis is no goin' ta get better from here 'til da threat be six feet in da ground."

Rook's brow lifted, and I could feel his annoyance before he spoke. "I told you, I'm in for the long haul, and no asshole will change my mind." Rook crossed his arms.

My gaze fell on Elewyen, who looked down at Caitlin and then back to me. "Dis be da same as dose dat burned da villages?"

"Aye, I be pretty certain it is," I said.

"Den I be goin' nowhere but wit ya. Killin' innocent babes and girls ta send a message be evil. I hunt dose dat do dis kind of cruelty. I'ma no' gonna be stoppin' now."

"I'ma needin' ta take her body to her home. I cannie leave her lyin' dere like dat. It be wrong an' disrespectful," I said.

I would find whoever was attacking us and destroy them. The question was, would I live through it, or would it also be the end of me?

My stomach twisted in knots knowing that Rook would die with me after the final ritual happened. I couldn't face that possibility. We needed to find and stop these people before the final ceremony. The next ritual moon was coming fast.

I needed to move faster.

Chapter 44

Elewyen

Rhys disappeared when we arrived at Glentruan. He showed me the way to my room—I asked to stay in my own for now—and I haven't seen him since. Rook came to check in with me today, but I wanted to talk to Rhys about the coven and Keeva. Mari said that he would agree, but I wanted to hear the words from his mouth.

Thinking about Keeva, I gripped my necklace and smiled when she answered. My heart felt full with her in my life. If she couldn't come here, then I wouldn't stay. Peering out of my room, I realised that the castle was noisy. Unlike the castle where Mari lived, where the quiet made the place feel lonely, Glentruan was full of activity. Two servants walked down the hall with linen and did a little bow as they passed. Someone else played an instrument somewhere in the castle. Whatever it was, I heard dying animals that sounded healthier.

Searching for Rhys, I reached the stairs that led down just as a girl with the same colour hair as Mari reached the top.

"Hello, I be Elewyen,"

The girl glared and looked me up and down before holding up one of the talking devices that all the people from the castles seemed to have.

"I'm on da phone. Do ya mind?"

I wasn't sure how to answer the question. Did I mind if she was on the phone?

"Why would me mind?" I asked. Apparently, that was the wrong answer because her eyes narrowed.

"All ya forest folk be so thick." She rolled her eyes. "And no' one of ya 'ave a sense in taste. What do ya call what yer wearin'?"

I looked down at the outfit Mari had given me. I quite liked the simple dress and warm sweater. "I'za…"

"I'za dinnie care," she drawled out slow and marched away as she continued to talk into the phone thing.

I must have offended her somehow, but I wasn't sure what I'd done.

Down the stairs, I heard laughter and crept towards the door. There was a man I'd never seen before standing by a massive fire in a rock hole. There were twenty people or more sitting around talking and drinking. Not seeing Rhys or Rook, I backed away from the partially open door and continued my search.

I just about gave up when I ventured down a long hall that got quieter the farther I walked. Metal men with weapons stood on either side of the hallway like they were guarding the space, and I stopped at one and gently tapped the shiny silver.

"How odd," I mumbled and continued on, looking in each room as I came to it.

Finally, in the last room at the end of the hall was Rhys at a massive wooden table with books and papers stacked around him. I leaned against the door and watched him in his element. He looked so handsome, even with his brow knit together in concentration like the papers were angering him. His cream-coloured shirt opened at the throat and was rolled up his arms to show off the dark tattoos.

My nerves got the better of me as little wings took flight in my stomach. Before I turned away, his eyes flicked up to where I was standing, and my heart stopped. His face changed when he spotted me, and warmth spread throughout my body.

"Ya comin' in?" Rhys asked and slowly stood.

My mouth ran dry as he stretched and rolled his large shoulders. I stepped into the room and looked at the items on the shelves and the pictures on the walls. They didn't seem like they belonged to Rhys for some reason.

"Sowry ta be botherin' ya," I said. "Did ya wanna talk later?"

Rhys smiled, and even though he reminded me of calm waters while Rook was like a wildfire, he still made me nervous.

"Ya neva be botherin' me," he said and walked around the table. With each step he got closer, the fluttering in my stomach got worse until I was fidgeting. "I should be apologizin' ta ya. I'ma sowry dat I've no' been around much since ya came to us."

He rubbed the back of his neck, and I clenched my fists to keep my hands to myself. I had an overwhelming urge to touch him and ease the strain in his eyes.

"I'ma no sure dat I can even say I've been a very good host."

"Wat be a host?"

He smiled widely and held out his hand for me to take. I stared at it like it was going to bite.

"Yer afraid of me?"

"Naw, jus nervous dat me brain no remember why I came ta find ya once I be touchin' ya," I said.

He laughed, and the sound was warm and rich as it flowed over my body. It was the kind of sound you wanted to wrap yourself in and hold all night long.

"Well den, ya best be tellin' me what ya came 'ere for before I be touchin' ya." He stepped in close enough that I could feel the heat of his body and could smell the fresh soap on his skin. "Cause I'ma likin' da idea of distractin' ya."

Clearing my throat, I lifted my gaze to his. "I was talkin' wit Mari..." I said.

His smile slipped to become an emotionless mask. "Aye?"

"I be tellin' her dat I will only stay if me sista, Keeva, and da rest of da coven can be comin' 'ere. She said dat ya would be good wit it, but I need ta hear da words comin' from yer mouth."

His body language changed, and he relaxed. The tension fled like the room had taken a deep breath. "Aye, she be right. Dat is fine wit me. How many be in yer coven?"

"Twenty-tree, includin' me and Keeva," I said as a wave of relief washed over me.

Rhys held out his hand again, and I slipped mine into his. The contact made me sigh, and I had the strongest urge to rub against him like a cat. It was just as strange of a reaction to him as Rook.

"Da castle has more den enough room for dat many. More, if need be."

I pointed out the door. "Ya sure? Dere be a lot of people in da room wit da fire."

512

Rhys grumbled something under his breath that I didn't catch. "Dat be me Uncle Rayland. He be more into entertainin' than runnin' da Faction. Never be mindin' him an' if the likes of any be mean ta ya, let me know. Yer da lady of da house, and dey should be showin' ya respect." His jaw tensed like he was grinding his teeth. "My cousins 'ave a knack for not bein' so friendly."

I wasn't sure what that meant, but it sounded like I was important to him, and that made me smile. Rhys ran his thumb over the back of my hand, and it tickled with magic.

"Ever play chess?" he asked.

I shook my head. He tugged me over to a small table by the window with two large chairs and an unusual board with squares and miniature statues lined up along the top.

"Dis was me father's office before he was killed. I like ta come sit in 'ere ta work, 'cause it makes it feel like he still be close and helpin' me when I be lost."

"Yer lost? But ya be at yer home."

Rhys laughed again, and it lit up his whole face. It made me blush with images I blamed Rook for putting in my head.

"I'ma only feelin' lost, not dat I cannie find me way around. Here, I'ma goin' show ya how ta play," he said and went to sit down, but I gripped his hand to stop him.

"I need ta be askin' ya somethin' else." Lifting my chin, I stared him in those slivery depths that could carry you away as surely as the turbulent, rolling clouds outside. Before I lost my nerve, I blurted out the question. "Ya still be lovin' Mari?"

His face blanched, and his eyes went wide. With a flick of his hand, the door to the office closed with a bang, making me jump.

"I dinnie tink dis be a conversation we should be havin'," he said, but didn't pull away. "Movin' here be our new start." He pointed back and forth between us.

Pulling my hand away from his, I crossed my arms over my chest and gave him a hard stare. "I dinnie know if dis is gonna work," I said, surprised with my own anger.

His mouth fell open, and he looked outside. "I'ma no' sure what ta say. I'm wantin' us ta work, Elewyen, and me be puttin' da past in da past."

I held up my hand. "Ya do still be in love wit her? Aye or no?"

He licked his lips and looked like he'd rather jump out the window than be in the same room with me. "Um...I'ma workin' toward da future wit ya and Rook." He crossed his arms over his big chest and looked down at the ground. I didn't like how he was dancing around the answer.

I shook my head as the anger bubbled higher. How could I be with someone and trust them when they could throw away the person they loved? What did that say about how he would treat me?

"I be tinkin' it be best if me go." Rhys stepped in my way.

"I be sowry, Elewyen. I cannie help it."

I poked him in the chest. "How are ya expectin' me ta trust ya when ya so easily trow dose ya claim ta love away from yer heart?" I could picture the pain in Mari's eyes. "I'za git dat dis has ta be da way it is, but real feelin's cannie just be turned off like yer fancy taps. Mari said ya only 'ave honour in her heart, but I be tinkin' her feelin's be couldin' her judgement. "

He shook his head, his brow pulling down, and I wasn't sure if he was angry or confused. "Wait...." He held up a hand and closed his eyes for a moment. "Ya be wantin' me ta still have feelin's fir Mari? I be so confused."

"It no be dat confusin'. Da bond I saw in her eyes be dat of someone dat would lay down their life fir da other. Ya seem like ya be wantin' ta sweep wat ya shared away, and dat be cruel. Now dinnie be mistakin', I know dat dis wit da three of us can't be somethin' she can be part of—she explained dat ta me—but..."

Before I could get out another word, Rhys cupped my face and dropped his lips to mine. The kiss was soft and yet sent a powerful surge through my body, but it was the tears that landed on my cheeks that had me holding still rather than pulling away.

"Ya be so different from Rook," he said, breaking the kiss with a sad smile on his lips.

"I be hopin' so. I dinnie 'ave a peen," I said.

He stepped away and laughed so hard that he had to lean against the chair.

"What!? It be da truth?" I wasn't sure why everyone laughed when I spoke the truth. Were they all used to lies?

"Aye, yer right. Ya dinnie have a peen." He smirked and smiled as he wiped away the stray tear rolling down his cheek. "I'ma gonna tell ya how I feel and what I tink, but I be askin' we no talk about it again."

I nodded as he came back to me and held out his hands. Uncrossing my arms, I slowly placed my hands in his.

"I'ma sayin' yer different, no' in a bad way. Yer jus very opposite, which be good, jus' unexpected. As fir yer da question about Mari." He sucked in a deep breath, and I could feel the air in the room shift as he gathered his thoughts. "Love like what da two of us shared be somethin' dat never dies. It be somethin' dat shifts and can change over time 'cause it must, but it never disappears. So da answer be aye, dere is and will always be something, but it needs ta shift from what it was ta somethin' different now." His hands were so warm as they held mine, and I could once more feel the pull to lean into him. "Dis

515

here wit ya and Rook be me new life. I'ma needin' ta walk forward and no' look back, or tings become confusin' and causin' pain ta everyone includin' Mari. Does dat make sense?"

"Aye, and me glad ta hear dat once ya be lovin' me, ya cannie jus be tossin' me aside when yer feelin' like it."

"Yer unusual, Elewyen. Ya tink different from anyone else I 'ave met, but in a good way. Keep dat, and always see da beauty, 'cause dis world has enough dark already." I shivered as his hands left mine and softly ran up my arms to cup my face. "I'ma gonna kiss ya again, if dat be all right?"

"Aye," I said as my heart hammered.

I didn't realize until now how much I wanted to know his touch. My skin tingled and felt alive under his firm, patient hands. Where Rook brought out a wildness in me, Rhys made me want to melt.

His lips were as warm as the rest of his body, and I sighed as they touched mine. The kiss deepened, and I gripped the front of his shirt. My head felt light, like it might blow away. I moaned into his mouth, and the kiss became more desperate.

He slid one of his hands down to press into my lower back, bringing me closer to him until there was only the feel of our bodies and his lips. It seemed wondrous to me that not long ago, I thought these two men were evil, but now everything was turned on its head. The emotions that Rhys emitted were kind and compassionate. He was full of warmth and understanding, with strength under it all.

The door to the office opened, and I jumped a little when it hit the wall.

"Well, isn't this heartwarming?" Rook said, and I blushed as I met his heated gaze.

"Ya mind? Ya interrupted a moment," Rhys said, his lip curled up with a teasing grin.

"You know what you're doing to me, right?" His eyes were trained on Rhys as he asked the question. "You know I can feel what you're doing, and now I'm sporting this." He pointed to where his peen was, and I saw the bulge under the black bottoms.

"Aye, well, as temptin' as dat is, ya better not be thinkin' dat we be turnin' dis into more."

"You're going to make me walk around like this? Again?" Rook asked. Rhys smirked. "You really are a sadist under all that nice thing you have going on."

Rhys laughed as he glanced at the thing on the wall they called a clock. "We 'ave a schedule ta keep. We have trainin', and Sam is gonna help Elewyen pick out some new clothes so she no be havin' ta wear someone elses."

"You're really think I'm going to get through training aching like this?" Rook grumbled.

Rhys only laughed. "If ya no notice, it stands up almost as much as da trees outside," Rhys said, and I smirked as Rook laughed. "I be pretty sure dat we can be gettin' it up again easy enough later."

I knew they were talking about laying with one another. I was tempted to join them at night, but even after the amazing time with Rook, I felt nervous joining them in the same room. It was not for lack of trying on Rook's part, mind you. He came by and asked at least three different times over the past two nights.

"Who's Sam, anyway?" Rook asked.

"Did someone say me name?" Sam said as he marched into the room and right past Rook like he wasn't there. "I be preferrin' ta be called Sammy taday. It 'as a better ring."

He introduced himself when we arrived the other day and told me that he was my person. There were so many things that I still didn't know what they meant. Being my person was one of them, but

I nodded as he chatted happily and then forced me to sit while he brushed and braided my hair.

"Come wit me, my dear. We got some clothes pickin' ta do," Sammy said with just as much excitement as the other day. He smiled and held out his elbow while his soft green eyes glittered with merriment. He was like a wild wind all by himself.

I looked up at Rhys, much preferring the idea of training than doing anything with clothes. As if reading my thoughts, he smiled.

"Belle be by later ta continue trainin' ya wit da smaller sword."

"What 'bout Mari?" I asked, excited to see her.

He shook his head. "Belle said dat she be gone to da mainland an' won't be back fir a few days. No worry, as soon as yer done with Sam ya can be meetin' us out back fir ya trainin'."

"Dis is gonna be so much more fun den trainin'," Sammy said as I took his offered elbow. Then he led me out the door like his feet were aflame.

As nice and helpful as Sammy seemed, was it wrong that I preferred to roll around in the dirt with Rook and Rhys? Taking a deep breath, I prepared myself for what I felt would be a battle of a different kind.

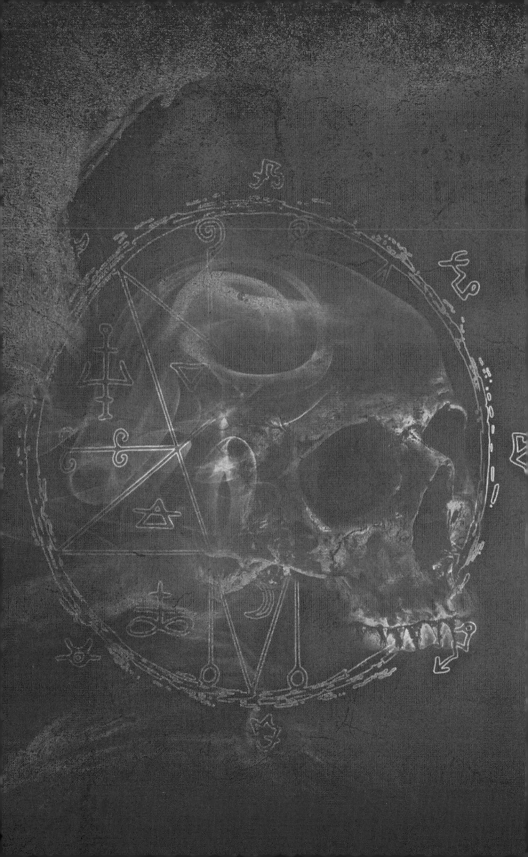

Chapter 45

Rook

"Fuck," I yelled as the hardwood cracked me in the elbow, and sent a jolt up my arm, making my fingers numb. Whatever happened to a good old-fashioned fistfight? This canne and sword work was for the birds.

"Yer dead again," Rhys said, holding the tip of the wooden sword under my chin. "Ya need ta quicken yer feet. Yer clumsy when ya tink ta much," he snarled, then marched away.

I bit back the angry retort I planned on spewing only because I knew that, despite the smile he put on his face, he wasn't over his friend being killed.

We took Caitlin's brutally mangled body to her parents. The look on her father's face when he answered the door was an image I would never forget. It was morbid and something I never wanted to experience again.

Rhys was trying to open up to me, but he was still too quiet and closed off. Even our connection during sex was strained with sadness. I was an extrovert when it came to my emotions. If I was angry, you fucking knew it. If I was sad…Oh, you definitely knew it. If I was broody…Well, I was broody a lot, so who knows? But Rhys? He held it all in, and I fucking felt all his turmoil, too. I hadn't thought about that in the library. Not that I would take the merge back, but I wasn't prepared. I was left with all the feelings and none of the context.

He wore a mask of stone and went about his day like the maelstrom of pain inside didn't bother him. The issue was that I felt the shit storm brewing in him like a cyclone headed for shore. In this case, I was the shore.

"Fuck, man, you are pissing me off today," I grumbled and rubbed at my sore arm.

"Yer slow. Ya be dead in an instant," Rhys said.

I spotted Riegan on a balcony, and she smiled as soon as my eyes found her. Too many damn R names in one place, if you asked me. Ronan was cool in a creepy way, but Riegan gave me a once-over that I knew well. You learned those looks when touring. The ones that said all you have to do is nod toward the VIP area. She was smokin', and a few short weeks ago, I would've been all up in her business.

Now here I was, the dutiful partner while Rhys cracked me with a fucking wooden sword like he was enjoying the bruises he was putting all over my body. Then again he probably was and here I thought I was the one that enjoyed doling out pain.

At least Elewyen was having a better time with Belle. I watched the two women in the other training area as they sparred, and my blood pounded a little harder at the sight of that short kilt and her long legs.

Taking a deep breath, I tried for calm and reasonable—two things that were not my strong character traits.

"I managed to block you for a solid five minutes before you hit me, Rhys," I said as I shook my arm to regain feeling.

"Aye, but it no' good enough," he said and then took a sip of water. "Let's go again. I'ma wantin' ya ta be able to handle a solid twenty before we move on ta somthin' else."

"Twenty! Have you lost..." I bit my lip to hold back the last part of the sentence. "Fine, but I need a break. My fingers are still tingling," I said, then I felt the anger in my chest.

My head snapped up to look at Rhys. His eyes narrowed into thin slits as he tossed his water bottle down on the ground and marched towards me, his wooden weapon spinning in his hand.

"Back off, Rhys," I said, but he kept coming, and I knew, by the look on his face, he was going to take the swing at me no matter what I said. "Rhys."

I brought my arm up at the last second and blocked the blow with the thick leather armour on my forearm, but it could only block so much of the pain, and I winced with the force of the strike.

"Rhys, what the fuck?" I tried again, but it was like he couldn't hear me or didn't give a fuck.

With a yell, he swung again, this time for my side, and I twisted awkwardly to avoid the blow. He didn't relent, and soon I was on my heels and backing up as I moved my wooden sword to counter the attack. The sound of wood cracking echoed in the still evening air.

Unlike at Injebreck, Glentruan had a large training facility with multiple areas and obstacles in the way. I used a tree to dart around and duck as the weapon came for my head. Little bits of bark flew off and hit me. That was a deadly blow, regardless of whether the sword was wood.

"Rhys, cut it out," I tried again as he rounded the corner. "Enough, man! I get it!"

But nothing slowed him down, and the anger I felt coming off him burned brighter than before. My pleas only made him more aggressive rather than less.

Crack, crack, crack!

The wood smacked together loudly as I forced my tired arm to work and feebly block each hit.

"I said, cut it out," I growled, my anger reaching the same boiling point his was already at.

Blocking the next swing, I grabbed his arm and shoved him back hard, until he stumbled away from me.

"What the fuck is wrong with you?" I panted, my chest heaving from the hours of physical exertion. "You trying to kill me?"

Little puffs of smoke rose in the air from our mouths like we were both getting ready to breathe fire.

Rhys tossed the wooden sword down, then plowed into me, taking me by surprise. He gripped me around the waist, ripping my feet from the ground, and slammed my back on the hard dirt. The impact forced all the air out of my lungs and left me slightly dazed. I shook it off quickly, unsure what the hell he was going to do next.

I would use my power to subdue him if I had to. Rhys would be pissed, but this was going too far.

"Do ya no' get it," Rhys said, his hands fisted into the front of my black sweater. "They be comin' for me, which means they be comin' for ya and Eley as well, and I'll be damned if I'm losin' either one of ya." His forearms flexed as he gave me a shake. I could feel the anger in his chest melt away and morph into fear.

"I'ma no' losin' ya," Rhys said again, and then crushed our lips together.

There was desperation in the kiss. It felt like he was terrified to let go, or I might disappear. Breaking the kiss, he lifted his head enough that I could stare into his stormy grey eyes that matched the overcast sky. "I cannie lose ya. Do ya understand?" His eyes flicked to where Elewyen was and then back to me. "I cannie lose either of ya."

I knew what he was trying to say, even though the words didn't leave his mouth. I was all up in my feelings where he was concerned too. I never knew love, not really. Aside from loving my brothers, as big of fucking dickheads as they were, I never felt anything more than a general sexual interest toward anyone. That was until Rhys. And now I added Elewyen, who crept into my blood, to join the mix.

My heart pounded like a caged animal trying to get out when Rhys was near, and I was restless and wanted to touch him whenever we were separated. I genuinely enjoyed his company and the thought of him hurt or dying made me murderous. All things I never knew before. All things that I couldn't figure out how to voice. All things that stared back at me from his eyes and swirled around inside him.

"You're not going to lose me. Besides, soon enough, if something were to happen to me, it's yourself you better worry about," I teased.

"Dat's no' funny," he said, and rolled himself off me.

We lay there staring up at the sky that promised either rain or snow and were quiet for a long time.

"You're right it wasn't. I'm sorry about your friend and your pub," I said, looking over at Rhys. It was the first time I acknowledged what happened that day.

"So am I," he said and rubbed his face. "It's me fault she's dead. If I hadna' introduced her to da Factions, she would'na been caught in da middle of dis feud."

"That's not true," I said. Rhys turned his head to stare at me. "Let's pretend for a moment she had no idea about the Factions and simply worked at your pub as a bartender, waitress, or even manager. She would've done exactly what she did on her way to work when she saw that the pub was up in flames. She was in the wrong place at the worst possible time, but she would have called you anyway. If it wasn't her, it would've been someone else who worked for you. Do ya think ya had anything to do with the villages and all those innocent people who didn't know ya?"

"Aye, I guess yer right. It jus' be hard ta let it go, ya know?" Rhys smiled. "Did ya just say ya three times?"

I snapped my mouth shut as I thought about what I said, then rubbed my face as Rhys began to laugh. "I blame you for that. Listening to you talk all the time, I'm starting to mimic ya—no, you. Shit. Next thing you know, I'll be saying dis, dere, and dat."

Rhys laughed a little harder before sitting up. "Could be worse, ya know. Ya could sound like a stuffy Faction Four wit dere propa English. You simply must lift your pinky finger when holding a cuppa," he said, putting on a Faction Four accent and making us both laugh.

It was the first real smile on his face since moving here. Sobering, I sat up and slowly pushed myself to my feet, which were killing me. Everything freaking hurt, but I held out my hand for Rhys to take. Helping him to his feet, I refused to let go of his hand until he looked at me.

"I know how serious this is, and I'm not taking it lightly, but you need to ease up a little, I'm not going to learn any faster with you angry at me," I said. "Besides, there are other ways you can torture me, even when my arms don't want to lift this fake sword anymore."

"Aye, and what might dat be?" He lifted an eyebrow like he

expected me to say something naughty. Fair point. My mind was always focused on getting naked.

"I'm thinking you can help me find the books I started to read at Injebreck. I had to leave them behind, and this library is even larger. I'm lucky I can find my way out of that maze, let alone find a book I want."

A sly smile crossed Rhys's face. "I'ma thinkin' yer just wantin' ta get me naked on some books again."

"Fucking brilliant idea. It was certainly the best time I've ever had in a library," I said, making us both smirk.

"Aye, but dat cleanup... I bet Illiam is still swearin', tryin' ta get all da books back into dere proper spots on da shelves."

A guard started ringing a bell and yelling something.

"What's going on?" I asked.

"Nothin' good," Rhys answered, his eyes fixed on the guards running from all over the property.

The front property entrance erupted in noise, followed by an explosion. We fell a step back, then ducked as little chunks of debris landed where we stood like dangerous rain.

The cloaking spell that Rhys wore at all times disappeared, showing off the real weapons. They were the same ones strapped to his body, but for some reason, it sunk in just how dangerous he was.

Rhys whipped out the sharp sword at his hip and set his feet into a fighting stance as he stepped in front of me. He would die for me. I knew it, but like the weapons on his body, it only just registered what that meant. It was one thing to say *I'd die for you.* It was another to put yourself in the line of danger.

Rhys looked over his shoulder at me, and the look on his face pulled me out of the fog my brain had been stuck in.

"Dere be intruders. Take dis. I'ma gonna use me axe," he said and pulled the double-sided axe from the straps on his back.

I looked to the other arena and saw four guards surrounding Belle and Elewyen, ready to fight and protect them.

"Oh, fuck," I said, wrapping my hand around the hilt of the sword as a horde of people stormed the training area. They were dressed in tight outfits similar to those who had attacked us at the pub. This bunch only wore black, and under their hoods, they wore bright white masks. Blood flew in all directions as the enemy collided with the guards. A group broke away from fighting the guards to run in our direction, and my hand tightened on the thin metal vines that encircled the sword's handle.

Adrenaline made my heart hammer in my chest while fear froze my legs. My muscles twitched as they sped across the grass and closed in on our location. Rhys was right. They were after us. I glanced at him out of the corner of my eye. They were after him.

Rhys roared as he ran at the group, not waiting for them to surround us. The sound sent a chill down my spine. It was the battle cry of a warrior. It was a cry of death, and it called to my soul. With one swing of his axe, the blade gutted three of the attackers. Each of them crumpled to the ground, holding the grotesque wounds, but it would do them no good. Their internal organs spilled out onto the grass, along with their blood.

Rhys spun, his kilt and heavy cloak flaring as the massive weapon he wielded cut through two more before they could get out of the way. As the great axe rose into the air, the unique Celtic engravings on the blade glinted in the dull light a breath before it decapitated its next victim.

Warm blood splattered my face, and I looked down to see the hot, wet streaks on my clothes. I wasn't scared, but I couldn't stop the adrenaline from racing and causing tremors that made my hands shake. The noise made my pulse pound harder with each passing second. I sucked in a deep breath, and my body trembled as the magic my bloodline was known for stirred within me.

It was death. It was calling to me like the sound of sweet song on the wind.

Spinning the blade in my hand, I blocked one of the guys trying to sneak around the others. He held two long knives that could've passed for short swords and was fast—much faster than I was used to dealing with—and I suddenly understood what Rhys had been talking about. While he moved like he was part of the breeze, I felt like a snail, my movements heavy and slow. My already sore arms screamed as I fought off the intruder, and unlike with the wooden swords, this battle was for keeps.

The metal clanged and echoed against the huge stone walls of the castle, beneath the darkening sky. It wasn't until I let my body go and began fighting with instinct that I was able to push the guy back on his heels. I stupidly thought that things were going better until two more of the strange invaders joined, and I knew I was outmatched.

I stared at the three masked faces. The only thing visible was their eyes, and they were filled with rage and hate.

One suddenly jerked before falling forward. Dead. I blinked in confusion for a moment as I stared at the arrow sticking out of the side of his head. A flash of tan and red hair told me that Elewyen had broken away from her guards or they were dead, but she had just joined the fight.

Another arrow flew through the air as I blocked a deadly blow, and another of the intruders fell to their knees, an arrow protruding from his chest. His hands went to the wooden shaft like he intended to pull it out, but a moment later, he collapsed, his eyes no longer seeing.

I was panting hard, and yet more and more people dressed in black poured onto the property. Our guards were tiring and being beaten back from the sheer volume of invaders. I could feel Rhys's fatigue in my chest. Could feel his movements slowing. I reached for my power, which was begging to be set free, no longer caring if it summoned all of the next fucking Faction or every hunter in the entire world. It rippled under my skin, ready.

I watched in horror as Rhys almost took a blade across the face, the poisonous tip of the sword almost delivering his demise, and a roar that sounded more animal than man ripped from my mouth as rage and fear fuelled me.

No one was going to hurt what was mine.

I dropped the sword, and the man I was fighting looked down, then back up at me. He stepped in my direction, thinking that I was giving up. His step faltered when I snarled at him. My eyes glowed so brightly that the light reflected off the shiny white mask he wore. My body vibrated as my power reached out along the ground like a bloodhound hunting for its prey. It was no harder than taking a breath to absorb the souls of those who fell into my system. The dead and their blood seeping into the dirt added to my power and filled every part of me with a desire for *more*.

The man raised his twin swords to strike, and I held out my hand in his direction, freezing him in place. He dropped his swords and gripped at his throat as I squeezed my hand closed. With a quick twist of my fist, his neck snapped with a distinct sound. He collapsed at my feet. His soul hovered over the hard dirt, confusion still on his face.

You're dead. I thought a wicked curl lifting my lip. *That's what happened, and now you will end up in the purgatory of nothingness.*

That was what happened when you used the souls of others to fuel your power. It was why it was normally banned unless it was extenuating circumstances. But to me, this was an extenuating circumstance. No one was fucking with my triad and those I loved.

I could taste the souls around me like dark brandy on my tongue, and I eagerly swallowed the flavour down. Letting out a shuddering breath, I called the newest soul to me, and it joined the torrent of others already coursing under my skin.

A wild fury filled me as Rhys leapt out of the way of a sword that would've ended his life. Elewyen jumped on the man's back and drove a knife through his throat before Rhys took his head. The two stood shoulder-to-shoulder and faced the next wave.

A growl rippled from my throat as I stared at the coming threat. I was through with this game. I protected what was mine.

I released my hold on the power with a groan.

Rhys looked over, shocked, as our eyes met when I floated past where he stood. I could feel the eyes of all, friends and foes, turning in my direction as my hovering body drew their attention.

The tall gate might say McGregor, but this was my home now. The clamour of battle was dulled by the whooshing of magic, and it swirled like smoke around my hands and feet. Knives, swords, and arrows flew in my direction, but they all disintegrated into dust before they reached my skin. Holding my palms up, I stared at those who stormed my home and knew their souls would be mine.

"Rise, my shadows. Rise and feast on what I offer," I said.

The ground rumbled like an earthquake was coming, and everyone stumbled, trying to remain upright. Spectral hands, as dark as only those from the demon fade could be, rose from the dirt. The

531

first shrill scream that reached my ears sounded like music. More screaming rose into the night sky as those ghastly, smoky hands wrapped around the legs of those who had invaded my home and tried to kill us. Claws tore at clothing and skin as the intruders tried to run, tried to get away from the death coming for them.

But it was inevitable.

I could feel their deaths on my fingertips and taste the destruction of their souls in my mouth.

I wanted them to suffer. Wanted them to know who they crossed before they died. Wanted those who sent them to understand what it meant to make an enemy of Rook Adair. I bowed down to no one. I took what I wanted. And right now, what I wanted was their fear.

The ground rumbled. The sky darkened. Thick shadows pulled away from the trees and rocks to join in the battle. Wild cries of pain and tearing flesh filled my ears. Blood splattered my face as the shadows clawed relentlessly at my enemies. Bones snapped, and bodies were torn apart, piece by piece.

Pleas and begging reached me but fell on deaf ears. Their cries of pain and suffering only added to the thrill of the kill. They started this, but I intended to finish it.

"Take them," I yelled. "Take them all. I give them all to you."

The shadows cut off those who almost reached the gate, and their terror-filled cries echoed off the stone walls of the immense castle. Guards backed away, and I could feel their fear that they were next.

It was tempting. Oh, so tempting.

I wanted more.

I wanted all the souls that I could take.

A hand touched my hand, and the warm buzzing that accompanied Rhys's touch travelled up my arm. The simple touch had me closing my eyes to take a steadying breath. Another hand touched my other hand, and Elewyen's presence, soft warmth, and calm kindness filled me. Their essence pushed down the rage fuelling me until it retreated into the depths of my soul, where it lingered on a low simmer.

As the power dissipated, the shadows evaporated and disappeared to become one with the world around us. Ever watching and waiting to be called. Drifting down to the ground, I looked at Rhys and then at Elewyen before I collapsed to my knees in the moist grass.

Lifting my shaking hand, I stared at it and blinked as I registered that it was soaked bright red. Red with the blood of my enemies. Red with the death of dozens.

What have I done? I wondered as my eyes fluttered closed and darkness consumed me.

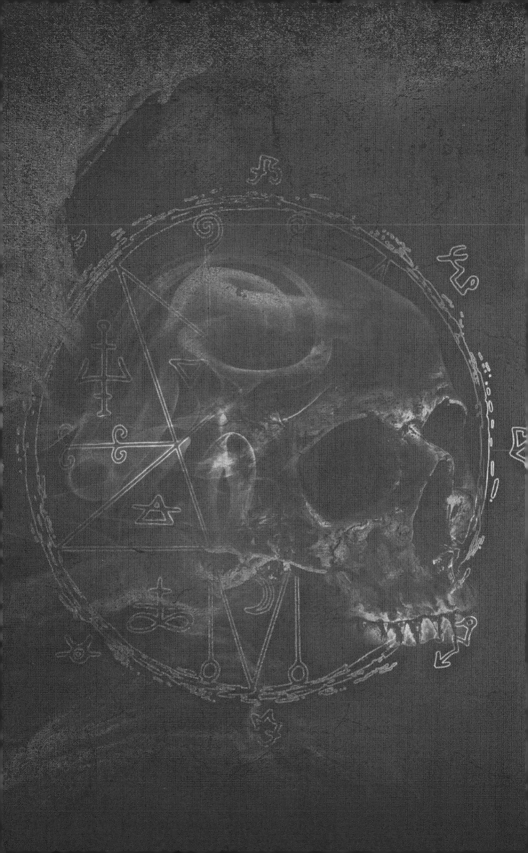

Chapter 46

E lewyen

"I'z never seen anythin' like dat before," I said to Rhys.
His cousin Ronan was helping carry Rook into the castle.

"Aye, dat was somethin' beyond me knowledge," Rhys answered.

I followed as they took Rook up the stairs to our wing.

"Dat be some seriously fierce shite," Ronan chimed in when we reached the top floor.

Ronan had the same black hair and grey eyes as Rhys, but his were more like the colour of a small grey mouse. Although he was only two years younger than Rhys, he seemed very chiseler. It was the feeling I got from his energy.

What happened with Rook may have seemed fierce—which I assumed meant great—but it felt dangerous. That was the darkest of dark magic, and a strange lingering pull tempted us from the shadows. It was as if the dark fade was whispering and calling to Rook as he channeled the deaths. I could hear their harsh, enticing words, like claws lightly scraping along my skin, making me shiver.

I'd never seen such carnage, except for the villages, but those people were burned. These were ripped to shreds by hands, not of the living or that of the dead. They were from the inky space that lingered in between worlds. The space that no one ever wanted to end up and filled us all minds with terror. Chills raced through my body, and the hair on my neck stood in warning when his power had rose like a creature from the depths of the fade.

"Dat no be fierce," Rhys said, echoing my thoughts as they laid Rook on the large bed. "Tanks, Ronan, but me got it from 'ere," Rhys stripped off his bloodied shirt.

"Whaddya want me ta do wit all da...parts?" Ronan asked from the door.

"I'm no' sure. I guess git da guards ta try an' wash da blood off da grass and burn what be left of da bodies. We no need anyone ta see dat, and da stench of da day's heat will 'ave us all wantin' ta move."

"Washin' body parts off da lawn. No' somethin' I ever pictured happenin'. Best feckin' day ever. Glad ta 'ave ya home cousin," Ronan said, far too cheerily before closing the door.

"Elewyen, ya mind grabbin' some cool, damp washcloths and a change of clothes for Rook?" His voice was calm and reassuring as he stripped his soiled clothing.

"Aye." I ran to the washroom, grabbed the small towels not much bigger than my hand off the shelf, put them in the sink, and turned on the cold water. We did this back at my coven for those running a fever. This was more convenient than water from a stream.

While the water cooled, I dashed into the closet. Searching through the piles until I found a black T-shirt and a pair of soft bottoms that Rook liked to wear in the evening. Rhys would want a set too, so I grabbed two of everything.

My steps faltered as Rhys dropped the last of his garments onto the floor. I froze, staring at the back of his hard, naked body and the massive Celtic symbol of power.

I never saw more than his face and a bit of his abs when his shirt would rise. Like Rook, dark artwork travelled along his arms, over his shoulders, and down the sides of his body, stopping at his hips. I licked my lips at the sight of him as my eyes continued to roam. He was built similarly and yet differently from Rook. They were equal in their more-than-average height, but Rook was less bulky. Rhys had wide shoulders and legs like trees, just as cut as the rest of his body. His arse flexed as he bent over to remove his boots, and my body flushed hot as everything hanging below the belt was suddenly on display.

He looked around his arm like he sensed me staring. My cheeks flamed hotter as our eyes locked. Those intense stormy eyes pulled me in and made my heart sputter in my chest. Clearing my throat, I walked towards him as he stood and turned in my direction. I held out the clothes and forced my eyes to stay on his face, away from anything tempting below his waist.

"I'za got dis fir both of ya. I dinnie know what he'd wanna wear," Rhys took the clothes.

Our fingers brushed, and his brooding expression in his office came to mind. Even though nothing showed on his face or in his tone, I could sense he was worried. He just stared at me like he was trying to communicate silently. I couldn't decipher the look, but I didn't have to.

Rook moaned, drawing our attention.

"I be needin' ta shower before I git changed," he mumbled, staring at Rook.

"I'za gonna go get da cloths," I turned away, but Rhys grabbed my arm.

"Tank ya. Fir many tings, but ya were amazin' out dere," he said.

He hesitated like he wanted to say more but let go and looked away. Swallowing down the heated feelings that crept up my throat, I went back to the cooling cloths trying to decide if I needed one of these for myself. I turned off the water and squeezed out the cloths before returning to the bedroom. At the last moment, I grabbed a much larger version of the small cloth off the shelf.

"Whaddya want me ta do?" I asked and held out the large cloth for him to put on as I averted my gaze.

"Tanks," he said and wrapped it around his waist before taking the small damp ones and sitting them aside. "I'ma gonna get ya ta help me ta take off da sweater. I already got the rest off," he said.

That was when I noticed that Rook was under the blankets from the waist down.

Climbing onto the bed, I waited until he sat Rook up and then began fighting with the clothing. He was worse than a small child, his limbs heavy as I tried to work without help from Rook, who was still very unconscious. I finally managed to get the sweater and damp shirt off one arm, then felt silly for panting so hard.

"It be harder den it looks," I said as Rhys smirked.

It was easier to straddle his body to continue, so I did. I got the sweater off his head and pulled the material down his other arm when Rook jerked in my hold. His head slowly tilted up to look at me and his eyes were no longer a pretty shade of blue. I shivered as I stared into the solid black depths.

Rook growled a sound that was not of this plane, and I tried to jump off his body when his hands clamped painfully on my hips. A shriek ripped from my throat as he rolled with such force that we landed hard on the floor with him on top of me. My head hit the stone, and air pushed out of my chest as my back screamed from the harsh impact.

"Rook," I said, my voice small as he growled again and opened his mouth like he was going to bite me.

My hands were trapped at my sides, and panic clawed at my throat. I closed my eyes, ready for what I knew would happen when his weight disappeared. I heard a loud thump, then a vicious snarl. My eyes snapped open to see Rhys holding Rook up against the wall.

If this weren't such a terrifying moment, I would've spent more time admiring the sheer strength of Rhys as he braced himself and growled back at Rook, his eyes glowing a silver so pure they looked white. Every muscle flexed and the tattoos on his arms seemed to shimmer.

"Enough! Leave him be," Rhys ordered, and a shudder travelled down my spine with the command. He slammed Rook against the wall again so hard that a picture rattled and fell to the ground.

"Demon a beheith imithe! Demon a beheith imithe! Demon a beheith imithe," Rhys roared, his eyes glowing brighter each time he repeated the banishing spell.

A terrifying screech ripped from Rook's mouth as Rhys continued to chant as Rook thrashed and snapped at Rhys face. The tattooed snake on Rook's arm and chest shimmered and shifted on his skin. With a hiss it pulled free and came alive. I screamed and pushed myself back along the floor, unable to believe my eyes. I looked around for a weapon. Spotting the long knife peeking out from beneath Rhys's discarded clothes, I crawled across the floor and pulled it free.

I didn't know if this snake was part of the demon's or Rhys doing. Shooting to my feet with the knife in hand, I tried to figure out the best way to help Rhys without killing Rook. What kind of dark magic made artwork on your body come alive?

"Demon a beheith imithe," Rhys yelled one more time, and the snake, which was as long as I was tall and as thick as Rhys's arm, opened its mouth to attack.

I leapt on the bed, ready to intervene, when the snake struck. It sank huge fangs, that were unnaturally long, into the flesh over Rook's heart. His body jerked and bowed away from the wall. The sight made my chest hurt, and I put my hand were my heart was and stared at Rook, unable to decide what to do. My hand shook as it tightened around the knife. I couldn't look away from the massive snake, stunned that Rhys didn't seem to care.

"Aye, take it. Heal him," Rhys cooed, encouraging the massive creature. "Poison da darkness," he said, close to the snake's head.

Inky black fluid drooled from the corner of Rook's mouth, dripping from his nose and ears as his body trembled in Rhys's hold. I squeezed the knife's handle to reassure myself but made no move to kill the snake that seemed to be helping. This was dark demon fade magic. That was the only explanation for what I was witnessing.

Rook stopped growling and shrieking as his eyes shifted back to his blue. As the great snake released its hold, I stared wide-eyed at the fangs as long as my hand and dripping with black blood. Rook began to make retching noises as he jerked in Rhys hands. Rhys lowered him to the floor and supported him as he threw up a vile-smelling black liquid. I stepped closer to the edge of the bed, unsure how to describe what I'd witnessed. Had he been possessed? Was he infected with a demon? What exactly did this snake do?

The great snake rose from where it lay across Rook's shoulders, like a pet, to stare me in the eyes. I swallowed hard as bright blue eyes that matched Rook's blinked. Its forked tongue slipped from its mouth, testing the air as if inspecting me. It looked at my hand clenching the knife and I followed its stare.

"I'za no gonna use it," I said, feeling like I needed to explain.

Those eerie blue eyes found mine once more and fear paralyzed me in place. The snake stayed like that for only a moment before slowly lowering itself down and sliding along Rook's skin. I watched in fascination as it spread out along his arm and once more became one with Rook.

"Aye, dat's it," Rhys said as he braced Rook and rubbed circles on his back. This was the side of Rhys that Mari saw. He could toss a man up against the wall in one breath and then comfort him in the next. He was as delicate in his care as he was fierce in battle. My heart bloomed with warmth that this was the type of man that the spirts chose to pair me with.

"That stuff tastes like shit," Rook said and coughed some more.

"Aye, I'd suspect it would. Come on. I'll help ya git ta the loo and git ya cleaned up. I'll worry about da floor later."

"Fuck, I hate throwing up," Rhys helped him to his feet. Rook was so unstable Rhys practically carried him to the loo.

I jumped off the bed, taking my first real breath since whatever happened outside, and felt useless. The guys were already in their routine, and because I purposely kept myself separate, I didn't know what to do in this room that wasn't mine.

Out in the hall, I searched for one of the dozens of servants who lurked around every corner.

"Sam," I called out tentatively. "Or Sammy?"

"Aye," he said from right behind me. I jumped and spun around, holding the knife to his face. "Sorry, me lady, I did'na mean ta scare ya," he said, and I slowly lowered my arm.

"Sowry, but no scarin' me like dat, I'z afraid ta hurt ya." I stuck the knife through the belt around my waist. "Do ya have secret passages or magic ta know when yer wanted?" I asked and looked around at the stone walls. It seemed impossible, but he just appeared where and when I needed him.

A small smile lifted the corners of the man's cherubic face. "Magic spell, no, but da passages may be a real ting," he whispered. "Da servents 'ave little ta no real magic me Lady."

"I'za no' supposed ta know about da passages?" I asked.

"Well, dey would'na be much of a secret if ya knew, would dey?" His smile made his soft green eyes sparkle with carefree mischief. He held up a finger. "Me just might be talked inta tellin' ya where dey be and where dey lead, but only 'cause I be tinkin ya may be needin' ta know one day."

I wasn't sure what that meant, but it seemed like a conversation for another time.

"Tanks, but I'za be needin' a bucket o' water and some cloths ta wipe da floor. Ya know where I'za can find 'em?"

"Me lady, I would'na be Samual freakin' Magee if I could'na help ya with a simple wee request like dat."

Turning on his heel, he trotted down the hall. I jogged to keep up with his quick pace. He pushed open a plain wooden door and revealed a room with jugs, buckets, and brooms.

"Dis be da cleanin' supplies for dis wing of da castle."

Sam bent over, grabbed a bucket, and put it under a tap. I watched carefully to see what he used as he picked up a jug and poured a healthy dollop into the water before shutting the tap off. Then he took a wooden handle with what looked like thick strands of woman's hair off a hook and held it out to me.

"Whaddya do wit dis?" I asked, staring at the strange thing close up.

"Dat be called a mop, me Lady. Come, den. I'll be showin' ya how ta use it. Not dat ya need to, ya know. Ya can jus ask me ta do it for ya. I be yer person, after all." He puffed up his chest. The shiny material of his purple outfit made him look dashing.

"Aye, I'ma no used to such treatment, Sam. I be meanin' no disrespect," I said and bowed my head.

"No, me Lady, dinnie be bowin' ta me," he said aghast. "Yer gonna be da next queen of da McGregors. Dat means ya bow ta no one. No eva, ya understand? Da sharks in dis place will eat ya if ya show a smidgin of fear." He looked around and whispered, "Keep yer back straight and yer fist firm."

Nodding, I looked around, unsure what he meant and terrified there were sharks roaming the castle. This place had strange magic indeed.

Sam chatted happily by my side as we walked toward Rook and Rhys room as if the bloody battle outside had never happened. He chirped on about the gossip of the house and the weather that was expected to blow in.

Rhys and Rook were still in the bathroom when we reached the room, and I pointed out the foul liquid on the floor.

"Oh, deary me. Someone had demselves a bit of a time wit a demon, dey did," Sam said, then whistled as he cleaned up the mess.

I hated just standing there watching him, so I walked over to the pile of soiled clothes. They looked like they would never be clean again, stained from the thick coating of blood. Carefully, I pulled the weapons and holders away from the clothes, and Sam gasped.

Worried that we were once more under attack, I looked around the room. Instead, the man stared at my hands and marched toward me with a frown.

"Me lady, for da last time, ya no do dis work no more," Sam scolded. "Dis be me job. Are ya tryin' ta take me job? Do ya no' want me ta have a way ta feed me family?"

"Naw, I'ma just wantin' help," I said, horrified that he would think such a thing. The dark frown lifted as he laughed.

"I be only joshin' wit ya. I dinnie 'ave a family," and laughed harder at the look on my face. "It be what all us servants say when someone new like ya comes 'ere. But in all seriousness, ya need ta be givin' me da pile and stop tryin' ta help. Come den, hand it over. We be g'tting' a tad bit pissy when da royals git in our way."

He took the pile, then picked up the other discarded clothes, tucking them under one arm, before grabbing the bucket and mop. Whistling, he placed it all out in the hall and then came back in and stripped the bed.

I stepped in to help, and he lifted a brow, challenging me to come closer. In a blink, all the sheets were clean, and new blankets were in place before he disappeared out the door.

I was going to have a really hard time getting used to this. That much was for sure. The bathroom door opened, and Rhys emerged, helping a weak-looking Rook. He looked a little better and had showered, but his skin was still very pale. Wanting to help, I went to his other side. He must have felt worse than he looked because he leaned heavily on Rhys and me as we got him into bed.

"I'za gonna go shower. I need ta git dis blood washed off," I said as Rhys went to the other side of the bed and got under the covers. I watched Rhys's hand travel through Rook's hair as Rook leaned into him and closed his eyes.

"Aye, I din't wanna stay in me clothes one second longer wit the sticky blood either," he said softly. "Even fir me dat be just too much. Are ya really okay?"

I nodded, unsure why the horror I witnessed didn't bother me to the depths that it should. A part of me thought it was wrong to feel so little, but they came here to hurt us. They weren't innocents forced to do this or wee children, they were men with a mission, and that mission was to kill one of us or all. I couldn't bring myself to care.

"I be good," I said. I reached the door when Rhys's voice stopped me.

"Tanks for gettin' da mess cleaned up."

"Sam, he be doin' all da hard stuff, but yer welcome."

The room felt small as Rhys's eyes found mine. "Ya can stay if ya want, ya know. Yer free ta use da shower and sleep with us. I'ma jus' no' wantin' ta push ya when ya made it clear yer no' ready to be 'ere wit us."

"Aye, I be gonna go and see once me gets cleaned up how I be feelin' on the topic."

I kicked myself in the ass all the way down the hall and into my room. Rhys offered his shower for me to use. But no, I let the nervousness get the better of me and left the room.

What in the name of the Great Mother was wrong with me? I wandered into my bathroom and got undressed. I be a fool.

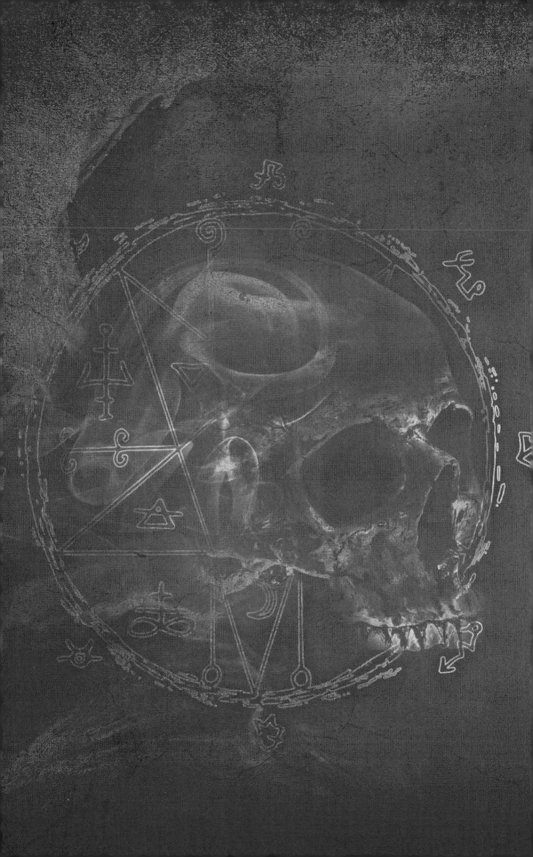

Chapter 47

Elewyen

I was staring at the ceiling when my necklace did its nightly glow. Gripping it in my hand, I responded in kind. My smile spread as I thought about Keeva here in this castle. She'd love the room with all the books. There were so many that you could read a book a day for years and still not make it through them all. She would also love the large green field and barn that held horses for riding. I'd never seen so many horses up close, but they all loved to get their daily treats of carrots and their necks scratched.

The little necklace dulled, and it pulled at my heart that she wasn't here yet. Pushing myself onto my elbows, I glanced around at the room that was way too large for one person, and my eyes landed on Barry curled up in a little ball on my pillow.

It was time I told Book and Rhys I was staying for good. After what I saw tonight, I knew I couldn't leave them to fight off this threat alone. With that decision came confidence. Sam was right about one thing. I needed to act like this was my home too, and not that I was a stranger passing through.

If I was going to do this, I needed to be in the same room with them. Staying separate wasn't helping me feel connected.

Hopping off the bed before I thought about it too long and changed my mind, I slipped into one of the long black T-shirts Rook gave me to sleep in. He liked how I looked wearing them, and the material was soft against my skin.

Peeking out into the hall, I made sure no one wandered the dark space. There were strange noises in the castle. It was the same at Injebreck. Little echoes of noise and low whispers, like the walls were telling all the day's secrets. It felt as if there were eyes in every corner.

Certain I was alone, I stepped out into the hall. Barry shot out of the room just before the door caught his wee tail.

"Whaddya doin'?" I opened the door for him to go back into the room, but he sat down. "Really? Dat's da way it's goin' ta be?" Bending down, I held out my hand, and he jumped into my palm. "Ya be needin' ta behave," I warned as I put him on my shoulder. "I be tryin' ta make a connection wit dem and ya cannie be throwin' stuff all da time." He nuzzeled my cheek. "Dinnie be actin' all innocent like, I be seein' ya."

Barry twisted his little head to the side as he looked at me. He was gonna do whatever he wanted anyway.

Outside Rook and Rhys's room, I wiped my hand on the bottom of my shirt before twisting the heavy metal handle. The latch clicked. I pushed open the door and poked my head inside. I was shocked to see Rhys still sitting up in bed. He lifted his head from the wall, those intense eyes finding mine. They seemed haunted in the soft glow of the single candle burning on the night table.

"I'z be tinkin' dat it may be okay ta sleep in 'ere if ya still be havin' me."

"Aye, yer always welcome," Rhys said quietly and held out his hand.

My heart pounded hard in my chest as the nervous little wings once more took flight in my stomach, as I closed the door. Each step brought a spark of the connection magic to life. I nibbled on my lip to keep from rubbing my arms as it licked over my skin.

"I'ma gonna say yer nervous ta be in 'ere," Rhys voice was soft as my hand slipped into his.

He was warm to the touch, and my body warmed from the gentle contact. A small charge lingered under each finger, like his touch created a tiny storm throughout my body.

"Jus' a wee bit," I said, not wanting to admit that my heart was pounding as hard as a drum. The nervousness told me I should be running from the room, not crawling into bed with him.

Rhys turned my hand in his and ran his thumb over my wrist.

"Do ya tink I'ma goin' ta hurt ya?" he gave my hand a gentle tug.

I licked my parched lips to get moisture back into my suddenly dry mouth.

"Naw," I said.

His eyes traced down my body and up again. "Yer beautiful," he said, and the compliment made me flush hot.

"Rook said da same ting."

Rhys smiled and drew me closer. "He no be wrong. Dinnie be tellin' him I said dat, it will go ta his head." Rhys glanced down at Rook, still peacefully sleeping. "I'ma thinkin' his ego be big enough." I covered my mouth as I laughed softly.

Barry took that moment to jump off my shoulder. Rhys watched as he scampered up the bed and across the pillows to curl up by Rook's neck.

Rhys smirked. "Seems me cuddlin' job has been takin care of."

He rolled onto his side and lifted the blankets. I could feel the warmth from the man holding them like a hand reaching out to grab me. I was drawn to Rhys and quickly got under the covers. Despite the immense heat, I shivered as my body came into contact with his chest. He lowered the blankets, and I was trapped against his large frame.

"Tank ya, by da way. I been meanin' ta say dat."

I turned to him. He looked so relaxed with his head resting on his hand while I felt like I could jump out of my skin.

"For?"

"For bein' so kind. Ya came here wit no knowledge other than bad tings about us and ya gave us a chance when many would no' have bothered. Den ya comforted me about me pub and friend, and yer jus' very carin'."

"Oh, dat was notin', just bein' a decent person," I fiddled with the edge of the heavy blanket. Rhys lowered his head to my hair, and I bit my lip.

"Ya smell like honey and lemon tea."

"Dat a bad ting?"

"Naw, it be makin' me mouth water," he said, making me squirm. "Ya wantin' me ta touch ya, or ya preferrin' fir me ta keep me distance?" His breath fanned my ear, but he made no other move.

I longed to feel his hands on my skin. The urge to touch him was as strong as it was with Rook. And now that my guard slipped, his proximity was pushing on the rest of the crumbling wall.

"I dinnie know," I said honestly.

Out on the trail, I was sure of myself. I would hunt, forage and challenge anyone who tried to hurt me or an innocent. But put me in this bed with Rhys and Rook, and I became a scared kitten. I hated that. If I'd been a cat then I didn't know if I wanted him to scratch behind my ear or if I should be hissing and swatting at him. It was an awkward way to feel. My one night with Rook was all my experience, and my insecurity about what I wanted was glaring.

"Dat's fine. Do ya wanna talk? Tell me about yer coven and who all ya want ta come 'ere." Rhys said.

I rolled onto my left side and stared into his eyes. Not sure that was a good idea as my blood sang hotter and felt like it was dancing in my veins.

"Whadd'ya be wantin' ta know?"

Rhys lifted his shoulder casually and seemed like a he was lounging in the sun. How did he look so darn calm while I was a twisted mess inside?

"Tell me wha' it be like. Tell me about da people or ya sista. Tell me whadeva ya be wantin' ta share."

"Me be thinkin' ya will be findin' it borin'. It no like here," I said.

Rhys reached out and ran his thumb gently across my cheek. I sighed, and little sparks soared where he touched. It made me wonder how someone so powerful could be so gentle.

"Ya dinnie give yerself enough credit, Eley. Din't ever be sellin', yerself short. It be a straight shot to feelin' like yer lesser than another. Even though this be a no' so popular opinion among da top in da Factions, I be a firm believer dat no one lad or lass be more or less den another."

For reasons I couldn't explain, my eyes pricked with tears that I fought hard to keep back. "Ya are who ya are, Eley, and dat is a person who I'ma keen ta get to know.

Does dat make sense ta ya, luv?"

He wiped away the lone tear that I couldn't contain. I watched in fascination as he brought his thumb to his mouth and licked the tiny droplet off.

"Even yer tears be as sweet as ya are."

"I like dat," I said, and he smirked. It lit up his whole face.

"Ya like me tastin' yer tears?" he asked cheekily.

I smiled at him, and a little of the tension inside of me disappeared. "Naw, although I be kinda likin' dat, too." It was strangely sexy and sweet and made my body shiver. "I'ma likin' da fact dat ya call me Eley. I'za never had meself anotha name. Da coven gave me my name, an' me likes it, but da way ya say it makes me feel like it be special. Me dinnie 'ave a second name like ya and Rook do. I be just Elewyen."

"Ya are special, and when we go for da union ritual, ya get Rook's second name. Ya get ta be an Adair." He smiled, and I blushed.

"Woulda be okay if me chose ta take da name McGregor instead?" Rhy's eyes widened, and I quickly carried on. "I no mean ta hurt Rook, but when da names play along me tongue it is da McGregor name dat calls ta me."

Rhys smiled wide like I said something special. "I'll speak ta Rook, and we'll make yer wish work."

There was a long pause, and it took all my control not to look away from his eyes.

"I'ma sorry dat ya all be livin' like out dere like dat. Scared of us and dose who live in da villages. It no' right, an' I no be much betta. I din't give da covens much thought until ya came along. I be thinkin' like everyone else dat I'd march around and hunt ya down and bring ya back." He bit his lip. "It be a terrible way ta find da person yer ta love."

Just when I thought I understood the depths of his kindness, he surprised me. He was genuine. He was sharp steel when needed, but he ruled his heart with a kindness that drew me in and left me wanting more.

Without another thought, I leaned forward and kissed his lips. I tried to fight the spell that drew the three of us together, but the battle was lost the moment I chose to stay. My heart was tumbling down a hill, and there was no stopping it.

Rhys moaned as the magic flowing between us became insistent and moved to our joined lips. I had no idea where the bravery came from, but I deepened the kiss, parched for more of him. Rhys tasted like dark cherries and the rich scotch he liked to drink. He was addictive. Rook was all-consuming, but Rhys was a treat I couldn't stop wanting more. He ran his hand through my hair and gripped a handful. I shifted closer to his body, needing to feel more of him.

My body was alive with the connection and desire I now understood. The ache between my legs was as delicious as the man himself, and a carefree abandon was in my soul.

"I be thinkin' dat I wanna do more den talk," I said, breaking the kiss long enough to get the words out before kissing him again.

Wrapping my leg around his, I realized he wasn't wearing anything as his peen pressed into my stomach.

Rhys broke the kiss and growled, sending a fresh wave of heat rippling through my body.

"Fuck, Eley. We cannie 'ave sex yet, but yer temptin' me beyond measure."

"I'ma sowry," I said, but didn't really mean it, and kissed his chest.

The rules of the triad and the ritual were a distant memory as I touched him and ran my hands over his hard muscles. The little groans he made as I nipped at his skin encouraged me and drove me to explore more.

"Harder, Eley. Ya can bite me harder. It be what I love," he said.

Even though I was sure it hurt, I bit harder into the muscle of his chest, and he shuddered. The fist holding my hair pulled back on my head until I was forced to let go, and I stared into the grey eyes that seemed wild with the same emotions I was feeling.

My arms were lifted over my head as we rolled so I was on my back. My legs naturally parted, and the pressure of his body only made me frantic for more. I wiggled my hips under him and felt what could only be his manhood pressing against me right where I wanted him. It felt like I needed him to complete what my body was craving. I tried to press down into the sensation, and he closed his eyes.

He was fighting to hold off, yet his hips shifted and ground against me. The head of his peen rubbed as his hand would, and my back arched. Moaning, I shamelessly begged for more. The spark of magic formed between us was a raging fire throughout my body. The sensation made me not care about the consequences. All that mattered was completing the act, making us one, and giving my body what it craved.

"Fuck, Eley, fuck. Yer drivin me mad. I should move away, but...." Rhys didn't finish what he was saying before he kissed me again. The firm hold on my wrists kept my body from inching down so he could slip inside me.

"Don't you fucking dare, you cocksucker," Rook growled.

Rhys and I jumped at Rook's harsh voice, and we turned our heads to look at him.

"Don't you two fucking look at me like that. I know what you were about to do. After the lecture I got from Rhys about preserving your virginity, you two don't get to fuck shit up now. Besides, Rhys, you'd hate yourself afterward," Rook said, and I could feel Rhys reining himself in as he pulled away.

"Please. Me body be on fire," I ached all over.

"Don't worry, I plan on making you come. Get up here and sit on my face," Rook growled, his eyes commanding.

Rhys shifted off of my body. I sat up, and he grabbed the edge of the T-shirt, lifting it over my head to toss aside. I wasn't sure what Rook meant by sit on his face, and Barry was not too impressed when I nudged him awake. With a dirty look, he jumped off the bed and buried himself in the discarded shirt.

"I no' sure what yer wantin'," I said.

Rook shifted so he was in the centre of the large bed.

"Face that way." He pointed towards his feet. "But straddle my face." He tapped my knee to demonstrate where he wanted it to be. I felt his tongue down there before and could picture what he wanted. I shivered with anticipation.

Rhys slipped off the bed, and a whimper left my mouth.

"Dinnie worry. I'ma comin' back," he said. He opened a drawer and pulled out a bottle and one of the silver eggs I saw in the strange sex dungeon back at Injebrek.

I straddled Rook the way he wanted and watched as Rhys poured a clear liquid on the silver thing and groaned as he pressed it into his arse. I was about to ask what he was doing when Rook's hands pulled me down harder. My body jerked as both pleasure, and the connection ripped through my body.

I yelled and arched my back as Rook's tongue performed the same magic as the other night.

My eyes were drawn to Rhys, and I couldn't help feasting on the sight of him naked and excited. The tattoos travelling down his sides to his hips were arousing in the moonlight shining through the window. He crawled on the bed and pulled the blankets off Rook.

Rook lifted his hips so Rhys could take off the soft bottoms he wore, but his tongue never let up. I was already panting heavily, and my hands gripped my breasts and began to pinch my nipples in time to his swirling tongue.

"Ya sure yer up for dis?" Rhys asked .

Rook broke contact with a growl.

"I'm fucking sure of it. Put my cock in your mouth already," Rook demanded.

Rhys smiled widely and gripped Rook in his hand. This was an entirely new experience. I wondered how the three of us would even work. It wasn't something that was discussed back in the coven. They stayed away from men at all costs. The idea of lying with two of them at the same time was unheard of and horrifying.

I watched as Rhys's tongue teased the top of Rook's cock, as he called it. A tingling started in my body, and I knew I was getting close to that special cliff that would end with a rush like nothing else.

"Oh my," I said, as much about the nearing orgasm as watching Rook's large cock disappear into Rhys's mouth.

It was too much for my senses to handle all at once, and I yelled as I came. The wave of release crashed through my body and demanded the attention of all my senses. I closed my eyes, my mouth hanging open in a silent scream. The magic didn't let up. It danced higher inside of me as it pushed for more. The golden spell I saw and felt before spiralled around the room as Rook groaned and gripped my hips tighter.

Rook didn't relent as he feverishly licked at my womanhood. Each flick of his tongue created chaos. I wanted more, and it was far too much at the same time. Rook's fingers would tighten around my hips, holding me in place whenever I moved away to take a much-needed deep breath. The swirling magic around the room glowed and throbbed in time with my body like it was attached to the blood pounding hard within me.

Slumping forward, I braced myself on Rook's chest.

"Ya be wantin' me ta move?" I asked as soon as my brain could figure out words. I never wanted to move. I wanted to sit here and have him do that again and again.

His voice was deep and rough as he spoke. "No, we're going to play a game tonight." Rook's words ended with a groan as Rhys moved faster on his cock.

"A game?"

"Yes, we're going to play the game of how many times can I force you to come before you pass out from exhaustion and pleasure. Now get back into position," he ordered.

A thrill travelled down my spine. I wasn't sure I wanted to know what my body would feel like after this game, but I was keen to play.

"Oh shit! Yes, you fucking asshole. Suck my cock," Rook yelled before I could get into position. His back arched off the bed, and I knew he was coming. "You weren't supposed to make me come that fast," he bit out as Rhys slowly lifted his head with a grin.

"Aye, but I know ya can keep it up, and why should Eley be da only one forced ta play da game? I tink dis be fair."

"Prick," Rook said, and I jerked as he dove back into my womanhood like he was eager to see how fast he could make me come again.

Rhys's eyes found mine, and I decided I wanted to learn his skill. To have that kind of power over either of their bodies was thrilling. He straddled Rook's body and got up on his knees so he could look me in the eyes. Our noses touched as he leaned in towards me.

"Mmm, ya smell so good," Rhys said, and gently nipped at my lower lip.

Rhys cupped my face kissing me deeply. I could taste Rook on his tongue. I moaned into his mouth and wanted to know what he tasted like. Would it be the same or different from Rook? My panting got heavier, and it was as if Rhys was feasting off the noise as he continued to kiss me hard.

My lips felt puffy, and my head was spinning when I broke the kiss. It was so beautifully sexy, commanding, and yet somehow sweet. He pulled away, and I wanted to reach out, grab him and tell him not to leave, but he turned around and bent over before I could form words.

"Eley, would'a do me a favour?" Rhys asked.

I tried to answer, but Rook picked that moment to add a finger to what he was doing, and I could only gasp and nod. Rhys pointed to the metal piece that was poking out of his arse.

"Can ya pull dat out fir me?"

Reaching out, I grabbed the small silver piece and began to pull. It was much harder to remove than I thought it would be. Rhys didn't seem to mind, though, and groaned the entire time.

"Oh, dat be amazin'. Play wit it a little," he said. "Like push it in and out."

My movement was tentative at first, but the groaning sounds he made and him wiggling closer to me gave me more courage.

"Yes, Eley, jus like dat." Rhys's voice was rough as he rocked into me.

Gripping the metal tighter, I picked up the pace, and soon the thick piece of metal was sliding in and out of his arse. I loved the sounds he was making and that I was causing it. My passion began to soar once more.

"Okay, yeah, better take it out before I come," Rhys said.

I was tempted to keep going to see how much longer it would take to make him lose control, but my body was beginning to twitch as Rook pushed another finger inside me. Before I forgot what I was supposed to do, I pulled the silver out and handed it over.

"Tanks," Rhys said and took it from me. I was suddenly curious to try another time.

The release Rook built within me made my body shake.

Rhys chose that moment to return, and I stared as he rubbed a clear liquid all over Rook's still, very hard cock. I knew from experience how many times the man could come in a night.

What shocked me was when Rhys stood on the bed and faced me. His cock was in my face but just out of reach without leaving the pleasure of Rook's mouth. Rhys straddled Rook's legs and lowered himself until he hovered over his body. I understood then that the silver thing was some toy to warm him up before he did this.

The sight of him gripping Rook in his hand and the deep, manly noises of pleasure that Rhys made as he sank down on that huge cock were a jolt to my system, and my release raced towards completion.

My eyes were glued to where the two men were joined and Rhys's hand on his own shaft. I thought I couldn't see a sexier sight than these men without their clothes, but this image was at the top of my list.

"Ya like dat, do ya?" Rhys asked, and my eyes flicked up to stare into his. "Ya like ta watch," he said, and I swallowed hard. "Din't be ashamed."

He beckoned me closer, and I leaned forward so he could wrap his hand in my hair.

"Din't ever be ashamed of watchin' or doin' whateva ya want with us," he said and kissed me hard. Our tongues battled as we tasted one another.

The power in the room surged brighter like it was encouraging us to continue and complete the union. All I could picture was having them both inside me, and I whimpered into Rhys's mouth.

Rhys began to move on Rook, still kissing me. Unable to help myself, I grabbed Rhys's hand as he stroked his cock. He changed our hands so that mine was touching him, and he gripped my hand tight. It seemed like it would be too much pressure, but Rhys squeezed my hand tighter. The feel of him sliding under my fingers was beyond anything words could describe.

Rhys growled a sound that pushed me right to the edge of that glorious drop off, and I sat there, teetering, until Rook groaned beneath me. The vibration pushed me over the edge, and I yelled into Rhys's mouth.

I broke the kiss and leaned my head forward onto Rhys's shoulder as he continued to move on Rook. I forgot for a moment that I still had Rhys's cock in my hand.

I wanted to try something different but not get myself into trouble, so I wiggled into a position that still gave Rook access to my womanhood while I stroked Rhys a few more times before slipping him into my mouth.

I closed my eyes and let myself drift in the sea of pleasure coursing through my body. There was no way to explain what it felt like to be with these two men. No one could have warned me about the danger of their touch. Now that I tasted them, I never wanted it to end. It was a different danger than the coven described. This was addicting.

I was nearing my next orgasm when Rhys gripped my hair harder and pressed down on the back of my head. I knew he was close to coming and picked up my pace, moaning when he came in my mouth. I drank him down and marvelled at how he tasted. So different from Rook and yet equally delicious.

"I dinnie know if I'ma gonna be able ta take anymore," I said, pulling Rhys from my mouth.

"I don't care," Rook said, and I knew he meant it. "You'll keep coming until you have nothing left, because the two of you almost fucked up this triad. This is your punishment. Now lie on your back. It's Rhys's turn to taste you while I fuck him the way I want."

Rhys and I shuddered at the same time, like Rook's words had power over us. I didn't know how much more I could handle as I stiffly rolled off Rook's face to do what he said. Yet, as Rhys settled between my spread thighs, grey eyes shining at me, as he slowly drew his tongue up my womanhood, I knew it wouldn't matter. I would go until, I indeed, passed out.

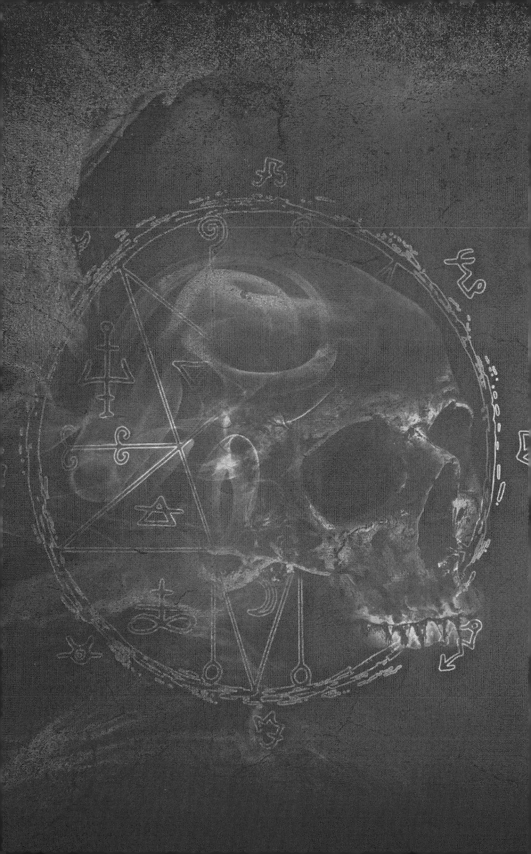

Chapter 48

Rhys

I paced the massive office and rubbed at my sore temples. The conference call was loud as all those on the line continued to talk over one another. One look at Rook told me exactly what he thought of the discussion. None of it was good. He told me he would do whatever I needed but wanted nothing to do with the call or his father. The only reason he was in here was to make sure I didn't lose my cool. I was the face of the McGregors, and couldn't give them any reason to doubt my leadership qualities. I listened to one excuse after the other as to why we shouldn't spend extra money, and it sank in that I needed to prove why I belonged at the big boy table. I knew I would be forced to take control of more aspects to do with the Faction, but today was not the day I expected

"Cannie everyone no' speak one at a time?" I probably would've had better luck talking to the wall than this pack of braying donkeys. My control slipped, and I slammed my fist down on the massive wooden desk.

"Fuckin' enough," I bellowed.

I was shocked when everyone on the line quieted. I leaned in so that I would be heard clearly over the speaker.

"This fightin' is doin' none of us any good. First, I din't give a crap about how much it is gonna cost. Those who are gonna be named or have been named, in me and Rook's case, need extra protection. We will be hirin' as many as it takes to protect the next triads, or ya might as well hand over da keys ta another Faction now and maybe if we be lucky dey won't be slittin' our throats."

Straightening up, I crossed my arms over my chest. "Second, we be needin' food. No' in a month, but now. Villagers da survived da attacks are wanderin' in from all over da place lookin' fir food and refuge. We need ta help 'em. Flitters or no, dey still be in our care an' dey normally grow our feckin' food. Angus, we be needin' ya send da plane with as many provisions as ya can. Fly it in here dis week and next, which will tide da island over until we can get a ship 'ere."

"Rhys, we do not take orders from you," Nigel said, his tone as condescending as ever. "You're not properly unioned, or had the ritual to make you officially the head of the McGregor family, and yet you're talking like you're the head of all our families. Seems a bit arrogant of you, don't you think?"

"Aye, ya be right. I dinnie run all da families, but can even one of ya tell me dat dis is a bad plan?" Only silence greeted me this time. "Naw, I din't tink so. Unless, Nigel, ya plan on savin' jus' yerself and leavin' da rest of us ta starve. If dat be yer plan, den by all means, please speak up an' let us know so we can be weedin' out who our real allies be."

"Don't be preposterous. Of course I don't mean that I want the people on the island to starve."

"Well, I be beginnin' ta wonder. Ya've made it pretty well-known dat ya din't like me as head of da McGregor family. Now yer arguin' over sendin' food and supplies dat are essential ta all dose livin' 'ere. Seems ta be a little suss ta me."

"What are you trying to say, Rhys?" Nigel asked, his voice rising with his own anger.

"That is enough, you two. Blaming one another is not going to help anything. Rook, do you have anything to add to this conversation?" Angus asked, and I looked over at Rook, who didn't bother to blink away from what he was reading. "I mean, you are supposed to be the One, are you not?"

"No, Father, I have nothing to add. Rhys is doing a fine job. He's doing exactly what I asked him to do as my Two, and that's to deal with this meeting," Rook called across the room, his voice full of disdain and boredom. I knew he hated the conference calls and was happy to let me take control which worked out well. I was the planner. I laid out the maps and sat the pieces on the board to figure out our next move. Rook wanted me to point him in the right direction and tell him and the others what to do. Once more, I marvelled at how well we balanced.

I could feel Rook's anger simmering under the surface of his calm façade, and underneath that was hurt. His father was quick to insult him, and I now understood where some of his insecurity lay and why he openly revolted against anything Faction.

I wanted to say something, but it would only look like Rook couldn't stand up for himself. Rook needed to control the meeting at some point to shut them all up, but I wasn't going to force it today. That required a wee bit of massaging or me giving him a blow job at the same time. That had distinct dirty fantasy possibilities. If I did that, I might eventually get him to agree.

Rook looked up as I chuckled and gave me a wink, the anger disappearing.

"I guess that is fine then," Angus pronounced each word like he was saying, fuck you too. This was the first time I was a part of any of their interactions, and I couldn't help wondering what happened to put such a rift between them.

"Rhys does have a point," Angus continued. "We all have sons and daughters who are at the age where they will be paired up, and they all need more protection. The other Factions and even the Hunters have been quiet for a long time. The fact that they have suddenly gotten so active and are attacking as openly as they have means they consider us a threat and are not about to stop without a fight. If they weaken us, then we are all as good as dead."

"Aye, it does. It also means dat as soon as we 'ave supplies ta make it thru da winter, we can focus on which Faction is tryin' ta take us down," Caleb offered. It was nice to know that my friend had my back.

"No one be takin' us down," Lochlin growled into the line. The noise was followed by the sound of fists banging on wood.

"So, da question remains...Angus, are ya goin' ta be sendin' da jet?" I asked.

"Yes. The pilot will radio when he is an hour out. Hopefully, we can keep it secret until the last minute that the plane is coming. Crispin has offered to help arrange the arrival plans since he has the most knowledge of the air traffic routes and how best to keep our loads secret," Angus said, and everyone mumbled their agreement.

I wanted to know how Angus learned to command a room the way he did. I tried to assert my authority, but there was always pushback. Was there pushback when he was my age, or did everyone naturally follow him because he was an Adair? The name Adair held a slightly different weight than the rest of us, no matter what our accomplishments were. At one time, the thought was like a burr under my ass, annoying and prickly, but I learned to accept it as normal as the sun rising in the east. I wished so many times over the last couple of years that my father was still around for me to ask. Rayland was as useless as a wet noodle in the rain.

As everyone was finalizing the plans to get supplies and more guards to the island, I glanced at Rook. He was still reading the massive leather-bound book. Angus could pound salt. Rook was an excellent One, even if it took him time to come around, and he was still growing. Rook was instrumental in getting those who survived and were made homeless by fires situated in new lodgings and even found a way to use his band as cover to get more supplies here. He was smart. I just wished he saw how smart he was.

I watched his leg swing back and forth over the padded armrest. There was something sexy about the pose with the massive book while he sipped a scotch. I suddenly wanted to lay him out on the desk and fuck him while everyone was still on the line. Now that was a statement.

I leaned over and hit end when I realized the call was over.

Turning back to Rook, I leaned against the desk. "Ya wanna sing wit me?"

"Sorry, I missed that. What?" Rook asked, his eyes meeting mine.

All he needed was a set of glasses to give him the ultimate sophisticated badass look. He was wearing ripped jeans and a black T-shirt.

With his shitkickers on, it was a perfect juxtaposition to the old leather-bound book in his hands.

"I wanna sing wit ya. I dinnie 'ave me pub no more, but we can jam," I said, and he smirked.

"I thought you said you didn't like the crap I sing," he teased, but the tone set my blood racing.

"Who says we are gonna be singin' yer crap?" Rook cocked a brow at me, and I smiled. "It also could'a been a slight exaggeration on me part. There be a good chance dat I was wantin' ta git under yer skin." I pushed away from the desk.

"Well, you certainly did that and more," Rook said, and I reminded myself that we needed to get actual work done today.

Although locking the door was certainly appealing, Eley may kill us for getting at it while she was having to endure another round of Sam and his over-eagerness.

Glancing at the title he was reading, my eyebrow rose.

"Yer readin' about dark rituals? Dat is dangerous shit," I said, suddenly worried about what he was thinking.

"Get that look off your face. I'm not thinking about doing anything crazy. Well…not too crazy."

I crossed my arms and waited for him to continue. There was no point in saying what I was feeling. The bastard felt everything I did now, which was proving to be annoying as fuck.

"I'm reading up on what I did with the shadows. It's an actual ritual, but from what I've been able to find, it's never been done outside of a ritual scenario with all the proper preparations, including being down in the catacombs to keep the dark contained."

"Aye, gee, I'ma wonderin' why…Ya were taken over by some demon or spirit, and it had no good intentions. We still din't know if dere be any long-term effects."

Rook swung his legs around to sit forward in the chair. "I'm looking more at how to prevent that from happening if I were to do that spell again. If I could even do it again."

"Ugh, dinnie be thick, Rook. Ya shouldna be tryin', no matter what," I said as Rook's phone rang.

He dug around in his pocket and pulled it out, then groaned as soon as he saw who was calling. He hit the video option, but I stayed out of the line of the camera. Devlin looked completely distraught.

"Devlin, to what do I owe the pleasure?" Rook drawled.

"Geez us you sounded exactly like dad." He made a gagging noise. "What the hell is that? Now I'm fucking positive they're drugging you, I'm going to come and save you, brother, don't you worry," Devlin said.

Rook seemed just as confused as I felt. "What are you babbling on about?" he asked, placing a bookmark in the pages and snapping the book shut.

"Oh, dear spirits, you used the word babbling, and is that…Oh, my god. You are reading." Devlin sounded truly horrified. "It wasn't just my eyes playing tricks on me."

"This is why you called me? What? Father has decided to treat you like crap since I'm not there, so you've decided to pick up the mantle and insult me instead? I'm hanging up now," Rook said.

"No, wait!" Devlin looked around and got close to the phone, so all I saw was part of his nose and an eye. "I wanted to know if you'd come to your senses about the whole triad thing. Rhys has always been a pill, but he sounded like a real dick on the phone. I mean, you don't want to be tied to that for the rest of your life, do you?" Devlin was so busy ranting that he didn't notice when Rook smirked and looked at me.

"A real dick...What do you mean?" Rook asked, baiting his brother.

"What do you mean, what do I mean? The guy was a total prick on the call. I mean, who the hell does he think he is, ordering our father, the head of the Adair family, around? I wouldn't take orders from him. I don't care if he is named the official head of the McGregor family."

"I thought it was fucking sexy the way he got everyone to shut up and stop arguing. Besides, Dad can handle himself, and it was nice to hear someone stand up to the pompous asshat," Rook said.

"Sexy? Have you lost your mind? Look, I know Dad forced you to go there, but we can still get out of this. Your union ritual isn't for two days, and I know that if we put our heads together, we can come up with a plan to get rid of our little problems."

I couldn't help but smile as I held Rook's gaze. He seemed content to let his brother wallow in the steaming pile of shit he was creating.

"Is that so? What did you have in mind? Swap partners out? Maybe drown them all? Oh, I've got it. Let's put them on Dad's jet and then poison the pilot, so he crashes it and kills them all." Rook's eyes went wide as he nodded at the camera.

"I was kind of thinking more along the lines of rejecting the ceremony and standing up to Dad together, but your way works too, I guess," Devlin said, his voice no longer sounding confident.

I chuckled at the look on Devlin's face. Rook grabbed me by the shirt and pulled. I knew what he was doing. Our lips met, and it wasn't a little peck type kiss. Rook kissed me like no one was watching as he attacked my mouth. I gripped the back of his neck and returned the ferocity of his kiss, making sure to taste every corner of his mouth, and then nipped his bottom lip as we parted.

Turning my head to look at the camera, I smiled at Devlin, whose mouth was hanging open.

"Hey'ya, Devlin. I be hearin' dat we're gonna see ya soon 'ere on da island fir a visit. After all dose glowin' comments ya be givin' me, I cannie wait ta see ya in person." I straightened, loving the stumbling and swearing Devlin did before he hung up on Rook.

"That was too much fun. Fucking with my brother is one of my favourite pastimes," Rook said, reaching for me again.

Even though there was a ton of work to be done, the moment he touched me, I was ready never to leave the room again. The power no longer consumed us, but it hummed and came alive as soon as we were close enough. It was more a constant thrum of energy just below the surface of my skin, like it was reminding me that Rook and Eley were mine.

I leaned in for another kiss when the door to the office opened and Eley poked her head inside.

"I'za cannie leave ya two alone for a moment wit out ya gettin' all hot, which makes me all hot, ya should know." She closed the door and leaned against it. "I'za snuck off on Sam. He gonna kill me, but I no wanna put on da poofy lace dress." She lowered her voice to whisper, "It be hideous."

"Well, yer certainly welcome ta join us," I offered.

"Temptin', truly, but…"

I watched her walk across the room and peer out the window before pulling the heavy curtains in place to block out the darkening sky. She then proceeded to check all the doors to make sure they were locked.

"We be alone?" We nodded our heads at the same time. "Dere be somethin' dat I'za tink ya need ta see, but me thinkin' dat ya should be pretendin' dat ya dinnie know 'bout it."

I looked at Rook to see if he understood if what she said made any sense to him, but he lifted a shoulder, confused as I felt. Usually, I understood what she was saying, but it was as though she was talking in tongues.

"Sorry, Eley, but I'ma no' sure what ya mean."

She got closer but kept looking at the corners of the room like a monster might jump out.

"I dinnie wan' ta take ya out dere in da dark," she said, nibbling at her bottom lip.

So much time passed during the meeting, and it felt like a lot had happened, but I got nothing done.

"Dere be somethin' important ya need ta see, but no one can know," she said.

My interest was piqued. "Aye, ya no we no' be sayin' anytin'," I said.

"Same here. What's going on?" Rook asked, standing.

"Follow me, but if we be seen, make it look like yer just fixin' ta have a tiddle and poke session out by da trees."

She waved us over and opened the door to walk out, a wide smile on her face. I wasn't sure why, but she giggled like I said something funny before looping her arm through mine. This was becoming curiouser by the second.

We wandered through the castle, out the front doors, and down the steps to the forest path near the gates. Then took the scenic route and meandered through the gardens. The guards weaved their way through the darkness. Their eyes glowed softly with their unique ability to see in the dark.

Before we stepped into the shadows of the forest, Eley looked up at me.

"Kiss me," she whispered.

Not bothering to question why, and all too happy to taste her sweet lips, my head dropped to hers, and I kissed her long and slow.

"Hey, I want in on this," Rook said.

I broke the kiss long enough to kiss Rook before he kissed Eley. It was unbelievably hot, and my mind was already off in fantasy land, imagining everything I wanted to do once we got back to the bedroom.

Eley giggled again—which was so not like her— and pulled on our hands, tugging us into the forest until we could no longer see the castle. It was almost pitch black in here, the overcast sky not offering much light, but I could see her fake smile fall.

"It be over here," she said, and her hand tightened on mine.

She looked worried, and I prepared to pull on my power or sword. We went around a bend, and Eley guided us off the trail to a large tree before tugging my arm to make me stop. Rook followed beside me.

"Whadda are we lookin' at?"

Eley pointed to the open hole in the tree that was just higher than my head. "Din't be puttin' yer hand in dere. Jus' take a look."

The hair stood all over my body as a trickle of unease flowed through me. Eley released my arm, and I stepped up to the tree, stretching enough to see in the hole. My mouth dropped. Stepping back so Rook could look, my eyes found Eley's concerned expression.

"How did ya find dat?"

"Barry. He be playin' out here and snoopin' around like he always be doin', but he came and got me. Jus' would'na leave me alone until I came ta see. I taught it was gonna be a big nut, but instead me find dat."

"What the fuck is that?" Rook asked as he turned to stare at us.

573

"Dat be a talisman of dark power," I said, as my mind began to whirl. "Dat maybe yer answer as ta why da power shifted so violently and left ya exposed ta da pull of da dark fade. Dat also be explain' why da gates never slowed da attack like dey should 'ave. Dis be interruptin' da power on da whole property," I said. "Fuck."

This meant that the traitor had been here or was still here. Rage filled me as I stared at Rook and Eley.

"A war be comin' from within, I cannie feel it, but we be ready fir when da day comes."

"What do you want to do with that?" Rook asked quietly.

"For now, nothin'. We dinnie wanna let da traitor know dat we found dis, but more importantly, we din't know what might happen if we touch it. Wit a talisman, ya never know what magics ya be dealin' wit. We'll come back in daylight and make sure we know which one we be dealin' wit and den destroy it once we be knowin' how."

"Should we put a shield or something around the tree or try to do something to stop the power?" Rook asked.

I tapped my chin as I thought. "A warnin' shield, fir sure. Eley, what da ya tink?"

She lifted one shoulder gracefully. "Dark magics be tricky. Ya can set off all sorts of evil if ya dinnie be doin' it right. I'ma gonna say just da shield fir now. Me only concern is if dere is gonna be anotha attack before da ritual."

"I'ma gonna make a call when we git back inside. I have an idea fir more help. I be unsure if it will be 'ere in time though."

Rook growled, and I felt the rage building in him. "No one hurts what is mine," he said.

I shivered at the tone of his voice. There was a feeling I couldn't shake. I didn't doubt that Rook would kill whoever this person was, but he was going to have to beat me to it because this was about me. Whoever this was, didn't like that I was the next McGregor head of the family. I had my suspicions, but I needed to prove it, and it was going to be tricky since I suspected they were a member of the council.

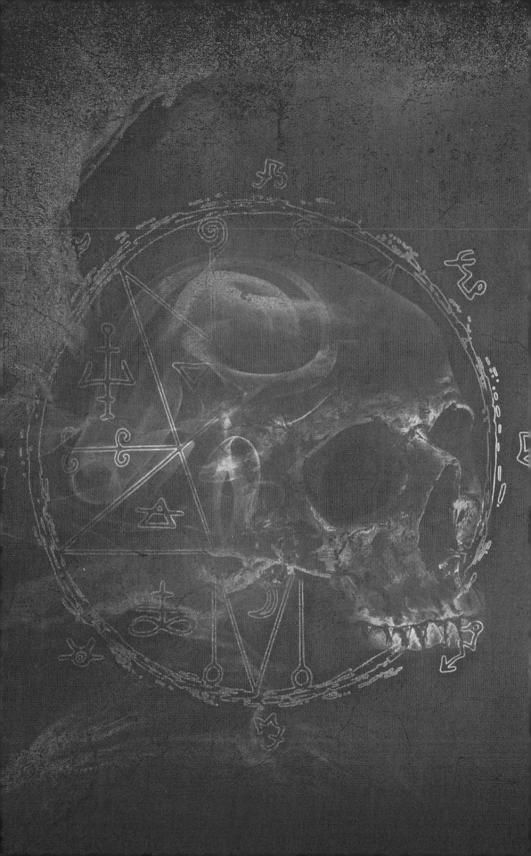

Chapter 49

R ook

Things were tense with Rhys for the last two days. His normal over-protective obsession had become all-consuming, a wild storm inside of him. He barely ate, didn't come to bed until Eley and I were asleep, and trained harder than ever.

We weren't fighting, but I felt the worry growing into something that was twisting him inside out. He was bristly, like an old bear poked with a stick, over the simplest of questions.

The traitor still hadn't shown themselves. We didn't dare touch the talisman after discovering that it was designed like a bomb. Not the explosive kind, but one that, if messed with, could kill everyone on the property. We placed an invisible barrier around the tree to block any signal it might emit. Rhys said that the spell he found should hold, and we would know when someone tried to take it. That hadn't happened yet, and it was frustrating.

I hadn't realized how much of an over-thinker and worrier Rhys could be until now. It made me wonder what he looked like when I initially rejected the pairing. The thought of him pacing the floor all night for weeks with a crippling pain in his chest made me look away from my reflection in the mirror.

It was hard to get ready for our triad union ritual when the nervous energy was amplified between the two of us. Elewyen seemed to be taking everything in stride. She really was the calm and focused one of the three of us. My hands shook as I tried once more to clasp the large Celtic brooch of my family crest in place and ended up stabbing myself.

"Shit," I swore and put my thumb in my mouth.

"I will do dat for ya," Elewyen said as she walked into the room.

I was speechless as I stared at her in the elegant yet simple white gown. Her waist-length red hair lay in soft waves down her back while a white cloak draped over her shoulders and brushed the floor. Since she didn't have a family crest, she wore the symbol of unity at her throat, and I had to admit that it was fitting.

Elewyen was fast becoming the glue that kept us together. Although, the angry make-up sex with Rhys when he sniped something sarcastic was fucking incredible. The image of us rolling around on the bed as we fought for dominance last night made my soul burn hot, and my heart pounded harder than I thought possible. Elewyen wisely kept her distance until it was out of our systems. I wasn't sure I could've held back from fucking her if she'd crawled on the bed.

I shook myself out of the little reverie before I did something that would make all of us miss the ritual.

"You look beautiful," I said.

It was strange that, with as many people as I dated and slept with, I couldn't remember when I gave anyone a genuine compliment. Yet now they came so easily with Rhys and Elewyen. Having this woman for real and sharing her with Rhys made me feel like the king of the world. Of all the things I wanted and knew needed to happen, all I wanted right now was to make her ours finally.

Elewyen's cheeks blushed a bright pink that only added to her beauty and made her green eyes sparkle. Not long ago, she tried to take my head off with her cane. We'd come far in such a short time.

She took the ends of my cloak from my hands and focused hard on attaching the two ends with the tricky pin. Elewyen smiled and dropped her hands away, but I grabbed them before she could move. Staring her in the eyes, I slowly sucked one of her dainty fingers into my mouth, savouring the heated look that crossed her face.

"You ready for what's about to happen?" I asked, moving on to the next finger.

I wondered that same question a million times. Was I more prepared now—to be united with the same two people until one or all of us died— than when I first arrived? It was a dark thought, and yet it was true. We would be tied in a way that would make the connection feel like child's play. As many times as I asked the question, I always got the same answer. My mind would say it didn't know, while my heart screamed that it was exactly what I wanted.

What did ten years look like? What did twenty or thirty or eighty? Would we all want to kill one other by then? Would we have all fallen in love by then? Would we still be in love? Would Elewyen and Rhys still look at me with as much desire as this moment?

No clue.

One thing was certain, though. I couldn't picture my life without them in it. As hard as I tried to visualize a future where I left them here and went off to continue my life as it was before meeting Rhys the first time, the images wouldn't come.

"I dinnie know, but me likes you and Rhys a lot. Ya make me feel very different, and I be happy wit ya," she said, in her typical honest and nonchalant manner that made me smile.

"You only *like* us a lot?" I asked, emphasizing the word like as I teased her.

The pink deepened to a red, and the smile that pulled at her mouth made me smirk.

"Maybe a wee bit more den like," she said.

Pulling her in close, my arms slipped around her body, and I instantly grew hard with her pushing up against me.

"Yer gonna make us late. Rhys no' gonna be happy if dat happens," she said, her voice wispy as I lowered my mouth to hers.

"We won't be late." I captured those full lips that begged to be kissed and appreciated this moment alone without those from the ritual watching. "I can't wait to have you for real, to make you ours," I said, breaking the kiss. I stared into her eyes, eyes that reminded me of spring.

"Din't be forgettin' dat ya will become mine as well." Her eyes glittered, and the excitement thrummed through my body as she claimed me as hers.

"Oh, I haven't forgotten. I'm looking forward to it, but what's this I hear you don't want my name?" Eley's eyes cast to the ground.

"Are ya angry?"

I was hurt by the thought when Rhys spoke to me. After I thought about what the name meant to me and how I shunned it my entire life, I decided that the proud way Rhys said his last name was what I wanted for her as well. She should be proud, I was still unsure whether mine deserved the respect it got.

"No, I'm not angry." I gave her lips another soft kiss. "Do you know what's going to happen at the ritual? Did Rhys explain it all?"

"Aye." She looked away from my eyes. "I no be likin' da human sacrifice—dat just be wrong—but he said dat he din't make da rules. Dat the spirits demand it." She shook her head slowly. "Yer spirits be cruel ta demand the blood of an innocent."

"The person won't be innocent, at least not in the traditional way. They're chosen from those who have wronged the Faction or have committed a crime."

"Aye, he told me. Still seems wrong ta do, an' I'za dinnie know if I want ta be layin' wit ya fir real fir da first time in front of all dose men. Why do dey 'ave ta watch?" She shuddered a little in my hold, and I tightened my arms around her.

"I'll make sure that you remain as covered as possible and just look at either Rhys or me. You'll never have to do this again, I promise."

We stood quietly and held onto one another until my reminder went off on my phone.

Elewyen looked around the room. "Where be Rhys?"

I lifted a shoulder and let it drop. "Rhys said he wanted to get changed privately and collect his thoughts before the ceremony," I didn't mask my fear well. Elewyen stepped back and narrowed her eyes at me.

"Ya be tinkin' he be havin' doubts?" She shook her head at me as she looked me up and down like I was crazy. "And ya tink because of Mari, din't ya?"

I shrugged again. "Honestly, I just can't figure out which feelings are mine and which are Rhys's anymore. He's so worried all the time, and I can't make heads or tails of what is going on with him."

"Wat ya be feelin' now?"

I sighed and rubbed the back of my neck. "I feel confusion, panic, and a little fear. That doesn't seem like a good combination going into a union."

Running my hand through my hair, I wandered to the window and stared down at the massive courtyard that was alight with tall torches, their flames dancing in the darkness.

"I dinnie know for sure what be in his mind and heart, ya would know betta, but he din't seem like the type ta back out. And, Rook da way he looks at ya. It be like ya hang da moon in da sky and ya be da air he breathes. I dinnie see him runnin'. I tink Mari be yer fear, an' no' Rhys's now."

"You could be right. What would you do if he left? I'm not saying he will, but will you go?"

I glanced over my shoulder at Elewyen. She was chewing on her bottom lip but never looked away from my stare.

"Naw, I'za wanna stay. If Rhys be kickin' me out, den dat be a different story. I no stay where I'm no' wanted, but if yer still wantin' me, well, den I still be wantin' ya."

I smiled at her. "Rhys kicking you out, now that I do doubt, but even if he did kick both of us out, we will always have a home at Injebreck. We would just go there, and that includes your sister and whoever else."

"So ya would be stayin'? Ya wouldna leave in da big metal bird?" Eley asked, and I laughed at the image she conjured.

"I may come and go, but you can come with me. Keeva can too. I think we're getting ahead of ourselves though."

"Aye, yer right. Tonight be about da union and only dat."

The lights of a car appeared, coming up the long drive. As soon as the man got out of the vehicle, I recognized my uncle Gregory. The rituals usually happened at Maughold, but with all the attacks happening, everyone thought it was best if we stayed here instead.

Rhys argued to go to Maughold since it was our normal process and a great source of power, with more of the ancestors buried there. The elders disagreed, and we were outnumbered. So, here we were, still at Gelentruan, and I felt uneasy. Or was it Rhys that felt uneasy? I rubbed my eyes, trying to sort through the confusion.

"Do ya wanna head down and jus' meet Rhys dere?" Elewyen asked, her hand touching my shoulder.

It was clear that Rhys had no intention of returning to the room for the three of us to go to the ritual rooms below the castle together, and I hoped he could feel how pissed I was with him. Confused or not, worried or not, he decided to build a future with us. Fuck, he was the one who insisted on it, and now I felt like I was the one barely holding us together at times. How in the ever-loving fuck did that happen?

"Yeah, I guess we should," I sighed.

Elewyen slipped her arm through mine and walked out of the bedroom, closing the door behind us. This wing of the castle we were staying in reminded me of royalty. There was no such thing—not for generations—but I saw pictures in books from the libraries. I secretly liked to read, but I would be damned if anyone knew that little secret. The pictures were incredible.

Our feet echoed off the walls of the cavernous stone hallway, and I looked up at the massive banners that lined the walls. Every other one had been switched out so that they now had the black and silver banner of the Adair family mixed in with the burgundy and gold of the McGregor family. They looked striking together.

Armour lined the hall from different eras, and each shone in the torchlight.

The magical torches that turned on and off on their own were one of the many little marvels I was still getting used to on this island. Living on the island his whole life, Rhys took all the oddities in stride, but Elewyen and I continued to stare around at things that would make most people run for the hills.

Injebreck had power flowing through everything, but this place was supercharged. As if on cue, one of the curtains blew inward as we passed, but the window wasn't open. Some hallways raised all the hair on my body and sent shivers racing down my spine when I walked down them. Servants watched us pass and bowed their heads, knowing what was to transpire tonight. Our main quarters were set up for a celebration and with extra comforts for when we returned. I rubbed the spot over my heart with a growing feeling of concern.

I pictured Rhys stepping up to the dais, then bolting for the door. Anger brewed in my chest, preparing myself for the rejection that seemed to be rolling toward me like a boulder.

Rhys certainly hadn't seemed like he was going to make a run for it like a groom with cold feet last night. In fact, after the rigorous session that we all shared, we showered and passed out. It was the calmest I felt him since the connection first linked us together.

The stairs seemed to go on forever, and we passed the cut-off to the cells. It made me think of when I tossed Eley in a cell. As if she sensed me thinking about her, Elewyen glanced up as I looked down into her eyes. She gripped my arm a little tighter, but it seemed more for my benefit than hers.

She was a marvel to me. She was practically plucked out of the wild and learned to use modern terms and amenities, and she agreed to join a union with two men she barely knew. Elewyen was braver than I was. If roles were reversed, I would've told them all to fuck off and gone home. Hell, I would've done that if the plane hadn't left me here.

She sucked in a sharp breath as we stepped through the first of the three shields that led to the ritual area.

"Dat be strong magic," she whispered.

"Yes, and they only get stronger from here. The third is the worst. It feels like insects running under your skin all over your body," I said and was greeted by a horrified expression. Maybe that wasn't the best thing to say, but I wanted to be honest with her.

We stepped through the second barrier and shivered as the power flowed through us, searching to make sure that we were friend and not foe. The outer area was set up for the preparation, and I guided her to a chair to sit.

Picking up the bowl, I bent and slipped off the dainty slippers to wash her feet and legs. I set the bowl aside and picked up the black onyx stone that seemed normal but, like everything in our world, was far from it. Laying it against her skin where she told us she wanted the symbol, I began drawing a line. It hurt a bit. It always did when the magical black ink was applied. These first two symbols were the symbols that represented Rhys and me.

I looked around, but I saw no sign of him. Now that we were in amongst all the shields, the ability to feel him was distorted, and I couldn't pick up his feelings as clearly.

Elewyen hissed when I traced back over lines already created in the design. They were more sensitive. Once I finished my symbol, I drew Rhys's for him, even though he was supposed to do it. Designs complete, I helped Elewyen stand, readjusted her dress, and helped her with the slippers before drawing up the large white hood that covered her face so completely in shadow that I could no longer see any features.

Pulling my hood up into place, I held out my hand for her to take.

"Remember, you are the sun. When they call you forward, you step up to the dais and stand on the symbol."

She nodded, and I turned to the final shield. We needed to ask for passage and state our purpose. It was like the shields could decipher what was in our hearts and match it with our words.

"Spirits, we ask for safe passage," I said in English and then again in the old language.

We made the symbol of the spirit at the same time. I was once more impressed with how quickly Elewyen had picked everything up.

"We have come to join our spirits."

We held up our hands as if to show off our intention.

"We are here for the ritual of three becomes one. Éiríonn triúr ar cheann," I finished and looked at Elewyen to see if there was any lingering doubt. Not seeing any, I looked over my shoulder, but the tunnel remained quiet and empty.

"You better already be in there, Rhys," I mumbled.

The barrier shimmered and sparkled to let us know we could safely step through. As we did, Elewyen pressed herself up against me. The feeling of that final barrier was something that I never got used to. No matter where you were, they were all the same.

We couldn't hear the chanting before crossing the barrier, but now we could make out multiple voices. The tunnel split, and I paused and pointed to the tunnel that had a sun etched into the stone.

"You'll be fine, I promise," I said.

She nodded and squeezed my hand before letting go and stepping into the darkness of the tunnel.

I stayed and watched until the white of her cloak disappeared, then continued until I reached the tunnel with the symbol of death carved into it. This was my tunnel, and as I entered, images from my life danced before my eyes. Was this a way to ensure that this was what we really wanted? Show us what we were giving up with each step.

I saw cheering crowds and women and men lined up outside my dressing room door. Everything from laughing with my brothers to flying here in the jet came to me. Then, like granules of sand in a storm, one by one, they blew away, leaving me feeling blank, like this was truly the beginning of my life and everything else was nothing but passing the time.

There was a mark on the floor that reminded me of a starting box for sprinters. Were we supposed to dash out and wave to the crowd? Now that the time had come, I didn't feel like having sex in front of the group that was gathered. Not that I ever had a problem fucking someone in public—hell, I'd done it more than I could count—but this felt different. This was supposed to be meaningful, and instead, it was as if we were nothing more than farm animals needing to be supervised to ensure we did the job properly.

I understood that they called upon the spirits to bless and unify the union, but after that should be our time. Gregory's deep voice stood out from the rest as he began the blessing. Even hooded, I knew which one he was. He stepped forward with Rhys's uncle Rayland to represent the two families. It was pretty fucking ironic that my father insisted that I come here and create this union to become the next great triad but couldn't be bothered showing up for it.

Here, son, I'm going to stud you out to the top McGregor and build up more power for the Faction, but don't expect me actually to give a shit.

A sour taste settled in my mouth. My father never showed up for anything. Why I was still surprised was beyond me.

"It is now time," Gregory said and held up a crystal that glowed so brightly that it looked like the moon had busted a small hole through the wall and was now shining into the dark ritual area with us.

"I call upon the sun," he said, and the power flowing through the crystal throbbed like it was blinking.

I could make out Elewyen's shadow moving across the floor. Anticipation notched up in my system as the connection spell binding us swirled around the room like it was ready to lasso us together as soon as all three of us were out there.

Elewyen stepped up onto the raised platform, her head lowered and hands clasped, but the white of her cloak reflected the glow of the crystal, and she became a beacon in the centre of the room. She was a symbol of hope and purity, and I licked my lips, wanting so badly to taste her. I was suddenly excited for them to call Rhys and me out so we could make this happen.

"We call upon the shadow," Gregory said.

I watched the floor, waiting for the same shadow to cross into the light as Elewyen had, but no one came. My stomach sank, and panic mixed with anger began to rise.

"We call upon the shadow," Gregory said again, louder this time, but still, no one walked across the floor.

My hands balled into fists, and I stomped out into the ritual area. All hoods turned in my direction. I didn't hesitate as I stomped across the floor to where Rhys should be standing, but even before I stepped inside the dark tunnel, I knew he wasn't there.

"Son of a bitch," I growled out under my breath.

Whipping around, I faced the room, and slowly, everyone began to push back their hoods, but no one said anything.

Was this payback? Is that what this was? I stood him up at the ritual and rejected him, so he waited until this moment to humiliate me the same way. No, that wasn't like him. Was it? Fuck.

I wanted to yell and scream and throw everything in the room. I gave up everything in my life to come here, and then I handed over my heart—the one thing I'd never given to anyone else—and this was what he did to me?

The anger was all-consuming, and the flames around the room began to rise as my power rippled out from my tight hold. Elewyen jumped off the platform and was by my side, gripping my arm in hers. I calmed slightly, but the betrayal ran deep.

My mind screamed that he ran, that he took off and left us here, and I fucking hated that it hurt. The thought hurt more than I ever wanted any emotion to affect me, yet here I was, with the pain so sharp in my chest that I could barely breathe.

"Rook, look at me," Elewyen said, her voice soft.

My eyes found hers, and I was at a loss as to what to say. If Rhys didn't show up in the next hour, it was over. There would be no union. At least not for another three months, and I wasn't sure I wanted to be a part of the triad after this.

"Rook, do ya hear me?"

"Yeah," I said.

"I dinnie tink he be doin' dis on purpose," she said, but she didn't feel the cluster of emotions I felt coming off him earlier. "Naw, I'ma meanin' it."

"What makes you so sure?"

"Search yer heart, Rook. Yer time in da library, the smiles he gives only ya. Has Rhys ever seemed like da kind of man dat would do

589

somethin' like dis? Does he seem dat unloyal? Do he seem like he 'ave no honour?"

I mulled over our interactions and what he said to me in the training area before the attack, how he held me after and whispered words of endearment, apology, and comfort every night, no matter how scared or snarly he'd been. I thought about how he kissed me before he left to change and the look in his eyes.

"No, he doesn't," I said quietly so only she could hear.

"Can ya feel him in 'ere?" she asked.

I shook my head no.

"Son, what would you like us to do?" Gregory asked.

Grabbing Elewyen's hand, I moved toward the exit. "If I'm not back by the time the moon has shifted out of position, then leave, and I'm sorry."

Not waiting for a response, Elewyen and I jogged through the barriers and out into the outer chamber, but there was still nothing. We ran up the impossibly long flight of stairs until we reached the main floor, then we stopped to catch our breath.

I looked at Elewyen, and a cold dread flowed through my veins. I could barely get the words out as panic gripped my throat.

"I can't feel him at all."

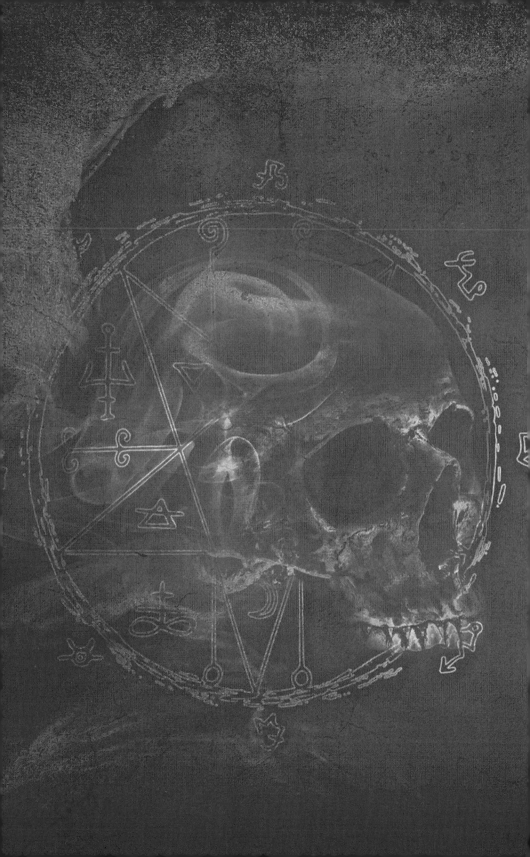

Epilogue

Rhys

My face was freezing cold, and my body was stiff and ached all over. My shoulders screamed in pain, and I tried to pull on my hands, but they wouldn't move. I tried to open my mouth, and it wouldn't open. Was I dead? It seemed to hurt too much to be dead.

As hard as I tried, my mind was muddled, and I couldn't put together a single coherent thought. My brain whirred back in time as I tried to piece together what had happened.

I was in the bedroom with Rook, and as nervous as I was, I looked forward to the triad union. The night finally arrived. I stopped to see Eley as she was getting ready and kissed her softly. She looked so pretty in her gown. Then I went down to the lower level to get my

It was just a piece of material, but I wanted to use his ceremonial cloak for the occasion. Something about the thought made it feel like he was giving his blessing, that he was there with us instead of Rayland. My uncle was a decent enough man, but he wasn't my father. He also didn't like much to do with the Factions or the daily running of the businesses. In a word, he was lazy, but he was the only McGregor elder left to stand in for my father.

I walked into the study and opened the closet door. I had to rummage around for the cloak, which was shoved to the far back corner of the closet. Then there was a sharp pain that had my back arching with a silent scream.

And then blackness.

It was almost impossible to sneak up on me, but someone had that much I knew. And something was wrong because I couldn't move my arms or legs. I felt the chill of a spell squeezing me tight, like a snake squeezing the life out of its prey. The pressure made it hard to breathe, but I forced myself to remain calm and pushed down the unease clawing at me and encouraging me to fight whatever this spell was. I'd never felt this spell before, so the counter to it was something I didn't know. Use the wrong counter, and you could be dead faster.

I managed to open my eyes, but all I could see was the dark silhouette of bars and a set of boots just beyond in the dull light. I tried to feel my power or Rook or anything, but there was nothing.

I was in a cell. It was the only thing that could block everything. The floor was hard and smelled of mould and old dirt. It was unyielding, and a rough spot was digging into my cheek.

"Twisted vines with thorns grow on your home," a deep voice I didn't recognize said. "Rest up. You're going to need it."

The boots walked away. I tried to open my mouth, and this time it moved. Whatever I was hit with had paralyzed me and was just now beginning to wear off.

A heavy door slammed, and the sound of a lock turning reached my ears. There was a distinct vibration, and I heard the dull thud of boots walking away. A tear slipped from my eye as I thought about Rook and Elewyen and how last night might have been our last time together. This was all my fault. I knew something was coming. I felt it in my heart. Mari warned me that she'd *seen* something, and I still failed.

I gazed up at the lone torch burning in the area outside of my cage. I wouldn't die here in this place. Last night wouldn't be the last time I saw those I loved. Quieting my mind, I rested my aching body and prepared myself for whatever was to come.

*A*lso check out book 1 in the same world by T.L. Hodel Backfire Book 1 of 3

CHARACTER INFORMATION

Alexander Kelly:
Al-ex-an-d-er – Son of Norris (Deceased) Kelly – Brother to Olivia Kelly

Ashlin McKinnon:
Ash-lyn – Daughter of Wallace McKinnon – Sister of Owen McKinnon

Angus Adair:
An-guss – Head of the Adair Family - Father of Rook, Devlin, Magnus and Wyatt Adair – Brother to Gregory Adair

Avril McKinnon:
Ah-v-ril – Daughter of Kingsley McKinnon – Sister to Falcon and Rylan McKinnon

Barry:

Bar-ee – Red Squirrel

Belle Adair:
B-ell - Daughter of Gregory Adair – Sister to Mari Adair

Blaine McGregor:
Bl-ay-ne - Son of Rayland McGregor – Brother to Ronan and Riegan McGregor

Caleb McCabe:
Kay-lub – Son of Sullivan McCabe – Brother to Leon McCabe

Camryn McKinnon:
Cam-ryn – Son of Keith McKinnon – Brother to Kayayn McKinnon

Charmaine Ricci:
Sh-ar-main – Mother of Sydney Ricci and wife of Rosco Ricci

Cora:
Cor-a – No Last Name – History Unknown

Crispin Kelly:
Krisp-in – Son of Nigel Kelly - Brother to Flynn and Fabian Kelly

Devlin Adair:
Dev-lyn - Son of Angus Adair - Brother to Rook, Magnus and Wyatt Adair

Elewyen:
Ell-ew-wen – No Last Name – History Unknown in Book 1

Fabian Kelly:
Fay-b-in – Son of Nigel Kelly – Twin brother to Flynn Kelly and brother to Crispin Kelly

Falcon McKinnon:
Fal-con – Son of Kingsley McKinnon – Brother of Rylan and Avril McKinnon

Fiona McGregor:
Fee-o-na – Daughter of Rian McGregor – Sister of Rhys McGregor

Flynn Kelly:
F-lynn – Son of Nigel Kelly – Twin brother to Fabian Kelly and brother to Crispin Kelly

Gregory Adair:
Greg-or-ee – Father to Mari and Belle Adair – Brother to Angus Adair

Haylee:
Hay-lee – No Last Name – History Unknown

Illiam:
Ill-ee-um - Servant at the Adair Castle - Personal Servant to Gregory Adair

Kayayn McKinnon:
Kay-anne – Daughter of Keith McKinnon – Sister of Camryn McKinnon

Keeva:
Kee-va – No Last Name - Non Blooded Sister to Elewyen – History Unknown

Keith McKinnon:
Kee-th – Father of Kayayn and Camryn McKinnon – Brother of Kingsley and Wallace McKinnon

Kingsley McKinnon:
King-s-lay – Head of the Mckinnon Family – Father to Falcon, Avril and Rylan McKinnon – Brother to Kingsley and Wallace McKinnon

Leon McCabe:
Lee-on - Son of Sullivan McCabe – Brother to Caleb McCabe

Liam:
Lee-im - Servant at the Adair Castle - Personal Servant to Rook

Lochlan Kelly:
Lock-lyn – Son of Niall Kelly – Brother of Reese Kelly

Magnus Adair:
Mag-nus – Son of Angus Adair – Brother to Rook, Devlin and Twin Brother to Wyatt

Mari Adair:
Ma-ree – Daughter of Gregory Adair – Sister to Belle Adair

Niall Kelly:

Nee-all – Father of Lochlan and Reese Kelly – Brother to Nigel and Norris (Deceased) - Kelly

Nigel Kelly:
Ni-gel – Head of the Kelly Family – Father of Crispin, Flynn and Fabian Kelly – Brother to Niall and Norris (Deceased) Kelly

Norris Kelly:
Nor-iss – Deceased – Father of Olivia and Alexander Kelly – Brother of Niall and Nigel Kelly

Olivia Kelly:
Oh-liv-i-a – Daughter of Norris (Deceased) Kelly – Sister to Alexander Kelly

Owen McKinnon:
Oh-win – Son of Wallace McKinnon – Brother of Ashlin McKinnon

Pascello Ricci:
Pass-cell-o – Uncle to Sydney Ricci - Brother to Rosco Ricci

Rayland McGregor:
Ray-land – Temporary Head of the McGregor Family – Father of Ronan, Riegan and Blaine McGregor

Reese Kelly:
Ree-ce – Son of Niall Kelly – Brother to Lochlan Kelly

Rian McGregor:

Ri-an – Deceased – Father of Rhys and Fiona McGregor – Brother to Rayland and Riddick McGregor

Riddick McGregor:

Rid-dick – Exiled - Father of Unknown – Brother of Rian and Rayland McGregor

Riegan McGregor:

Ree-gan – Daughter of Rayland McGregor – Sister to Ronan and Blaine McGregor

Ronan McGregor:

Ro-nan – Son of Rayland McGregor – Brother to Riegan and Blaine McGregor

Rook Adair:

Ro-ok – Son of Angus Adair – Brother to Devlin, Magnus and Wyatt Adair

Rhys McGregor:

Ri-ze – Next Head of the McGregor Family – Son of Rian McGregor – Brother to Fiona McGregor

Rylan McKinnon:

Ry-lyn – Son of Kingsley McKinnon – Brother of Falcon and Avril McKinnon

Samuel aka Sam aka Sammy:

Sam-u-el - Servent at McGregor Castle - Personal Servant to Elewyen

Shyla McCabe:
Shy-la – Exiled - Sister of Sullivan McCabe

Sullivan McCabe:
Sull-i-van - Head of the McCabe Family – Father of Leon and Caleb McCabe Brother to Shyla McCabe

Sydney Ricci:
Syd-nee – Daughter of Rosco and Charmaine Ricci

Wallace McKinnon:
Wall-ass – Father to Owen and Ashlin McKinnon – Brother to Kingsley and Keith McKinnon

William:
Will-ee-am - Head Servant to the McCabe family

Wyatt Adair:
Why-att – Son of Angus Adair – Brother of Rook, Devlin and Twin Brother to Magnus Adair

Wynter:
Win-ter – No Last Name – History Unknown

THANK YOU

Thank you to all those that decided to pick up this book and read it. It is only with readers continued support that Indie Authors, such as myself, are able to keep writing which is why your reviews mean so much to us. If you enjoyed this book, please consider leaving me a review.

BROOKLYN

If you like it dark and edgy then look no further. Brooklyn Cross has always had a deep passion for writing that stemmed from a wild imagination. When she is not busy typing away about the next character you will fall in love with, you can find her walking with her dogs on the farm and sipping a hot cup of coffee.

In addition to getting her degree in business she was highly competitive in the equestrian sport of dressage, with aspirations of an Olympic dream. She is an entrepreneur at heart and has coached and trained many of a riding enthusiast or their wonderful mounts, but always found herself drawn to writing full-time.

"Writing is what I love. I just want to be authentic with my characters. To tell a story that others can immerse themselves in and enjoy, but also relate too. If I can make you smile, laugh, cry, or your heart pound then I have done my job. To drop people into my worlds and for a short time have you live alongside my characters, is what I have always wanted."

CROSS

Below are the links that you can use to find me if you'd like to follow me on my social media platforms.

Book Bub: <u>Brooklyn Cross Books - BookBub</u>
Goodreads: <u>Brooklyn Cross (Author of Dark Side of the Cloth) |</u>
<u>Goodreads</u>
TikTok: <u>Author Brooklyn Cross (@authorbrooklyncross) TikTok |</u>
<u>Watch Author Brooklyn Cross's Newest TikTok Videos</u>
IG: <u>Brooklyn Cross (@author_brooklyncross) • Instagram photos</u>
<u>and videos</u>
FB Group: <u>Crossfire - A Brooklyn Cross Reader Group | Facebook</u>

Made in the USA
Middletown, DE
29 July 2023

35910207R00378